P9-CMF-101

THE RECEPTION AT BERG'S

ORIGINAL DRAWING BY E. H. GARRETT

THE COMPLETE WORKS OF

LYOF N. TOLSTOÏ

War and Peace

VOLS. III–IV

THOMAS Y. CROWELL COMPANY

PUBLISHERS : : : NEW YORK

WAR AND PEACE

VOL. III

CONTENTS

PART VI

PART VII

WAR AND PEACE

PART SIXTH

CHAPTER I

IN the year 1808 the emperor went to Erfurt for another interview with the Emperor Napoleon, and in the upper circles of Petersburg much was said about the magnificence of this solemn meeting.

In 1809 the intimacy between these two "arbiters of the world," as Napoleon and Alexander were called, reached such a point that when Napoleon that year declared war against Austria, the Russian troops crossed the frontier to support their former enemy, Bonaparte, against their former ally, the emperor of Austria; and there was also talk in high life of a possible marriage between Napoleon and one of the Emperor Alexander's sisters.

But, besides these external political combinations, the attention of Russian society was at this time occupied with especial interest with the internal reforms which were inaugurating in all parts of the imperial dominion.

In the meantime, life, — the ordinary life of men, — with its own concerns of health, illness, labor, recreation, with its interest in philosophy, science, poetry, music, love, friendship, hatreds, sufferings, went on as always, independent and outside of political alliance or enmity with Napoleon Bonaparte, and outside of all possible reforms.

Prince Andreï had been living uninterruptedly for two years in the country. All those enterprises on his estates, such as Pierre had devised on his and had brought to no result, constantly changing as he did from one plan to another, — all those enterprises had been accomplished by Prince Andreï without any display, and without noticeable exertion.

He had to a high degree that practical tenacity of purpose which Pierre lacked, and which gave impetus to any enterprise, without oscillation or undue effort on his own part.

On one of his estates, the three hundred serfs were enrolled as free farmers; this was one of the first instances of the sort in Russia: on others, the forced husbandry service was commuted for *obrok*, or quit-rent. At Bogucharovo, a *babka*, or midwife, was engaged at his expense to help in cases of childbirth, and a priest was employed at a salary to teach the children of the peasants and household servants.

Half of his time, Prince Andreï spent at Luisiya Gorui with his father and son, who was still in the care of nurses; the other half he spent at his "Bogucharovsky monastery," as his father called his estate.

Notwithstanding the indifference which he had affected in Pierre's presence to all the outside events of the world, he eagerly followed them; he read many books, and was often amazed to remark when men came fresh from Petersburg, from the very vortex of life, to visit his father or himself, that these men were far behind him in their knowledge of what was going on in politics at home and abroad, though he had not once left the country. In addition to his enterprises on his estates, and his general occupations in reading the most varied books, Prince Andreï spent his spare time in composing a critical account of our last two unfortunate campaigns, and a project for a change in our military code and establishment.

In the spring of 1809 Prince Andreï went to the neighborhood of Riazan, where his son, whose guardian he was, had estates.

As he sat in his calash, he enjoyed the warmth of the spring sun, and looked at the young grass, the first foliage of the birches, and the first curling clouds of the spring flying over the clear blue sky. He simply did not think, but gazed on all sides, full of joy, and free from care.

He came to the ferry where he and Pierre had talked together the year before. He came to a filthy village, barns, a vegetable garden, a slope with the remains of a snowdrift by the bridge, a hillside where the clay was hollowed into runnels, strips of stubble-field and of shrubbery where the catkins were beginning to show, and finally reached a birch forest which extended along both sides of the road. It was almost sultry in the woods; there was not a breath of wind; the birches, all covered with young, green, sticky leafage, did not even rustle. Out from under the last year's leaves, lifting them up, came the first green bracken and the violets. Scattered here and there among the birches, small evergreens, with their somber hues, unpleasantly reminded one of winter. The horses snorted as they entered the woods, and their coats were streaked with sweat.

The footman, Piotr, said something to the coachman; the coachman replied in the affirmative. But it was evident that Piotr got very little sympathy from the coachman; he turned round on the box toward his barin.

"Your illustriousness, how nice it is!" said he, with a deferential smile.

"What?"

"Nice, your illustriousness!"

"What did he say?" wondered Prince Andreï. "Oh, yes! probably about the spring," he communed to himself, glancing all around. "And how green everything is already! .... so early! The birches and the wild-cherries and the alders are already out. .... But I don't see any oaks. Oh, yes, there's one, there's an oak!"

By the roadside stood an oak. It was evidently ten times as old as the birches of which the forest was mainly composed; it was ten times as large round and twice as high as any of the birches. It was enormous, two spans around in girth, and with ancient scars where huge limbs, evidently long ago lopped off, had been, and with bark stripped away. With monstrous, disproportioned, unsymmetrically spreading, gnarled arms and branches, it stood like an ancient giant, stern and scornful, among the smiling birches. Only this oak and the slender evergreens scattered through the woods, with their hue symbolical of death, seemed unwilling to yield to the fascination of the spring and to look at the sun and the spring.

"The spring and love and happiness!" this oak seemed to say. "And how can it be that ye still like to cheat yourselves with that stupid and senseless delusion? It's forever the same old story, and a mere delusion. There is no spring, no sun, no happiness. Look here at these mournful, lifeless evergreens, always unchanged; and here I, too, spread out my mutilated, excoriated branches, from my back and my sides, where they grew, just as they grew; and here I stand, and I have no faith in your hopes and illusions!"

Prince Andreï looked back several times at this oak, as he rode along the forest, as if he were expecting it to say something to him. The flowers and grass were under the oak; but it stood among them as before, frowning, immovable, monstrous, and inexorable.

"Yes, that oak is right, he is a thousand times right," said Prince Andreï to himself. "Let others, younger men, once more hug this delusion; but we know what life is; our life is done."

A whole new series of pessimistic ideas, agreeable from their very melancholy, arose in Prince Andreï's mind, suggested by the sight of the old oak. During all the rest of his journey he seemed once more to live his life over in thought, and he came back to his former comforting and at the same time hopeless conclusion that there was nothing more for him to undertake, that he must live out his life, refrain from working evil, and not worry, and not expect anything.

CHAPTER II

Prince Andreï was compelled by his obligations as trustee of the Riazan property to call upon the district *predvodityel*, or marshal of the nobility. The marshal was Count Ilya Andreyitch Rostof; about the middle of May, Prince Andreï went to see him.

By this time the weather had become very warm. The woods were now in full leaf, it was dusty, and it was so hot that, as he drove by water, he had a powerful desire to take a bath.

Prince Andreï, in anything but a happy frame of mind, and absorbed in thinking of the business which he had to transact with the marshal, drove into the tree-shaded avenue leading up to the mansion of the Rostofs at Otradnoye. At his right, he heard behind the trees the gay sounds of women's voices, and saw a bevy of young girls running down as if to cut off his calash. In front of the others, and therefore nearest to him, ran a very slender, indeed a strangely slender, maiden, with dark hair and dark eyes, in a yellow chintz dress, with a white handkerchief around her head, the locks escaping from it in ringlets. This maiden shouted something as she approached the calash; then, seeing that it was a stranger, she ran back again with a merry laugh, not looking at him.

Something akin to pain affected Prince Andreï at this incident. The day was so beautiful, the sun so bright, everything all around was so cheerful! But this slender, pretty young girl knew not, and had no wish to know, aught of him, and was content and happy in her separate, most likely stupid, but still gay and careless, existence. What was there for her to be merry about? What were her thoughts? Certainly not about the military code, or about Riazan quit-rents! What, then, was she thinking about? And why was she happy? Such questions involuntarily arose in Prince Andreï's mind.

Count Ilya Andreyitch was spending the summer of

1809 at Otradnoye in the same way as he had always done; that is, entertaining almost all the residents of the government with hunting-parties, theatricals, dinners, and music. He welcomed Prince Andreï most hospitably, as he did every new guest, and almost by main force compelled him to stay for the night.

During the course of the wearisome day, monopolized by his elderly hosts and the most distinguished of the guests, who happened to be present in large numbers on account of the old count's approaching name-days, Bolkonsky many times was attracted to Natasha, who was among the merriest and most entertaining of the younger members of the household, and kept asking himself, "What can she be thinking about? Why is she so gay?"

At last, finding himself alone that night, in a new place, it was long before he could go to sleep. He read for a time, then put out his candle, then lighted it again. It was hot in the room with the shutters closed from within. He was annoyed at "that stupid old man," as he called Rostof, for having detained him by the excuse that the necessary papers had not yet come from the city; and he was vexed with himself for having remained.

Prince Andreï got up and went to the window to open it. As soon as he threw back the shutters, the moonlight, as if it had been on the watch at the window and long waiting the opportunity, came pouring into the room. He opened the window. The night was cool and calmly beautiful. In front of the window was a row of clipped trees, dark on one side and silver-bright on the other. At the foot of the trees was some sort of succulent, rank vegetation, the leaves and stalks covered with silvery dew. Farther away, beyond the trees, was a roof glittering with dew; farther to the right, a tall tree, with wide-spreading branches, showed a brilliant white bole and limbs; and directly above it the moon, almost at her full, shone in the bright, almost starless, spring night. Prince Andreï leaned his elbows on the window-sill, and fixed his eyes on that sky.

Prince Andreï's room was on the second floor: the rooms overhead were also occupied, and by people who were not asleep. He overheard women's voices above him.

"Only just once more," said a voice which Prince Andreï instantly recognized.

"But when are you going to sleep?" replied a second voice.

"I will not, cannot sleep; what can I do? Come! this is the last time."

The two female voices broke out into a snatch of song, forming the final phrase of a duet.

"Akh! how charming! Now, then, let's go to sleep; that's the end of it!"

"You go to sleep, but I can't," replied the first voice, approaching the window. She evidently thrust her head quite out of the window, because the rustling of her dress was heard, and even her breathing. Everything was calm and stone-still, like the moon and her light, and the shadows. Prince Andreï feared to stir, lest he should betray his involuntary presence.

"Sonya! Sonya!" again spoke the first voice. "Now, how can you go to sleep! Just see how lovely it is! Akh! how lovely! Come, wake up, Sonya!" said she again, with tears in her voice. "Come, now, such a lovely, lovely night was never seen!"

Sonya made some answer expressive of her disapproval.

"No, but do look! what a moon! Akh! how lovely! Do come here! Sweetheart! darling,[1] come here! There, now, do you see? If you would only squat down this way, and rest yourself on your knees.... a little closer.... we must squeeze together more.... there, if one tried, one might fly away! Yes, that's the way!"

"Look out! you'll fall!"

A little scuffle was heard, and then Sonya's discontented voice saying: —

"See! it's two o'clock!"

[1] *Dushenka, galubushka.*

"Akh! you only spoil it all for me! now go away, go away!"

Again all became still, but Prince Andreï knew that she was still there; he could hear from time to time a little rustling, from time to time her sighs.

"Akh! dear me! dear me! it is too bad! To bed, then, if I must!" and the window was closed.

"And my existence is nothing to her!" thought Prince Andreï, while he was listening to their talk, somehow or other hoping and fearing that she would say something about him. "It's the same old story! And done on purpose!" he thought. And suddenly there arose in his soul such an unexpected throng of youthful thoughts and hopes, opposed to the whole current of his life, that he felt himself too weak to analyze his condition, and so he went to sleep immediately.

CHAPTER III

THE next day, taking leave only of the count, and not waiting for the ladies to come down, Prince Andreï went home.

It was already the first of June, and on his way home Prince Andreï once more drove through the birch wood, where the gnarled old oak had so strangely and memorably attracted his attention. The little bells on the horses sounded with still less resonance now through the forest than they did the fortnight before; all the spaces were full of thick leaves, shadows, and shrubbery; and the young fir trees scattered through the woods were no longer an exception to the general beauty, and but partook of the universal characteristics of the season, and showed a soft green at the ends of their succulent young sprays.

The whole day had been hot; now and again there had been threats of thunder-showers, but only small masses of clouds had scattered a few drops over the dusty highway and the sunny leaves. The forest on the left was dark, in shadow; that on the right, with branches glistening with diamond drops and gently swaying in the breeze, was full of sunlight. Everything was in flower; the nightingales broke out in gushing melody, and answered one another from far and near.

"Yes, in this forest here stood the oak whose mood seemed to agree with mine," said Prince Andreï to himself. "Yes! there he is," he thought, as he looked along at the left of the road, and found himself, before he knew or realized it, admiring the old oak of which he was in search. The old oak, as if transfigured, spread out a mighty tabernacle of dark, sunny green, and seemed to swoon and sway in the rays of the afternoon sun. Nothing could be seen of the gnarled branches, or of the scars, or of the old unbelief and grief. Through the rough, century-old bark had pierced the smooth, succulent young foliage; it was incredible that this patriarch should have produced them.

"Yes, this is the very same oak," said Prince Andreï to himself; and suddenly there came over him an unreasonable, joyous feeling of delight and renovation. All the most sacred moments of his life came back to him at one sweep, — Austerlitz, with that unfathomable sky, and the dead, reproachful face of his wife, and Pierre on the ferry-boat, and the maiden enjoying the beauty of the night, and that night itself, and the moon; everything suddenly crowded back into his mind.

"No! life is not ended at thirty-one," suddenly said Prince Andreï, with resolute, unalterable decision. "It is a small thing that I myself know what is in me; all others must know it also; Pierre, and that girl who wanted to fly up into the sky; all of them must learn to know me, so that my life may not be spent for myself alone, in order that they may not live so independently of my life, that it may send its reflection over all other lives, and that they may all live in union with me!"

On his return from his journey, Prince Andreï made up his mind to go to Petersburg in the autumn, and he excogitated various reasons in support of this decision.

A whole series of convincing and logical arguments in favor of his return to Petersburg and even reëntering the army were all the time coming to his aid. It now passed his comprehension that he could ever have doubted the necessity of going back to active life, just the same as a short month before he could not comprehend how the idea could ever occur to him of leaving the country.

It seemed clear to him that all his experiments of life would surely be wasted, and without reason, unless he were to put them into effect and once more take an active part in life. He now could not understand how, on the strength of such wretched arguments, he had convinced himself that it would be humiliating himself, after all his lessons in life, to believe in the possibility of getting profit, and the possibility of happiness and love. Now his reason showed him the exact contrary.

After this journey of his, Prince Andreï began to feel tired of the country; his former occupations no longer interested him; and often, as he sat alone in his cabinet, he would get up, go to the mirror, and look long at his own face. Then he would turn away, and gaze at the portrait of his late wife, Liza, who, with her little curls *à la grecque*, looked down upon him, with an affectionate and radiantly happy expression, from the golden frame. She seemed no longer to say to her husband those terrible words; she simply gazed at him with a merry and quizzical look. And Prince Andreï, clasping his hands behind his back, would walk long up and down the room, sometimes scowling, sometimes smiling, thinking over the preposterous, inexpressible, mysterious, almost criminal ideas connected with Pierre, with glory, with the maiden at the window, with the old oak, with the beauty of women, and love, which were changing his whole life. And at such moments, when any one came to see him, he was generally dry, stern, and short, and disagreeably logical.

"*Mon cher,*" the Princess Mariya once said, happening to find him in such a state, "Nikolushka can't go out to-day; it is very chilly."

"If it were warm," Prince Andreï replied to his sister, "then he might go out in nothing but his shirt; but since it is cold, you will have to put some warm clothes on him, as might have occurred to you. Now, there is no sense in keeping the child indoors because it is cold, when he needs the fresh air."

He would say such things with all the logic in the world, as if he were punishing some one else for all this illogical reasoning that was secretly working in his mind. Under such circumstances, it was not strange that the Princess Mariya said to herself: —

"How this intellectual work dries men up!"

CHAPTER IV

PRINCE ANDREÏ reached Petersburg in August, 1809. This was the time when the young Speransky was at the apogee of his glory and zeal for the reforms which he had undertaken.

This same month of August, the emperor, while out riding in his calash, was upset, and hurt his leg; he was confined at Peterhof for three weeks, and the only person he would see was Speransky.

During this time two ukases, or rescripts, of extreme importance and most alarming to society, were prepared: the one was in regard to the doing away of court *chin*, or rank; and the other, in regard to the passing of examinations for the rank of Collegiate-Assessor and Councillor of State.[1] The scheme also provided for a complete imperial constitution, destined to revolutionize the existing departments of Justice, Administration, and Finance, from the Council of State even down to the tribunals of the Volosts, or Cantons, throughout the empire.

Now began to materialize and take shape those vague liberal dreams with which the Emperor Alexander had

[1] In the civil service, the *kollezhsky assessor*, having personal nobility, corresponds to major; *statskj sovyetnik*, having hereditary nobility, ranks above colonel in the army.

mounted the throne, and which he had vainly endeavored to bring about with the aid of his assistants, Czartorisky, Novosiltsof, Kotchubey, and Strogonof, whom he in jest called "the Committee of Public Safety."

Speransky was then the general representative for civil affairs, and Arakcheyef for all things connected with the military.

Prince Andreï, immediately after his arrival, appeared at court, and at his majesty's levee, in his capacity as chamberlain. The sovereign twice, on meeting him, did not vouchsafe him a single word. Prince Andreï had always before felt that the sovereign did not approve of him, that his face and general appearance did not please his majesty. By the cold look of disfavor which the sovereign gave him, Prince Andreï was still more confirmed in his former supposition. The courtiers explained to Prince Andreï that the emperor's neglect of him was due to his majesty's displeasure at Bolkonsky's leaving the service in 1805.

"I know very well how little control we have over our likes and dislikes," said Prince Andreï to himself. "And, therefore, there is no use in thinking of personally presenting to his majesty the emperor my Memorandum on the military code; but I must let its merits speak for themselves."

He mentioned his work to an old field-marshal, a friend of his father's. The field-marshal gave him an appointment, received him more than courteously, and promised to lay the matter before the sovereign. Several days later, Prince Andreï was notified to present himself before the minister of war, Count Arakcheyef.

At ten o'clock on the morning of the day set, Prince Andreï went to Count Arakcheyef's.

Prince Andreï did not know the minister of war personally, and had never seen him; but from all that he had ever heard of him he was disposed to hold this man in very slight esteem.

"He is minister of war, the confidant of his majesty

the emperor; no one need be concerned with his personal characteristics; it is his business to examine my Memorandum; moreover, he is the only person who can put it into execution," said Prince Andreï to himself, as he sat with a number of other visitors of more or less note waiting in Count Arakcheyef's reception-room.

Prince Andreï, during the period of his military service, generally as aide, had seen the reception-rooms of many notabilities, and the various characteristics of those reception-rooms were very distinct in his mind. Count Arakcheyef's reception-room had an entirely different character from anything that he had ever seen. The faces of the less notable individuals who were waiting their turn for an audience with Count Arakcheyef wore an expression of shame and humility; those of higher rank gave a general impression of awkwardness vainly hidden under a mask of ease and ironical derision of themselves, their position, and those who were likewise waiting. Some walked pensively back and forth, some whispered and laughed together; and Prince Andreï overheard the sobriquet *Sila Andreyitch*, "Andreyitch the Strong," and the expression *Dyadya Zadast*, "Uncle Push," applied to the count. One general, a man of note, was evidently annoyed because he was kept waiting, and sat with his legs crossed, smiling sarcastically at himself.

But, whenever the door opened, all faces instantly expressed one and the same sentiment — fear! Prince Andreï for a second time asked the officer on duty to take in his name; but he received a scornful, impertinent stare, and was told that he would be summoned when it was his turn. After several persons had been escorted in and out of the war minister's cabinet, an officer, whose frightened and humiliated face had already struck Prince Andreï, was shown through the dreaded door. This officer's audience lasted a long time. Suddenly the bellowing of a disagreeable voice was heard on the other side of the door, and the officer came out, pale, and with trembling lips, and, clasping his head with his hands, hastened through the reception-room.

Immediately after this, Prince Andreï was ushered into the audience-chamber; and the officer on duty whispered, "To the right, next the window."

Prince Andreï went into the meanly furnished cabinet, and saw, sitting by the table, a man of forty years of age, with a long waist, and a peculiarly long head, closely cropped hair, a face covered with deep wrinkles, brows contracted over grayish green, heavy-looking eyes, and a drooping red nose. Arakcheyef turned his head toward the newcomer without looking at him.

"What was it you wanted?" asked the count.

"I have nothing to ask for, your illustriousness," replied Prince Andreï, gently. Arakcheyef's eyes fastened on him.

"Sit down," said Arakcheyef; "Prince Bolkonsky?"

"I have nothing to ask for; but his majesty the emperor deigned to put into your hands my Memorandum, your illustriousness...."

"Please give me your attention, my dear sir: I have read your Memorandum," interrupted Arakcheyef, speaking the first words with a certain courtesy; then again, staring into his face, and assuming more and more of a querulous and scornful tone, he went on, "You propose new regulations for the army? Plenty of regulations now. No one fulfils the old ones. Nowadays everybody's writing new regulations; it's easier to write 'em than to carry 'em out!"

"I have come at his majesty the emperor's request, to learn what you propose to do with my Memorandum," said Prince Andreï, respectfully.

"I have indorsed my decision upon your manuscript, and sent it to the committee. I do *not* approve of it," said Arakcheyef, getting up and taking a slip of paper from his writing-table. "Here!" and he handed it to Prince Andreï.

Across the paper these words were written in pencil, without capitals or punctuation marks, and ill-spelt:—

"without basis in common cence as it is only an imitation of the french military coad and no need of changing our own articles of war."

"To what committee has my Memorandum been given?" inquired Prince Andreï.

"To the Committee on the Revision of the Military Code, and I have added your nobility to the list, but without salary."

Prince Andreï smiled.

"I should wish no salary."

"An honorary member, without salary," reiterated Arakcheyef. "I have the honor of .... Hey there, come in! Who 's next?" he shouted, bowing to Prince Andreï.

CHAPTER V

WHILE waiting for the formal notification of his appointment as a member of the committee, Prince Andreï took pains to renew former acquaintances, especially with persons who, as he knew, were in power, and might be of assistance to him. He now experienced in Petersburg a feeling analogous to that which he had experienced on the eve of a battle, when a restlessness and sense of curiosity had invincibly attracted him toward those lofty spheres where the future is prepared, on which depends the fate of millions.

By the angry criticisms of the older men, by the curiosity of the uninitiated, by the reserve of those who knew, by the eagerness and activity of all, by the portentous increase in committees and commissions, — new ones being, as he knew, appointed every day, — he felt certain that there and then, in the year 1809, in Petersburg, some mighty civil conflict was in preparation, and that the presiding genius of it was to be a personage as yet unknown to him, endowed in his fancy with mysterious qualities, with genius, — Mikhaïl Speransky. And this vaguely understood fact of reform, and Speransky, its leader, began to interest him so intensely that the matter of the military code was very soon relegated to a secondary place in his mind.

Prince Andreï found himself in the most advantageous position for being well received in the most varied and lofty circles of the Petersburg society of that day. The party pledged to reform welcomed him cordially, and did their best to win him to their side, — in the first place, because he had a reputation for intelligence and great learning; in the second place, because, by having of his own free will emancipated his serfs, he had gained himself the reputation of being a liberal.

The party of the old men, the discontents, naturally turned to him for sympathy in their criticisms of reform, as being the son of his father. The generality of women, society, gladly welcomed him, because he was a rich man, and illustrious, and yet practically a novelty, with that aureole of romance with which he was crowned, on account of his supposed death and the tragic end of his wife. Moreover, all those who knew him in days gone by confessed with one accord that he had greatly changed for the better during the last five years, that time had softened down his asperities, that he had lost all that old pretense, pride, and sarcastic manner, and had now acquired the serenity which comes only with years. He was talked about, people were interested in him, and all were anxious to see him.

On the day after his interview with Count Arakcheyef, Prince Andreï was at a reception at Count Kotchubey's. He had been telling the count about his reception by "Sila Andreyitch." That was the nickname by which Kotchubey called Arakcheyef, with the same expression of masked contempt that Prince Andreï had noticed in the way others spoke of him at the minister of war's reception-room.

"My dear fellow, even in this affair of yours, you can't get along without Mikhaïl Mikhaïlovitch.[1] He can do everything. I will tell him. He promised to come this evening...."

"But what has Speransky to do with military matters?" asked Prince Andreï.

[1] Speransky: of obscure origin; his family name possibly Russified by the priests; from the Latin *spero*, hence, the "Hopeful"; one of the greatest men of Alexander's time; from foundling to prime minister; intrigued against, banished; and afterward one of the governors of Siberia.

Kotchubey, with a smile, shook his head, as if amazed at Bolkonsky's innocence.

"He and I were speaking of you only a day or two ago," continued Kotchubey, "and about your free laborers...."

"Ah! and so you have been emancipating your muzhiks?" asked an old man of Catherine's time, turning scornfully upon Bolkonsky.

"It was a very small estate, which brought in a very meager income," replied Bolkonsky, trying to palliate his action, in his presence, so as not to irritate the old man to no purpose.

"You seem to be in a great hurry," said the old man, glancing at Kotchubey. "There's one thing I do not understand," continued the old man. "Who is going to plow the land, if they are emancipated? It's easy to make laws, but hard to execute them. If it is all the same to you, count, I will ask you who is going to be the deciding judge when all have to pass examinations?"

"Those who succeed in passing them, I suppose," replied Kotchubey, shifting from one leg to the other, and glancing around.

"Now, there is Pryanitchnikof, an excellent man, true as gold, but he is sixty years old: will he pass an examination?"

"Yes, that is where the difficulty lies, since certainly education is not at all wide-spread, but...."

Count Kotchubey did not finish his sentence. He got up, and, taking Prince Andreï by the arm, led him forward to meet a tall, bald man of forty years, with white hands, with a broad, open forehead, and an extraordinarily strange pallor on his long face. The newcomer wore a blue coat, the ribbon of an order around his neck, and a star over his heart.

This was Speransky.

Prince Andreï instantly knew who it was, and a peculiar feeling stirred his heart, as usually happens at significant moments in life. Whether it were caused by respect, envy, expectation, he could not tell. Speransky's whole figure was of a peculiar type, so that it was impossible for a moment ever to mistake him. Never had Prince Andreï seen any one in the spheres where he had moved, who was so remarkable for the calmness and self-assurance of his motions, though they were awkward and ungainly; or any one who had such a steady, and at the same time gentle, gaze, from his half-closed and rather moist eyes; or any one with such determination expressed in an insignificant smile; or with such a delicate, gentle, monotonous voice; and, above all, such an ethereal pallor of face, shared also by the hands, which were rather broad, but extraordinarily plump, soft, and white. Such white and ethereal delicacy of complexion Prince Andreï had never seen, except in the case of soldiers who had been long at the hospital.

This, then, was Speransky, the emperor's secretary, the sovereign's factotum, and his companion at Erfurt, where more than once he had met and talked with Napoleon.

Speransky did not glance around from one person to another, as men usually do, involuntarily, on first entering a large company; and he did not hurry about speaking. He spoke quietly, assured that he would be listened to, and he looked only at the man with whom he was speaking.

Prince Andreï followed Speransky's every word and motion with the keenest attention. As usually happens to people, especially to those who are inclined to judge their fellows severely, Prince Andreï, on meeting a new personage, like Speransky, for instance, whom he knew by reputation, naturally expected to find in him the full complement of human perfections.

Speransky told Kotchubey that he was sorry at not being able to come earlier, but that he had been detained at the palace. He did not say that it was the sovereign who had detained him. And Prince Andreï remarked this affectation of modesty. When Kotchubey presented Prince Andreï, Speransky slowly turned his eyes upon Bolkonsky, without altering his smile, and continued to gaze at him in silence.

"I am very happy to make your acquaintance; I have heard of you, as every one else has," said he.

Kotchubey gave a brief account of Bolkonsky's reception by Arakcheyef. Speransky smiled more noticeably.

"The chairman of the Commission for Revising the Military Statutes, Mr. Magnitsky, is an excellent friend of mine," said he, carefully dwelling on each syllable and each word. "And if you would like, I can give you a personal interview with him." Here he came to a full stop. "I hope that you will find him sympathetic, and willing to further all that is reasonable."

A little circle had immediately gathered around Speransky; and the same old man who had spoken of his chinovnik, Pryanitchnikof, turned to the minister with the same question.

Prince Andreï did not take part in the conversation, but contented himself with observing all the motions of Speransky, that man who but a short time since had been an obscure seminarist, and now held in his hands, those white, plump hands, Russia's fate. He was struck by the extraordinary, contemptuous calmness with which Speransky answered the old man. It seemed as if he stooped down from an immeasurable height to grant him a condescending word. When the old man began to speak louder than the occasion justified, Speransky smiled, and said that he could not judge of the utility or futility of what the sovereign deigned to approve.

After conversing for some time with the group generally, Speransky got up, and, joining Prince Andreï, drew him aside to another corner of the room. It was plain that he considered it necessary to pay some attention to Bolkonsky.

"I have n't had a chance to talk with you yet, prince, owing to the lively discussion into which I was drawn by that worthy old gentleman," said he, with his blandly contemptuous smile, seeming to imply by this smile that he and Prince Andreï appreciated the insignificance of the people with whom he had just been talking. This treatment was very flattering to Prince Andreï.

"I have known of you for a long time, — in the first

place, through your treatment of your serfs, the first example of the sort, I believe, and one which I should like to see generally followed; and in the second place, because you are the only one of the chamberlains who has not considered himself abused by the new ukase, concerning the court ranks, which has produced so much talk and criticism."

"Yes," replied Prince Andreï. "My father did not wish me to take advantage of this prerogative; I began with the lowest step in the service."

"Your father is a man of a bygone generation; he evidently stands far above the men of our day, who are so severe in their judgments upon this measure, and yet it aims simply to reëstablish genuine justice."

"I am inclined to think, however, that there is some ground for these criticisms," said Prince Andreï, striving to free himself from Speransky's influence, of which he was beginning to feel conscious. It was distasteful for him to agree with him at every point; he felt a strong desire to contradict him. Prince Andreï, who generally spoke fluently and well, now found some difficulty in expressing himself while talking with Speransky. He was too much occupied with his study of the personality of this distinguished man.

"The ground of personal vanity, maybe," quietly suggested Speransky.

"Partly, and also for the sake of the government," replied Prince Andreï.

"What makes you think so?" asked Speransky, slightly dropping his eyes.

"I am a disciple of Montesquieu," said Prince Andreï. "And his maxim, 'The fundamental principle of monarchies is honor,' seems to me incontrovertible. Giving the nobility certain rights and privileges seems to me to be the means of maintaining this sentiment."

The smile faded from Speransky's pallid face, and his expression gained greatly by the change. Evidently Prince Andreï's thought seemed to him worthy of consideration.

"If you take up the question from this point of view,"

he began, finding it evidently rather difficult to express himself in French, and speaking still more deliberately than in Russian, and yet with absolute self-possession, "Montesquieu says that honor, *l'honneur*, cannot be maintained by prerogatives that are injurious to the service; that honor, *l'honneur*, is either the negative concept of refraining from reprehensible actions, or it is the true fountain-head of impulse for the winning of approbation, and the rewards that are the fruit thereof."

His arguments were succinct, simple, and clear.

"An institution which maintains this honor, this source of emulation, an institution like the *Légion d'Honneur* of the great Emperor Napoleon, is not prejudicial, but advantageous to the success of the service, but that is not true of social or court prerogatives."

"I do not quarrel with that, but it is impossible to deny that court privileges have always tended toward the same end," said Prince Andreï. "Every courtier considers himself bound to support his position worthily."

"But you have not cared to take advantage of them, prince," retorted Speransky, his smile showing that, having worsted his opponent in the argument, he was now ready to cut short this special mark of his favor. "If you will do me the honor of calling on me Wednesday," he added, "then I shall have had a talk with Magnitsky, and may be able to tell you something of interest; and, moreover, I shall have the pleasure of a more circumstantial conversation with you."

Then, closing his eyes, he made him a low bow, and slipped from the room *à la Française*, without taking leave, so as not to attract attention.

CHAPTER VI

During the first part of his stay in Petersburg, Prince Andreï was conscious that the whole system of thought which he had elaborated during his solitary life in the country was entirely obscured by the petty occupations with which he was now engaged in the city.

Every evening, when he returned to his lodgings, he jotted down in his note-book four or five indispensable visits or appointments for the next day. The mechanisms of his life, the arrangement of the twenty-four hours, so as to allow him to be always punctual, was at the cost of a goodly portion of his mental energy. He accomplished nothing; he neither thought nor had time to think; and whatever he said in conversation — and said well — was what he had been able to think out for himself in the country.

He occasionally remarked with dissatisfaction that, on appearing at different gatherings on one and the same day, he repeated himself. But he was so absorbed all day long, that he had no time to think out anything new.

Speransky, as at his first meeting with him at Kotchubey's, so also on Wednesday, at his own home, received Bolkonsky graciously, had a long and confidential talk with him, and made a powerful impression on him.

Prince Andreï looked upon so many men as contemptible and beneath contempt, he had such a powerful desire to discover in another the living ideal of the perfection toward which he was striving, that it was easy for him to believe that he had discovered in Speransky his ideal of a perfectly reasonable and virtuous man. If Speransky had sprung from the same class in society to which Prince Andreï belonged, if he had had a similar education and mental processes, Bolkonsky would have soon discovered his weaknesses, his human instead of his heroic side; but now this strangely logical bent of mind aroused his esteem from the very fact that he did not fully understand him.

Moreover, Speransky, either because he prized Prince Andreï's talents, or because he felt that it was necessary to attract him to himself, displayed before Prince Andreï his cool, easy intellect, and flattered Prince Andreï with that delicate flattery which appeals to a man's self-conceit, by tacitly taking for granted that he is the only other man capable of comprehending the full depth of stupidity of all the rest of the world, and the reasonableness and depth of their own ideas.

During the time of their long conversation on Wednesday evening, Speransky more than once said, "With *us* there is a chance to look on everything that rises above the common level of the commonplace routine;" or, with a smile, "But *our* idea is that the wolves should be fed well, and yet the sheep kept whole;" or, "*They* cannot comprehend this;" and all the time his expression seemed to imply, "*We* — that is, you and I — understand who they are, and who we are."

This first long conversation with Speransky merely served to confirm the feeling produced in him at his first interview with him. He saw in him an intelligent, severely logical man, of immense talent, energy, and tenacity of purpose, who desired to obtain power which he would wield solely for the good of Russia. Speransky was, in Prince Andreï's eyes, the man most able to explain by his intellect alone all the phenomena of life, accepting as of any importance only what appealed to his reason, and, in all circumstances, capable of applying the rules of logic in a way which he had always longed to be able to do. Everything was placed before his mind so lucidly through Speransky's exposition, that he found himself involuntarily agreeing with him on every point. If he raised objections, and entered into discussions with him, it was simply because he was anxious to be independent, and not a mere echo of Speransky's opinions.

Everything was just as it should be, everything about him was good; but there were one or two things that struck Prince Andreï unpleasantly: such were Speransky's cold, mirror-like, inscrutable eyes, and his white, plump hand. Prince Andreï could not help looking at them, just as one is always drawn to look at the hands of those men who are in the possession of power. These mirror-like eyes and that soft hand somehow irritated Prince Andreï. He was also offended by the overweening contempt for men which he had remarked in Speransky, and at the various shifts in his arguments which he used for the buttressing of his ideas. He made use of all possible weapons of thought, especially affecting metaphors; and it seemed to Prince Andreï that he leaped from one to another with too great audacity. Sometimes he set himself up as a practical worker, and flouted visionaries; then as a satirist, and made ironical sport of his antagonists; then he would become severely logical; then suddenly he would rise into the domain of pure philosophy. (This last weapon of proof he was especially fond of employing.) He would take questions to the heights of metaphysics, indulge in definitions of space, time, and thought, and, finding counter arguments in them, he would come back to fresh discussions.

On the whole, the chief trait of Speransky's intellect, and one that amazed Prince Andreï, was his unswerving, unquestioning faith in the power and validity of the intellect. It was evident that Speransky never dreamed of harboring such thoughts as were habitual with Prince Andreï, as to the impossibility of expressing all that came into his mind, or that he had ever doubted whether all that he thought and all that he believed were not vanity. And it was this very characteristic of Speransky's intellect that especially attracted Prince Andreï toward him.

During the first period of his acquaintance with Speransky, Prince Andreï conceived a passionate admiration for him, analogous to that which he had formerly experienced for Bonaparte. The circumstance that Speransky was the son of a priest, which many looked upon as derogatory, scorning a man as a *kuteïnik*, a priestling, — or a *popovitch*, the son of a pope, — undoubtedly made Prince Andreï particularly cautious in indulging this feeling toward Speransky, and unconsciously strengthened him in it.

On that first evening that Bolkonsky spent with him, they got to talking about the Committee for the Revision of the Laws; and Speransky told Prince Andreï, with a touch of irony, how this committee had existed a hundred and fifty years, had cost millions, and yet had not accomplished anything; that Rosenkampf had merely stuck labels on all the articles of comparative legislation. "And that is all the result that the government has received from those millions," said he. "We want to give new judicial powers to the Senate, and we have no laws. Therefore it is a sin for such men as you, prince, not to serve at the present time."

Prince Andreï replied that for this it needed a legal training, which he did not possess.

"But there is no one who has, so what are you going to do about it? This is a *circulus viciosus*, and we must break away from it by main force."

Before a week was over, Prince Andreï was appointed a member of the Committee on Revising the Military Code, and, much to his surprise, *nachalnik*, or president, of one section of the Special Commission on the Revision of the Laws. At Speransky's special request he took up the study of the "Revised Civil Code," and with the aid of the "Code Napoléon," and the "Institutes of Justinian," set to work on the section entitled "The Rights of Individuals."

CHAPTER VII

Two years before this, Pierre, on his return to Petersburg, from his tour among his estates, found himself involuntarily at the head of the Petersburg Freemasons. He established dining lodges and burial lodges, he gained over new members, labored for the union of various lodges, and for the acquisition of original documents. He gave his money freely toward the building of a Masonic temple, and, as far as it lay in his power, pushed forward the collections for charity, in regard to which the majority of the members were penurious or unpunctual. He supported almost unaided the almshouse established by the order in Petersburg.

His life, in the meantime, went on the same as before, with the same inclinations and dissipations. He liked the pleasures of the table, — good eating and wines; and although he looked upon it as immoral and degrading, he could not keep himself from the gayeties of his bachelor friends with whom he mingled.

Amid the fog of all his various occupations and enterprises, Pierre, however, before a year was over, began to be conscious that the Masonic ground on which he stood was giving way faster and faster under his feet, the more he tried to maintain himself on it. At the same time, he felt that the more the ground on which he stood yielded under him, the more inextricably he was committed to it. When he first entered Freemasonry, he experienced the sensations of a man who unquestioningly sets foot on the smooth surface of a bog. On bearing his weight upon it, he begins to sink. In order fully to persuade himself of the solidity of the ground whereon he stands, he sets down another foot, and slumps in more deeply than before, and, being caught in it, he, in spite of himself, wades in up to the knee.

Osip, or rather Iosiph Alekseyevitch, was no longer in Petersburg. Of late, he had done with the Petersburg lodges, and lived exclusively at Moscow. All the brethren, the members of the lodges, were Pierre's acquaintances in every-day life, and it was hard for him to see them as merely brothers, according to Freemasonry, and not as Prince B——, and not as Ivan Vasilyevitch D——, whom he knew in society, for the most part, as weak and insignificant men. Under their Masonic aprons and insignia, he could not help seeing their uniforms and the decorations which they had obtained in the world. Often when collecting the contributions and counting the twenty or thirty rubles received — for the most part in promises — from a dozen men, half of whom were as able to pay as he himself was, Pierre remembered the Masonic oath, whereby each brother bound himself to give all his possessions to his fellow-men, and then doubts would arise, though he would strive not to dwell upon them.

He divided all the brethren whom he knew into four categories. In the first he placed those who took no interest in the transactions of the lodges, or in human affairs in general, but were exclusively absorbed in the mysterious doctrines of the order, absorbed in questions as to the threefold nature of God, or the three primordial elements of matter, — sulphur, mercury, and salt, — or as to the significance of the Cube, and all the symbolism of Solomon's Temple. Pierre reverenced this class of Masons, to which belonged principally the older members of the brotherhood, — and Iosiph Alekseyevitch, in Pierre's opinion, — but he could not share in their pursuits. His heart was not attracted by the mysterious side of Masonry.

In the second category he reckoned himself, and those like himself — seekers, inclined to waver, not yet successful in walking the straight and intelligible way of Masonry, but all the time striving to walk in it.

In the third category he placed the brethren — and they formed the majority — who saw in Freemasonry nothing but superficial formalities and ceremonies, and who insisted on the strenuous fulfilment of these external forms, caring nothing for their real essence and significance. Such were Villarski, and even the Grand Master of the Supreme Lodge.

In the fourth category, finally, were reckoned also the great mass of the brethren, and especially those who had been recently admitted. These were men who, according to Pierre's observation, believed nothing, and desired nothing, and entered the brotherhood simply for the sake of bringing themselves into intimate relations with rich young men endowed with influential connections, of whom there were many in the lodges.

Pierre began to feel dissatisfied with his activity. Masonry, at least Masonry such as he knew it in Russia, it sometimes seemed to him, was founded on mere formalities. He did not dream of doubting Masonry itself, but he was persuaded that Russian Freemasonry was on the wrong track, and had turned aside from its first principles. And, therefore, toward the end of the year, Pierre went abroad to become initiated in the highest mysteries of the order.

In the summer of 1809 Pierre returned to Petersburg. Through correspondence carried on between our Masons and those abroad, it became known that Bezukhoï had succeeded in winning the confidence of many persons standing in the very highest ranks of the order, had been initiated into the deepest secrets, had been raised to the very highest degrees, and was bringing back to Russia notions of the greatest advantage for the confraternity. The Petersburg Masons all flocked around him, trying to get into his good graces; and it seemed to all that he was keeping some weighty secret which he was getting ready for them.

A solemn meeting was called of the lodge of the second degree, and Pierre promised to communicate the message with which he was charged by the supreme directors of the order. The session was crowded. After the ordinary business was concluded, Pierre got up and began his speech.

Beloved brethren [he began, flushing and hesitating, and holding in his hand his address already written], it is not enough to keep our secrets in the privacy of the lodge room, it is necessary to act.... to act. We have fallen into a state of torpor, and we must act.

Here Pierre took to his manuscript and began to read: —

For the propagation of pure truth, and for securing the triumph of virtue [he read], we must purge men of their prejudices, and spread abroad regulations consonant with the spirit of the time; we must undertake the education of the young, and make ourselves one by indissoluble bonds with men of intellect; we must boldly, and at the same time prudently, contend with superstition, infidelity, and folly; we must organize among the men devoted to our cause bands of workers, united together by singleness of aim, and possessed of power and strength.

For the furtherance of these ends, we must weight the scale, so that virtue, and not vice, will tip the beam; we must strive to make it possible for the virtuous man, even in this world, to receive the eternal rewards for his good deeds. But these mighty undertakings find a tremendous obstacle in existing political institutions. What, then, are we to do in such a state of affairs? Shall we use revolutionary methods? Shall we overturn all things? Oppose force with force? .... No, we are very far from advising that. All violent reforms deserve censure, because they can never do away with evil as long as men are what they are; and, therefore, it is the part of wisdom not to employ violence.

The whole aim of our fraternity should consist in making men consistent, virtuous, joined together in the unity of a conviction, a conviction that it is their duty everywhere and with all their might to oppose vice and folly, and the wasting of their talents and virtues; to raise worthy men from the dust, and unite them into our brotherhood. Only then our fraternity will secure the power of insensibly binding the hands of those who work disorder, and of directing them so that they will not be aware of it. In a word, it is necessary to found a universal, dominant form of government, which shall propagate itself over the whole world, without destroying social ties, or preventing other forms of government from still continuing to maintain their own special rights, and do everything except stand in the way of the mighty object of our fraternity, — which is to make virtue triumph over vice. This was the aim proposed by Christianity itself. It taught men to be wise and good, and, for their own advantage, to follow the example and precepts of the best and wisest men.

At a time when all were immersed in darkness, it was sufficient, of course, to have preaching alone: the novelty of the truth constituted its peculiar strength; but at the present day we are obliged to make use of far more powerful means. It is necessary now that a man, guided by his senses, should find in virtue a genuine charm. It is impossible to eradicate the passions; one must, therefore, strive to guide them to salutary ends; and, accordingly, it is requisite that every man should satisfy them within the limits of virtue, and our fraternity should furnish the means for this end.

As soon as we have enrolled a considerable number of worthy men in every land, each one of them will bring around him two others, and all will be straitly united together; then all things will be possible for our fraternity, which has already been able to do much, through working secretly, for the advantage of humanity.

This discourse produced not only a deep impression, but even excitement, in the lodge. The majority of the brethren affected to see in it the dangerous doctrines of the Illuminati,[1] and Pierre was amazed at the coldness with which it was received.

The Grand Master began to raise objections to Pierre's theories. Pierre, with more and more heat, tried to defend them. It was a long time since they had had such a stormy session. The members were divided into parties: some accused Pierre and criticised him for preaching the mystical doctrines of the Illuminati; others supported him. Pierre, for the first time, at this meeting, was struck by the endless variety of human minds, the result of which is that no truth presents itself alike to any two men. Even those who seemed to be on his side accepted him in their own way, with mental reservations and changes, with which he could not agree, since his chief desire was nothing else than to transfer his thought to others, exactly as he himself understood it.

Toward the end of the meeting, the Grand Master, with some ill-feeling, ironically called Bezukhoï's attention to his display of temper, and remarked that it was not so much love toward humanity, as it was the impulse of quarrelsomeness, that had dragged him into the discussion. Pierre made no reply to this, and asked bluntly whether his scheme would be accepted. When he was told no, Pierre, without waiting for the usual formalities, left the lodge and went home.

CHAPTER VIII

Pierre again found himself victim of the old melancholy which he dreaded so much. He spent the three days that followed the reading of his discourse

[1] A famous secret society devoted to deistic and republican principles, founded by Professor Adam Weishaupt, at Ingolstadt, Bavaria, in 1776, and numbering two thousand members, many of whom were Freemasons; it spread through Europe and aimed at emancipation from all despotisms. It was prohibited by the Bavarian government in 1784.

at the lodge at home on his divan, seeing no one, and not once stirring out of doors.

At this time he received a letter from his wife, who begged him to grant her an interview, described her sorrow at what had happened, and her desire to devote her whole life to him.

At the end of the letter, she informed him that she was about returning to Petersburg from abroad.

Shortly after the receipt of this letter, one of the Masonic brethren, whom he respected less than the others, broke in on his solitude, and, leading the conversation to Pierre's domestic grievances, took it on him to say to him, in the way of brotherly advice, that his severity toward his wife was unjust, and that Pierre had swerved from the first rules of the brotherhood by not pardoning the penitent.

At the same time, also, his mother-in-law, the wife of Prince Vasili, sent for him, begging him to call on her, if only for a few minutes, in regard to a matter of supreme importance. Pierre saw that he was destined to be overpersuaded, that they were bound to have him reconciled to his wife; and indeed this was not wholly disagreeable to him in the state of mind in which he found himself. It was all the same to him. He now felt that nothing in life was of great importance, and under the influence of the low spirits which had ruled him, he prized neither his own freedom nor his obstinate determination to punish his wife.

"No one is right, no one is to blame, and of course she was not to blame," he said to himself. If Pierre did not immediately agree to a reconciliation with his wife, it was simply because in this condition of melancholy in which he found himself, he had not the energy to take the first step in the matter. If his wife had come to him, he would simply not have driven her away. In comparison with what now occupied him, was it not a matter of supreme indifference to him whether or not he lived with his wife?

Making no reply either to his wife or to her mother, Pierre, late one evening, started off and went to Moscow, in order to have a consultation with Bazdeyef. This was what Pierre wrote in his diary: —

Moscow, November 29.

I have only just come from the Benefactor's, and I make haste to transcribe all my experiences with him. Iosiph Alekseyevitch lives in extreme poverty, and has been suffering for two years past with a painful affection of the bladder. No one has ever heard him utter a groan or a word of complaint. From morning till late at night, except during those hours when he is eating his most simple meals, he devotes himself to scientific work.

He received me courteously, and I sat down on the bed where he was lying. I gave him the grip of the Knights of the East and of Jerusalem. He replied with the same, and with a benignant smile asked me what I had learned and experienced in the Prussian and Scottish lodges. I told him everything that I knew; then I related to him the proposal which I had brought before our Petersburg lodge, and described the unfriendly reception which it had received and the rupture which had arisen between me and the brethren. Iosiph Alekseyevitch said nothing for some little time, and was lost in thought; then he expounded his views in regard to the whole matter, so that all the past was made plain to me as well as the way which lay stretched out before my feet. He surprised me by asking if I remembered the threefold object of the fraternity: —

(1) The conservation and study of the mysteries;

(2) Self-purification and regeneration so as to be able to receive them; and

(3) The regeneration of the human race through striving after such purification.

What is the first and chief of these three aims? Of course it must be self-purification and regeneration. Only thereby can we strive and make our way onward, independent of all circumstances. But at the same time this very aim constrains us to the most arduous labors, and therefore, being deceived by our pride, we lose sight of this aim, and strive either to penetrate the mystery which we are incapable of accepting on account of its purity, or else we make an effort toward improving humanity, when we merely show in ourselves an example of turpitude and depravity. "Illuminism" is not pure doctrine, precisely for the reason that it has been carried away by the charms of social activity and has become puffed up with pride.

From this standpoint, Iosiph Alekseyevitch criticized my discourse and all my activity. I agreed with him in the depths of my soul.

During the course of our conversation we touched on my domestic troubles, and he said to me:—

"The chief obligation of a true Mason, as I told you once before, consists in the perfecting of self. But we often imagine that if we were freed from all the hardships of our lives, we should soon attain this end; on the contrary, my dear sir," said he, "only in the tumults of life can we attain the three chief ends:—

"(1) *Self-knowledge*, for a man can learn to know himself only through comparison;

"(2) *Perfection*, which is obtained only by battling; and

"(3) The chief virtue,—*Love of death.*

"Only the vicissitudes of life can teach us its falsity and stimulate our innate love of death, or our new birth into another and better life."

These words were all the more impressive from the fact that Iosiph Alekseyevitch, in spite of his severe physical sufferings, has never felt the burdens of this life, and yet he loves death, though in spite of all the purity and loftiness of his nature, he never feels that he is as yet sufficiently prepared for it.

Then the Benefactor fully explained to me the grand Square of Creation and demonstrated that the numbers three and seven were the foundation of all other things. He counseled me to avoid a breach with the Petersburg brethren, to take upon myself only the obligations of the second degree, and while winning the brethren away from the dominion of pride, to strive to keep them on the straight road toward self-knowledge and perfection. Moreover, he advised me, above all things, to keep a strict watch over myself, and for this purpose he gave me this note-book, in which I am now writing, and in which I am henceforth to keep an account of all my actions.

PETERSBURG, December 5.

Again I am living with my wife. My mother-in-law, with tears in her eyes, came to me and said that Ellen had returned, and that she begged me to hear her, that she was innocent, that she was unhappy at my putting her away, and many such things. I was well aware that if I once allowed myself to see her, I should not have the force to refuse her request. In my perplexity, I did not know whose help and advice to seek. If the Benefactor had been here he would have told me. I shut myself up alone in my room, read over Iosiph Alekseyevitch's letters, recalled my conversations with him, and, taking all things together, I came to the conclusion that I had no right to refuse her request; and that if it was my duty to offer the hand of help to every one, all the more was it to a person so closely united to me, and that I was in duty bound to bear my cross. But if I pardoned her for the sake of right-doing, then my reunion with her must have merely a spiritual end and aim. And thus I made up my mind, and thus I wrote to Iosiph Alekseyevitch. I told my wife that I would beg her to forget all the past, that I would beg her to pardon me for anything in which I had been blameworthy toward her, and that I had nothing to forgive. It was a pleasure for me to tell her that. No need for her to know how trying it was for me to see her again. I have taken up my abode in the upper rooms of the great mansion, and I rejoice in a pleasant sense of regeneration.

CHAPTER IX

In those days, as has always been the case, "high society," which met at court and at the fashionable balls, was divided into a number of inner circles, each having its own distinctive peculiarities. The most extensive of these cliques was the "French circle," based on the Napoleonic alliance, and led by Count Rumyantsof and Caulaincourt. Ellen immediately took a most prominent position in this clique, as soon as she and her husband began living together again at Petersburg. Her *salon* was frequented by the gentlemen of the French legation, and by the great collection of people distinguished for their amiability and wit, who belonged to that set.

Ellen had been at Erfurt at the time of the notable meeting between the emperors, and had there made acquaintance of all the Napoleonic celebrities of Europe. She had enjoyed a most brilliant success. Napoleon himself remarked her presence at the theater and said of her, "*C'est un superbe animal.*"

Pierre was not surprised at her success, as far as beauty and elegance were concerned, because, as time went on, she grew more beautiful than ever. But he was amazed that his wife, in the course of two short years, should have succeeded in acquiring the reputation of being "a charming woman, as clever as she is beautiful."

The distinguished Prince de Ligne wrote her eight-page letters. Bilibin treasured up his witticisms so as to get them off for the first time at the Countess Bezukhaya's. To be received at her *salon* was regarded as equivalent to a diploma of cleverness. Young men read books previous to making their appearance there, so as to have some special subject to talk about; and the secretaries of legation, and even the ambassadors, confided diplomatic secrets to her, so that Ellen was a power in a certain way.

Pierre, who knew that she was really stupid, had a strange feeling of perplexity and fear when he appeared, as he sometimes did, at her receptions and dinner-parties, where the conversation ran on politics, poetry, and philosophy. On such occasions, he experienced a feeling such as a juggler must have, who is all the time afraid lest somehow or other his deception should be found out. But either because stupidity is the one thing needful in the management of such a *salon*, or because those who are deceived find a certain amount of satisfaction in the deception itself, the secret was not betrayed, and Elena Vasilyevna Bezukhaya's reputation of being *une femme charmante et spirituelle* was so firmly established that she could say the most astonishing trivialities and nonsense, and all professed themselves charmed with every word that fell from her lips, and discovered in them a depth of thought which she herself did not begin to suspect.

Pierre was precisely the kind of a husband which such a brilliant woman of the world ought by good rights to have. He was a queer, absent-minded fellow, a *grand seigneur* of a husband, interfering with no one, and not only not spoiling the lofty tone proper to such a drawing-room, but serving as an admirable background, against which to display his wife's elegance and tact.

Pierre, during these two years, — in consequence of perpetually concentrating his mind on transcendental interests, and of his genuine contempt for all things else, — assumed in the, to him uninteresting, society which his wife gathered round her, that tone of abstraction and absent-mindedness, combined with affability toward all, which cannot be acquired by art, and which somehow commands involuntary respect. He walked into his wife's drawing-room as if it were the theater; he knew every one, toward all he was equally cordial and equally reserved. Sometimes he joined in the conversation if it interested him, and then he blurted out his opinions with that thick utterance of his, regardless of the inappropriateness of his ideas, or the presence of the gentlemen from the embassies. But it was a foregone conclusion in regard to "that queer husband" of the most distinguished woman of Petersburg, that no one should take his idiosyncrasies seriously.

Among the young men who daily frequented Ellen's mansion after her return from Erfurt, Boris Drubetskoï, who was now on the highroad to success in the service, was the most assiduous in his visitations at the Bezukhoïs'. Ellen called him *mon page*, and treated him as if he were a boy. The smiles that she gave him were just like those that she showered on all the rest, but occasionally Pierre had an unpleasant feeling at the sight of it.

Boris treated Pierre with a peculiar dignified and rather grave deference. This shade of deference also disquieted Pierre. He had suffered so keenly three years before from the affront that his wife had put on him, that now he saved himself from the possibility of a repetition of it, in the first place, by renouncing the idea of being his wife's husband, and in the second place, by not allowing a suspicion of her to enter his head.

"No, now that she has become a *bas bleu*, a bluestocking, she will never be troubled again with such temptations," he would say to himself. "There is no example of a *bas bleu* having love-affairs," he would assure himself, as if it were an axiom in which he must infallibly believe, though he could not have told where he obtained it.

But, strangely enough, Boris's presence in his wife's drawing-room — and he was there almost constantly — affected him physically: it seemed to paralyze all of his limbs, to waken all his self-consciousness, and take away his freedom of motion.

"Such a strange antipathy," thought Pierre, "and yet he used to please me very much."

In the eyes of the world, Pierre was a great barin, the somewhat blinded and ridiculous husband of a distinguished wife, a queer genius, who accomplished nothing, did no one any harm, and was on the whole a very fine and good young man. But in the depths of Pierre's soul, during all this time, there was going on the complicated and arduous labor of internal development, which brought him into the knowledge of many secrets, and made him pass through many joys and many doubts.

CHAPTER X

He continued his diary, and here are some extracts from what he wrote at that time: —

December 6. — Rose at eight o'clock, read in the Gospels, then went to a committee meeting ...."

Pierre, by his Benefactor's advice, had entered the service as a member of one of the committees.

Came back to dinner, dined alone (the countess had many guests, who were disagreeable to me), ate and drank moderately, and after dinner copied some documents for the brethren. In the afternoon I went down to the drawing-room and related a ludicrous story about B——, and only when it was too late, and every one was laughing heartily, did I remember that I should not have done so.

Went to bed in a happy and contented frame of mind.

Almighty Lord! help me to walk in thy paths!

(1) To conquer angry passions by gentleness and moderation.

(2) Carnal desires by self-restraint and aversion.

(3) To shun vanity, but not to shut myself off from (*a*) the conditions of service of the State; (*b*) from family affairs; (*c*) from dealings with friends; (*d*) and from domestic economy.

DECEMBER 7.—Arose late, and after I woke up lay for a long time indulging in slothfulness. My God! help me and strengthen me, so that I may walk in thy ways. Read the Holy Gospels, but without the proper feeling. Brother Urusof came; we talked about the vanities of the world. Told about the emperor's new plans. I began to criticize them, but remembered our regulations, and the words of the Benefactor in regard to the obligations of a genuine Mason,—to be a zealous worker in the government when his services are required, and a calm observer of what he cannot approve. My tongue is my enemy. Brothers G——, V——, and O—— came to see me; it was a meeting preparatory to the initiation of a new brother. They insisted upon clothing me with the office of Rhetor. I feel myself weak and incompetent.

Then the conversation turned on the significance of the seven pillars and seven steps of the Temple. Seven sciences, seven virtues, seven sins, seven gifts of the Holy Spirit. Brother O—— was very eloquent.

The initiation took place in the evening. The new arrangement of the lodge room made a magnificent spectacle. Boris Drubetskoï was the adept. I was his sponsor, and I was also Rhetor. A strange feeling agitated me while I was with him in the dark room. I detected in myself a feeling of hatred toward him, which I vainly strove to overcome. And I should wish really to save him from evil and win him over to the side of truth, but hard thoughts about him arose in my mind. It seemed to me that his sole aim in joining the fraternity was that he might get into closer relations with certain men, creep into favor with those who belong to our lodge. Besides the fact that he has several times asked me whether N—— or S—— belonged to our lodge—which I could not answer him—and the fact that, from my observation of him, he is not qualified to feel proper reverence for our holy order and is too much occupied and content with the external man to desire the improvement of the spiritual, I had no grounds to base my objections upon; but he seemed to me insincere, and all the time that I was alone with him in the dark chamber, it seemed to me that he was scornfully smiling at my words, and I had a strong temptation really to pierce him with the sword which I held at his bared breast. I could not speak with any fluency, and I could not frankly confess my doubts to the brethren and the Grand Master. May the Great Architect of the Universe aid me to find the true way which leads from the labyrinth of lies!

After that there was a gap of three pages in the diary, and then came what follows:—

Had an instructive and long talk to-day with brother V——, who advised me to hold fast by brother A——. Many things were revealed to me, though I am so unworthy. Adonai is the name of the Creator of the world! Elohim is the name of the One who directs the universe. The third name, the unspeakable name, means the All. These talks with Brother V—— strengthen me, enlighten me, and confirm my feet in the path of virtue. In his presence there is no chance for doubt. How clear to my mind is the distinction between the wretched knowledge of the general sciences and our sacred, all-comprehensive teaching! Human science subdivides everything, so as to comprehend; destroys everything, so as to scrutinize. In the holy science of our brotherhood everything is coördinated, everything is recognized by its unity and its life. The Trinity is the three primordial elements of all things — sulphur, mercury, and salt. Sulphur has an unctuous and fiery quality; taken in conjunction with salt, its fiery nature arouses a longing in it, by means of which mercury is attracted, seizes it, and from the combination arise various bodies. Mercury is the living and volatile, spiritual being, — Christ, the Holy Spirit, *He*.

DECEMBER 15.—Awoke late, read the Holy Gospels, but was apathetic. Afterward, I went out and walked up and down the hall. Tried to think, but instead my imagination brought up an occurrence that happened four years ago. After our duel, Mr. Dolokhof and I met in Moscow, and he said that he hoped that I was now enjoying complete peace of mind, in spite of the absence of my wife. At that time I made him no answer. Now I recalled all the circumstances of our meeting, and in my heart of hearts I reviled him with the most angry words and the most cutting sarcasms. I came to my senses and banished this thought only when I found myself stirred up to wrath; but I have sufficiently repented of this.

After this, Boris Drubetskoï came in and began to relate of various "adventures." From the first instant, I was annoyed at his visit, and contradicted him. He retorted. I grew angry, and said a great many disagreeable and even hateful things. He said no more, and I recollected myself only when it was too late. My God! I cannot tell at all how to treat him. The cause of this is my self-conceit. I regard myself as superior to him, and consequently I behave a thousand times worse than he does, since he condones my rude behavior, while I feel nothing but contempt for him. My God! enable me in his presence better to realize my own shortcomings, and so to order my life that he too may find advantage in it. After dinner I had a nap, and while I was going to sleep I distinctly heard a voice saying in my left ear, "*Thy* day."

It seemed to me in my dream that I was walking in darkness, and suddenly I was surrounded by dogs; but I proceeded without fear; suddenly one small one seized me by the left thigh, and did not let go. I tried to throttle him. And I had just succeeded in getting rid of him, when another, still larger, began to snap at me. I tried to lift him up, and the higher I lifted him, the larger and heavier he grew. And suddenly Brother A—— came along, and, taking me by the arm, drew me with him, and brought me to an edifice, to enter which it was necessary to cross a narrow plank. I stepped on it, and the plank tipped and fell, and I tried to climb a fence, the top of which I could hardly reach by stretching up my arms. At last, after great efforts, I hoisted my body up in such a way that my legs were on one side and my trunk on the other. I managed to look around, and saw that Brother A—— was standing on the fence and directing my attention to a great alley and garden, and within the garden was a large and beautiful edifice.

Then I woke up.

Lord, mighty Architect of Nature! help me to defend myself from the dogs — my passions — and from the last of them, who united in himself the strength of all the others, and aid me to enter that temple of virtue, the sight of which I attained in my vision.

December 19. — In a vision, it seemed to me that Iosiph Alekseyevitch was sitting in my house, and I felt very glad, and was anxious to entertain him.

It seemed to me that I went on chatting irrelevantly, and

suddenly remembered that this would not be pleasing to him, and I felt anxious to approach him and embrace him. But as soon as I came close to him, I saw that his face was transfigured; he appeared youthful, and in a low tone repeated something from the teachings of the order, so low that I could not understand what he said. Then we seemed all to leave the room, and a marvelous thing occurred.

We were sitting or lying on the floor. The Benefactor said something to me. And I seemed to be anxious to manifest my tenderness toward him, and, without listening to his discourse, I tried to realize the condition of my inner man, and the mercy of God, which had overshadowed me. And the tears stood in my eyes, and I was glad that he noticed it. But he glanced at me with a look of annoyance, and sprang up, breaking off his discourse. I was crestfallen, and asked if what he had said applied especially to me; but he made no reply; then he turned a benignant face upon me, and immediately we seemed to be in my sleeping-room, where stands a double bed. And he seemed to ask me, "Tell me honestly, what is your strongest temptation? Have n't you ever confessed it to me? It seems to me that you have."

I was mortified at his question, and replied that sloth was my chief sin. He shook his head incredulously, and I seemed to be still more confused, and replied that, though I lived with my wife, as he had advised, still, I did not live with her as a husband with a wife. To this he replied that a man ought not to deprive his wife of the affection which was her due, and gave me to feel that this was an obligation. But I replied that I was ashamed to begin now, and suddenly everything vanished.

When I awoke, I found myself repeating the text of Holy Writ: "*And the life was the light of men, and the light shineth in darkness, and the darkness comprehended it not.*"

Iosiph Alekseyevitch's face was youthful and bright. On that very same day I received a letter from the Benefactor, in which he wrote of the obligations of the married state.

DECEMBER 21.—I had a dream from which I awoke with a throbbing heart. I seemed to be in my own mansion in Moscow, in the great divan-room, and Iosiph Alekseyevitch seemed to be coming out of the dining-room. And I immediately saw that a strange change had taken place in him, and I hastened to meet him. And it seemed to me that I kissed his cheek and his hand, and he said:—

"Have you noticed that my face looks different?" I gazed

at him while still holding him in my embrace, and it seemed to me that his face was youthful, but there was no hair on his head, and his features were greatly altered. And it seemed to me that I replied, "I should have known you had I met you anywhere," and at the same time I ask myself, "Am I telling the strict truth?" and suddenly I see that he has fallen like a corpse; then he gradually came to his senses, and went with me into the great library, holding a great parchment book in manuscript in the Alexandrian style. And he seemed to say, "This I have written."

And he replied to me with an inclination of his head. I opened the book, and on all the pages of this book were exquisite illustrations. And it seemed to me that I recognized that these pictures represented the adventures of the soul with her beloved. And among them I seemed to see one representing a beautiful damsel flying through the clouds in diaphanous raiment, and with a transparent body. And I seemed to be aware that this damsel illustrated the Song of Songs. And as I looked at these pictures, it seemed to me that I was doing wrong, and yet I could not tear myself away. Lord, aid me! My God, if this, Thy abandonment of me, is Thy work, then Thy will be done. But if I myself am to blame, then teach me what I must do. I must perish in my own corruption, if Thou wholly abandonest me!

CHAPTER XI

THE Rostofs' financial affairs had not improved in the course of the two years while they had been living wholly in the country.

Although Nikolaï had persistently kept to his resolve, and continued to serve in an obscure regiment, where he had no chance of advancement, and therefore spent comparatively little money, still, the scale of life at Otradnoye was so large, and, above all, Mitenka's management was so bad, that the debts rolled up more and more each year. The old count evidently saw but one means of relief, — that was a government position, and he went to Petersburg to get a situation, and at the same time, as he expressed it, to give the girls one last season's amusement.

Shortly after the Rostofs reached Petersburg, Berg had proposed for Viera, and his proposal had been accepted.

In spite of the fact that in Moscow the Rostofs moved in the highest society, without thinking or inquiring what the society was to which they belonged, they found in Petersburg that their position was somewhat absurd and undefined. In Petersburg they were regarded as provincials, and many people who had accepted their hospitality at Moscow without question now did not deign to notice them.

The Rostofs entertained as freely at Petersburg as they had done at Moscow, and around their board gathered a very mixed company: neighbors of theirs at Otradnoye, landed proprietors of good standing but not rich, and their daughters and a Freïlina Peronskaya, Pierre Bezukhoï, and the son of their district postmaster, who had a government appointment at Petersburg. Among the men who were on a footing of familiarity at the Rostofs' were Boris, Pierre, whom the old count had met on the street one day and brought home with him, and Berg, who spent whole days at the Rostofs', and showed the Countess Viera those attentions which every young man is expected to show on the eve of a proposal.

Not without effect had Berg shown every one the right arm wounded at Austerlitz, and affected to hold his wholly unnecessary sword in his left hand. He described the occurrence so persistently, and made it a matter of such grave importance, that all came to believe in the genuineness and merit of his action, and Berg received two rewards after Austerlitz.

In the campaign in Finland he had also succeeded in distinguishing himself. He picked up a fragment of shell which had just killed one of the general-in-chief's aides, and carried this fragment to the chief. And in exactly the same way as after Austerlitz, he persisted in giving every one such detailed accounts of his behavior, that all came finally to believe with him that this must have taken place also; and again, after the war in Finland, he received two rewards. In 1809 he was already captain of the Guard, and held a most advantageous place in Petersburg.

Though there were some skeptics who smiled significantly when Berg's merits were mentioned in their presence, it was impossible not to admit that Berg was a strict, brave officer, of excellent standing at headquarters, and a highly moral young man, with a brilliant career before him, and already enjoying an exceptional position in society.

Four years before, Berg, happening to fall in with a comrade, also a German, in the parterre of one of the Moscow theaters, had called his attention to Viera Rostova, and said in German, "*Das soll mein Weib werden* — She is to be my wife," and from that moment he had laid his plans to marry her. Now that they were in Petersburg together, he compared his own position with the Rostofs', and came to the conclusion that his time had come, and he proposed.

Berg's proposal was received at first with a surprise not flattering to him. It seemed at first thought strange that the son of an obscure Lifland nobleman should offer himself to a Countess Rostova! But one of Berg's most characteristic traits was such a naïve and good-natured egotism, that the Rostofs began involuntarily to feel that it would be an excellent arrangement, if he himself were so firmly convinced that it was an excellent, a very excellent arrangement! Moreover, the Rostofs' affairs were in great disorder, so that there was little attraction for wooers; and, worse than all, Viera was twenty-four, and, although she had been everywhere, and was undoubtedly pretty and sensible, she had never before received an offer. So the consent was granted.

"Now you see," said Berg to a comrade whom he called his "friend," simply because he knew that it was fashionable for men to have friends, "you see I have weighed it all carefully, and I should not think of marrying if I had not thought it all over, or if it interfered with any one. But now, on the contrary, my father and mother are provided for. I have secured for them that leasehold on the Baltic frontier, and I can live in Petersburg on my salary, together with what comes from her estate, for I am careful and economical. We can live very well. I don't marry her for her money; I don't call that sort of thing honorable, but it 's no more than fair for the wife to contribute her portion and the husband his. I have my appointment; she, her connections and her little property. That 's something in these days, is n't it? But, best of all, she is a lovely girl, of good character and she loves me." ....

Berg reddened, and added with a smile, "And I love her because her character is well-balanced .... very admirable. Now there 's her sister, of the same family, but a very different person .... a most disagreeable character, and no sense at all, and that kind of thing, you know .... disagreeable. But my affianced .... well," continued Berg, "you 'll come to us some day to see her." He had it in mind to say, "to dine," but he bethought himself and said, "to tea," and, doubling up his tongue, he deftly sent forth a little ring of tobacco-smoke, absolutely typical of his dreams of happiness.

After the first feeling of dissatisfaction which Viera's parents felt at Berg's proposal, the festivity and happiness usual in such circumstances were redoubled; but the joy was not genuine, it was artificial. In the feelings of the relatives regarding this alliance there were mingled elements of perplexity and mortification. Their consciences pricked them because they had never been fond of Viera, and were now so glad to get her off their hands. The old count, most of all, was perplexed. He probably would not have been able to tell what was the cause of this perplexity, but the real cause of it was his finances. He really did not know how he stood or how much he owed, and what he should be able to give as Viera's dowry. When the daughters were born, each had received as a portion about three hundred serfs; but one of these estates had been already sold, and the other was mortgaged and the payments were so behindhand that it was bound to be foreclosed, and therefore could not be granted as a dower. Nor was there any money to spare.

Berg had already been the accepted bridegroom for more than a month, and only a week remained before the wedding, and still the count had not been able to face the dreaded question of the dowry, and had not broached the subject to his wife. At one time, the count thought of giving Viera his Riazan property; at another, of selling a forest; then of raising money on a note.

One morning, a few days before the wedding, Berg came early to the count's private room, and with a pleasant smile respectfully asked his future father-in-law what he was going to give as the Countess Viera's marriage portion. The count was so confused at this long-anticipated question that he answered at haphazard whatever first came into his head.

"I like it in you that you are careful, I like it; you shall be satisfied."....

And, patting Berg on his shoulder, he got up, thinking to end the conversation then and there. But Berg, still smiling pleasantly, explained that, unless he could know definitely what would be Viera's dowry, and unless a portion of it, at least, were paid over beforehand, he should be under the necessity of withdrawing from the offer.

"You will certainly agree with me, count, that if I should permit myself to marry without having a definite knowledge of what means I shall have for the maintenance of my wife, I should be acting abom...."

The conversation ended by the count, who wished to be generous, and also to avoid future demands, saying that he would give him a note for eighty thousand rubles. Berg, sweetly smiling, kissed him on the shoulder, and declared that he was very grateful, but that he could never make himself ready for his new life unless he had thirty thousand in ready cash. "Or only twenty thousand would do, count," he added. "And in that case, the note would be for only sixty thousand."

"Well, very good," said the count, hastily. "Only you

will allow me, my dear fellow, to give you the twenty thousand, and the note for eighty thousand besides. That 's the way we 'll do it! Kiss me!"

CHAPTER XII

NATASHA was now sixteen, and the year 1809 was the very one to which she had counted up on her fingers four years before, at the time when she and Boris had exchanged kisses. Since that time she had not once seen Boris. Before Sonya, and always with her mother, when Boris was mentioned, she had freely declared that all that had gone before was childish nonsense, as if it were a settled matter, of which there was no use talking, and long ago forgotten. But in the deepest depths of her heart she was tormented by the question whether the promise that bound her to Boris was to be considered in jest or in earnest.

From the very time when, in 1805, Boris had first left Moscow and joined the army, he had not met the Rostofs. He had been at Moscow several times, and had passed not very far from Otradnoye, but not once had he been to see his old friends.

It had several times occurred to Natasha that he was trying to avoid her, and her surmises had been strengthened by the melancholy tone in which her elders spoke of him.

"In these degenerate days, old friends are easily forgotten," said the countess, more than once, when Boris had been mentioned.

Anna Mikhaïlovna had also been more rarely of late at the Rostofs'; she seemed to hold herself especially on her dignity, and always spoke enthusiastically and boastfully of her son's merits, and the glittering career which he was now pursuing.

When the Rostofs came to Petersburg, Boris went to call on them.

He went to their house with some emotion. His romance with Natasha was the most poetical recollection of his youth. But at the same time he went there with a firm determination to give both her and her parents clearly to understand that those youthful relations between him and Natasha could not be considered binding on either of them. He had a brilliant position in society, thanks to his intimacy with the Countess Bezukhaya, a brilliant position in the service, thanks to the patronage of an eminent personage whose confidence he fully enjoyed, and he had now fully elaborated plans for a marriage with one of the wealthiest heiresses in Petersburg, which, indeed, he might very easily do.

When Boris reached the Rostofs', Natasha was in her room. When she was informed of his presence, she went to the drawing-room almost on a run, blushing and beaming with a more than gracious smile.

Boris remembered Natasha as a little girl, in a short gown, with dark, flashing eyes under her clustering hair, and with a wild, merry laugh. That was just as he had last seen her, four years before; and consequently, when an entirely different Natasha came into the room, he was taken aback, and his face expressed solemn amazement. This expression on his face delighted Natasha.

"Well, would you have known your mischievous little playmate?" asked the countess. Boris kissed Natasha's hand, and said that he noticed a great change in her: —

"How handsome you have grown!"

"Why should n't I?" replied Natasha's mocking eyes.

"Don't you think that papa seems much older?" she asked.

Natasha sat there without joining in the conversation between Boris and the countess, and silently studying the husband of her childhood's ideal, even to the minutest particulars. Boris was conscious of her steady and affectionate gaze fixed upon him, and occasionally he stole a glance at her.

His uniform, his spurs, his cravat, the cut of his hair, all were most fashionable and *comme il faut*. Natasha instantly noticed this. He sat somewhat toward the edge of the easy-chair, nearest the countess, with his right hand smoothing the immaculate, neat-fitting glove that he wore on his left, and he spoke, with a peculiarly delicate compression of the lips, about the gayeties of Petersburg high life, and he called to mind the old times in Moscow, and his Moscow acquaintances, with a gentle irony. Natasha felt sure that not without design he mentioned the names of the highest aristocracy, whom he had met at the ambassador's ball, or his invitations to the N. N.'s' and the S. S.'s'.

Natasha sat silent all the time, looking keenly at him. This glance of hers confused and troubled Boris more and more. He kept turning frequently toward her, and stumbling in the midst of his stories. He did not stay more than ten minutes, and then got up to take his leave. All the time those keen inquisitive eyes, full of mockery, looked at him with a peculiar challenging expression.

After this first visit of his, Boris confessed to himself that Natasha was just as fascinating to him as ever, but that it was his duty to renounce this feeling, because to marry her, an almost dowerless maiden, would be the ruin of his career, and the renewal of their former friendship without intention of marrying her would be a base trick. Boris resolved in his own mind to avoid meeting Natasha; but, notwithstanding this resolution, he went again in a few days, and kept going more and more frequently, and at last spent whole days at the Rostofs'. He kept trying to persuade himself that he would soon have a chance to come to an explanation with Natasha, and tell her that what was past must be forgotten, that, in spite of everything, she could not be his wife, that he had no property, and their friends would never consent to their union. But he kept putting it off, and finding it more and more awkward to bring about this explanation. Each day he became more and more perplexed.

In the opinion of her mother and Sonya, Natasha was just as much in love with Boris as ever she had been. She sang for him all her favorite pieces, showed him her album, begging him to write in it; but she never allowed him to talk about the past, giving him to understand how charming the new relationship was, and each day he entered deeper into the fog, never saying what he had resolved to say, not knowing what he was doing, or why he went there, and how it would all end. He even ceased to frequent Ellen's, though he daily received reproachful notes from her; but still he spent most of his spare time at the Rostofs'.

CHAPTER XIII

One evening, when the old countess, in nightcap and dressing-sack, with her false curls removed, and with one thin little wisp of white hair escaping from under her white calico cap, was performing the low obeisances of her evening devotions on a rug, sighing and groaning, the door of her room creaked on its hinges, and Natasha came running in, with her bare feet in slippers, and also in dressing-jacket and curl-papers.

The countess glanced around and frowned. She went on repeating her last prayer, "*If this couch become my tomb.*" Her devotional frame of mind was destroyed. Natasha, with rosy cheeks and full of animation, when she saw her mother at her devotions, suddenly paused, made a courtesy, and involuntarily poked out her tongue, to express her annoyance at her carelessness. Then, perceiving that her mother still went on with her prayer, she ran to the bed on tiptoes, kicked off her slippers by rubbing one dainty little foot against the other, and sprang into that couch which the countess was so afraid would be her tomb. This couch was a lofty feather-bed, with five pillows, each smaller than the other. Natasha jumped into the middle, sinking deep into the feather mattress, rolled over next the wall, and began to creep under the bedclothes, snuggling down, tucking her knees up to her chin, then giving animated little kicks, and laughing almost aloud, now and again uncovering her head and looking at her mother.

The countess finished her prayers, and with a stern face came to the bed; but seeing that Natasha's head was hidden under the bedclothes, she smiled her good, amiable smile.

"Nu, nu, nu," said the mother.

"Mamma, can we talk now? Say yes!" cried Natasha. "There now, one kiss in thy neck; just one more and that will satisfy me!" and she threw her arms around her mother, and kissed her under the chin. In her treatment of her mother, Natasha seemed to be very rough in her manner; but she was so dexterous and graceful, that, whenever she seized her mother in her arms, she always did it in such a way as not to hurt her, or disturb her at all.

"Well, what have you to tell me to-night?" asked the countess, settling back on the pillows, and waiting until Natasha, rolling over and over, should nestle down close to her, drop her hands, and become serious.

These visits from Natasha, which took place every night before the count came from his club, were a great delight to both mother and daughter.

"What is there to tell to-night? I want to tell you about...."

Natasha stopped her mother's mouth with her hand.

"About Boris?.... I know," said she, gravely. "That's why I came. Don't speak, I know! No, but you may tell me." She took away her hand. "Go on, mamma; he's a dear, isn't he?"

"Natasha, you are sixteen years old; at your age I was already married. You say that Boris is a dear. He is a very dear boy, and I love him like a son, but what do you wish?.... What are you thinking about? You have entirely turned his head, that's evident."....

As she said this, the countess looked at her daughter. Natasha lay looking fixedly at one of the carved mahogany sphinxes that ornamented the bedposts. The countess could only see her daughter's profile. It seemed to her that the sweet face had a peculiarly grave and thoughtful expression.

Natasha was listening and pondering.

"Well, what is it?"

"You have entirely turned his head. What made

you do so? What do you want of him? You know that you cannot marry him."

"Why not?" asked Natasha, without altering her position.

"Because he is young, because he is poor, because he is a relative.... because you yourself are not in love with him."

"How do you know I'm not in love with him?"

"I know. Now, this is not right, darling."

"But if I wish...." began Natasha.

"Do cease talking nonsense!" said the countess.

"But if I wish...."

"Natasha, I am in earnest...."

Natasha did not allow her to finish; she seized the countess's plump hand and kissed it on the back, and then on the palm; then turned it over again and began to kiss it on the knuckle-joint of each finger in succession, then on the middle joints, then again on the knuckles, repeating in a whisper, "January, February, March, April, May.... Tell me, mamma, why don't you go on? Speak!" said she, looking at her mother, who with affectionate eyes gazed at her daughter, becoming so engrossed in this contemplation that she apparently forgot what she was going to say.

"It is n't proper, dusha moya! People won't remember anything about your affection as children, but if he is seen to be so intimate with you now, it might injure you in the eyes of other young men who come to the house; and, worst of all, it is torturing him all for nothing. Perhaps he might, by this time, have found some rich girl to marry, but now he is quite beside himself."

"Beside himself?" repeated Natasha.

"I will tell you my own experience. I once had a cousin...."

"I know — Kirill Matveyitch, but he's an old man, is n't he?"

"He has n't always been old! But see here, Natasha, I am going to talk with Boris. He must not come here so often...."

"Why must n't he, if he likes to?"

"Because I know that this cannot come to any good end."

"How do you know? No, mamma! you must not speak to him. What nonsense!" exclaimed Natasha, in the tone of one who is about to be deprived of a possession. "Well, I won't marry him; but do let him come, for he enjoys it, and so do I." Natasha looked at her mother with a smile. "Not with any intentions, but this way," she repeated.

"What do you mean, my dear?"

"Why, *this way.* It is perfectly understood that he is not to marry me.... but *this way!*"

"Yes, this way, this way," repeated the countess; and she went into an unexpected fit of good-natured laughter, her whole body shaking.

"Come, mamma, stop laughing at me!" cried Natasha. "You make the whole bed shake. You are awfully like me. You laugh just as easily as I do..... Do stop!" ....

She seized the countess's two hands, kissed the joint of the little finger of one of them for June, and went on kissing July and August on the other hand.

"Mamma, but is he ever and ever so much in love?.... you think so, do you?.... Was any one ever as much in love with you?.... And he's a dear boy, very, very dear boy, is n't he? Only, he's not quite to my taste — he's so narrow, just like the dining-room clock. You know what I mean, don't you? narrow, you know.... grayish and polished." ....

"What nonsense you do talk!' exclaimed the countess.

Natasha went on: "Don't you understand what I mean? Nikolenka would understand me..... There's Bezukhoï, — he's blue, dark blue and red, and he is four square."

"And are you coquetting with him too?" asked the countess, laughing again.

"No; he's a Freemason; I found it out. He is splendid, dark blue and red. How can I make you see it?" ....

"Graphinyushka — little countess; are n't you asleep

yet?" cried the count at this moment at the door. Natasha jumped out of bed, seized her slippers in her hand, and escaped barefooted to her own room.

It was long before she could go to sleep. She kept thinking how strange it was that no one could ever understand things as she understood them, or read what was in her mind.

"Sonya?" she thought, gazing at the young girl, who, with her hair in a tremendous long braid, lay asleep curled up like a little kitten. "No, not even she! She is amiable! She is in love with Nikolenka, and that's all she cares about. And mamma can't understand either!.... It is so strange; how clever I am and how .... she is pretty," Natasha went on, speaking of herself in the third person, and imagining that some very intelligent, some most intelligent and most handsome man, was saying this about her. "She has everything, everything," this man of her imagination was saying. "She is extraordinarily clever, lovable, and pretty, besides .... extraordinarily pretty and graceful; she can swim, she can ride horseback splendidly, and what a voice! One might say, a marvelous voice!"

She sang her favorite snatch from a Cherubini opera, threw herself into bed, smiling at the happy thought that she should be asleep in a moment, called to Dunyasha to put out the light; and even before Dunyasha had left the room, she had already passed across into that other, still happier world of dreams, where all things were just as bright and beautiful as in reality, but still more fascinating, because so different.

On the next day, the countess, calling Boris to her, had a talk with him, and from that time forth he ceased to be a frequent visitor at the Rostofs'.

CHAPTER XIV

On the thirty-first of December (O.S.), on the very eve of the new year, 1810, *le réveillon*, a ball was given by a grandee of Catherine's time. The diplomatic corps and the emperor had promised to be present.

The grandee's splendid mansion on the English Quay was illuminated with countless windows, all ablaze. At the brilliantly lighted, red-carpeted entrance stood a guard of police, comprising not alone gendarmes, but even the chief of police and half a score of officers. Carriages drove away, and new ones kept taking their places, with red-liveried lackeys, and lackeys with plumes in their hats. From the carriages descended men in uniforms, and men adorned with stars and ribbons; and, as the steps were let down with a bang, ladies in satins and in ermine cloaks hastily and noiselessly went up the carpeted entrance.

Almost every time when a new equipage drove up, a flurry of excitement ran through the crowd, and hats were removed.

"The sovereign?" .... "No, a minister." .... "Prince so and so." .... "An ambassador." .... "But did you see his plume?"

Such were the remarks heard in the crowd. There was one man, better dressed than the rest, and he seemed to know who everybody was, and called by name the famous grandees of the time.

Already a third of the guests had arrived; but at the Rostofs', who were also invited, hasty preparations were still making.

In the Rostof family there had been much discussion and excitement over this ball; many were the apprehensions lest they should not get their invitation, lest their dresses should not be ready, lest everything should not be as it ought to be.

Marya Ignatyevna Peronskaya, an old friend and relative of the countess, was to accompany the Rostofs to the ball. She was a lean and sallow lady-in-waiting to the empress dowager, and took charge of her country cousins, the Rostofs, in their entry into Petersburg high life.

They were to call for her at ten o'clock in the evening at the Tavrichesky Sad, and now it lacked only five minutes of ten, and the ladies were not yet dressed.

This was the first great ball which Natasha had ever attended. She had got up at eight o'clock that morning, and had been all day long in a state of the wildest excitement and bustle. All her energies, from earliest morning, had been expended in the effort to have all of them — herself, Sonya, and her mamma — dressed to perfection. Sonya and the countess trusted themselves entirely to her hands. The countess was to wear a dark red or *masaka* velvet gown; the two girls white crêpe gowns with pink silk overskirts, and roses in their corsages; their hair was to be arranged *à la grecque.*

The most important part had been already done: their feet, hands, arms, necks, and ears had been washed, perfumed, and powdered with extraordinary care. On their feet they wore open-worked silk stockings, and white satin slippers with bows. Their toilets were almost finished. Sonya was already dressed, and so was the countess; but Natasha, who had been helping the others, was behindhand. She was still sitting in front of the mirror in a *peignoir* that covered her slender shoulders. Sonya, already dressed, was standing in the middle of the room fastening on a last bow with a pin that hurt her dainty fingers as she tried to press it, squeaking, through the ribbon.

"Not that way, not that way, Sonya," cried Natasha, turning her head suddenly, and putting her hands up to her hair, which the maid, who was dressing it, had not yet had time to finish. "Don't put the bow that way, come here!"

Sonya sat down in front of her. Natasha pinned the bow in a different position.

"If you please, baruishnya, I can't arrange your hair this way," exclaimed the maid, still holding Natasha's braids.

"Oh, good gracious, wait then! There, that's the way, Sonya!"

"Are you almost ready?" the countess was heard asking. "It's ten o'clock already."

"In a minute, in a minute. And are you all ready, mamma?"

"Only have my toque to put on."

"Don't you do it without me!" cried Natasha. "You won't get it right!"

"Yes, but it's ten o'clock!"

It had been decided upon that they should reach the ball-room at half-past ten, and Natasha had still to get on her gown, and they had to drive to the Tavrichesky Sad.

As soon as her hair was done, Natasha, in her short petticoat, which showed her ball-slippers, and wearing her mother's dressing-jacket, ran to Sonya and examined her critically; then she hurried to her mother. Bending her head down she put the toque on it, and, giving her gray hair a hasty kiss, she scurried back to the maids, who were putting the last touches to her skirt.

The delay had been caused by Natasha's skirt, which was too long; two maids were at work on it, hastily biting off the ends of the thread. A third, with her mouth full of pins, was hastening from the countess to Sonya; and a fourth was holding up high in the air the completed crêpe gown.

"Mavrushka, hurry up, you old dove."[1]

"Give me the thimble, baruishnya."

"Are you almost ready?" asked the count, coming to the door. "Here is some perfume for you. Peronskaya will be in a fume."

"There! it is done!" cried the maid, lifting up with two fingers the completed crêpe dress, and giving it a puff and a shake, by this motion expressing her sense of the airiness and purity of what she held.

Natasha began to put the garment on.

"In a minute, in a minute; don't come, papa," she cried to her father, who was just opening the door. Her

[1] *Galubushka.*

head at that very moment was disappearing under the cloud of crêpe. Sonya closed the door. But in a moment the count was admitted. He wore a blue dress-coat, short clothes, and buckled shoes, and was scented and pomaded.

"Oh! papa, how handsome you look! Charming!" cried Natasha, as she stood in the middle of the chamber and adjusted the folds of her skirt.

"Excuse me, baruishnya, excuse me," said one of the maids, who was on her knees pulling the skirts; and she shifted the pins from one side of her mouth to the other, with a deft motion of her tongue.

"Mercy on us!" cried Sonya, with despair in her voice, scrutinizing Natasha's dress. "Mercy on us! it 's too long now!"

Natasha made a few steps so as to look into the pier-glass. The skirt was indeed too long.

"Good gracious! sudaruinya, it is n't too long, at all," said Mavrusha, crawling along on the floor after her young mistress.

"Well, if it 's too long, then let us tack it up; we can do it in a second," said Dunyasha, in a decisive tone, taking a needle from the bosom of her dress, and again sitting on the floor, to baste up the bottom of the skirt.

At this instant, the countess, in her toque and velvet robe, came timidly into the room with noiseless steps.

"Oo! Oo! my beauty!" cried the count. "You are the best of them all!"....

He tried to give her a hug and a kiss, but she blushed and pushed him away, so as not to rumple her dress.

"Mamma, your toque wants to be more to one side," cried Natasha. "I will pin it on," and she sprang forward so quickly that the maids, who were at work on the skirt, did not have time to let go, and a piece of the crêpe was torn.

"Good heavens! what has happened?.... Truly, it was not my fault."....

"No matter; it won't be seen," said Dunyasha.

"O my beauty! a real queen!" cried the old nurse,

looking in at the door. "And Sonyushka, too; well, they are beauties!" ....

By quarter-past ten, finally, all were seated in the carriage and on their way. But they had still to stop at the Tavrichesky Sad.

Peronskaya was all ready and waiting for them. Notwithstanding her advanced age, and her lack of charms, almost exactly the same thing had taken place in her case as with the Rostofs, though, of course, with no haste and flurry, for this was an old story with her; but her unbeautiful old body had been washed and scented and powdered in just the same way, and she had been just as scrupulous in washing behind her ears; and just as at the Rostofs', her ancient maid had enthusiastically contemplated the adornment of her mistress, when, dressed in her yellow robe with the monogram, she had come down into the drawing-room.

Peronskaya praised the Rostofs' toilets and the Rostofs extolled her taste and her toilet; and at last, at eleven o'clock, taking great care of their hair and their gowns, they stowed themselves away in the carriages, and drove off.

CHAPTER XV

NATASHA, since that morning, had not had a moment's freedom; and not once had she taken time to think of what was before her.

In the raw, chill atmosphere, in the narrow, dimly lighted, swaying carriage, she, for the first time, vividly saw in her imagination what was waiting for her there, at the ball, in the lighted halls, — the music, the flowers, the dances, the sovereign, all the brilliant youth of the city. Fancy pictured it in such attractive colors, that she could hardly believe that it was going to be realized; it was all in such vivid contrast with the impression of the chill, the narrowness, and darkness of the carriage. She realized all that was awaiting her only at the moment when, having passed along the red-carpeted entrance, she went into the vestibule and took off her shuba, and, together with Sonya, preceded her mother up the grand staircase lined with flowering plants. Then only it came over her with what propriety she must behave at a ball, and she tried to assume that dignified manner which she felt to be the proper thing for a young maiden on such an occasion.

But, fortunately for her, she was conscious that her eyes were wandering; she could not distinguish anything clearly; her heart was beating a hundred a minute, and her pulses throbbed almost painfully. It was impossible for her to assume any such manner, and it would have been ridiculous in her; and so she walked along, trembling with excitement, and trying with all her might to hide it; and this was the very manner which, more than any other, was becoming to her. Behind them, and in front of them, other guests were mounting the stairs, also talking in low tones, and dressed in ball costumes. The mirrors on the landings reflected visions of ladies in white, blue, and pink gowns, with diamonds and pearls on their bare arms and bosoms.

Natasha glanced into the mirrors, but in the reflection she could not distinguish herself from among the others; all were commingled and confused in one glittering procession. As they reached the door leading into the first ball-room, an unbroken roar of voices, footsteps, and greetings deafened Natasha; the lights and brilliant toilets still more dazzled her. The host and hostess, who had been half an hour standing near the entrance and repeating over the same words of welcome, "*Charmé de vous voir,*" met the Rostofs and Peronskaya in the same way.

The two young girls, in their white gowns, each with a single rose in her dark locks, went in and courtesied exactly alike; but involuntarily the hostess let her glance rest longer on the slender little Natasha. She looked at her and smiled on her alone with a special graciousness; to the others she was only the hostess. As she looked at her, she perhaps remembered the golden days of her girlhood, which would never more return, and her own first ball. The host also followed Natasha with his glance, and asked the count which of the two was his daughter.

"*Charmante!*" said he, kissing his finger-tips.

In the great ball-room, the guests were crowded together near the entrance, awaiting the coming of the sovereign. The countess took her place in the front row of this group. Natasha had had her ears open, and was conscious that several had asked who she was, and had looked at her. She realized that she was making a pleasant impression on those whose attention she had attracted, and this fact somewhat calmed her agitation.

"There are some just like ourselves, and some not so good," she thought.

Peronskaya was pointing out to the countess the most notable personages in the ball-room.

"There! that's the Dutch ambassador, see, — that gray-headed man," said Peronskaya, directing the countess's attention to a gentleman with abundant curly hair, silver-white. He was surrounded by ladies, whom he had just set to laughing by some remark.

"Ah! and there is the tsaritsa of Petersburg, the Countess Bezukhaya," she exclaimed, indicating Ellen, who had just entered. "How handsome she is! she does not stand second even to Marya Antonovna. Just see how young and old stare after her. She's both handsome and intelligent. .... They say Prince —— has gone daft about her. And see those two, there! They are not pretty at all, but what a following they have!"

She indicated a lady and her extremely plain daughter, who were just crossing the ball-room.

"That girl is the heiress to millions," said Peronskaya; "and there are her suitors. That's the Countess Bezukhaya's brother, Anatol Kuragin," said she, calling attention to a handsome young cavalryman, who was just then passing them, holding his head very high, and not deigning to give the ladies any recognition. "How handsome he is! is n't he? They say he's going to marry this heiress; and your cousin, Drubetskoï, is also after her; they say she has millions. .... Who? Oh!

that is the French ambassador himself," she replied to the countess, who asked who Caulaincourt was. "Just see, he is like some tsar! And yet they are all so pleasant, so very pleasant — these French. Ah! and there *she* is! After all, there is no one who can be compared to our Marya Antonovna. And how simply she is dressed! Charming! — And that stout man yonder, in spectacles, is the universal Freemason," said she, pointing out Bezukhoï. "Compare him with his wife! what a ridiculous creature!"

Pierre walked along, his stout form swaying, and pushed through the throng, bowing to right and left, carelessly and good-naturedly, as if he were making his way through the swarms of a market-place. He passed along, evidently in search of some one.

Natasha was glad to see Pierre's well-known face, even if he was "a ridiculous creature," to use the words of Peronskaya; and she knew that it was her party, and herself in particular, of whom Pierre was in search. Pierre had promised that he would attend the ball and find partners for her.

But before he reached where they stood, Pierre stopped near a short and very handsome dark-featured cavalryman, in a white uniform, who was standing by the window and conversing with a tall man with stars and a ribbon. Natasha instantly recognized the short young man in the white uniform: it was Bolkonsky, who seemed to her to have grown younger, gayer, and handsomer.

"There 's another of our acquaintance — Bolkonsky — do you see him, mamma?" asked Natasha, indicating Prince Andreï. "Do you remember? he spent a night with us at Otradnoye."

"Ah, indeed! so you know him, then?" asked Peronskaya. "I cannot endure him. *Il fait à present la pluie et le beau temps!*[1] There's no end to his pride. He 's like his father. And now he 's hand in glove with Speransky; they are concocting all sorts of schemes.

[1] "From him now we must look for our good weather or our rain;" a French proverb, signifying his success. — AUTHOR'S NOTE.

See how he treats the ladies! one just spoke to him, and he turned his back on her! I 'd give him a lesson if he treated me as he did those ladies."

CHAPTER XVI

SUDDENLY there was a general stir: a whisper ran through the throng, which pressed forward and then divided again, making two rows, between which came the sovereign, to the strains of the band which just then began to play. He was followed by the host and hostess. The sovereign passed along, hastily bowing to the right and left, as if he were anxious to have done as soon as possible with these first formalities. The musicians played a polonaise then famous, on account of the words which had been set to it. These words began, "*Aleksandr, Yelizavyeta, you enrapture us.*" ....

The sovereign entered the drawing-room. The throng pushed toward the doors; several personages, with anxious faces, in great haste, rushed hither and thither. The throng again moved away from the drawing-room door, where the sovereign made his appearance, engaged in conversation with the hostess. A young man, with an expression of annoyance on his face, came along and begged the ladies to step back. Several ladies, with eager faces, showing absolute disregard of all the conventional rules of good breeding, pushed forward, to the imminent risk of their toilets. The gentlemen began to select partners, and get into position for the polonaise.

Space was cleared; and the sovereign, with a smile, stepping out of time, passed into the ball-room, leading the lady of the house by the hand.

They were followed by the host, with Marya Antonovna Naruishkina; then ambassadors, ministers, and various generals, whom Peronskaya indefatigably called by name.

More than half of the ladies had partners, and were already dancing or beginning to dance the polonaise.

Natasha felt that she and Sonya, as well as her mother,

were neglected with that minority of ladies who lined the walls, and were not invited to take part in the polonaise. She stood with her slender arms hanging by her sides; with her maidenly bosom, as yet scarcely defined, regularly rising and falling with long inspirations; and she looked straight ahead with brilliant eyes full of alarm, indicating that she was ready for the greatest enjoyment or the greatest disappointment.

She was not interested now in the sovereign, or in any of those distinguished personages whom Peronskaya was calling their attention to; she had only one thought, —

"Is n't any one coming to invite me? Can it be that I am not going to be taken out for the first dance? Won't any of those men notice me? — of those men who now do not seem to see me; or, if they see me, look at me as much as to say, 'Oh, she's nothing, — she's nothing to look at!' No, it cannot be!" said she to herself. "They must know how I am longing to dance, and how splendidly I dance, and how much they would enjoy it if they danced with me!"

The strains of the polonaise, which had now lasted some little time, began to have a melancholy cadence in Natasha's ears, — as if connected with sad memories. She felt like having a good cry. Peronskaya had left them; the count was at the other end of the ball-room; she and Sonya and the countess were as much alone, in this throng of strangers, as if they were in the woods; no one took any interest in them, or looked out for them.

Prince Andreï passed them with a lady on his arm, and evidently did not recollect them. The handsome Anatol, smiling, said something to the lady with whom he was promenading, and looked into Natasha's face as one looks at a wall. Twice Boris passed them, and each time turned his head away. Berg and his wife, who were not dancing, joined them.

Natasha felt mortified to death at this family gathering, there, at the ball; as if they had no other place for family confidences than in a ball-room. She did not look at Viera, or listen to what she had to say about her emerald-green dress.

At last the sovereign sat down near his last partner — he had danced with three — and the music ceased. An officious aide bustled up to the Rostofs, begging them to move back a little more, and this although they almost touched the wall; and then from the gallery was heard the rhythmical, smooth, and enticing sounds of the waltz.

The sovereign, with a smile, glanced down the ball-room. A moment passed, and no one had as yet begun. The aide, who acted as master of ceremonies, approached the Countess Bezukhaya, and asked her to dance. She accepted with a smile, and then, without looking at him, laid her hand on his shoulder. The aide, who was a master of his business, calmly, deliberately, and with all self-confidence, placing his arm firmly about her waist, at first started off with her in the *glissade* around the edge of the circle; then, when they reached the end of the ball-room, he took her right hand with his left, turned her around, and, while the sounds of the waltz grew more and more rapid, the clicking of the aide's spurs could be heard, as his agile and skilful feet beat the time of the rhythm; while on the third beat, at every turn, his partner's velvet dress floated out and seemed to fly. Natasha gazed at them, and was ready to weep that it was not she herself who was leading this first waltz.

Prince Andreï, in the white uniform of a colonel of cavalry, in silk stockings and shoe-buckles, stood, full of life and radiant with happiness, in the front row of the circle, not far from the Rostofs. Baron Firhof was talking to him about the first meeting of the Imperial Council, which had been appointed for the next day. Prince Andreï, as an intimate friend of Speransky, and one who had shared in the labors of the Legislative Committee, might be able to give authentic information in regard to the approaching session, concerning which there were various rumors. But Prince Andreï was not listening to what Firhof was saying, and looked now at the sovereign, and now at the various gentlemen who were all ready to dance, but had not the necessary courage to take the floor.

Prince Andreï was observing these gentlemen, who showed such timidity in the presence of their sovereign, and the ladies, whose hearts were sinking within them with desire to be invited.

Pierre came up to Prince Andreï and took him by the arm.

"You are always ready for a dance. My *protégée*, the little Rostova, is here; do invite her!" said he.

"Where?" asked Bolkonsky. "I beg your pardon," he added, turning to the baron. "We will finish this conversation at another time; but at balls it is our duty to dance."

He went in the direction indicated by Pierre. Natasha's despairing, melancholy face attracted Prince Andreï's attention. He recognized her, and divined her feeling; and, realizing that she was just "coming out," and remembering her conversation, he went with a beaming countenance up to the Countess Rostova.

"Allow me to make you acquainted with my daughter," said the countess, with a blush.

"I have had the pleasure of meeting her before, but perhaps the countess does not remember me," said Prince Andreï, with a low and respectful bow, entirely belying Peronskaya's spiteful observation about his rudeness. Approaching Natasha, he started to put his arm around her waist, even before he had actually invited her to dance with him. Then he proposed that they should take a turn of the waltz. Natasha's face, with its melancholy expression, ready to sink to despair or become radiant, was suddenly lighted up with a happy, childlike smile of gratitude.

'I had been waiting long for you,' this timid and radiant young maiden seemed to say, by this smile flashing out from under the tears that had been almost ready to start, as she put her hand on Prince Andreï's shoulder. They were the second couple that ventured out upon the floor. Prince Andreï was one of the best dancers of his time. Natasha danced exquisitely; her dainty little feet, shod in her satin slippers, performed their duty with perfect ease and agility, independently of her volition; and her face beamed with triumphant delight.

Her bare neck and arms were thin and far from pretty, compared with Ellen's charms. Her shoulders were slim, her figure undeveloped, her arms slender; but Ellen seemed to be already covered with an enamel left by the thousand glances that had glided over her form, while Natasha seemed like a maiden who for the first time appeared in a low-necked gown, and would feel very much mortified if she were not assured that it was the proper thing.

Prince Andreï liked to dance, and, as he wanted to escape as soon as possible from the political and intellectual remarks with which all approached him, and to break up, as soon as possible, that tiresome circle of people abashed by the presence of the sovereign, — he was ready to dance; and he chose Natasha because Pierre had suggested her, and because she happened to be the first among all the pretty women who attracted his attention. But as soon as he clasped her slender, supple form, and she began to move so close to him, and smiled up into his face, the wine of her fascination mounted to his head; he felt a renewed energy and fresh life when, having released her, he stopped and began to look at the other dancers.

CHAPTER XVII

FOLLOWING Prince Andreï's example, Boris came and invited Natasha to dance with him; also the master of ceremonies, who had opened the ball, and several other young men; and Natasha, turning her superfluity of partners over to Sonya, flushed and happy, did not miss a single dance throughout the rest of the evening.

She had eyes for nothing else, and she did not notice what had attracted the attention of every one else at the ball. She did not once remark how the emperor had a long conversation with the French ambassador; or how he showed signal favor to a certain lady who was present; or how Prince So-and-So and So-and-So said and did this, that, and the other thing; or how Ellen enjoyed a brilliant success and attracted the special attention of such and such a person: she did not even see the sovereign, and only noticed that he had withdrawn by the fact that, after his departure, the ball became livelier than ever.

Just before supper, Prince Andreï danced one of the jolliest of cotillions with Natasha. He reminded her of their first meeting on the Otradnoye driveway, and how she could not go to sleep that moonlight night, and how he had involuntarily overheard what she said. Natasha blushed at this reminiscence, and tried to excuse herself, as if there were something of which she ought to be ashamed in the consciousness that Prince Andreï had accidentally overheard her.

Prince Andreï, like all men who had grown up in society, liked to meet any one that was free from the stereotyped imprint of fashionable high life; and such a person was Natasha, with her admiration, her enjoyment, and her modesty, and even her mistakes in speaking French.

He treated her, and spoke to her, with a peculiar delicacy and affectionate courtesy. As he sat next to her, talking on the simplest and most insignificant topics, Prince Andreï admired the merry gleam in her eyes, and her smile, answering not to what was said to her so much as to her inward happiness. If, by chance, Natasha was invited to dance, and got up with a smile, and went dancing across the room, Prince Andreï found especial delight in watching her fawn-like grace. In the midst of the cotillion, Natasha, having just danced out one figure, came back to her place, still panting. A new partner again invited her out. She was tired and out of breath, and evidently at first inclined to refuse; but instantly placed her hand on the cavalier's shoulder, and gave Prince Andreï a smile.

'I should like very much to get my breath, and sit with you, — I am tired, — but you see how I am in demand; and that pleases me, and I am happy, and I love you all, and you and I understand it all;' this, and much more besides, this smile of hers seemed to say. When her partner released her, Natasha glided across the room to choose two ladies for the figure.

"If she speaks to her cousin first, and then to the other lady, she will be my wife!" said Prince Andreï, unexpectedly even to himself, as he looked at her.

She went to her cousin first!

"What nonsense sometimes enters one's head!" said Prince Andreï to himself. "But it is quite evident that this maiden is so sweet, and so unlike anybody else, that she won't be kept dancing here for a month; she 'll be engaged or married..... There 's no one like her here!" he thought, as Natasha, smoothing out the crumpled petals of a rose in her corsage, came back and resumed her place next him.

At the end of the cotillion the old count, in his blue coat, came up to the dancers. He invited Prince Andreï to call and see them, and he asked his daughter if she had been having a good time. Natasha at first did not reply, except by a smile which had a sort of reproach in it, as much as to say, 'How can you ask such a question?'

"The jolliest time I ever had in my life," said she; and Prince Andreï noticed how she made a quick motion to raise her slender arms, as if to embrace her father, and instantly dropped them again. Natasha was happier than she had ever been in her life before; she had reached that lofty height of bliss, when a person becomes perfectly good and lovely, and cannot believe in the existence or the possibility of wickedness, unhappiness, and sorrow.

Pierre, at this ball, for the first time had a realizing sense of the humiliating position in which he was placed by the status occupied by his wife in court society. He was morose and absent-minded. A deep frown furrowed his brow; and, as he stood by the window, he glared through his spectacles, and yet saw nothing.

Natasha, as she went down to supper, passed by him

His gloomy, unhappy face struck her. She paused in front of him; she felt a desire to help him, to share with him the superfluity of her own happiness.

"How jolly it is, count," said she. "Is n't it?"

Pierre gave her a distracted smile, evidently not understanding what she said.

"Yes, I am very glad," he replied.

"How can any one be dissatisfied with anything?" wondered Natasha. "Especially such a good fellow as that Bezukhoï."

In Natasha's eyes, all who were at the ball were alike good, sweet, lovely men, full of affection toward one another; hatred was out of the question, and therefore all ought to be happy.

CHAPTER XVIII

On the next day Prince Andreï remembered the ball of the evening before, but it soon passed out of his mind.

"Yes, it was a very brilliant ball; and besides .... yes, the little Rostof girl was very captivating. There's something peculiarly fresh about her, very original and un-Petersburg-like!"

That was the extent of the thought that he gave to the ball; and, after he had drunk his tea, he sat down to his labors. But, either because of his weariness, or his sleepless night, the day was unpropitious for work and he could not accomplish anything; he kept finding fault with his own work, as was often the case with him, and he was glad when word was brought that some one had come to see him.

The visitor was Bitsky, who had served on various committees, and frequented all the different cliques of Petersburg society. He was a zealous supporter of the new ideas and of Speransky, and was an indefatigable gossip-monger: one of those men who follow the fashion in their opinions as in their clothes, and who, for that very reason, are regarded as the most eager partisans of the latest doctrines.

Scarcely giving himself time to remove his hat, he

rushed eagerly into Prince Andreï's room, and, on the instant, rattled off into a stream of talk. He had only just learned the details of the session of the Imperial Council, that had taken place that morning, opened by the sovereign in person, and he began to tell about it with enthusiasm. The sovereign's speech had been extraordinary; it was such a speech as only a constitutional monarch could have uttered.

"The emperor said, in so many words, that the council and the senate were now the *members* of the government: he declared that the administration should have its basis, not on arbitrary will, but on firm principles. The sovereign declared that the finances should be reorganized, and the budgets made public," said Bitsky, laying a special emphasis on the important words, and opening his eyes significantly. "Yes, the event of to-day marks an era, a magnificent era, in our history," he said in conclusion.

Prince Andreï listened to the story of the opening of the Imperial Council, which he had been looking forward to with so much impatience, and to which he attributed so much importance; and he was amazed that this event, now that it was really accomplished, not only did not stir him, but even seemed to him worse than idle. He listened to Bitsky's enthusiastic account with quiet irony. The most obvious thought that came into his head was, "What concern is it to me or to Bitsky, — indeed, what concern is it of ours, — what the sovereign deigned to say in the council? Can it make me any happier, or any better?"

And this obvious criticism suddenly destroyed for Prince Andreï all the interest that he had formerly taken in the reforms.

Prince Andreï had been invited to dine that day at Speransky's, "*en petit comité*," as he himself expressed it when he gave him the invitation.

The idea of this dinner, in the intimate and home circle of a man for whom he felt such an admiration, had before this been exceedingly attractive to Prince Andreï, the more from the fact that hitherto he had never seen

Speransky in his family life; but now he lost all desire to go.

At the hour set for the dinner, however, Prince Andreï reached Speransky's own small house, near the Tavrichesky Sad. Prince Andreï, a little late, was shown into the parquetry-floored dining-room of the modest little residence, — distinguished for its extraordinary, its rather monastic, primness, — where all the gentlemen constituting Speransky's *petit comité*, being his most intimate friends, had promptly assembled at five o'clock. There were no ladies present, except Speransky's young daughter, who had a long face just like her father's, and her governess. The guests were Gervais, Magnitsky, and Stoluipin.

Even while Prince Andreï was in the anteroom, he heard loud voices, and a clear, precise ha-ha-ha: a laugh like that affected by actors on the stage. Some one, whose voice sounded like Speransky's, rang out distinctly: ha-ha-ha. Prince Andreï had never heard Speransky laugh heartily, and the clear, ringing laugh of the great statesman struck him strangely.

Prince Andreï went into the dining-room. All the company were standing between two windows, around a small table, spread with the zakuska. Speransky, in a gray coat, with a star, and wearing the same immaculate white waistcoat and high white stock in which he had appeared at the memorable meeting of the Imperial Council, stood at the table, his face beaming with pleasure. The gentlemen formed a circle around him. Magnitsky, addressing Mikhaïl Mikhaïlovitch, was relating an anecdote. Speransky listened, and began to laugh even before Magnitsky reached the point of his story. At the moment Prince Andreï entered the room, Magnitsky's words were drowned in another roar of merriment: Stoluipin's deep voice rang out, as he nibbled a morsel of bread and cheese; Gervais bubbled over with tinkling laughter; and above all rang out Speransky's loud, deliberate ha-ha-ha.

Speransky, still laughing, gave his soft white hand to Prince Andreï.

"Very glad to see you, prince," said he. "One minute,".... said he, turning to Magnitsky, and interrupting the story he was telling. "We have an agreement today: dinner is for recreation, and not a word about business."

And again he turned to the narrator, and again broke out into laughter..

Prince Andreï, with surprise and sorrowful disillusionment, listened to his guffawing, and gazed at the hilarious Speransky. It seemed to Prince Andreï that it was not Speransky, but another man. All the mystery and charm that he had hitherto discovered in Speransky suddenly seemed commonplace and repulsive.

The conversation at the table did not flag for a moment, and seemed to consist of little more than a string of ludicrous stories. Magnitsky had scarcely time to cap the climax of his story, when some one else manifested his readiness to tell something that was even funnier. The anecdotes were for the most part, if not exactly confined to the world of officialdom, at least related to the individuals in the service. It seemed as if, in this gathering, the insignificance of such characters was so thoroughly taken for granted, that the only way in which it was worth while to speak of them was to cover them with good-natured ridicule.

Speransky related how at the council meeting that morning, one of the statesmen, who happened to be deaf, on being asked his opinion, replied that he was entirely agreeable. Gervais related a long incident in connection with the census, wherein remarkable stupidity had been shown by all persons concerned. Stoluipin, who had an impediment in his speech, joined the conversation, and began with some heat to speak of the abuses of the former order of things; but, as this threatened to give a too serious character to the talk, Magnitsky chaffed him on his earnestness. Gervais made a pun, and again the talk assumed its former hilarious character.

Evidently Speransky, after his labors, liked recreation,

liked to divert himself with a gay circle of friends; and all his guests, knowing this characteristic of his, did their best to make him enjoy himself, and at the same time to enjoy themselves. But this gayety seemed to Prince Andreï forced, and the opposite of gay. The ringing tones of Speransky's voice impressed him unpleasantly, and his incessant laughter had a false ring to it which strangely wounded his sensibilities. Prince Andreï could not laugh, and he was afraid that he should appear like a killjoy in the company. But no one noticed that he did not participate in the general merriment. All of them, it seemed, were extremely gay.

He tried several times to put in his word; but each time it was tossed back, as it were, like a cork tossed out of the water, and he could not jest like the others.

There was nothing wrong or ill-judged in what they said; wit and sense were displayed, and it ought to have been really worth laughing at, but something, the very thing that constitutes the salt of gayety, was lacking; but, worse than all, they did not seem to realize that it was.

After dinner, Speransky's little daughter, with her guvernantka, withdrew. Speransky caressed the little girl with his white hand, and kissed her. Even this action seemed to Prince Andreï full of affectation.

The gentlemen, after the English fashion, remained sitting at table over their port wine. The conversation had turned on Napoleon's management of affairs in Spain, and all were of one and the same mind in their approbation of it; but Prince Andreï took it on him to disagree with them. Speransky smiled, and, evidently wishing to change the subject, told a story which was totally irrelevant. Then silence ensued for several moments.

Before they left the table, Speransky recorked a bottle in which a little wine was left, and saying, "Good wine is expensive these days,"[1] handed it to the servant, and got up.

All arose, and, still talking noisily, passed into the

[1] "Good wine goes in fine boots," a variant of a Russian proverb.

drawing-room. Speransky was handed two envelops brought by a courier. He took them and went into his private room. As soon as he had left, the general gayety subsided, and the guests began to talk together in subdued tones on matters of real interest.

"Well, then, now for a recitation!" exclaimed Speransky, coming back from his private room. "Wonderful talent," he said, addressing Prince Andreï. Magnitsky immediately assumed an attitude, and began to recite some satirical verses which he had written in French on certain well-known personages in Petersburg, and several times he was interrupted by applause. At the end of this recitation, Prince Andreï went to Speransky to take leave.

"Where must you be going so early?" asked Speransky.

"I promised to spend the evening...."

All were silent. Prince Andreï looked into Speransky's mirror-like and impenetrable eyes, and it seemed to him ridiculous that he had ever expected anything great from this Speransky, or of the work that he had undertaken to perform, or how he could ever have attributed any importance to what Speransky was doing. It was long before that dry, measured laugh of his ceased to ring in his ears, even after he had taken his leave of Speransky.

On his return home, Prince Andreï began to live over his life in Petersburg during the four months past, as if it were something new. He recalled his labors, his rounds of solicitation, the history of his project of the military code — which had been brought to notice, and then quietly laid on the table, for the sole reason that another one of very wretched character had already been compiled and placed before the sovereign; he recalled the meetings of his committee, of which Berg was a member; he recalled how strenuously and at what length everything that touched upon the outside forms and proceedings of their meetings had been discussed, and how careful they had been to avoid everything that reached the essence of the matter; he recalled his judicial labors, and what pains he had taken to translate articles on the

Roman and French course of procedure into Russian; and he grew ashamed of himself.

Then his imagination vividly brought up before his mind his estate of Bogucharovo, his projects in the country, his journey to Riazan; he recalled his muzhiks, and their head man, Dron, and he applied to them his theory of the individual rights which he had so carefully elaborated into paragraphs; and he was amazed at himself that he could have wasted so much time in such idle work.

CHAPTER XIX

On the following day Prince Andreï went to make calls at several houses where he had not been as yet, and in the number at the Rostofs', whose acquaintance he had renewed at the last ball. Not only was he required by the laws of politeness to call at the Rostofs', but he also had a strong desire to see in her own home this original and lively young girl, of whom he had such pleasant recollections.

Natasha was the first who came down to see him. She wore a simple blue morning-dress, and it seemed to Prince Andreï that it was even more becoming to her than the one she had worn at the ball. She and the rest of the family received Prince Andreï simply and hospitably, as an old friend. The whole family, which he had at first been inclined to criticize severely, now seemed to him charming, simple-hearted, and cordial people. The old count showed such genuine and unbounded hospitality, and his good nature was so contagious, especially there in Petersburg, that Prince Andreï could not with good grace refuse his invitation to dinner.

"Yes, they are excellent people," said Bolkonsky to himself. "Of course they cannot appreciate what a treasure they possess in Natasha; but they are good, kindly people, and they make a most admirable background against which to bring out all the charm of this wonderfully poetical young girl, so overflowing with vivacity."

Prince Andreï felt that in Natasha existed a peculiar and unknown world, full of unrealized delights, — that unknown world of which he had caught the first glimpse as he drove through the Otradnoye avenue, and then again at the window that moonlight night, when he had been so stirred by it. Now this world no longer excited his curiosity, no longer was it a strange world; but, as he entered into it, he realized that new delight was awaiting him.

After dinner, Natasha, at the count's request, went to the clavichord and began to sing. Prince Andreï stood by the window and listened, occasionally exchanging words with the other ladies. In the middle of a phrase Prince Andreï stopped talking, and, to his amazement, found that he was choked with tears, a thing which he would not have believed possible for him. He looked at Natasha as she sang, and a new and joyous feeling arose in his heart. He was happy, and at the same time melancholy. He had really nothing to weep about, but he was ready to burst into tears. For what? his former love?.... For the little princess?.... For his disappointed illusions?.... For his hopes of the future?.... Yes and no! The chief reason that he felt like weeping was the sudden awakening to that strange and vivid contradiction between the boundlessly immense and infinite that existed in him, and the narrow and limited world to which he felt that he himself, and even she, belonged.

This contrast tormented and rejoiced him while she was singing.

As soon as Natasha finished her song, she went to him and asked him frankly how he liked her voice. She asked the question, and was overwhelmed with confusion the moment she had spoken, realizing, when it was too late, that she ought not to have asked it. He smiled as he looked at her, and replied that he liked her singing just as he liked everything else that she did.

It was late that evening before Prince Andreï left the

Rostofs'. He went to bed as usual, but soon found that he had a sleepless night before him. Relighting his candle, he sat up in bed a little while; then he got up; then he lay down again; still, he was not in the least oppressed by this sleeplessness; his soul was so full of new and joyful sensations, that it seemed to him as if he had just emerged from a sultry chamber into God's free world. Nor did it once occur to him that he was in love with the young Countess Rostova; he did not think of her, he only imagined her himself; and the consequence of this was that all his whole life presented itself to him in a new light.

"Why am I struggling, why am I toiling and moiling in this narrow, petty environment, when life, all of life, with all its pleasures, is open before me?" he asked himself.

And for the first time for long months, he began to devise cheerful plans for the future. He decided that it was his duty to undertake personally the education of his son, to find him an instructor, and put him into his hands; then he would quit the service and travel abroad, and see England, Switzerland, and Italy.

"I must make the most of my freedom, since I feel myself so overflowing with strength and energy," said he to himself. "Pierre was right in saying that one ought to believe in the possibility of happiness, and now I believe it is so. Let the dead bury their dead; but, while we are alive, let us live," he thought.

CHAPTER XX

One morning, Colonel Adolph Berg, with whom Pierre was acquainted, just as he was acquainted with every one in Petersburg and Moscow, came to see him. He was dressed in an immaculate and brand-new uniform, with little pomaded love-locks curling round over his temples, just as the sovereign wore them.

"I have just come from calling on the countess, your wife, and I was so unfortunate in not being able to have my request granted! I hope, count, that I shall be more successful with you," said he, with a smile.

"What would you like, colonel? I am at your service."

"I am now quite completely settled in my new rooms, count," pursued Berg, evidently convinced in his own mind that this communication could not fail to be an agreeable piece of news. "And, consequently, I wanted to have a little reception for my friends and my wife's." He smiled more effusively than ever. "I wanted to ask the countess and yourself to do me the honor to come and take a cup of tea with us, and — and have supper."

Only the Countess Elena Vasilyevna, who considered the society of such people as the Bergs beneath her, could have had the heart to refuse such an invitation. Berg explained so clearly why he desired to gather around him a small and select company, and why it would be pleasant to him, and why he grudged money spent on cards, and other disreputable occupations, but was willing to go to large outlay in entertaining good company, that Pierre could not think of refusing, and agreed to be present.

"Only don't come late, count, if I may be so bold as to beg of you; at ten minutes to eight, I beg of you. We will have cards; our general will come, — he is very good to me. We will have a good supper, count. So please do me the favor."

Contrary to his usual habit of being late, Pierre that evening reached the Bergs' at quarter to eight, five minutes before the appointed time.

The Bergs, having made every provision for the reception, were all ready and waiting for their guests to come.

Berg and his wife were sitting together in their library, all new and bright, and well provided with statuary and paintings and new furniture. Berg, in a nice new uniform, tightly buttoned up, was sitting near his wife, explaining to her that it was always possible and proper to have acquaintances among people of high station, that being the only real advantage in having friends. "You can always find something to imitate, and can ask any sort of advice. You see, that 's the way I have done ever since I was first promoted." — Berg did not reckon his life according to his years, but according to the various steps of promotion. — "My comrades are still of no account, but, at the first vacancy, I shall be made regimental commander; and then, I have the happiness of being your husband." He got up and kissed Viera's hand, but, before he did so, he straightened out the corner of a rug that was turned up. "And how have I accomplished all this? Principally, by exercising a choice in my acquaintances. Of course, though, one has to be straightforward and punctual."

Berg smiled with the consciousness of his superiority over a weak woman, and relapsed into silence, saying to himself that his wife, lovely as she was, was, nevertheless, a feeble woman, unable to appreciate the full significance of the dignity of being a man — *ein Mann zu sein!*

Viera, at the same time, smiled with a similar consciousness of her superiority over her good, worthy spouse; who, nevertheless, like the rest of his sex, was quite mistaken, she thought, in his understanding of the meaning of life.

Berg, judging by his wife, considered that all women were weak and unintellectual. Viera, judging by her husband alone, and making wider generalizations, supposed that all men considered no one but themselves wise, and at the same time had no real understanding, and were haughty and egotistical.

Berg got up, and, embracing his wife carefully, — so as not to rumple her lace pelerine, for which he had paid a high price, — kissed her on the center of the lips.

"There is one thing, — we must not begin to have children too soon," said he, by an unconscious correlation of ideas.

"Yes," replied Viera. "That 's exactly what I do not want. We must live for society."

"The Princess Yusupovaya has one exactly like this,"

said Berg, laying his finger on the lace pelerine, with his honest, happy smile.

At this time Count Bezukhoï was announced. The young couple exchanged congratulatory glances, each appropriating the honor of this visit.

"This is what comes of understanding how to form acquaintances," said Berg. "This comes of having tact!"

"Now, I beg of you, don't interrupt me when I am talking with guests," said Viera. "Because I know how to receive each one, and what to talk to them about."

Berg also smiled.

"Of course; but sometimes, among men, there must be conversation for men," said he.

Pierre was shown into the new drawing-room, where one could not possibly take a seat without destroying the symmetry, neatness, and order that reigned there; and, consequently, it was perfectly comprehensible and not to be wondered at that it required much magnanimity of Berg to allow this symmetry of chair or sofa to be disturbed for his beloved guest; or that, by reason of finding himself in a state of painful irresolution in regard to it, he should have allowed his guest to solve the problem in his own way. Pierre, accordingly, broke into the symmetry by pushing out a chair; and immediately after, Berg and Viera began their reception and began to talk, each interrupting the other, and trying to entertain their guest.

Viera, deciding in her own mind that Pierre would naturally be interested in the French embassy, immediately began to talk about it. Berg, deciding that a more virile subject must be chosen, broke into his wife's discourse by raising a question in regard to the war with Austria; and found himself involuntarily digressing from the abstract topic to various concrete proposals which had been laid before him in regard to taking part in the Austrian campaign, and the reasons which had led him to decline them.

Although the conversation was desultory, and Viera

was indignant that this masculine element should have been introduced, both husband and wife had a feeling of satisfaction that, though as yet there was only one guest, still the evening had begun auspiciously, and that their reception was going to be like every other reception — with talk, tea, and brightly lighted candles — as like, in fact, as two drops of water.

Shortly after, Boris appeared, he having been Berg's former comrade. He treated Berg and Viera with a shade of superiority and condescension. Boris was followed by a colonel and his lady, then Berg's own general, then the Rostofs; and the reception by this time, without a shadow of a doubt, began to resemble all other receptions.

Berg and Viera could not refrain from a blissful smile at the sight of this stir in the drawing-room, at the clatter of disconnected snatches of conversation, at the rustle of silken gowns, and the greetings.

Everything was just as it would be everywhere else; especially so was the general, who could not find enough to say in praise of Berg's apartments, and patted him on the shoulder, and with fatherly authority arranged the disposition of the tables for Boston. The general then set down next Count Ilya Andreyitch, as being, next to himself, the guest of the greatest importance. The old people gathered in groups by themselves, the young people by themselves; the hostess took her place at the tea-table, which was laid out with exactly the same kind of macaroons, in a silver cake-basket, as the Panins had had at their reception; in fact, everything was exactly the same as at all receptions.

CHAPTER XXI

PIERRE, as one of the most distinguished guests of the evening, naturally had to play Boston in the set with Count Ilya Andreyitch, the general, and the colonel. It happened that his place at the table brought him opposite Natasha, and he could not help being struck by the strange change that had come over her since the evening of the ball. She spoke scarcely a word, and was not so pretty as she had been at the ball; indeed, she would have looked plain, if it had not been for her sweet expression of resignation.

"What is the matter with her?" Pierre wondered, as he looked at her. She was sitting next her sister at the tea-table, and, with an air of utter indifference and without even looking at him, answered some remark that Boris had made to her. Having played out a whole suit, and taken five tricks, greatly to his partner's satisfaction, Pierre, as he gathered up his cards, was again led to look at her, by hearing complimentary greetings, and then the steps of some one entering the room.

"What has happened to her?" he asked himself, with even more wonder than before.

Prince Andreï, with an expression of protecting affection, was now standing in front of her, and saying something to her. She had lifted her head, and was gazing at him with flushed cheeks, and apparently striving to restrain her rapid breathing. And the brilliant light of a strange inner fire, till then suppressed, again flashed up in her. She was wholly transfigured: instead of being plain, she was as radiantly beautiful as she had been at the ball.

Prince Andreï came toward Pierre, and Pierre noticed a new and youthful expression in his friend's face.

Pierre changed his seat several times during the game, sometimes being before Natasha, and sometimes behind; but, during all the time of the six "rubbers," he kept watching her and his friend.

"There is something very serious going on between them," said Pierre to himself; and a feeling of mingled joy and sadness stirred him, and made him forget his own grief.

After the sixth rubber the general got up, declaring that it was an impossibility to play in such a way, and Pierre regained his freedom. Natasha, on one side, was talking with Sonya and Boris; Viera, with a slight smile on her face, was talking to Prince Andreï about something or other.

Pierre joined his friend, and, asking what secret they were discussing together, took a seat near them. Viera, having noticed Prince Andreï's attention to Natasha, had decided that that evening, that very evening, it was an unavoidable necessity for her to drop some shrewd insinuations in regard to the feelings; and so she took advantage of a moment when Prince Andreï was alone to begin a talk about the sensibilities in general, and about her sister in particular. With such a clever man as she knew Prince Andreï to be, she knew she must here use her diplomatic arts.

When Pierre joined them, he noticed that Viera was talking with great eloquence and self-satisfaction, while Prince Andreï seemed rather confused, — which was a rare thing with him.

"What is your opinion?" asked Viera, with her slight smile. "You have such keen insight, prince, and are so quick to read people's characters: what do you think of Natalie? Would she be likely to be constant in her attachments? would she be like other women," — Viera had herself in mind, — "and love a man once, and remain forever faithful to him? That is what I call genuine love. What do you think, prince?"

"I have too slight an acquaintance with your sister," replied Prince Andreï, with a satirical smile, under which he tried to hide his confusion, "to decide such a delicate question; and then, I have noticed that the less attractive a woman is, the more likely she is to be constant," he added, and looked at Pierre, who had just at that instant joined them.

"Yes, that is true, prince; in our days," pursued Viera, — speaking of "our days" in a way affected by narrow-minded people who labor under the delusion that they are the only ones to discover and appreciate the peculiarities of their time, and that the human nature changes with the changing years, — "young girls have so much freedom, that the pleasure of being wooed — *le plaisir d'être courtisée* — often stifles their true feelings.

And Natalie, it must be confessed, is very susceptible to it."

This reference to Natasha again caused Prince Andreï to scowl disagreeably; he was about to rise, but Viera proceeded with a still more subtle smile: —

"I think no one has ever been more *courtisée* than she has," said Viera. "But no one had ever really seriously succeeded in pleasing her, until very recently. You must know, count," said she, addressing Pierre, "even our dear Cousin Boris has, between ourselves, gone very, very far into the land of sentiment."....

Prince Andreï, still scowling, said nothing.

"You and Boris are friends, are you not?" asked Viera.

"Yes, I know him."....

"I suppose he has told you about his boyish love for Natasha?"

"Ah! so it was a boyish love, was it?" suddenly asked Prince Andreï, unexpectedly reddening.

"Yes! You know sometimes this intimacy between cousins leads to love; cousinhood is a risky neighborhood! that 's true, is n't it?"

"Oh, yes, without doubt," said Prince Andreï; and suddenly, becoming unnaturally excited, he began to rally Pierre on his duty to be on his guard against any intimacy with his fifty-year-old cousins in Moscow; and then, right in the midst of his jesting talk, he got up, and, taking Pierre by the arm, drew him aside.

"Well! what is it?" asked Pierre, amazed at his friend's strange excitement, and remarking the look which, as he got up, he threw in Natasha's direction.

"I must, I really must, have a talk with you," said Prince Andreï. "You know our gloves," — he referred to the Masonic gloves, which a newly initiated brother was to present to the lady of his love. "I.... but no.... I will talk with you about it by and by." And, with a strange light in his eyes, and a restlessness in his motions, Prince Andreï crossed over to Natasha and sat down. Pierre saw how he asked her some question, and how she blushed as she answered him

But just at that moment Berg came up to Pierre and urged him to take part in a discussion between the general and the colonel, on Spanish affairs.

Berg was satisfied and happy. Not once did the smile of pleasure fade from his face. The reception had been a success, and exactly like other receptions which he had attended. The parallelism was complete. The nice little gossipy chats among the ladies; the cards, and the general raising his voice over the game; the samovar and the macaroons! One thing only was lacking, which he had always seen at receptions, and which he wished to imitate: that was a loud conversation between the men, and a discussion over some grave and momentous question. The general had begun this conversation, and now Berg carried Pierre off to take part in it.

CHAPTER XXII

THE next day, Prince Andreï went to the Rostofs' to dinner, in accordance with Count Ilya Andreyitch's invitation, and spent the whole evening there.

All in the house had an inkling of the reason of Prince Andreï's visits, and he made no secret of it, but tried to be in Natasha's company all the time.

Not only Natasha, in her heart of hearts frightened and yet blissful and full of enthusiasm, but all the household also, felt a sort of awe, in the anticipation of a great and solemn event. The countess, with melancholy and gravely wistful eyes, gazed at Prince Andreï as he talked with Natasha, and, with a sort of timidity, tried to introduce some indifferent topic as soon as he turned to her. Sonya was afraid to leave Natasha, and equally afraid that she was in their way, when she was with them. Natasha grew pale with fear and expectation if by chance she was left alone with him for a moment. Prince Andreï's timidity amazed her. She felt certain that he had something to say to her, but had not the courage to speak his mind.

In the evening, when Prince Andreï had taken his departure, the countess went to Natasha.

"Well?" said she, in a whisper.

"Mamma, for pity's sake, don't ask me any questions now. It is impossible to tell."

Nevertheless, that night, Natasha, at one moment full of excitement, at the next full of trepidation, lay for a long time in her mother's bed, with eyes fixed on space. Now she would tell her mother how he praised her, and how he said he was going abroad, and how he asked her where they were going to spend the summer, and how he had asked her about Boris.

"Well, it's so strange, so strange!.... I never knew anything like it before," said she. "But I have such a feeling of terror when he is here; I always feel afraid when I am with him; what does it mean? Does it mean that it is really and truly....? Mamma, are you asleep?"

"No, dusha moya; I confess to the same feeling of terror," replied the mother. "Go, now!"

"I shan't go to sleep, all the same. How silly it would be to go to sleep! Mamasha, mamasha, nothing like it ever happened to me before," said she, in amazement and awe at the feeling which she was now experiencing. "How could we possibly have imagined...."

It seemed to Natasha that even as long ago as when Prince Andreï had come to Otradnoye, she had fallen in love with him. She was terror-stricken, as it were, at that strange, unexpected happiness in meeting again with the very man whom she had — as she persuaded herself — chosen for her husband then, and feeling that he was not indifferent to her.

"And it had to be that he should come to Petersburg just at the time when we were here; and it had to be that we should meet at that ball. It was our fate. It is evident that it was our fate, that it all led to this — all this. Even when I saw him first, I felt something peculiar."

"What is it he has said to you? What were those verses? Repeat them to me," said the countess, trying to recall some verses which Prince Andreï had written in Natasha's album.

"Mamma, it 's nothing to be ashamed of because he is a widower, is it ?"

"Don't talk nonsense, Natasha. Pray to God! Marriages are made in heaven!"

"Sweetheart![1] mamasha! how I love you, how good you are!" cried Natasha, shedding tears of bliss and emotion, and hugging her mother.

At that same time, Prince Andreï was at Pierre's, telling him about his love for Natasha, and his firm intention of marrying her.

That same evening, the Countess Elena Vasilyevna had given a rout. The French ambassador had been there; the foreign prince who for some time had been a frequent visitor at the countess's had been present; and a throng of brilliant ladies and gentlemen. Pierre had come down and wandered through the rooms, attracting general notice among the guests by his concentrated, distracted, and gloomy looks.

Pierre, ever since the time of the ball, had been conscious that attacks of his old enemy, hypochondria, were imminent; and, with the energy of despair, he had struggled to get the better of them. Since this prince had become the countess's acknowledged admirer, Pierre had unexpectedly been appointed one of the emperor's chamberlains; and from that time forth he began to feel a great burden and loathing in grand society, and more often his former gloomy, pessimistic thoughts, about the falsity of all things human, began to come back to him.

At this particular time, this tendency to gloominess was accented by the discovery of the sympathy existing between his little *protégée* Natasha and Prince Andreï, and by the contrast between his own position and his friend's. He vainly struggled to banish the thought about his wife, and about Natasha and Prince Andreï. But everything began once more to seem insignificant

[1] *Galubushka.*

in comparison with eternity, and again the question arose, "To what end?"

Night and day he compelled himself to toil over his Masonic labors, hoping to exorcise the evil demon that hovered near him.

At midnight, Pierre came from the countess's apartments to his own low-studded room, which smelled of stale tobacco, and had just sat down at the table in his soiled khalat, and started to finish copying some original documents from Scotland, when some one came into the room.

It was Prince Andreï.

"Oh, it's you, is it?" said Pierre, in an abstracted and not over-cordial manner.

"Here I am at work, you see," said he, pointing to his copy-book, and his face showed that he was trying to find in it salvation from his troubles. Unhappy folk always look at their work with that expression. Prince Andreï, his face radiant with enthusiasm and new life, came and stood in front of Pierre; and, not noticing his friend's unhappy face, smiled down on him with the egotism of happiness.

"Well, my dear," said he, "last evening I wanted to tell you something, and now I have come for that purpose. It is something wholly unprecedented in my experience. I am in love, my friend."

Pierre suddenly drew a deep sigh, and stretched his clumsy form out on the divan near Prince Andreï.

"With Natasha Rostova, I suppose?" said he.

"Yes, yes; who else could it be? I should never have believed it, but this feeling is stronger than I. Last evening I was tortured, I was miserable; but this torture I would not exchange for anything in the world. I have never lived till now. Only now do I live, and I cannot live without her. But can she love me?.... I am too old for her. What should you say?"....

"I? I? What could I say?" suddenly exclaimed Pierre, springing up and beginning to pace the room. "I have always thought.... This girl is such a treasure, such a.... she is a rare maiden.... my dear fellow: I be seech you, don't reason about it, don't let doubts arise, but marry her, marry her, marry her, ... and I am convinced that you will be the happiest man alive!"

"But how about her?"

"She loves you!"

"Don't talk nonsense...." said Prince Andreï, with a smile, and looking straight into Pierre's eyes.

"She loves you, I know she does," cried Pierre, bluntly.

"Now listen!" said Prince Andreï, holding him by his arm. "Do you know what a position I am in? I must tell some one all about it!"

"Well, well, go on, I am very glad," said Pierre, and in reality his face had changed; the frown had smoothed itself out, and he listened to Prince Andreï with joyous sympathy. Prince Andreï seemed, and really was, another and wholly new man. Where had vanished his melancholy, his contempt of life, all his disillusion? Pierre was the only man in whose presence he could speak with absolute frankness, and hence he poured out before him the fullness of his heart. Then he fluently and boldly made plans for the future, declaring that he could not think of sacrificing his happiness to his father's caprices, and expressing his hope that his father would consent to their marriage, and would come to love Natasha; then he expressed his amazement at the strange and uncontrollable feeling that dominated him.

"If any one had predicted the possibility of my being so deeply in love, I should not have believed it," said Prince Andreï. "It is an entirely different sentiment from the one that I had formerly. The whole world is divided for me into two portions: the one is where she is, and there all happiness and hope and light are found; the other is where she is not, and there everything is gloom and darkness." ....

"Darkness and gloom," repeated Pierre. "Yes, yes, and how I appreciate that!"

"I cannot help loving light, and I am not to blame for it. And I am very happy. Do you understand me? I know that you sympathize with my joy."

"Yes, indeed, I do," said Pierre, earnestly, gazing at his friend with tender, melancholy eyes. Prince Andreï's fate seemed to him all the brighter from the vivid contrast with the darkness of his own.

CHAPTER XXIII

PRINCE ANDREÏ required his father's sanction for his marriage, and the next day he set out for his home.

The old prince received his son's communication with external unconcern, but with wrath in his heart. As his own life was nearing its close, he could not understand how any one could wish to make such a change in his life, to introduce into it such a new and unknown element.

"If only they would let me live out my life in my own way! then, when I am gone, they can do as they please," said the old man to himself. With his son, however, he made use of that diplomacy which he employed in matters of serious import. Assuming a tranquil tone, he summed the whole matter up: —

In the first place, the match was not brilliant, as to the birth, fortune, or distinction of the bride's family. In the second place, Prince Andreï was not as young as he had once been, and his health was feeble, — the old prince laid especial stress on this, — and she was very young. In the third place, he had a son, whom it would be a shame to give over to the mercy of a young stepmother.

"In the fourth place, finally," said the father, giving his son an ironical look, "I beg of you to postpone the affair for a year, go abroad, go through a course of treatment, find a good German tutor for Prince Nikolaï; and then, if your love, passion, stubbornness, whatever you call it, is as strong as ever, — why, marry her. And this is my last word, remember; absolutely my last word," concluded the old prince, in a tone that signified that nothing could ever change his mind.

Prince Andreï clearly saw that the old prince hoped

that either his sentiments or his prospective bride's might not withstand the test of a year, or else that he himself — since he was an old man — might die meantime; he, accordingly, determined to obey his father's wishes, to offer himself, and then postpone the wedding for a year.

Three weeks after his last call at the Rostofs', Prince Andreï returned to Petersburg.

The day following her confidential talk with her mother, Natasha waited anxiously for Bolkonsky; but he did not come. The second day, and the third day, it was precisely the same. Pierre, also, failed to come; and Natasha, not knowing that the prince had gone to see his father, could not explain his absence.

Thus passed three weeks. Natasha had no desire to go anywhere, and she wandered like a languid and mournful shadow through the rooms; evenings, she hid herself away from the others, and wept, and no longer came to her mother's bedchamber. She frequently flushed, and her temper grew peevish. She had an impression that everybody knew about her disappointment, and was laughing at her and pitying her. This grief, born of pride, added to her misery, all the more from the fact that it was hidden grief.

One time she went to the countess, and tried to say something, but suddenly burst into tears. Her tears were like those of a child who has been punished without knowing for what reason.

The countess tried to calm her; but the young girl, though she at first began to listen, suddenly interrupted her: —

"Do stop, mamma; I do not understand and I cannot understand. .... He came, and then he stopped coming .... he stopped coming .... "

Her voice faltered, she almost wept; but she controlled herself and went on: —

"I have n't any desire at all to be married; and I have been afraid of him all the time: I 'm perfectly content now, perfectly content." ....

On the day following this conversation, Natasha put on an old gown for which she had an especially tender feeling, owing to the gay times which she had enjoyed when wearing it in days past; and from that morning she once more resumed the occupations that she had dropped since the time of the ball. After she had drunk her tea, she went into the ball-room, which she liked on account of its powerful resonance, and began to practise her solfeggios and other exercises. After she had finished her lesson, she stood in the middle of the room and repeated a single musical phrase which pleased her more than others. She joyfully listened to the charming and apparently unexpected way in which these notes reverberated through the empty spaces of the ball-room, and slowly died away; and suddenly her heart grew lighter.

"What is the use of thinking so much about it all! it is good as it is," said she to herself, and she began to pace up and down the room, not content with simply walking along the echoing inlaid floor, but at every step — she wore her favorite new slippers — setting her little heels down first, and then her toes, and finding as much enjoyment in the regular clapping of the heel and the creaking of the toe, as in the sounds of her voice. As she passed by a mirror, she glanced into it.

'What a girl I am!' the expression of her face, as she caught sight of the reflection in the glass, seemed to say. 'It's all good! I need no one.'

A lackey was on the point of coming in to make some arrangements in the ball-room; but she sent him away, closing the door after him, and then continued her walk. Now again, this morning, she resumed her former favorite habit of loving and admiring her own sweet self.

"How charming this Natasha is!" she was saying, as if the words were spoken by some third person, the man of her imagination. "Pretty, a good voice, young, and she does not interfere with any one; only leave her in peace!"

But even if she had been left in peace, she could not

have been calm; and of this she was immediately made aware.

The front door into the vestibule was opened, and some one asked: —

"Are they at home?" and then a man's steps were heard. Natasha was gazing into the mirror, but she did not see herself. She heard voices in the vestibule. When she looked in the mirror again her face was pale.

It was *he!* She was sure of it, though she could barely distinguish the voices through the closed doors.

Pale and frightened, Natasha ran into the drawing-room.

"Mamma, Bolkonsky has come," she cried. "Mamma! this is dreadful! this is unendurable! I will not be.... tortured so! What shall I do?"....

Before the countess had time to answer her, Prince Andreï, with a grave and anxious face, was shown in. As soon as he caught sight of Natasha, a flash of joy lighted it. He kissed the countess's hand, and Natasha's, and took a seat near the divan.

"It is a long time since we have had the pleasure...." the countess began to say, but Prince Andreï interrupted her. He answered her implied question, and was evidently anxious to speak what was on his mind as soon as possible.

"I have not been to see you all this time, for the reason that I went to see my father; I had to confer with him regarding a very important matter. I returned only yesterday evening," he said, glancing at Natasha. "I should like to have a little conversation with you, countess," he added, after a moment's silence.

The countess, drawing a long sigh, dropped her eyes.

"I am at your service," she murmured.

Natasha knew that it was her duty to leave the room, but she found it impossible to stir; something choked her, and she stared at Prince Andreï, almost rudely, with wide eyes.

"What! so soon? this very moment?.... No, it cannot be!" she said to herself.

He again looked at her, and this glance told her that beyond a peradventure she was not deceived.

Yes, her fate was to be decided instantly, that moment, then and there!

"Go, Natasha, I will send for you," whispered the countess.

Natasha, with startled, pleading eyes, looked at her mother, and at Prince Andreï, and left the room.

"I have come, countess, to ask your daughter's hand," said Prince Andreï.

The countess's face flushed, but she said nothing.

"Your proposal...." began the countess, gravely. Prince Andreï waited, and looked into her eyes. "Your proposal"—she grew confused—"is very pleasing to us, and.... and I accept, accept your proposal, with pleasure. And my husband.... I hope.... but it will depend upon herself."

"I will ask her as soon as I receive your permission .... will you grant it?" said Prince Andreï.

"Yes," said the countess, and she offered him her hand; and, with a mixed feeling of alienation and affection, touched his brow with her lips, as he bent over her hand. She was ready to love him as a son; but she was conscious that he held her at a distance, and filled her with a sort of terror. "I am sure that my husband will give his consent," said the countess; "but your father.... "

"My father, to whom I have confided my plans, has consented, on the express stipulation that the wedding should not take place within a year; and this was the very thing that I wished to tell you," said Prince Andreï.

"It is true that Natasha is still young, but a year is so long."

"This cannot be otherwise," said Prince Andreï, with a sigh.

"I will send her to you," said the countess, and she left the room.

"Lord, have mercy upon us!" she repeated over and over, as she went in search of her daughter. Sonya said that Natasha was in her chamber. She found her sitting on her bed, pale, with dry eyes, gazing at the holy pictures, and swiftly crossing herself, and whispering to herself. When she saw her mother, she jumped up and rushed to her.

"What? Mamma?.... What is it?"

"Go, go to him. He has proposed for your hand," said the countess, coldly, so it seemed to Natasha. "Go!.... Go," reiterated the mother, drawing a long sigh, and looking with melancholy, reproachful eyes after her daughter, as she flew out of the room.

Natasha could not remember how she found herself in the drawing-room. But, as she went into the room, and caught sight of him, she stopped short.

"Can it be that this stranger is now all in all to me?" she asked herself; and the reply came like a flash, "Yes! he alone is dearer to me than all in the world."

Prince Andreï went to her with downcast eyes:—

"I have loved you from the first moment that I saw you. May I dare to hope?"

He looked at her, and the grave passion expressed in his face filled her with wonder.

Her eyes replied, "Why should you ask? Why should you doubt what you must surely know? Why should you speak, when it is impossible with words to express what you feel?"

She drew near to him, and paused. He took her hand, and kissed it: "Do you love me?"

"Yes, yes," exclaimed Natasha, with something that seemed almost like vexation; and, catching her breath more and more frequently, she began to sob.

"What is it? What is the matter?"

"Akh! I am so happy," she replied, smiling through her tears, and coming closer to him; she hesitated for a moment, as if asking if it were permissible, and then kissed him.

Prince Andreï held her hand, and gazed into her eyes, and failed to find in his heart his former love for her. A sudden transformation seemed to have taken place in his soul: there was none of that former poetical and mysterious charm of longing; but there was a feeling akin to pity for her weakness, as a woman, as a child; there was a shade of fear, in presence of her utter self-renunciation, and her fearless honesty; a solemn and, at the same time, blissful consciousness of the obligation which forever bound him to her. The present feeling, though it was not so bright and poetical as the former, was more deep and powerful.

"Has your *maman* told you that our marriage cannot be till a year has passed?" asked Prince Andreï, continuing to gaze into her eyes.

"Can it be that this is the little silly chit of a girl, as they all say of me?" mused Natasha. "Can it be that from this time forth, I am the wife, the equal, of this stranger, this gentle, learned man, whom even my father regards with admiration? Can it be true, can it be true that now, henceforth, life has become serious? that now I am grown up? that now I shall be responsible for every word and deed?.... Yes, but what was that he asked me?"

"No," said she aloud; but she did not know what he had asked her.

"Forgive me," said Prince Andreï. "But you are so young, and I have already had such long experience of life. I tremble for you. You do not know yourself!"

Natasha, with concentrated attention, listened to what he said, and did her best to take in the full meaning of his words; but it was impossible.

"How hard this year will be for me — deferring my happiness!" pursued Prince Andreï. "But during the time you will have made sure of your own heart. At the end of the year I shall ask you to make me happy; but you are free. Our betrothal shall remain a secret, and if you should discover that you do not love me, if you should love...." said Prince Andreï, with a forced and unnatural smile.

"Why do you say that?" asked Natasha, interrupting him. "You know that from that very first day that you came to Otradnoye, I loved you," said she, firmly convinced that she was telling the truth.

"In a year, you will have learned to know yourself."

"A who....ole year!" suddenly exclaimed Natasha, it now suddenly, for the first time, dawning upon her that the wedding was to be postponed. "And why a year? — why a year?"

Prince Andreï began to explain the reasons for this postponement. Natasha refused to listen to him.

"And is there no other way of doing?" she asked. Prince Andreï made no answer, but the expression of his face told her how unalterable his decision was.

"This is terrible! No, this is terrible, terrible!" suddenly exclaimed Natasha, and again she began to sob. "I shall die, if I have to wait a year; it cannot be, it is dreadful."

She looked into her lover's face, and saw that it was full of sympathy and perplexity.

"No, no, I will do everything you wish," she said, suddenly ceasing to sob. "I am so happy."

Her father and mother came into the room, and congratulated the affianced pair.

From that day forth, Prince Andreï began to visit the Rostofs as Natasha's accepted husband.

CHAPTER XXIV

THERE was no formal betrothal, and Bolkonsky's engagement to Natasha was not made public. Prince Andreï insisted on this point. He said that, as he was the cause of the postponement, he ought to bear the whole burden of it. He declared that he considered himself forever bound by his word; but he felt that he ought not to hold Natasha, and he granted her perfect freedom. If, within a half-year, she should discover that she did not love him, she should have perfect right to break the engagement.

Of course, neither the parents nor Natasha would hear to this, but Prince Andreï pressed the matter. Prince Andreï was at the Rostofs' every day, but he did not treat Natasha with the familiarity of the *zhenikh*, or bridegroom: he always addressed her by the formal *vui*, "you," and kissed only her hand.

Between Prince Andreï and Natasha, after the day of their betrothal, there came to be an entirely different relationship from before: one closer and more simple. It seemed as if they hitherto had never known each other; both of them liked to recall how they had seemed at the time when they were *nothing* to each other; now they both felt that they were entirely different beings; then everything was pretense, now it was simple and true. At first the family felt a certain awkwardness in their relations toward Prince Andreï: he seemed like a man from another world, and it took Natasha a long time to train the others to feel used to him; and she felt a pride in assuring them all that it was only in appearance that Prince Andreï was so different, and that he was really like every one else, and that she was not afraid of him, and that no one had any reason to fear him.

After some days the family got wonted to him, and felt no awkwardness in going on in his presence with the ordinary routine of life, and he also had a share in it. He could talk with the count about farming, with the countess and Natasha about wearing-apparel, and with Sonya about albums and embroidery. Sometimes the family, when by themselves, and even in Prince Andreï's presence, marveled that such an event had taken place, — that the prognostics of it had been so apparent: thus, Prince Andreï's visit to Otradnoye, and their coming to Petersburg, and the resemblance between Natasha and Prince Andreï, which an old nurse had remarked when he first came to Otradnoye, and many other portents of what had happened, were recalled by the family.

That poetical melancholy and silence which always mark the presence of an engaged couple reigned in the house. Often, when all were together, no word would be said. Sometimes the rest would get up and leave the room, and even then the two young people, though by themselves, would sit in perfect silence, as before. They rarely spoke about their future; Prince Andreï avoided it from dread, as well as from conscientious motives. Natasha shared his feelings, as, indeed, she shared all his feelings, which she was always quick to read.

Once, Natasha began to ask him about his little boy; Prince Andreï flushed, as he was apt to do at that time, — and Natasha particularly liked it in him, — and replied that his son would not live with them.

"Why not?" asked Natasha, in alarm.

"I could not take him away from his grandfather; and, besides...."

"How I should love him!" exclaimed Natasha, instantly divining his thought. "But I understand: you are anxious to avoid any excuse for misunderstandings between us."

The old count sometimes came to Prince Andreï, kissed him, and asked him his advice in regard to Petya's education, or Nikolaï's advancement in the army. The old countess would sigh as she looked at them. Sonya was always afraid that she was in the way, and tried to invent excuses for leaving them alone, even when this was not necessary. When Prince Andreï talked — and he was very admirable in conversation — Natasha would listen to him with pride; when she herself spoke, she noticed, with fear and joy, that he listened to her with attention, and scrutinized her keenly. She would ask herself in perplexity: —

"What is he searching for in me? What are his eyes trying to discover? Supposing he were not to find in me what he seeks to find?"

Occasionally she was attacked by one of those absurd fits of mirth, peculiar to her, and then it was a delight for her to see and hear him laugh. He rarely laughed aloud, but when he did indulge in merriment, he gave himself up entirely to it; and always, after such an experience, she felt that she had grown nearer to him. Natasha would have been perfectly happy, if the thought of their parting, which was now near at hand, had not filled her with vague alarm, — so much so that she grew pale and chill at the mere thought of it.

On the evening before his departure from Petersburg, Prince Andreï brought Pierre, who had not once called at the Rostofs' since the evening of the ball. Pierre seemed confused and out of spirits. He engaged in conversation with the countess. Natasha was sitting with Sonya at the checker-table and asked Prince Andreï to join them. He did so.

"You have known Bezukhoï for a long time, have you not?" he asked. "Do you like him?"

"Yes, he is a splendid man, but very absurd."

And, as was usually the case, when speaking of Pierre, she began to relate anecdotes of his heedlessness, anecdotes, many of which had been invented about him.

"You know, I have told him our secret," said Prince Andreï. "I have known him since we were boys. His heart is true gold. I beg of you, Natalie," said he, growing suddenly grave. "I am going away. God knows what may happen: you may cease to lo.... well, I know that I ought not to speak of this. One thing, though: in case anything should happen, after I am gone...."

"What could happen?"

"If there should be any misfortune," pursued Prince Andreï, "I beg you, Mademoiselle Sophie, if anything should happen, go to him for help and counsel. He may be a most heedless and absurd man, but his heart is the truest gold."

Not Natasha's father, or mother, or Sonya, or Prince Andreï himself, could have foreseen what an effect parting from her lover would have had upon Natasha. Flushed and excited, with burning eyes, she wandered all day long up and down the house, busying herself with the most insignificant things, as if she had no idea of what was going to happen. She did not shed a tear, even at the moment when he kissed her hand for the last time, and bade her farewell.

"Don't leave me," was all that she said; but these words were spoken in a voice which caused him to pause and consider whether it was really necessary for him to go away, and which he remembered long afterward.

Even after he had gone, she did not weep; but she stayed in her room for many days, not shedding a tear, and she took no interest in anything, and only said from time to time: —

"Akh! why did he go?"

But, a fortnight after his departure, most unexpectedly to the household, she woke up out of this moral illness, and began to seem the same as formerly; except that her whole moral nature was changed, just as the faces of children change during protracted illness.

CHAPTER XXV

Prince Nikolaï Andreyitch Bolkonsky's health and disposition grew much worse during the year that followed his son's absence. He became even more irritable than formerly; and all the explosions of his unreasonable anger were turned against the Princess Mariya. It seemed as if he tried to search out all the tender spots of her nature, so as to torture her as grievously as possible.

The Princess Mariya had two passions, and, therefore, two joys: her little nephew, Nikolushka, and religion; and both were favorite themes for the old prince's slurs and ridicule. Whatever subject of conversation arose, he managed to bring in some reference to old maids' superstitions, or to the spoiling and over-indulging of children.

"Do you wish to make him" — he referred to Nikolushka — "an old maid, like yourself? It 's all nonsense; Prince Andreï wants a son — not a girl," said he.

Or, turning to Mlle. Bourienne, he would ask her, in the princess's presence, how she liked our Russian popes and images, and again indulge in his bitter jests.

He seized every opportunity of cruelly wounding the Princess Mariya, but his daughter found no difficulty in forgiving him. How could she blame him, and how could he, her father, who she knew, in spite of all, loved her, be unjust to her? Yes, and what was justice? The princess never thought about that word "justice"—a concept born of pride. All the complicated laws of men, for her, were summed up in the one clear and simple rule of love and self-denial, imposed upon us by Him, who, though he was God, so loved the world as to suffer for it. What mattered to her, then, the justice or injustice of men? It was necessary for her to suffer and to love, and this she did.

During the winter, Prince Andreï had come to Luisiya Gorui, and was more cheerful, gentle, and affectionate than the Princess Mariya had seen him for a long time. She had a presentiment that something unusual had happened to him; but he said nothing to her about his love. Before he went away, he was closeted for a long time with his father, and the Princess Mariya noticed that each was displeased with the other.

Shortly after Prince Andreï's departure, the Princess Mariya wrote to her friend, Julie Karagina, who was at that time in Petersburg, and in mourning for her brother, who had been killed in Turkey. Like all young girls, the Princess Mariya had her dreams; and one of hers was that Julie would yet become her brother's wife.

Affliction, my dear and affectionate friend Julie, is evidently the common lot of us all.

Your loss is so awful that I can only explain it as being a special providence of God, who, in his love for you, has seen fit to try you and your excellent mother. Ah! my dear friend, religion, and religion alone, can—I will not say console us—but save us from despair; religion alone can make plain to us what, without her aid, it is impossible for man to comprehend: why, for what purpose, should beings who are good and noble, and best made to find happiness in life, who have not only never injured a living thing, but rather have sought only the happiness of others,—why should they be recalled to God; while the base and the vicious, or those who are only a burden to themselves and others, are left to live?

The first death which I ever witnessed—and I shall never forget it—was that of my dear sister-in-law, and it produced upon me a wonderful impression. Just as you are now asking Fate why your charming brother had to die, so did I ask why this angelic Liza should be taken away, when she had never done the slightest wrong to any one, and never had anything but the purest thoughts in her soul. And since then, my dear friend, five years have passed away, and, even with my humble intelligence, I begin clearly to see why she had to die, and how her death may be regarded as merely the expression of the Creator's infinite goodness, all of Whose works, though for the most part beyond our comprehension, are but the manifestation of His boundless love to His creatures.

I often think so, and perhaps her purity was too angelic to be compatible with the force necessary to carry all the obligations of motherhood. As a young wife, she was beyond reproach; possibly she might have failed as a mother. Now, although she has left us, and Prince Andreï in particular, the purest regret and sweetest memories, I am sure that she herself is in the enjoyment of that place which I dare not hope for myself to attain.

But, not to speak of her exclusively, this premature and terrible death has had a most salutary effect, notwithstanding all the sorrowfulness of it, on my brother and myself.

These thoughts at that time would have been impossible, — at that time I should have repelled them with horror; but now this is plain, and beyond a peradventure. I write this to you, my friend, simply hoping that it may persuade you of the Gospel truth, which I have taken as the rule of my whole life: that not one hair from our head shall fall without His will. And His will is conditioned only by infinite love toward us; and, therefore, all that happens to us is for our good.

You ask if we are going to spend next winter in Moscow? In spite of all my desire to see you, I think it most improbable; and, indeed, I cannot think that it is for the best. And you will be amazed when I tell you that the reason of that is — Buonaparte! And this is why: my father's health has been failing of late; he cannot endure any contradiction, and has grown irritable. This irritability, as you may know, is especially excited by political affairs. He cannot endure the thought that Buonaparte has so managed as to put himself on an equality with all the sovereigns of Europe, and especially with ours — the grandson of the great Catherine! As you know, I am perfectly indifferent to politics; but from words spoken by my father, and from his discussions with Mikhaïl Ivanovitch, I know all that is going on in the world, and particularly about all the honors attained by Buonaparte, who, I should think, is considered a great man, and not the least of the French emperors, all over the world, except at Luisiya Gorui!

And this is what my father will not admit! It seems to me that my father, precisely on account of his views of political affairs, and foreseeing the collisions which would infallibly take place, in consequence of his character, — taking no account of any one when he expresses his opinions, — feels unwilling to go to Moscow. All the gain that he would get, he would more than undo by the quarrels which would be sure to follow in regard to Buonaparte. At all events, the question is soon to be decided.

Our home life goes on in the old routine, except that my brother Andreï is away. As I have already written you, he has been very much changed of late. This year, for the first time since his affliction, he has begun to lead a perfectly normal life; he has become what he was when he was a child, as I remember him, kind, affectionate, and with a truly golden heart, the like of which I never knew. He has learned, so it seems to me, that his life, after all, is not yet ended. But, together with this moral change, his physical health has deteriorated. He is far worse than before, more nervous. I am troubled about him, and I am glad that he has decided to take the trip abroad which the doctor long ago prescribed for him. I hope that it will effect a complete cure.

You write me that he is spoken of in Petersburg as one of the most industrious, cultivated, and intelligent young men of the day. Forgive a sister's pride, but I have never doubted it. It is impossible to estimate the good which he has accomplished here, beginning with his own peasantry, and including the nobility of the district. In his life at Petersburg he has received only what was due him.

I am amazed that rumors should have come from Petersburg to Moscow, and especially such false rumors as what you wrote me in regard to the supposed marriage of my brother to the little Rostova. I do not believe that my brother will ever marry again; and certainly he will not marry her. And this is my reason for thinking so: in the first place, I know that, though he rarely mentions his late wife, yet he was too deeply afflicted by her loss ever to think of letting another fill her place in his heart, or of giving a stepmother to our little angel. In the second place, to the best of my knowledge, this young girl is not the sort of woman who would be likely to please Prince Andreï. I feel certain that he would not choose her for his wife, and I will frankly confess that I do not desire it.

But I have prattled too long, already: here I am, finishing my second sheet! Good-by, my dear friend. May God shield you under His holy and almighty wing. My dear companion, Mlle. Bourienne, sends her love.

MARIE.

CHAPTER XXVI

IN the middle of the summer, the Princess Mariya received a letter from her brother, from Switzerland, in which he confided the strange and surprising news of his engagement to Natasha. His whole letter breathed enthusiastic devotion for his "bride," and affectionate and trusting love for his sister. He wrote that he had never before loved as he loved now, and that now only did he realize and understand the meaning of life; he besought his sister to pardon him for not having said anything to her about this at his visit at Luisiya Gorui, although he had confided his intention to his father.

He had not told her because the Princess Mariya would have endeavored to persuade their father to grant his request; and if she had failed, it would have irritated him, and the whole weight of his displeasure would have come upon her.

Moreover [he wrote], the matter was not so definitely settled as it is now. Then, my father had set a term of probation — a year; and now, already, six months have slipped away, half of the designated term, and I remain firmer than ever fixed in my determination. If the doctors had not detained me here at the springs, I should have been back in Russia ere this; but now I must postpone my return for three months longer. You know me, and how I am situated in regard to my father: I really need nothing from him; I have been, and shall be always, independent of him; but to act contrary to his wishes, to incur his anger, when perhaps he has so short a time to remain among us, would destroy half of my happiness. I have just been writing him a letter in regard to this, and I beg of you, if you can find a favorable moment, give him this letter, and inform me how he receives it, and whether there is any hope that he will consent to shorten the term by three months.

After a long period of indecision, doubting, and prayer, the princess handed the letter to her father. The day following, the old prince said to her, without any show of excitement: —

"Write to your brother to wait till I'm dead.... it won't be long.... he'll soon be free."....

The princess tried to make some reply; but her father would not hear to it, and his voice began to rise higher and higher.

"Marry, marry, my little dove!.... Fine family!.... Clever people, ha? Rich? ha! Yes, a fine stepmother for the little Nikolushka she'll make. Write him that he may marry her to-morrow, if he wishes. She'll make a fine stepmother for Nikolushka, and I'll marry Bouriennka! Ha! ha! ha! so that *he* may have a stepmother as well! There's one thing, though, there's no room for any more women here; let him marry, and go and live by himself. Perhaps you'd like to go and live with him?" said he, turning to the Princess Mariya: "Go, then, in God's name: through ice and snow — ice and snow — ice and snow!"

After this explosion, the old prince said nothing more on that score, but his restrained vexation at his son's weakness was expressed in his treatment of his daughter. And he now had new themes for his sarcasm, in addition to his old ones; namely, stepmothers, and his admiration for Mlle. Bourienne.

"Why should I not marry her?" he asked his daughter. "She would make a splendid princess!"

And the Princess Mariya began to notice, with perplexity and amazement, that her father more and more tried to have the Frenchwoman about him as much as possible. The Princess Mariya wrote Prince Andreï how their father had received his letter; but she tried to comfort her brother, giving him to hope that her father might be dissuaded from this notion.

Nikolushka and his education, Andreï, and religion were the Princess Mariya's consolation and delight; but, as every human being must cherish some individual aspiration, so also the Princess Mariya had, in the deepest depths of her soul, secret dreams and hopes, which constituted a higher consolation even than the others. This consoling dream and hope was represented to her mind by the "Men of God," the pilgrims and fanatics who came to see her without the old prince's knowledge.

The longer the Princess Mariya lived, and the more experience she got out of life, by carefully observing it, the more she marveled at the short-sightedness of men who seek here on earth all their enjoyment and delight; who toil and moil, and battle and struggle, and do evil to one another, in order to follow these impossible, shameful phantoms of happiness. Prince Andreï loved his wife; she died: he was all ready to find his happiness in another woman. His father objected to this, because he desired for his son a more distinguished and wealthy alliance. And thus all men struggled, and suffered, and tortured themselves, and risked the loss of their souls, their immortal souls, for the sake of attaining joys which were merely transitory.

"Not only do we know this ourselves, but Christ, the son of God, came down to earth and taught us that this life is fleeting, a short probation; and yet we cling to it always, and expect to find happiness in it. How is it that no one comprehends this?" wondered the Princess Mariya. "None except these despised Men of God, who come to me with wallets on their shoulders, climbing the backstairs, for fear they should meet the prince, not to avoid suffering, but for the sake of preventing him from committing a sin. To forsake family and fatherland, and forswear all endeavor to get earthly good; to form no ties, and to wander under an assumed name, in hempen rags, from place to place, doing no harm to any one, and praying for people, praying for those who persecute them, as well as for those who give them protection, — there is no truth, and no life, higher than that!"

There was one pilgrim woman, Fedosyushka, — a little, gentle, pock-marked woman, fifty years old, — who had been for thirty years wandering about the world barefooted and wearing penitential chains. The Princess Mariya was especially fond of her. Once, in the solitude of her chamber, feebly illumined only by the lampadka or shrine lamp, when Fedosyushka had been telling about her experiences, the thought that the pilgrim woman had found the only true path of life suddenly came over her with such appealing force that she herself resolved to go on a pilgrimage. After Fedosyushka had retired to rest, the Princess Mariya long pondered the matter in her own mind, and at last resolved, no matter how unusual it was, that it was her duty to make this pilgrimage. She confided her resolve only to the monk, Father Akinfidja, her confessor, and the confessor approved of her project. Under the pretext that she was going to help some pilgrim, the Princess Mariya sent and purchased a pilgrim's complete outfit: shirt, lapti, or bast shoes, a kaftan, and a black kerchief. Frequently she would go to the curtained commode where she kept them, and stand irresolute, wondering whether the time had not yet come for her to carry out her project.

Often, when she heard the stories told by the pilgrims, she would be stirred by their simple narratives, which to her were full of profound meaning, though so mechanically repeated by them; till, oftentimes, she was ready to renounce everything and flee from her home. In her imagination she already saw herself and Fedosyushka, in filthy rags, tramping along with staff and birch-bark wallet, over the dusty highway, rambling about from one saint's shrine to another; without envy, without the love of her fellows, without desires; and, at the end of all, journeying thither where there is no regret and no tears, but eternal joy and felicity.

"I shall go to a place where there is a saint; I shall pray there; but, before I get attached to the place, or love any one, I shall pass on. And I shall keep wandering on until my limbs fail under me, and then I shall lie down and die anywhere; and then, at last, I shall reach that eternal haven of peace where there is no regret and no sorrow!" said the Princess Mariya to herself.

But later, when she saw her father, and especially the little Koko, her resolve lost its force; she shed a few quiet tears, and had the consciousness that she was a sinner: she loved her father and her nephew more than God.

PART SEVENTH

CHAPTER I

THE biblical tradition tells us that absence of work, idleness, constituted the first man's happiness before the fall. A love for idleness remains just the same, even in fallen man; but the curse still hangs over mankind, and it is impossible for us to be slothful and easy-going; not alone because we are required to earn our bread in the sweat of our faces, but because by the very conditions of our moral nature we cannot be idle and content. A secret voice warns us that to be idle is for us a sin. If a man could find a situation where he could feel that he was of use in the world, and fulfilling his duty while still remaining idle, he would have found one of the conditions of primeval bliss. And such a condition of obligatory and irreproachable idleness is enjoyed by a whole class of society — the military. And this state of obligatory and irreproachable idleness always has been and will be the chief attraction of military service.

Nikolaï Rostof had been enjoying this felicity to the full, having continued since 1807 to serve in the Pavlograd regiment; he was now commander of the squadron of which Denisof had been deprived. Rostof had grown into a rather rough but kindly young fellow, whom his Moscow acquaintances would have found sufficiently *mauvais genre*, but who was loved and respected by his comrades, his subordinates as well as his superiors; and he was well satisfied with his existence. Latterly, in 1809, in letters from home, he had found more and more frequent complaints from his mother that their pecuniary affairs were going from bad to worse, and that it would be seasonable for him to come home and give his old parents some joy and consolation.

In reading over these letters, Nikolaï felt a sensation of alarm at the thought of being torn from a condition of life where he found himself so quiet and tranquil, far removed from the busy turmoil of society. He had a presentiment that, sooner or later, he should be dragged again into that whirlpool of life, — with its wasteful expenditure, and rearrangement of affairs; with its accounts to verify; with its quarrels, intrigues, obligations; with the demands of society, and with Sonya's love, and the necessity of an explanation. All this was terribly difficult and confused; and he answered his mother's letters with cold formality, beginning, *Ma chère maman*, and concluding with *Votre obéïssant fils*, and studiously refrained from setting any time for his return home.

In 1810 he received a letter from his parents, who informed him of the engagement between Natasha and Bolkonsky, and that the wedding was put off for a year, on account of the old prince refusing his sanction. This news grieved and disgusted Nikolaï. In the first place he was pained at the thought of losing Natasha from the household, for he was fonder of her than the other members of the family; in the second place, he was annoyed, from his point of view as a hussar, that he had not been on hand to make this Bolkonsky understand that this alliance was not a very great honor, and that, if he loved Natasha, he might have married her, even without his scatter-brained father's consent.

For a moment he almost made up his mind to ask for leave of absence, so as to see Natasha before she was married; but just then came the army manœuvers, he remembered Sonya and the various entanglements, and once more he postponed it.

But in the spring of that same year he received a letter from his mother, who wrote without the count's knowledge, and this letter prompted him to go. She wrote that if he did not come, and did not assume the management of their affairs, their whole property would have to be sold by auction, and they would all be thrown on the world. The count was so weak, he had such confidence in Mitenka, he was so good-natured and so easily cheated by every one, that everything was going from bad to worse. "For God's sake, I beg of you, come immediately, unless you wish to make me and all the family unhappy," wrote the countess.

This letter had its effect upon Nikolaï. He was possessed of the sound common sense of mediocrity, and it told him that this was his duty.

Now, it was requisite that he should go either on leave of absence or on the retired list. He could not have explained why he had to go, but, after his siesta, he commanded his roan stallion Mars to be saddled — it had not been out for a long time, and was at any time a terribly fiery steed; and, when he brought it home all in a lather, he explained to Lavrushka, — Denisof's man had stayed on with Rostof, — and to his comrades who dropped in that afternoon, that he had obtained leave of absence, and was going home.

How hard it was for him to realize that he was going to absent himself from army life — the only thing that especially interested him — and fail to find whether he had been promoted, or granted the "Anna," for the last manœuvers! How strange it was to think that he was going away before he had sold that *troïka*, or three-span, of roans to the Polish Count Holuchowski, which they had been negotiating about, and which Rostof had wagered would bring two thousand rubles! How impossible to realize that he should miss the ball which the hussars were going to give to the Pani Pscazdecska, in order to pique the Uhlans, who had given a ball to their Pani Borzjozowska! He knew that he must leave, go away from all this bright, pleasant existence, and go where everything was trouble and turmoil.

At the end of a week he was granted his leave of absence. His comrades of the hussars, not only those of his regiment, but of the whole brigade, gave him a dinner which cost them fifteen rubles a head; they had two bands to play, and two choruses to sing for them. Rostof danced the trepaka with Major Basof; the tipsy officers "tossed" him, embraced him, and deposited him on the ground again; the soldiers of the third squadron once more "tossed" him and cried hurrah. Then they carried him to his sledge, and escorted him as far as the first station.

As is usually the case, Rostof's thoughts during the first half of his journey, from Kremenchug to Kief, were retrospective and connected with the affairs of his squadron; but, after he had gone half-way, he began to forget about the troïka of roans, his quartermaster Dozhoïveïk, and anxious questions began to arise in his mind as to what he should find at Otradnoye. The nearer he came to his home, the more powerfully he was affected by his forebodings; as if the inner feelings were subject to the law that conditions the swiftness of falling bodies to the square of the distance. At the Otradnoye station he gave the driver three rubles for vodka, and, all out of breath, rushed like a school-boy up the steps of the old home.

After the first enthusiastic greetings, and after that strange sense of vague disappointment at the reality falling short of expectation, — "Everything is just the same; why, then, have I hastened so?" — Nikolaï began to become wonted to the old home life again. His father and mother were the same, except that they had grown a trifle older. He detected a peculiar restlessness about them, and sometimes a slight coldness between them, which was a new thing, and which Nikolaï, as soon as he discovered it, attributed to the unfortunate condition of their affairs.

Sonya was now about twenty years old. She had reached the zenith of her beauty, and gave no promise that she would ever surpass what she already was; even thus, she was pretty enough. She simply breathed happiness and love from the moment that Nikolaï came home, and this maiden's faithful, unfaltering love for him had a delightful effect on him.

Nikolaï was more than all surprised at Petya and Natasha. Petya had grown into a tall, handsome, frolicsome, intelligent lad of thirteen, whose voice was already beginning to break. It was long before Nikolaï could get over his amazement at Natasha, and he said, laughing, as he gazed at her: —

"You're not at all the same!"

"What! have I changed for the worse?"

"Quite the contrary; but what dignity, princess!"[1] said he, in a whisper.

"Yes, yes, yes," exclaimed Natasha, gleefully.

Natasha told him of her romance with Prince Andreï, and about his visit to Otradnoye, and showed him her last letter from him.

"Tell me! Are you not glad for me?" she asked. "I am so calm, so happy now."

"Yes, very glad," replied Nikolaï. "He is a splendid man. And are you very much in love with him?"

"How can I tell you?" replied Natasha. "I was in love with Boris, and with my teacher, and with Denisof, and — but this is not at all the same. My mind is serene and decided. I know that there is not a better man to be found, and so I feel perfectly calm and happy. It is entirely different from what it used to be.... before...."

Nikolaï expressed to Natasha his dissatisfaction that the wedding was to be postponed a year; but Natasha, with some show of exasperation, contended that it could not have been otherwise, that it would have been disgraceful to force her way into his family against his father's will, and that she herself had wished it.

"You don't in the least, in the least, understand the necessities of the case," said she.

Nikolaï said no more, and acquiesced. He often marveled as he looked at her. She was absolutely unlike a girl deeply in love and separated from her betrothed. Her temper was calm and even, and she was as merry as in days gone by. This was a surprise to Nikolaï, and even made him look with some incredulity at her engagement with Bolkonsky. He could not make up his mind that her fate was as yet fully decided, the

[1] The point of this lies in his calling her *knyaginya*, the title of a married princess, as *knyazhna* is that of one unmarried.

more from the fact that he had not seen Prince Andreï with her. It seemed to him all the time that there was something that was not as it should be in this proposed marriage.

"Why this postponement? Why are they not formally betrothed?" he asked himself. Once, when speaking with his mother about his sister, he found to his surprise, and to a certain degree his satisfaction, that his mother also did not in the depths of her heart feel any great confidence in the engagement.

"This is what he writes," said she, showing her son a letter which she had received from Prince Andreï, with that secret feeling of discontent which a mother always has toward her daughter's future married happiness. "He writes that he will not be back before December. What do you suppose can detain him so? It must be he is ill. His health is very delicate. Do not say anything to Natasha. Don't be surprised that she is happy; these are the last days of her girlhood, and I know how it affects her whenever we get a letter from him. However, it is all in God's hands, and all will be well," she concluded; adding, as usual, "He is a splendid man."

CHAPTER II

The first days after Nikolaï's return, he was grave, and even depressed. He was tormented by the present necessity of making an investigation into the stupid details of the household economy, for which his mother had begged him to come home. On the third day after his return, in order to get this burden from his shoulders as soon as possible, he went, with contracted brows, sternly, and not giving himself time to decide what he was going to do, to the wing where Mitenka lived, and demanded of him the "accounts of everything." What he meant by the "accounts of everything," he had even less of an idea than Mitenka, who, nevertheless, was thrown into alarm and perplexity.

Mitenka's explanations about his accounts were soon

finished. The starosta of the estate, and the starosta of the commune, who were waiting in the anteroom, listened with terror and satisfaction at first, as the young count's voice began to grow fiercer and louder, while they could distinguish terrible words of abuse, following one upon another.

"You brigand, you ungrateful wretch!.... I'll whip you like a dog!.... You 're not dealing with my papenka this time," and words of the like import.

Then these men, with no less satisfaction and terror, saw the young count, all flushed, and with bloodshot eyes, dragging Mitenka by the collar, and reinforcing his efforts with very dexterous applications of his knees and feet, whenever the pauses between his words gave him a convenient chance; while he cried at the top of his voice:—

"Get out of here! you villain! Don't you ever show your face here again!"

Mitenka flew down the six steps head first, and landed in a bed of shrubbery. This shrubbery was a famous place of refuge for delinquents at Otradnoye. Mitenka himself, when he returned tipsy from town, was wont to hide in it; and many of the inhabitants of Otradnoye, trying to get out of Mitenka's way, knew the advantages of this place as a refuge.

Mitenka's wife and her sister, with terror-stricken faces, peered out of the door of the room, where a polished samovar was bubbling, and where the high-post bedstead affected by overseers could be seen, covered with a patchwork quilt.

The young count, all out of breath, and giving them no attention, strode by them with resolute steps, and went into the house.

The countess, who had heard from the maids all that had taken place in the wing, was, in one sense, delighted at the direction which their affairs were now evidently going to take; and in another she was disquieted at the way in which her son had taken hold of the matter.

She went several times on tiptoe to his door, and listened while he was smoking one pipe after another

The next day the old count called Nikolaï to one side, and with a timid smile said:—

"But do you know, my dear, you wasted your fire! Mitenka has told me all about it."

"I knew," thought Nikolaï, "that I should never accomplish anything here, in this idiotic world."

"You were angry with him because he did not reckon in those seven hundred rubles. But, do you know, they were carried over, and you did not look on the other page."

"Papenka, he is a scoundrel and a thief; I know he is! And what I have done, I have done. But if you don't wish it, I won't say anything more to him about it."

"No, my dear." The count was also confused. He was conscious that he himself had been a bad administrator of his wife's estate, and that he was to blame toward his children; but he did not know how to set things right. "No, I beg of you, take charge of our affairs; I am old, I...."

"No, papenka, forgive me if I have done anything disagreeable to you; I am less able to attend to it than you are.—The devil take these muzhiks, and accounts, and carryings over," he said to himself. "I used to know well enough what quarter stakes on a six at faro meant; but this carrying over to the next page, I don't know anything about it at all," said he to himself; and from that time forth he gave no more attention to their pecuniary affairs. Once, however, the countess called her son to her, and told him that she had a note of hand given her by Anna Mikhaïlovna, for two thousand rubles, and she asked Nikolaï's advice as to what ought to be done about it.

"This is what I think," replied Nikolaï. "You have told me that I was to decide the question. Well, I don't like Anna Mikhaïlovna, and I don't like Boris; but they have been friends of ours, and are poor. This is what we will do, then!" and he took the note and tore it in two; and this action made the old countess actually sob with delight.

After this, the young Rostof entirely forswore interference with their business matters, and entered with passionate enthusiasm into the delights of hunting with the hounds, for which the old count set him an example on a large scale.

CHAPTER III

Already the wintry frosts had begun, each morning, to chain up the soil, soaked by the autumnal rains; already there was green only in patches, and these made a vivid contrast against the strips of brownish stubble-fields, trodden down by the cattle, and the patches of winter or spring wheat, or the russet lines of the buckwheat fields. The forest tree-tops, which even as early as the end of August had been green islands amid the black fields of winter wheat and the corn stubble, were now golden and crimson islands amid the fields of bright green wheat.

The gray hare had already more than half changed his coat; the foxes were beginning to leave their holes, and young wolves were larger than dogs. It was the very height of the hunting season. The hounds belonging to that eager young huntsman, Rostof, were now in excellent training for their work; but they had been taken out so assiduously, that, by the general advice of the whippers-in, it had been decided to give them three days' rest, and to set upon the twenty-eighth of September for the hunt; at which time they would begin with a certain dense forest, where there was a litter of young wolves.

Such was the state of affairs on the twenty-sixth of September.

All that day the hunting train was at home. It had been bitter cold, but toward evening it grew warmer and began to thaw. On the morning of the twenty-seventh, when young Rostof went in his dressing-gown to his window, he looked out on a morning which could not have been better for hunting; the very sky seemed to be melting and flooding out over the earth. There was no sign of a breeze. The only motion in the air was that faint stir of microscopic drops of mist or fog, falling from above. On the bare limbs of the park trees transparent drops hung and fell on the leaves that carpeted the ground. The garden soil had a peculiar black and glistening appearance, like poppy, and within a short distance lost itself under the dim and moist curtain of fog.

Nikolaï stepped out upon the wet doorsteps, all covered with trails of mud. There was an odor of dying forest vegetation, and of dogs. Milka, the black-spotted bitch, with broad hind quarters, and big black goggle eyes, got up when she saw her master, stretched herself back, and lay down like a hare; then unexpectedly leaped up and licked his nose and ears. Another dog, a greyhound, seeing his master, came bounding up the garden path, arching his back, and impetuously raising his tail,[1] began to rub around Nikolaï's legs.

"O hoï!" rang out at this moment that inimitable huntsman's call, which compromises in itself the deepest bass and the clearest tenor, and around the corner appeared the whipper-in and hunter, Danilo: a grizzled, wrinkled man, with his hair cropped, leaving a knob, after the fashion of the Ukraïna, and carrying a long whip, with curling lash. He had that independent expression and scorn for all the world so characteristic of huntsmen. He took off his Circassian cap in his barin's presence, and looked at him scornfully. This expression of scorn was not meant to be insulting to the barin; Nikolaï knew that, scornful and superior as this Danilo seemed to be, he was, nevertheless, his devoted servant and huntsman.

"Danila!" said Nikolaï, with a timid consciousness that in this perfect hunting weather, with these dogs, and this huntsman, he was seized by that indefinable passion for hunting which makes a man forget all his former good resolutions like a fond lover in the presence of his mistress.

[1] *Pravilo*, rudder.

"What do you please to require, your illustriousness?" asked a deep, antiphonal bass, hoarse with shouting at the hounds; and two bright black eyes gazed out from under the brows at the silent barin. 'Well, and can't you resist?' these two eyes seemed to be asking.

"Fine day, is n't it? A chase and a race, hey?" asked Nikolaï, pulling Milka's ears.

Danilo said nothing, and winked his eyes.

"I sent Uvarka out at sunrise this morning to listen," said his deep bass, after a minute's pause. "He says *she's* drawn into the Otradnensky zakas, and they're howling there."

He meant that a she-wolf, which they both knew about, had gone with her whelps into the Otradnensky forest preserves, which was a small detached property, about two versts from the house.

"Well, we must go after them, must n't we?" said Nikolaï. "Come to me with Uvarka, will you."

"Just as you order!"

"See they are fed, then."

"All right!"

In five minutes, Danilo and Uvarka were standing in Nikolaï's great library. Though Danila was not very tall, the sight of him in the room irresistibly made one think of a horse, or a bear, surrounded by furniture and the conditions of civilized life; Danilo was himself conscious of this, and, according to his habit, stood as near the door as possible, striving to talk in an unnaturally low tone, and to keep from moving, lest he should break something, and saying what he had to say as rapidly as possible, so as to get out into the open air, under the sky instead of the ceiling.

Having asked the requisite number of questions, and elicited from Danilo — who was fully as anxious as himself to go — the information that it would not hurt the dogs, Nikolaï ordered the horses to be saddled.

But, just as Danilo was on the point of leaving the room, Natasha came hurrying in with swift steps, not having stopped to do up her hair, or finish dressing, but wearing her nurse's shawl. Petya came running in with her.

"Are you going?" asked Natasha. "I thought so! Sonya declared that you were not going. I knew that to-day was such a perfect day that you would have to go."

"Yes, we're going," curtly replied Nikolaï, who, as he intended to make a serious business of hunting that day, had no wish to take Natasha and Petya. "We are going, but after wolves only; it would bore you."

"You know that is just what I like best of anything," said Natasha. "It's too bad to be going yourself, and to have the horses saddled, and not say a word to us!"

"'Vain are obstacles to Russians!' let us go!" cried Petya.

"No, but you can't go; mamenka told you that it was out of the question," said Nikolaï, turning to Natasha.

"Yes, I am going; I certainly am going," insisted Natasha, firmly.

"Danila, have the saddles put on for us, and have Mikhaïla bring around my dogs," said she, addressing the whipper-in.

It had been trying and uncomfortable for Danilo to be in the confinement of the room; but to receive an order from the young lady seemed incredible. He cast down his eyes and made haste to go, pretending that it did not concern him, and striving not to strike against her in any way.

CHAPTER IV

The old count, who had always kept up an immense hunting establishment, had turned it over to his son's management; but on this day, the twenty-seventh of September, feeling particularly cheerful, he determined to be of the party.

In two hours the whole hunt was gathered at the front doorsteps. Nikolaï, with a grave and solemn face, which made it evident that he could not be distracted by trifles, walked right by Natasha and Petya, who were trying to say something to him. He personally inspected everything, sent forward the pack with the huntsmen, mounted his sorrel Donets; and, whistling to the dogs of his own leash, he started off through the threshing-floor into the field that stretched toward the Otradnensky preserves. The old count's steed, a dun-colored gelding, named Viflyanka, was in charge of the count's groom; he himself was to ride in his drozhsky straight to the muset which he had designated.

The whole number of hounds brought together was fifty-four, together with six whippers-in and feeders. Besides the gentlemen, there were also eight greyhound-grooms, followed by more than twoscore greyhounds; so that, with the master's dogs in leash, there were, all told, about one hundred and thirty dogs, and twenty mounted huntsmen.

Each dog knew who his master was, and answered to his call. Each man knew his duty, his place, and his work.

As soon as they had ridden beyond the hedge, all, without unnecessary noise or talking, galloped smoothly and evenly along the road, and then struck into the fields that led to the Otradnensky preserves.

As soon as the horses were out of the beaten track, they made their way across the field, as if it were a carpet of yielding grass, occasionally splashing through pools of water. The misty sky continued the same, and the moisture fell monotonously to the ground. The air was calm, mild, unresonant. Occasionally were heard a huntsman's whistle, the snorting of a horse, the crack of the long lash, and the whine of a dog which had left its place.

After they had ridden about a verst, suddenly out of the fog loomed five more riders with dogs, coming to meet the Rostofs. In front of them rode a hale and hearty old man, with heavy gray mustaches.

"Good-morning, 'little uncle,'"[1] cried Nikolaï, as the old man rode up to him.

[1] *Dyadyushka*, diminutive.

"Here's a how-de-do![1] I was sure of it," said the old man. He was a neighbor and distant relative of the Rostofs — a landed proprietor of small means. "I knew it, you could not resist it, and it's good you came. Here's a how-de-do!" This was a favorite phrase of the old man's. "Look out for the cover, double quick, for my Girchik reports that the Ilagins, and all their train, are in the stubble, and they might — here's a how-de-do! — might snatch the litter away from under our very noses!"

"That's where I am going. Say, shall we join packs?" asked Nikolaï.

They united all the hounds into one large pack, and the old man, whom Nikolaï called "little uncle," rode along by his side. Natasha, muffled up in shawls, out of which peered her eager face, with bright, glistening eyes, galloped up to them, followed by Petya and Mikhaïlo, the huntsman, who were her inseparable companions, and by a groom, who was delegated to attend her. Petya was full of glee, and kept whipping up and hauling in his horse. Natasha sat firmly and gracefully on her raven black Arabchik, and reined him in with a practised hand, though without effort.

The "little uncle" looked disapprovingly at Petya and Natasha. He did not believe in combining frivolities with the serious business of hunting.

"Good-morning, 'little uncle'; we are going too," shouted Petya.

"Good-morning to you, good-morning; don't ride the dogs down!" cried the old man, severely.

"Nikolenka, what a splendid dog Trunila is! He knew me!" said Natasha, pointing to her favorite greyhound.

"Trunila, in the first place, is not a dog, but a hound," mused Nikolaï, and gave his sister a stern glance, trying to make her realize the immense distance that separated them at that moment. Natasha realized it.

[1] *Chistoye dyelo marsch!* An almost meaningless semi-military phrase. Literally: "Clean thing! forward!" — invented by the speaker, and characteristic of him.

"Don't you imagine, 'little uncle,' that we shall be in any one's way," said Natasha. "We will stay in our own places and not stir."

"An excellent idea, little countess,"[1] said the "little uncle." "But mind you don't fall off your horse," he added. "For you see, — here 's a how-de-do! — you see you 've nothing to hold on by!"

The "island" of the Otradnensky preserves was now in sight, two or three hundred yards distant, and the cavalcade rode up toward it. Rostof and the "little uncle," having definitely decided where they should set in the hounds, and shown Natasha her post, a place where there was not the slightest chance of anything ever passing, crossed through a ravine into the woods.

"Well, little nephew, stand on solid ground," said the "little uncle." "Take care not to let her get by."

"That depends," replied Rostof. "Phüt! Karaï!" he cried, by this call answering the old man's words. Karaï was an aged, deformed, ugly-faced hound, famous for having once tackled by himself a she-wolf.

All got to their posts.

The old count, knowing his son's passionate zeal for hunting, had made good time, so as not to be behindhand; and the cavalcade had scarcely reached the preserve, when Ilya Andreyitch, cheerful and ruddy, with shaking cheeks, came jolting across the fields, behind his three black horses, and was set down at the muset which he had selected. Smoothing out his fur shuba, and getting his hunting equipment, he mounted his glossy Viflyanka, fat, kind, and steady, and as gray as himself. The horses and the drozhsky were sent home. Count Ilya Andreyitch, although not a keen huntsman at heart, nevertheless was well acquainted with the rules of venery; and he rode off to the edge of the forest, gathered up his reins, settled himself in the saddle, and, feeling conscious that he was all ready, glanced around with a smile.

Near him stood his valet, an old-fashioned but heavy rider, Semyon Chekmar. Chekmar held in leash three

[1] *Grafinyetchka.*

fierce-looking wolf-hounds, not less fat and sleek than master and horse. Two dogs, old and intelligent enough to be out of leash, stretched themselves out on the ground. A hundred paces farther along the edge of the forest was stationed the count's second whipper-in, Mitka, a splendid rider and passionate huntsman. The count, in accordance with time-honored custom, before the hunt began, drank a silver cup full of *zapekanotchka*, or root brandy, took a snack of lunch, and then drank a half-bottle of his favorite Bordeaux.

Ilya Andreyitch was a trifle flushed from the wine and the ride; his eyes grew moist and had a peculiar gleam; and as he sat in his saddle, muffled in his shuba, he had the aspect of a child who has been got ready for a ride.

The lean Chekmar, with sunken cheeks, having got things settled to his satisfaction, looked up at his barin, whose inseparable companion he had been for upwards of thirty years, and, perceiving that he was in good humor, waited for some pleasant talk. Just then a third person rode up cautiously — evidently the result of careful training — and, coming out from behind the woods, paused not far from the count.

This person was an old man, with a gray beard, in a woman's capote and high collar. This was the buffoon who bore the woman's name Nastasya Ivanovna.

"Well, Nastasya Ivanovna," said the old count to him in a whisper, and giving him a wink, "if you should dare to scare away the brute, Danila would give it to you!"

"I can defend myself," said Nastasya Ivanovna.

"Sh-sh-sh-sh-sh!" hissed the count, and, turning to Semyon, he asked, "Have you seen Natalia Ilyinitchna? — Where is she?"

"She and Piotr Ilyitch were stationed in the high grass[1] near Zharovo," replied Semyon, with a smile. "She's a lady, but she's going to have a great hunt all the same."

"And aren't you surprised, Semyon, to see how she

[1] *Buryan*, steppe-grass.

rides — hey?" asked the count. "She rides as well as a man!"

"Of course I'm surprised. Such daring! such skill!"

"And where is Nikolasha? On Lyadovo hill, I suppose?" asked the count, in a whisper.

"That's where he is. He knows well enough where the best places are. And he rides so cleverly, too; Danila and I were thunderstruck at him the other day," replied Semyon, knowing what would please the count.

"He rides well, does he? Hey? Fine fellow on a horse, is he? Hey?"

"Like a picture! How he run that fox t' other day out of the steppe at Zavarzino! How he did gallop out of the woods, 't was a caution! Horse worth a thousand, but the rider beyond price! 'T would be a hard job to find such another young fellow."

"It would, indeed," interposed the count, regretting that Semyon did not spin his story out longer. "'T would be a hard job, would it?" turning back the flap of his shubka, and searching for his snuff-box.

"Then the other day, coming out of mass, in all his regalia, when *Mikhaïl-to* Sidoruitch. ...."

But Semyon did not conclude his sentence, having distinctly heard, owing to the stillness of the atmosphere, the howling of a hound or two, signifying that the hunt was on; he bent down his head and listened, and gave a warning gesture to his barin.

"They are after the whelps!" he whispered. "They are making straight for Lyadovskaya."

The count, with the smile still lingering on his lips, gazed into the distance, along the dike, and held the snuff-box in his hand, forgetting to take a pinch. Instantly following the baying of the hounds came the sound of Danilo's heavy horn, the signal that the wolf was found. Then the pack united their voices with those of the first three hounds; and then they could hear the hounds breaking in, across the ravine, with that peculiar howl which is the sign to the huntsman that they have discovered the wolf. The riders had not yet begun to set on the dogs, but were uttering the uliuliu; and louder than all rang out Danilo's voice, now in bass, now in piercingly shrill notes; it seemed as if his voice filled the whole forest, and burst out beyond the forest bounds, and rang far over the fields.

After listening for a number of seconds in silence, the count and his groom were convinced that the hunt had divided into two packs. The larger half, vehemently giving tongue, were driving farther afield; the other pack were rushing along the forest past the count, while behind them was heard Danilo's uliuliu. The sounds mingled and melted together, but seemed to be growing fainter in the distance. Semyon sighed, and stooped down to disentangle his leash, a young puppy having got the cords mixed up. The count also sighed; and, noticing that he had his snuff-box still in his hand, opened it and took out a pinch of snuff.

"Back," cried Semyon to the young hound, which was trying to make for the woods. The count was startled, and dropped his snuff-box. Nastasya Ivanovna dismounted, and was just on the point of picking it up. The count and Semyon were looking at him. Suddenly, as often happens, the sounds of the hunt came nearer, and it seemed as if the baying mouths of the dogs and Danilo's uliuliu were directly upon them.

The count looked round, and at his right saw Mitka, who, with starting eyes, was staring at him, and, lifting his cap, directed his attention in front of him to the other side.

"Look out!" he shouted, in such a voice that it was evident that this word had been for some time painfully struggling to escape. And, letting loose his leash, he dashed in the count's direction. The count and Semyon sprang out from the cover, and saw at their left a wolf swinging easily along, and, with a noiseless lope, making for the very cover where they had been in hiding. The ferocious dogs yelped, and, tearing themselves free from the leash, flung themselves after the wolf, almost under the legs of the horses.

The wolf paused in his course, awkwardly, like one suffering with the quinsy, turned his head, with its wide forehead, in the direction of the dogs, and then again, with the same easy, waddling gait, gave one spring, and then another, and, shaking his "stump," disappeared in the cover.

At the same instant, with a roar that rather resembled a whine, from the opposite edge of the forest, appeared first one, then a second, then a third hound, and then the whole pack came pouring out into the field, in the very track by which the wolf had sneaked away and escaped. On the heels of the hounds appeared Danilo's horse, all black with sweat, breaking through the hazel bushes. Over his long back, bending forward, and doubled up like a ball, sat Danilo, hatless, with his gray hair disheveled and falling around his sweaty face.

"*Uliuliuliu! Uliuliu!*" he was shouting. When he saw the count, his eyes flashed fire.

"You sh...." he began, menacing the count with his upraised whip-handle. "You've lost that wolf! What hunters!"

And, as if scorning to have further conversation with the confused and startled count, he gave the wet flank of his chestnut stallion the wrathful blow which had been directed against the count, and dashed after the hounds. The count, like one who had been chastised, remained motionless; and, looking around with a scared smile, was going to try to gather sympathy for his situation from Semyon.

But Semyon had disappeared; he was riding in and out of the bushes, trying to start the wolf up from the thicket. The masters of the greyhounds also were beating up the brute from all sides. But the wolf had made his way into the bushes, and not a single hunter got sight of him.

CHAPTER V

Nikolaï Rostof, meantime, had not left his post, and was anxiously expecting the brute. By the nearer and more distant sounds of the hunt; by the baying of the hounds, whose voices he could distinguish; by the shouts of the whippers-in, advancing and retreating, — he had an idea of what was going on in the "island." He knew that the "island" sheltered growing and full-grown wolves; that is, old wolves and their whelps. He knew that the hounds had divided into two packs; that in one place they were on the right scent, and that elsewhere they had met with bad luck. He expected each second to see the beast making in his direction. He made a thousand different conjectures as to which side the brute would come out, and how he should attack him. His heart was filled with mingled hope and despair.

Several times he offered up a prayer to God that the wolf might come in his way; he prayed with that sense of passionate anxiety with which men are wont to pray under the influence of some powerful excitement, even though it may be due to the most trivial cause.

"Now what would it be to Thee," he said in his prayer, "to do this for me? I know that Thou art mighty, and that it is a sin to ask Thee for such a thing; but, for God's sake, let an old full-grown wolf come my way, and let Karaï get a death clutch on her throat, in sight of the 'little uncle' who keeps glancing over in this direction."

A thousand times during that half-hour, Rostof swept his eyes eagerly, restlessly, and with stubborn purpose, around that thicket of forest, where two mighty oaks looked down upon the aspen underbrush; and at the ravine, with its gullied banks; and at the "little uncle's" cap, just visible underneath the bushes on the right.

"No, I shan't have this luck," thought Rostof. "But how jolly it would be! No hope! always the same bad luck with me at cards, and in war, and everywhere."

Austerlitz and Dolokhof, in vivid but swift alternation, flashed through his mind.

"If I could only just once in my life run down a full-grown wolf, that is all that I would ask for!" he said to himself, straining his ears and his eyes, as his gaze swept the thicket from left to right, and as he tried to distinguish the slightest variation in the noise of the hunt.

Then again he glanced to the right, and beheld something swiftly moving across the open field in his direction.

"No, it is impossible!" thought Rostof, with a heavy sigh, as a man sighs when what he has been long looking forward to is practically accomplished. And here the greatest piece of good fortune was accomplishing so simply, so noiselessly, so undemonstratively, without a sign! Rostof could not believe his eyes; and this incredulity lasted more than a second. The wolf came running forward, and leaped clumsily over the ravine that lay across his path. It was an aged brute, with a gray back, and a clearly marked russet belly. He ran along at no great speed, evidently convinced that no one could see him. Rostof, not daring to breathe, glanced at his dogs; they were lying down or standing up all around, but had not yet discovered the wolf, or realized what was going on. Old Karaï, bending his head back, and showing his yellow teeth, occasionally snapping them together, was making a spiteful search for a flea, on his haunch.

"*Uliuliuliu!*" whispered Rostof, thrusting out his lips. The dogs, shaking their chains, and pricking up their ears, sprang to their feet. Karaï ceased his flea-hunting and got up, cocking his ears, and slightly wagging his tail, on which still hung a few shreds of hair.

"Shall I let 'em loose yet, or not?" queried Rostof, while the wolf was making in his direction, and steadily increasing his distance from the woods. Suddenly the wolf's whole appearance underwent a change: a thrill ran over him, at the sight of what he had never probably experienced before, a pair of human eyes fixed on him; and slightly raising his head toward the huntsman, he paused.

"Back or forward? Eh! it's all the same! Forward; we'll see," he seemed to say to himself; and, without looking around, he dashed ahead, with occasional leaps, easy and long, but decided.

"*Uliuliu!*" cried Nikolaï, in a voice that sounded not his own; his good steed, of her own accord, bore him forward down the slope, leaping the ravine, to cut off the wolf; and still swifter, entirely outstripping her, rushed the hounds. Nikolaï did not hear his own shout, was not conscious of the pace at which he was riding, saw neither the dogs nor the ground over which he was carried; saw only the wolf, which, quickening his speed, bounded on, without swerving, in the direction of the ravine. The black-spotted, wide-haunched Milka was the first to get close to the wild beast. Nearer, nearer, she seemed to press — there, she leaps upon him! But the wolf swerved a trifle toward her, and, instead of attacking, as was usually the case with her, Milka, suddenly raising her tail, came to point.

"*Uliuliuliuliu!*" cried Nikolaï.

The red Liubim leaped beyond Milka, impetuously flung himself on the wolf, and gripped him by the haunch; but, at the same instant, overcome by panic, he sprang to one side. The wolf crouched down, clapped his teeth together, then sprang up again, and bounded forward, followed at an arshin's distance by all the hounds, though they avoided getting closer.

"He'll escape! No, that's impossible!" mused Nikolaï, continuing to shout in a hoarse voice.

"Karaï! *Uliuliu!*" he screamed, trying to make out where the old wolf-hound was; he was now his only reliance. Karaï, with all the strength left him by his advanced age, bounding forward, looking at the wolf from the corner of his eyes, was running heavily side by side with the brute, trying to get in front of him. But, owing to the swiftness of the wolf, and the comparative slowness of the hound, it was evident that Karaï's calculation was to be mistaken.

Nikolaï now began to see the forest in front of him, which, if the wolf succeeded in reaching it, would probably prove his safety. Just then, in front of them, a pack of dogs and a huntsman came in sight, dashing almost directly toward him. Here again was a hope. A dark brown young dog, with a long body, belonging to a kennel unknown to Rostof, was flying eagerly forward, directly toward the wolf, and quite upset him. The wolf swiftly and most unexpectedly sprang up and threw himself upon the dark brown hound, chattered his teeth, and the hound, covered with blood, from a great gash in his side, with a pitiful howl, beat his head on the ground.

"Karaïushka! Oh, heavens!" mourned Nikolaï. The old hound, with the tufts of hair flying out from his haunches, had taken advantage of the pause that he had made to block the wolf's path, and was now within five paces of him. The wolf, apparently conscious of the peril, looked out of the corner of his eyes at Karaï, put his stump of a tail as far as possible under his legs, and went off at a mighty bound. But, at this instant, — Nikolaï saw that something extraordinary happened to the dog, — Karaï, quick as a flash, was on the wolf's back, and the two were rolling heels over head down into the ravine in front of them.

The moment that Nikolaï caught sight of the dog and the wolf rolling at the bottom of the ravine, in one indiscriminate mass, out of which could be resolved the wolf's gray hide, his hind leg stretched out, and his scared face, and panting, with laid-back ears (Karaï still held him by the gorge), — the minute that Nikolaï saw this was the happiest moment of his whole life. He was just grasping the saddle-bow to dismount and give the wolf his finishing stroke, when suddenly, from out of that mass of dogs, the brute's head was extended, then his fore paws were laid on the edge of the ravine. The wolf chattered his teeth — Karaï had now let go of his gullet — gave a mighty leap with his hind legs, and, flirting his tail, again got his distance from the dogs, and was off at full speed. Karaï, with bristling hair, apparently either bruised or wounded, crawled painfully out of the ravine.

"My God! what does it mean?" cried Nikolaï, in despair.

The "little uncle's" whipper-in started from the other side to cut off the wolf's course, and the dogs again brought the wolf to bay. Again they gathered round him.

Nikolaï, his whipper-in, the "little uncle," and his huntsmen circled around the wolf, crying their uliuliu, and screaming to the dogs, at each minute, whenever the wolf sat up on his haunches, expecting to dismount, and each time dashing forward, whenever the wolf shook himself free, and tried to dash toward the thicket, which was his only salvation.

At the very beginning of this wolf-baiting, Danilo, hearing the hunters' uliuliu, came galloping along the edge of the forest. He got there in time to see Karaï grapple with the wolf; and he pulled in his horse, expecting to see that the game was finished. But when the huntsmen did not dismount, and the wolf shook himself and made off, Danilo spurred on his chestnut; not indeed at the wolf, but in a straight line toward the thicket, in the same way as Karaï had done, so as to intercept the beast. By reason of this move, he caught up with the wolf just as the "little uncle's" hounds had brought him to a halt for the second time. Danilo galloped forward silently, holding an unsheathed dagger in his left hand; and like a flail fell the strokes of his whip on his chestnut's laboring sides.

Nikolaï had not seen or heard Danilo until his heavily panting chestnut dashed by; and then he heard the sound of a falling body, and saw that Danilo had flung himself into the midst of the dogs, back of the wolf, and was trying to clutch him by the ears. It was now manifest to the dogs, and to the huntsmen, and to the wolf, even, that all was over. The wild beast, timidly laying back his ears, was struggling to gather himself up once more; but the dogs formed a ring round him. Danilo, reaching forward, made a staggering step, and with all his weight threw himself upon the wolf, as if he were lying down to rest, and seized him by the ears. Nikolaï was going to stab him, but Danilo muttered: —

"Don't do it, we'll gag him!" and, changing his position, he placed his foot on the wolf's neck. Then they put a stake into the wolf's jaws, fastened him as if they were getting him into a leash, tied his legs, and Danilo twice rolled the brute over and over.

With weary but happy faces, they lifted the live,

full-grown wolf on the shying and whinnying horse; and, accompanied by the dogs, all yelping at him, they took him to the place of general rendezvous.

All hastened up and began to examine the wolf, which, with his great broad-browed head hanging down, with the stake in his chops, glared from his great glassy eyes at all that throng of dogs and men surrounding him. When he was touched, he would draw together his helpless paws, and glare fiercely, and at the same time steadily, at them all. Count Ilya Andreyitch also came riding up, and had a look at the wolf.

"Oh, what an old one," said he. "Full-grown, hey?" he asked of Danilo, who stood near him.

"Indeed he is, your illustriousness," replied Danilo, respectfully taking off his cap. The count remembered the wolf which had got past him, and his encounter with Danilo.

"Still, my boy, you were in a bad temper," said the count.

Danilo made no reply, and merely smiled with embarrassment — a childishly sweet and pleasant smile.

CHAPTER VI

THE old count rode off home. Natasha and Petya promised to follow immediately. The hunt went farther, as it was still early in the day. Toward noon they sent the hounds into a dell grown up with a dense young forest. Nikolaï, taking his position on the hillside, could overlook all his huntsmen.

On the other side from Nikolaï were fields; and there his whipper-in had taken his post alone, in a pit behind a hazel copse. As soon as the dogs were slipped, Nikolaï heard the sharp yelp of one of his favorite dogs — Voltorn; the other hounds also gave tongue, now ceasing, and then again taking up the cry. In a minute, from the forest, the cry to fox was heard: and the whole pack rushed off pell-mell toward the open, in the direction of the field and away from Nikolaï.

He saw the dog-feeders, in their red caps, dashing off along the edge of the overgrown dell; he saw, also, the dogs, and every instant he expected the fox to show himself in that direction on the field.

The huntsman stationed in the pit gave a start, and let loose the dogs; and then Nikolaï saw a strange-looking red fox crouching down, and hurriedly making across the field, with rumpled brush. The dogs began to close in upon her. Then, as they came closer to her, lo! the fox began to dodge about among them, in circles, making the circles ever shorter and shorter, and sweeping her furry brush (which the hunters call *truba*, a trumpet) around her; and then, lo! one, a white dog, flew at her; and this one was followed by a black dog; and then all were mingled in confusion, and the dogs, as they stood, scarcely swerving, made a sort of star, all their tails pointing outwards. A couple of huntsmen galloped up toward the dogs, one in a red cap, the other, a stranger, in a green kaftan.

"What can that mean?" queried Nikolaï. "Where did that huntsman come from? It's not one of 'little uncle's.'"

The men despatched the fox, and stood for a long time, without mounting or tying her to the straps. Near by, with projecting saddles, stood their horses, which they held by the bridle; and the dogs threw themselves down. The huntsmen were gesticulating and doing something with the fox. Then there rang out the sound of a bugle, the conventional signal of a dispute.

"That's one of Ilagin's hunters; and he's quarreling with our Ivan about something," said Nikolaï's whipper-in.

Nikolaï sent the man to fetch his sister and Petya; and then rode slowly, at a footpace, to the place where the dog-feeders had collected the hounds. Several huntsmen were galloping up to the scene of the dispute.

Nikolaï dismounted and stood near the hounds, with

Natasha and Petya, who had now come up, and waited till word should be brought as to the issue of the dispute.

Out from behind the skirt of the forest came the quarrelsome huntsman, with the fox at his saddle-straps, and galloped up to his young barin. While still at a distance, he took off his cap, and tried to speak respectfully; but he was pale and out of breath, and his face was wrathful. One of his eyes was blackened, but he was apparently unconscious of the fact.

"What was the matter with you there?" asked Nikolaï.

"What do you suppose! he would be after snatching it away from among our hounds! And it was my mouse-colored bitch, too, that had grabbed her! Come now, decide! He tried to get away our fox. Now I 'll have a whack at his foxes. Here she is, on the saddle-straps. Or would you like a taste of this?".... pointing to his dagger, and evidently imagining that he was still talking with his enemy.

Nikolaï, not stopping to discuss the matter with the huntsman, told his sister and Petya to wait for him, and rode off to the place where the rival hunt of the Ilagins was collected.

The victorious huntsman joined the throng of whippers-in; and there, surrounded by his sympathetic admirers, he related his exploit.

The truth of the matter was that Ilagin, with whom the Rostofs had, in days gone by, had some disputes, as well as lawsuits, was hunting in places usually preempted by the Rostofs; and, on this occasion, he had apparently given special orders to go to the "island" where the Rostofs were hunting, and allowed his whipper-in to snatch the game from his rival's dogs.

Nikolaï had never seen Ilagin; but, as was always the case, knowing no half-way in his judgments and feelings, and believing certain reports of the violence and arbitrary conduct of this proprietor, he hated him with all his heart, and considered him his worst enemy. He now rode up to him, full of angry emotions, and firmly grasping his long whip, ready for the most decisive and risky proceedings against his enemy.

He had just ridden up to a jut of the forest, when he saw riding in his direction a portly gentleman, in a beaver cap, on a handsome raven-black steed, and accompanied by two huntsmen.

Instead of an enemy, Nikolaï found in Ilagin a well-bred, representative barin, who manifested a special desire to make the young count's acquaintance. Riding up to Rostof, Ilagin raised his beaver cap, and declared that he was very sorry for what had taken place; that he had commanded the huntsman who had permitted himself to trespass on another's preserve to be punished. He craved the count's acquaintance, and invited him to hunt on his grounds.

Natasha, apprehensive lest her brother might do something terrible, came up in great anxiety, and drew up at a little distance behind him. When she saw that the rivals were greeting each other with friendly courtesy, she joined them. Ilagin lifted his beaver cap still higher as he saw Natasha, and, with a pleasant smile, said that the countess resembled Diana, both by her passion for hunting and by her beauty, of which he had heard many reports.

Ilagin, in order to smooth over his huntsman's indiscretion, pressingly urged Rostof to go to a steep hill-side of his, about a verst away, which he kept for his own private use, and which, on his word, was swarming with hares. Nikolaï consented; and the hunting party, doubled in numbers, swept on their way.

In order to reach Ilagin's preserve, they had to strike across country. The huntsmen made common cause. The gentlemen rode together. The "little uncle," Rostof, Ilagin, each stealthily examined the dogs of the other, striving not to let the others remark it, and anxiously searched for possible rivals among the dogs of the others.

Rostof was especially struck by the beauty of a small thoroughbred young bitch, spotted with red, and rather slender, with muscles like steel, with a delicate little muzzle, and with prominent black eyes. She belonged to Ilagin's pack. He had heard of the rarity of Ilagin's dogs; and in this pretty little dog he recognized a rival to his Milka. In the midst of a sedate conversation about the crops of the current year, which Ilagin had started, Nikolaï called his attention to this little spotted bitch.

"That 's a lovely little bitch you have!" said he, in a careless tone. "Full of mettle?"

"That one? Yes, that one 's a good dog! She 's a hunter," replied Ilagin, speaking with affected indifference of his red-spotted Yorza, for which he had paid a neighbor, the year before, three families of household serfs. "You did n't have much of a yield of grain, either, did you?" he asked, resuming the conversation that he had begun. And then, considering it no more than fair to mollify the young count, in the same way, Ilagin looked at his dogs, and picking out Milka, whose breadth of beam first attracted his attention, he said:—

"That black-spotted bitch of yours is a handsome one, too — well worth having!"

"Yes, pretty good, full of go!" replied Nikolaï. "If only an old gray hare would start across that field, I would show you what kind of a dog she is!" he thought; and, turning to one of his huntsmen, he said he would give a ruble if he would find a hare "on his form," that is, hiding in his nest.

"I cannot understand," pursued Ilagin, "how it is that sportsmen can be jealous of other men's game and dogs. I will tell you how it is with me, count. I enjoy going out to hunt; you see, you are apt to fall in with pleasant company, like this. For what could be better?" — he took off his beaver cap again to Natasha. "But as for merely counting the pelts — that 's a matter of indifference to me!"

"That 's a fact!"

"Or why should it trouble me that some other dog, and not mine, got on the scent first? I get just as much sport from looking on at the course; don't you, count? So I judge...."

Just at this time was heard the long halloo — "*Atoo-yevoa*," — from one of the greyhound-keepers, who had been set on the watch. He was standing half-way down the slope, on a hillock, with his whip upraised; and again he uttered the long-drawn "*A—too—yevoa.*"

This halloo, and the upraised whipstock, signified that he had caught sight of a couching hare.

"On the scent, I imagine," said Ilagin, carelessly. "What say you, count? Shall we give him a run?"

"Yes, we must be after him; certainly! All together, shall we not?" replied Nikolaï, glancing at Yorza and the "little uncle's" red Rugaï, the two rivals against which he had never as yet had a chance to pit his own dogs. "Now what if they get my Milka by the ears!" he thought to himself as, side by side with the "little uncle" and Ilagin, he galloped off toward the hare.

"A full-grown fellow, is n't he?" asked Ilagin, as they came up to the hunter who had discovered him, and, not without anxiety, whistling to his Yorza. "And you, Mikhaïl Nikanoruitch?" he asked, turning to the "little uncle."

The "little uncle" came up with a frown.

"Why should I meddle? It's your game! — here's a how-de-do! — why, your dogs cost a whole village! Thousand-ruble dogs! You two match yours, and I will look on! Rugaï! Na! na!" he cried. "Rugaïushka!" he added; involuntarily expressing by this endearing diminutive the hope that he placed upon his red hound.

Natasha could see and feel the excitement which these two old men and her brother tried vainly to conceal, and she herself was even more excited.

The huntsman on the hillock still stood with upraised whipstock; the gentlemen approached him at a foot-pace. The harriers, coming up to the same horizon, dashed off in the direction of the hare; the hunters, but not the gentlemen, also hastened after them. The whole movement was made slowly, and in due form.

"Which way is he heading?" asked Nikolaï, coming within a hundred paces of the hunter that had discovered him. But the beater had no time to reply, ere the gray hare, scenting the frost of the coming morn, was up and away. The harriers, still in leash, dashed with a howl down the slope after the hare: from all sides, the greyhounds, unleashed, dashed after the harriers and the hare. All these slowly stirring hunting attendants, shouting "stoï" (stay) to keep the dogs on the right scent, and the greyhound-keepers crying "atoo," to urge them on, swept across the field. Ilagin, with perfect coolness, Nikolaï, Natasha, and the "little uncle" flew along, not heeding how or whither they were going, with only the dogs and the hare in their eyes, and fearing only lest they should for a single instant lose the course of the hunt from sight.

The hare proved to be full grown and full of game. After springing out, he did not on the instant dash away, but cocked up his ears, listening to the shouts of the men, and the trampling of the horses, suddenly closing in upon him from all sides. He made a dozen springs, in no great haste, letting the hounds come quite close to him; and then, finally, having chosen his course, and realized his danger, he laid back his ears and was off like the wind. His form had been in the stubble; but the course he took was toward the meadowlands, where it was marshy. Two dogs, answering to the hunter who had discovered him, were the first to see the hare, and lay for him; but they were still a considerable distance behind when Ilagin's red-spotted Yorza outstripped them, came within a dog's length of him, sprang on him with frightful violence, snapped at the hare's tail, and, supposing that she had him, rolled over and over.

The hare, arching his back, darted off at a sharper pace than ever. Then the black-spotted Milka, broad of beam, dashed swiftly in front of Yorza, and began to gain on the hare.

"Milushka!—little mother!"—rang out Nikolaï's encouraging shout. It seemed as if Milka were just going to overtake and nip the hare, but she went too far, and went beyond. The hare had stopped short.

Again the pretty little Yorza came to the fore and seemed to hang over the hare's very tail, as if she were measuring the distance, so as not to be deceived again, before she should seize him by the hind leg.

"Yorzanka!—little sister!"—rang out Ilagin's voice, unnaturally, and as if choked with tears. Yorza heeded not his prayer; at the very instant that she might have been expected to seize her game, he swerved off and bowled away along the ridge, between the meadow and the stubble. Again Yorza and Milka, like two little pole-horses, dashed off neck and neck after the game; but this middle ground was better running for the hare, and the dogs did not gain on him so rapidly.

"Rugaï! Rugaïushka! here's a how-de-do!" cried still a third voice at this instant; and Rugaï, the "little uncle's" red, crook-backed hound, stretching out and doubling up his back, was seen catching up with the two other hounds, dashing beyond them, and falling, with terrible self-control, on the hare itself. He flung him from the stubble-ground into the meadow, leaped on him even more fiercely a second time, in the muddy marsh, into which he sank up to the knees; and then all that could be seen was that he rolled over and over with the hare, the mud staining his back.

The "star" of dogs clustered round them. In a minute the party gathered in a circle round the clustering dogs. The "little uncle," radiantly happy, alone dismounted, and cut off the hare's hind foot. Shaking the hare, so that the blood would drip off, he looked around excitedly, with wandering eyes, unable to keep his feet and hands quiet; and spoke, not knowing what he said, or whom he addressed.

"That's the kind of a how-de-do! That's a dog for you! Worth all of your thousand-ruble hounds! Here's a how-de-do!" said he, all out of breath, and fiercely glancing around, as if he were berating some one; as if all of them were his foes, and all had insulted him, and now, at last, he had come to his chance for getting even with them. "Look at your thousand-ruble dogs! Here's a how-de-do! Here, Rugaï, here's the foot!" he cried, flinging him the hare's paw, with the mud still clinging to it: "You 've earned it — here 's a how-de-do!"

"She 'd run herself all out: she cornered him thrice, all by herself," said Nikolaï, likewise not heeding any one, and not minding whether any one listened to him or not.

"That was a great way; he seized him by the back!" exclaimed Ilagin's groom.

"Yes, when she 's run him out, of course, any house-dog could grip him!" said Ilagin at the same instant; he was flushed, and what with the mad gallop, and the excitement, could scarcely draw his breath. Natasha, so great was her excitement and enthusiasm, also was screaming at the top of her lungs, and shrilly enough to make one's ears ring. With these shrieks of delight, she expressed what all the other sportsmen were expressing by their simultaneous exclamations. And these shrieks were so odd, that she would have been constrained to feel ashamed of herself, and all the others would have been amazed at it, if it had been at any other time.

The "little uncle" himself doubled up the hare cleverly, and boldly laid him over the crupper of his horse, as if, by this action, he were defying them all; and he mounted his fallow bay, and rode away, acting as if he had no wish to speak to any one.

All the rest, melancholy and disconsolate, separated; and it was only after some time had elapsed, that they recovered their former state of affected indifference. For some time, still, they gazed after the red, humped-back Rugaï; who, all spattered with mud, rattling his chain, trotted after the "little uncle's" horse, with the supercilious aspect of a victor.

'You see I am like all the rest of you, as long as there is no game to be after. Yes, and you had better keep at a respectful distance!' was what the aspect of this dog seemed to Nikolaï to say.

When, after some time, the "little uncle" rode back to Nikolaï, and began to talk with him, Nikolaï felt flattered that, after what had taken place, the "little uncle" was condescending enough to talk with him!

CHAPTER VII

WHEN, late in the afternoon, Ilagin courteously took his departure, Nikolaï found that they were so far from home that he was glad to accept the "little uncle's" proposition that their hunting party should spend the night at his little estate at Mikhaïlovko.

"Now if you should come to my place — here's a how-de-do!" — said the "little uncle," "that would be the best way: you see the weather is wet," added the "little uncle." "You could get rested; and the little countess can be driven home in a drozhsky."

The proposition was accepted; a huntsman was sent to Otradnoye, after the drozhsky, while Nikolaï, Natasha, and Petya went to the "little uncle's."

Five men, big and little, — the "little uncle's" house serfs, — rushed out on the front doorsteps, to welcome their barin home. A dozen women, of every age and size, thrust their heads out of the back porch to stare at the approaching cavalcade.

The appearance of Natasha — a woman, a *baruinya* — on horseback aroused the curiosity of the "little uncle's" household serfs to such a pitch that several of them, undeterred by her presence, approached her, stared at her, and freely made their observations, as if she were some curiosity on exhibition, and not a human being who could hear and understand what they said.

"Arinka, just ye look: she sits sidewise! Yes, sidewise; and her skirt dangles! .... And just see her horn!"

"Holy saints preserve us! and a knife too!" ....

"She's a real Tatar!"

"How is it you do not get thrown off?" asked the most audacious of them, turning directly to Natasha.

The "little uncle" dismounted from his horse at the doorsteps of his small country residence, which was built in the midst of an overgrown garden; and, glancing round on his domestics, he gave an imperative order for the supernumeraries to clear out, and for everything to be done necessary for the reception of his guests and the hunting train.

There was a general scattering. The "little uncle" helped Natasha to dismount, and, giving her his hand, led her up the precarious deal steps. The house, which was not plastered, and showed the rough timbers of the walls, was not remarkable for its cleanliness; it was plain to see that the inmates did not consider it the first duty of life to remove every trace of a spot, but there was no noticeable neglect. The entry was filled with the odor of fresh apples, and hung with the skins of wolves and foxes.

The "little uncle" conducted his guests through the antechamber into a small dining-room, with a folding table and red-painted chairs; thence into the drawing-room, where there were a round pine table and a divan; and finally into the library, where there were a ragged divan, a well-worn carpet, and portraits of Suvorof, of the proprietor's father and mother, and of himself in military uniform. The library smelt strong of tobacco and dogs.

Here the "little uncle" begged his guests to be seated and make themselves quite at home, and he left them. Rugaï, his back still covered with mud, came into the room, lay down on the divan, and began to clean himself with tongue and teeth. From the library led a corridor, in which could be seen a screen with its hangings full of rents; beyond the screen were heard the laughing and chatter of women.

Natasha, Nikolaï, and Petya threw off their wraps, and sat down on the divan. Petya rested his head on his arm, and was instantly asleep. Natasha and Nikolaï sat in silence. Their faces were flushed; they were very hungry, and in very good spirits. They exchanged glances; after the hunting was over and they were in the house, Nikolaï no longer considered it necessary to display his masculine superiority over his sister. Natasha winked at her brother; and both, after trying to restrain themselves for a moment, burst forth in a short and hearty peal of laughter, without even taking time to think what they were laughing at.

After a short absence, the "little uncle" came in, dressed in a Cossack coat, blue trousers, and short boots. And Natasha felt that this costume, which, to her amusement and amazement, she had seen the "little uncle" wear at Otradnoye, was a perfectly proper costume, in no respect worse than frock-coat or swallow-tail. The "little uncle" was also in the best of spirits: he was not only not offended by the brother's and sister's merriment, — it never entered into his head that they were laughing at his mode of life, — but he even joined in with their apparently causeless laughter.

"Well, the little countess is so young — here's a how-de-do! — never saw another like her!" he exclaimed, giving Rostof a long-stemmed pipe, and clutching another with a carved short stem between his three fingers, as his habit was.

"All day riding, just like a man, and as if it were quite the ordinary thing."

Shortly after the "little uncle" rejoined them, the door was opened by a young girl, apparently barefooted, to judge by the noiselessness of her tread; and in came a portly, ruddy-faced, handsome woman of forty, with double chin and full red lips, bearing in her hands a huge tray set out with dishes. With overpowering hospitality, dignity, and politeness beaming from her eyes, and expressed in her every motion, she contemplated the guests, and with a flattering smile made them a most respectful courtesy. In spite of her rather unusual portliness, which made bosom and abdomen unduly prominent, and caused her to hold her head very high, this woman, who was the "little uncle's" *ekonomka*, or housekeeper, moved about with amazing agility. She walked up to the table, set down the tray, and skilfully, with her white, plump hands, removed and arranged on the table the bottles and various dishes comprising the *zakuska* or lunch. Having done this, she started away and stood by the door, with a smile on her face.

'That is the kind of a woman I am! Now, do you

understand the "little uncle"?' her attitude seemed to Rostof to imply. How could he fail to understand? Not only Rostof, but even Natasha, understood the "little uncle," and the meaning of his furrowed brows, and the happy, self-satisfied smile which slightly curved his lips as Anisya Feodorovna entered the room. On the tray were *travnik* or herb brandy, liqueurs, mushrooms, wheat-flour cakes with buttermilk, fresh honeycomb, mulled wine and sparkling mead, apples, raw nuts, roasted nuts, and nuts cooked in honey. Then Anisya Feodorovna brought fruits preserved in honey and sugar, and a ham and a fowl just roasted.

All this was of Anisya Feodorovna's own preparation, and selecting, and setting forth. All this was redolent of Anisya Feodorovna, and had the mark of her genius and taste. All was in character with her scrupulous neatness, and cleanness, and whiteness, and her pleasant smile.

"Have a bite of something to eat, little countess," she insisted, handing Natasha first one thing and then another. Natasha partook of everything; and it seemed to her that she had never seen and never tasted such buttermilk cakes, or mulled wine with such a flavor, or nuts cooked so deliciously in honey, or such a fowl!

Anisya Feodorovna went out. Rostof and the "little uncle," while sipping their glasses of cherry liqueur, talked about hunting, past and to come, about Rugaï, and Ilagin's dogs. Natasha, with shining eyes, sat up erect on the divan, and listened to them. Several times she tried to rouse Petya to have something to eat; but he muttered incoherent words, and was evidently too sound asleep. Natasha felt so happy, she so keenly enjoyed the novel surroundings, that her only fear was that the drozhsky would come for her too soon. After one of those fortuitous silences that are almost inevitable with people who for the first time entertain their friends at home, the "little uncle," responding to a thought that must have occurred to his guests, remarked:—

"And this is the way I shall live out my days. You

die — here 's a how-de-do ! — and nothing is left. So what 's the sin ? "

The "little uncle's" face had grown very grave, and even handsome, as he made this remark. Rostof could not help thinking of the pleasant things his father and the neighbors had said of the old man. The "little uncle," throughout the whole government, had the reputation of being as noble-hearted and disinterested as he was eccentric. He was often called upon to act as arbiter in family disputes, he was chosen executor of wills, he was made the repository of secrets, he was elected judge, and called upon to fill other offices; but he stubbornly refused to enter active service: autumn and spring he rode about the country on his fallow bay stallion; in the winter he stayed at home; in the summer he lounged in his overgrown garden.

"Why don't you enter the service, 'little uncle'?"

"I have served and I 've given it up. It is no use — here 's a how-de-do ! — I can't make anything out of it. It 's well enough for you youngsters, but my wits could never grasp it. But hunting ! That 's quite another thing ! That 's the how-de-do ! Open that door, there !" he cried. "What did you shut it for ?"

The door at the end of the corridor — which the "little uncle" called "collidor" — led into a single room occupied by the hunting train. The bare feet swiftly slithered along, and an invisible hand pushed the door open into the "hunters' room," as this was called. The sounds of the balalaïka, or Ukraine guitar, were clearly heard through the corridor; some one who was a master hand at playing it evidently had hold of the instrument. It had been a long time since Natasha had listened to these sounds, and now she ran out into the corridor to hear more distinctly.

"That is Mitka, my coachman. I bought a beautiful balalaïka for him, I 'm fond of it," said the "little uncle." After coming back from his courses, the "little uncle" was in the habit of summoning Mitka into the "hunters' room" to play for him. The "little uncle" liked that kind of music.

"How good it is! It's excellent!" said Nikolaĭ, with a slight trace of involuntary scorn, as if he were ashamed of himself for confessing that he extremely enjoyed such sounds.

"Excellent!" repeated Natasha, reproachfully; she was conscious of the tone in which her brother spoke. "*Excellent* does not express it: it's charming, that's what it is!"

Just as the "little uncle's" pickled mushrooms, the hydromel, and the liqueur seemed to her the best in the world, so also did that tune on the balalaïka seem to her, at that moment, the very acme of all musical charm.

"Again, please, again," cried Natasha at the door, as soon as the sounds of the balalaïka had ceased. Mitka tuned the instrument, and once more began bravely to thrum out the *Baruinya*, or "The High-born Maid," with a clanging of strings and grappling of chords. The "little uncle" sat and listened, inclining his head to one side with an almost imperceptible smile. The theme of the *Baruinya* was repeated a hundred times. Several times the balalaïka had to be tuned, and then once more the same sounds trembled forth; and yet the listeners were not wearied, and wanted to hear this tune over and over again. Anisya Feodorovna came in, and leaned her portly frame against the door-lintel.

"Be kind enough to listen to him," said she to Natasha, with a smile strikingly like the "little uncle's." "He plays for us gloriously!" said she.

"That part is not done right!" suddenly exclaimed the "little uncle," with an energetic gesture. "It needs to be faster there — here's a how-de-do! — let it out!" ....

"And do you know how to play?" asked Natasha.

The "little uncle" smiled, but made no reply.

"Just you look, Anisyushya, if the strings are all on my guitar. I have not had it in my hands for some time — here's a how-de-do!"

Anisya Feodorovna gladly went to fulfil her lord

and master's command, and immediately brought the guitar.

The "little uncle," not looking at any one, blew off the dust, rapped with his bony fingers on the sounding-board of the guitar, tuned the strings, and straightened himself on his chair. He grasped the guitar above the finger-board, with a somewhat theatrical air, pushing back his left elbow; and, with a wink toward Anisya Feodorovna, he struck up, not the *Baruinya*, but a prelude of one clear, ringing chord; after which he began in a steady and precise, but still regularly accentuated *tempo*, to improvise variations on the well-known song, "On the pa-a-vement o-of the street."

At once the theme of the song began to sing itself rhythmically in the hearts of both Nikolaï and Natasha, with that peculiar sedate cheerfulness which Anisya Feodorovna's whole being exhaled. Anisya Feodorovna blushed, and, hiding her face in her handkerchief, she left the room with a laugh. The "little uncle" went on improvising on the song clearly, carefully, and with energetic steadiness, his glance, full of varying inspiration, fixed on the spot where Anisya Feodorovna had been standing. There was a barely perceptible *something*, betokening amusement, at one corner of his mouth, under his gray mustache; and this look intensified as the song went on, or as the accent grew more pronounced, and in such places as the strings almost snapped under his twanging fingers.

"Charming! charming, 'little uncle'! Some more, some more!" cried Natasha, as soon as he came to a pause. Then, springing up from her seat, she threw her arms around the "little uncle" and kissed him.

"Nikolenka! Nikolenka!" he cried, glancing at her brother, and, as it were, asking him if he appreciated it all.

Nikolaï also was greatly delighted with the performance. The "little uncle" once more struck up a tune. Anisya Feodorovna's smiling face again appeared in the doorway, and behind her were grouped still other faces.

"*Za Khalodnoï Kliutchevoï*
Kritchit: 'dyevitsa, postoï!'"[1]

was the tune which the "little uncle" played. Then he made one more skilful change of key, broke off, and shrugged his shoulders.

"There, there, 'little uncle!' you old darling!"[2] murmured Natasha, in such a tone of entreaty that one might have thought her life was dependent on its gratification. The "little uncle" stood up, and as if there were two men, — the one smiling a grave smile at the merry one, while the merry one performed a naïve and dignified antic in anticipation of the *plyaska*, or native dance.

"Now, then, my dear niece," cried the "little uncle," waving his hand toward Natasha, after striking a chord.

Natasha threw off the shawl which she had wrapped around her, glided out in front of the "little uncle," and, putting her arms akimbo, made a motion with her shoulders, and waited.

Where, how, when, had this little countess, educated as she had been by a French *émigrée*, imbibed the Russian spirit? Was it from the very atmosphere which she breathed? Where had she learned all those characteristic motions which the *pas de châle* might long ago have been supposed entirely to efface?

But the spirit and the motions were the very ones — inimitable, untaught, intuitive, thoroughly Russian — which the "little uncle" expected of her. The moment she got to her feet, with an enthusiastic, proud, and shrewdly gay smile, the first tremor of fear which seized Nikolaï and all the other spectators — the fear that she might not be able to perform it correctly — passed away, and gave place to sheer admiration.

Her performance was so absolutely perfect, and so entirely what was expected of her, that Anisya Feodorovna, who had immediately handed to her the handker-

[1] "At the crystal-flowing fountain
Cries a voice, 'O maiden, wait!'"

[2] *Galubchik.*

chief that played such an indispensable part in the dance, wept and laughed at once, as she gazed at that slender, graceful countess, from another world, as it were, educated in silks and velvets, who could understand all that was in herself — Anisya; in Anisya's father, Feodor; and in her aunt, and in her mother, and in the whole Russian people.

"Well, little countess — here's a how-de-do!" exclaimed the "little uncle," with a radiant smile, when the plyaska was finished. "Well done, niece! Now, all we need is to pick you out a fine young husband — here's a how-de-do!"

"Already picked out," said Nikolaï, smiling.

"Oho!" exclaimed the "little uncle," in surprise, with a questioning look at Natasha. Natasha, with a smile of pleasure, nodded her head in assent.

"And he's such a fine one!" said she.

But the moment these words had escaped her lips, a new train of thoughts and feelings arose in her mind: what signified Nikolaï's smile when he said, "Already picked out?" "Is he glad or sorry? Possibly he thinks that my Bolkonsky would not approve, would not understand, this gayety of ours. No, he certainly would not understand it all..... Where is he now, I wonder?" said Natasha to herself, and her face grew suddenly grave. But it lasted only a single second. "You must not think about it, you must not dare to think about it," said she to herself; and, with her face wreathed in smiles, she again sat down beside the "little uncle," and urged him to play something more.

The "little uncle" played still another song and waltz; then, after a short silence, he cleared his throat, and struck up his favorite hunting-song: —

> "*Kak so vetchera porosha*
> *Vuipadala khorosha.*"[1]

The "little uncle" sang as the people sing, with that full and naïve conviction that the whole meaning of the

[1] "As the evening sun sank low
Fell the white and beauteous snow."

song is to be found exclusively in the words; that the tune will go of itself, and that there is no special air, or that the air is merely for harmony's sake. The result was that this singing of the "little uncle's," so completely free from self-consciousness, like the songs of the birds, was particularly charming. Natasha was in raptures over his singing. She determined that she would not take any more lessons on the harp, but would henceforth play only on the guitar. She asked the "little uncle" to let her take the instrument, and immediately began to pick out chords for singing.

About ten o'clock a *lineïka*, or long, low carriage, and a drozhsky came for Natasha and Petya, and three mounted men, who had been sent to find them. The count and countess did not know what had become of them, and, as the messenger reported, were in a great state of agitation.

Petya was picked up and deposited in the lineïka, like a dead body; Natasha and Nikolaï took their places in the drozhsky. The "little uncle" muffled Natasha all up, and bade her farewell with a new and peculiar touch of affection. He accompanied them on foot as far as the bridge, which they had to abandon for the ford, and he commanded his hunters to precede them with lanterns.

"Good-by, *prashchaï*, — my dear niece," rang his voice from out the darkness — not the one which Natasha had known hitherto, but the one that had sung, "As the evening sun sank low."

The windows in the village through which they passed gleamed with ruddy lights, and there was a cheerful odor of smoke.

"How charming the 'little uncle' is!" exclaimed Natasha, as they bowled along the highway.

"Yes," said Nikolaï. "You are not cold, are you?"

"No, I'm comfortable, perfectly comfortable. Oh, I'm so happy!" replied Natasha, with a sense of perplexity. They rode for a long time in silence.

The night was dark and damp. They could not even

see the horses; they could only hear them splashing through the unseen mud-puddles.

What was going on in that girl's impressionable mind, which was so quick to catch and retain the most varied experiences of life? How was it possible to stow them all away in it? But she was very happy. As they drew near the house, she suddenly struck up the song, "As the evening sun sank low," the tune of which she had been trying all the way to catch, and at last succeeded in remembering.

"You've caught it, have you?" said Nikolaï.

"What were you thinking about just now, Nikolenka?" asked Natasha. They were fond of asking each other this question.

"I?" exclaimed Nikolaï, trying to recollect; "let me see! At first, I was thinking that Rugaï, the red hound, was like the 'little uncle'; and that, if he had been a man, he would keep the 'little uncle' about him all the time; if not for hunting, at least for his music; at all events, I would have kept him. How musical the 'little uncle' is! Is n't he? Well, and what were your thoughts?"

"Mine? Wait! wait! At first, I was thinking how we were riding here, and that we supposed we were on our way home; whereas, in reality, it is so dark that God only knows where we are going; and we might suddenly discover that we were not at Otradnoye at all, but in some fairy realm! And then I was thinking.... no, there was nothing else!"

"I know! you certainly were thinking about *him*," said Nikolaï, smiling, as Natasha knew by the tone of his voice.

"No," replied Natasha, though in reality she had been thinking about Prince Andreï, and wondering how he would have liked the "little uncle." "And there's one thing I have been repeating and repeating all the way," said Natasha, "and that is, 'How superbly Anisyushka marched about!'" And Nikolaï heard her clear, merry laugh, so easily excited by trifles. "But do you know," she suddenly added, "I am certain that

I shall never, never again be so happy, so free from care, as I am now!"

"What rubbish, nonsense, trumpery talk!" exclaimed Nikolaï; and he thought in his own mind, "How charming this Natasha of mine is! I shall never find another friend like her! Why should she think of getting married? We might travel all over the world together!"

"How charming this dear Nikolaï is!" thought Natasha. "Ah! there's a light in the drawing-room still," said she, pointing to the windows of the mansion, cheerfully shining out into the moist, velvety darkness of the night.

CHAPTER VIII

COUNT ILYA ANDREYITCH had resigned his position as *predvodityel*, or marshal of the district nobility, because this office entailed too great expenses. But still his finances showed no improvement.

Often Natasha and Nikolaï found their parents engaged in secret, anxious consultation; and they heard rumors about the sale of the magnificent ancestral home of the Rostofs, and their pod-Moskovnaya estate. Now that he was relieved from this office, it was not necessary for them to entertain so extensively, and life at Otradnoye went on more quietly than in former years; but the huge mansion, and the wings, were just as full of servants as ever, and more than twenty persons habitually sat down at table. And all these were the regular household, who lived there, practically members of the family; or those who were obliged, for some reason or other, to live at the count's expense. Such, for instance, were Dimmler, the music-master, and his wife; Vogel, the dancing-master, and his whole family; then, an elderly lady of quality,[1] named Bielova, who had her home there; and many others of the same sort: Petya's tutors and governors, the young ladies' former "guvernantka," and men and women who simply found it

[1] *Baruinya.*

better, or more to their advantage, to live at the count's than at home.

They had not quite as much company as formerly; but the scale of living was practically the same, for the count and the countess found it impossible to accommodate themselves to any other.

The hunting establishment was the same, nay, it had even been increased by Nikolaï: there were still fifty horses and fifteen coachmen in the stables; rich gifts on name-days were still given, and formal dinners, to which all the neighborhood were invited; the count still had his whist and Boston parties, at which, as he held his cards spread out so that every one could see them, his neighbors were enabled to go away enriched to the extent of several hundred rubles, every day, having come to regard it as an especial prerogative of theirs to make up a table at which Count Ilya Andreyitch should serve as their chief source of income.

The count marched along through the monstrous tangle of his affairs, striving not to believe that he was so involved, and at every step involving himself more and more, and feeling conscious that he had not the strength to rend the bonds that beset his feet, or the zeal and patience required to unravel them.

The countess, with her loving heart, was conscious that their fortunes were going to rack and ruin; but she felt that the count was blameless; that he could not help being what he was; that he himself was suffering, — though he tried to conceal it, — from the consciousness of the ruin that faced himself and his family, and was striving to devise means of rescue.

From her woman's point of view, the only means that presented itself was to get Nikolaï married to a wealthy heiress.

She felt that this was their last hope; and that if Nikolaï refused a certain match, which she proposed to arrange for him, it would be necessary to bid a final farewell to every hope of restoring their fortunes. This match was with Julie Karagina, the daughter of a most worthy and virtuous father and mother; a girl whom the Rostofs had known since she was a child, and who had lately come into a large fortune, by the death of the last of her brothers.

The countess had written directly to Madame Karagina, in Moscow, proposing a marriage between daughter and son; and she had received a most favorable response. Madame Karagina replied that she, for her part, was agreed; but that everything depended on her daughter's inclinations. Madame Karagina invited Nikolaï to come to Moscow.

Several times the countess, with tears in her eyes, told her son that now, since both of her daughters were provided for, her sole desire was to see him married. She declared that she would go to her grave contented, if this might be. Then she said that she happened to know of a very lovely young girl; and she wanted to know his ideas upon the subject.

On other occasions, she openly praised Julie, and advised Nikolaï to go to Moscow and have a good time during the Christmas holidays. Nikolaï was sharp enough to understand his mother's covert hints; and, during one of their talks, he managed to draw her out completely.

She told him that their whole hope of bringing their affairs into order was in seeing him married to the Karagina.

"But what if I loved a girl who was poor, *maman*, would you insist upon my sacrificing my feelings and honor, for *money?*" he asked, not realizing the harshness of his question, and simply desiring to show his noble feelings.

"No, you don't understand me," said his mother, not knowing how to set herself straight. "You misunderstood me, entirely, Nikolenka. All I desire is your happiness," she added; and she had the consciousness that she had not spoken the truth, that she was getting beyond her depth. She burst into tears.

"Mamenka! don't cry; simply tell me that this is your real wish, and you know that I would give my whole life — everything that I have — to make you happy," said Nikolaï. "I would sacrifice everything for you, even my dearest wishes."

But the countess had no desire to offer the dilemma: she had no wish to demand a sacrifice from her son; she would have preferred herself to be the one who should make the sacrifice.

"No, no, you did not understand me; we won't say anything more about it," said she, wiping away her tears.

"Yes, perhaps it is true, that I am in love with a penniless girl," said Nikolaï to himself. "Why should I sacrifice my sentiments and my honor, for the sake of wealth! I am amazed that mamenka should say such a thing to me! Is there any reason, because Sonya is poor, that I should not love her?" he asked himself, "that I should not return her true, generous love? And, most certainly, I should be much happier with her, than with such a doll as Julie! I can always sacrifice my feelings for my parents' good," said he to himself. "But to command my feelings is beyond my power. If I love Sonya, then my feeling is more powerful, and above everything for me."

Nikolaï did not go to Moscow. The countess did not again revert to her conversation with him about his marriage; but she saw with pain, and even with indignation, the signs of a constantly growing intimacy between her son and the dowerless Sonya. She reproached herself, but she found it impossible to resist heaping worriments upon Sonya, and finding fault with her: oftentimes unreasonably stopping her short, and addressing her with the formal *vui*, "you," and "*moya milaya,*" instead of by the usual tenderer epithets. What annoyed the worthy countess most of all was that this poor, dark-eyed niece of hers was so sweet, so gentle, so humbly grateful for all her kindnesses; and so genuinely, unchangeably, and self-sacrificingly in love with Nikolaï, that it was impossible to find anything really to blame her for.

Nikolaï stayed at home, waiting till his leave of absence should expire.

A letter was received about this time from Natasha's

lover, Prince Andreï, dated at Rome; it was his fourth. In it he wrote that he should long ere that have been on the way home to Russia, had it not been that the warmth of the climate had unexpectedly caused his wound to reopen, which obliged him to postpone his journey till the beginning of the next year.

Natasha was deeply in love with her "bridegroom": her character had been greatly modified by this love; at the same time, her nature was thoroughly open to all the joys of life; but toward the end of the fourth month of their separation, she began to suffer from attacks of melancholy, which she found it impossible to resist. She was sick to death of herself; she grieved because all this time was slipping away so uselessly; while she felt that she was only too ready to love and to be loved.

It was far from cheerful at the Rostofs'.

CHAPTER IX

THE Christmas holidays had come, and except for the High Mass, except for the formal and perfunctory congratulations of the neighbors and the household servants, except for the new gowns that every one had on, there was nothing that especially signalized the season; though the perfectly still atmosphere, with the thermometer at twenty degrees[1] below zero, the sun shining dazzlingly all day long, and at night the wintry sky glittering with myriads of stars, seemed to imply that nature at least gave special distinction to the Christmastide.

After dinner on the third day of the Christmas holidays, all the household had scattered to their respective rooms. It was the most tedious time of the day. Nikolaï, who had been out in the morning, making calls on the neighbors, was asleep in the divan-room. The old count was resting in his library. Sonya was sitting at the center-table in the drawing-room copying some designs. The countess was laying out her game of

[1] Réaumur.

patience. Nastasya Ivanovna, the buffoon, with a woe-begone countenance, was sitting at the window with two old ladies.

Natasha came into the room, and went directly up to Sonya, looked at what she was doing, then stepped across to her mother and stood by her without saying a word.

"Why are you wandering about like a homeless spirit?" asked her mother. "What do you want?"

"I want *him* .... instantly! this very minute! I want *him*," said Natasha, with gleaming eyes, but without a trace of a smile.

The countess raised her head and gave her daughter a steady look.

"Don't look at me! Don't look at me, mamma; I shall cry if you do!"

"Sit down, sit down with me here," said the countess.

"Mamma, I must have him. Why am I perishing so, mamma?"

Her voice broke; the tears started to her eyes, and in order to hide them she quickly turned away and left the room.

She went into the divan-room, stood there a moment lost in thought, and went to the maids' sitting-room. There, an elderly chambermaid was scolding a young girl, who had just come in from out of doors all out of breath.

"You might play some other time," the old servant was saying. "There is a time for all things."

"Let her be, Kondratyevna," said Natasha. "Run, Mavrusha, run."

And having rescued Mavrusha, Natasha went through the ball-room into the anteroom. An old man and two young lackeys were playing cards. They stopped their game, and respectfully stood up as their young mistress came in.

"What shall I have them do?" wondered Natasha. "Yes, Nikita, please go .... where shall I send him? oh, yes .... go into the barnyard and fetch me a cock; yes, and you, Misha, bring me some oats."

"Do you wish a few oats?" asked Misha, with joyous readiness.

"Go, go, make haste," said the old man, imperiously.

"And you, Feodor, get me a piece of chalk."

As she went past the butler's pantry, she ordered the samovar to be got ready, although it was not anywhere near the time for it.

Foka, the *bufetchik*, or butler, was the most morose man of all the household. Natasha took it into her head to try her power over him. He suspected that she was not in earnest, and began to ask her if she meant it.

"Oh, what a baruishnya she is!" said Foka, pretending to be very cross at Natasha.

No one in the house set so many feet flying, and no one gave the servants so much to do, as Natasha. She could not have any peace of mind if she saw servants, unless she sent them on some errand. It seemed as if she were making experiments whether she would not meet with angry answers or with grumbling, on the part of some of them, but the servants obeyed no one else so willingly as Natasha.

"Now, what shall I do? Where shall I go?" pondered the young countess, as she slowly passed along the corridor.

"Natasya Ivanovna, what sort of children shall I have?" she demanded of the buffoon, who, dressed in his woman's short jacket, was coming towards her.

"Oh, you will have fleas, dragon-flies, and grasshoppers!" replied the buffoon.

"My God! my God! it's this everlasting sameness! What shall I do with myself? Where can I find something to do?" and, swiftly kicking her heels together, she ran up-stairs to the quarters occupied by Vogel and his wife. Two governesses were sitting in the Vogels' room; on the table stood plates with raisins, walnuts, and almonds. The governesses were discussing the question whether it were cheaper to live in Moscow or Odessa.

Natasha sat down, listened to their conversation with a grave, thoughtful face, and then stood up.

"The Island of Madagascar!" she exclaimed. "Ma-da-gas-car," she repeated, laying a special emphasis on each syllable; and then, without replying to Madame Schoss's question what she said, she hastened from the room.

Petya, her brother, was also up-stairs; he and his tutor were arranging for some fireworks which they were going to set off that night.

"Petya! Petka!" she cried to him. "Carry me down-stairs!"

Petya ran to her and bent his back. She jumped upon it, threw her arms around his neck, and he, with a hop, skip, and jump, started to run down with her.

"No, thank you! that will do! The Island of Madagascar!" she repeated, and jumping off, she flew down-stairs.

Having made the tour of her dominions, as it were, having made trial of her power of command, and discovered that all were sufficiently obedient, but that everything was nevertheless utterly stupid, Natasha went into the ball-room, took the guitar, sat down in a dark corner behind a cabinet, and began to thrum the bass strings of her guitar, practising a theme which she remembered from an opera she had heard at Petersburg in company with Prince Andreï.

To those who were outside listening to her as she strummed on the guitar there seemed to be no sense to what she was playing, but in her imagination these sounds aroused from the dead past a whole series of recollections. As she sat in the shadow of the cabinet, with her eyes fixed on the pencil of light that streamed from the door of the butler's pantry, she listened to herself, and indulged in day-dreams. She was in the mood for day-dreaming.

Sonya, with a wine-glass in her hand, passed through the ball-room on her way to the butler's pantry. Natasha looked at her, at the bright chink in the door; and it seemed to her that on some occasion, long before, she had seen the light streaming through the chink in the pantry door, and Sonya crossing the room with a glass.

"Yes, and it was exactly the same!" said Natasha to herself. "What is this tune, Sonya?" cried Natasha, moving her fingers over the bass strings.

"Ah! Are you here?" cried Sonya, startled at first, and then stopping to listen. "I don't know. Is n't it 'The Storm'?" she suggested timidly, for fear that she was mistaken.

"Now, there! she gave a start in exactly the same way, she came up to me in exactly the same way, and her face wore the same timid smile when that took place," thought Natasha. "And in just the same way I felt that there was something lacking in her.—No! that is the chorus from the 'Water Carrier.'[1] You ought to know!"

And Natasha hummed the air over to recall it to Sonya's memory.

"Where were you going?" asked Natasha.

"To change the water in this glass. I am just copying a sketch."

"You are always busy; and here am I, not good for anything," said Natasha. "Where is Nikolaï?"

"Asleep, I think!"

"Sonya, do go and wake him up," urged Natasha. "Tell him that I want him to sing."

She remained sitting there, and wondering why it was that this had happened so; but, as it did not disturb her very much that she was not able to solve this question, she once more relapsed into her recollections of the time when she was with *him*, and he looked at her with loving eyes.

"Akh! I wish he would come! I am so afraid that he won't come! But, worst of all, I 'm growing old! that 's a fact! Soon I shall not be what I am even now! But, maybe, he will come to-day. Maybe he is here now. Maybe he has come, and even now is sitting in

[1] The Peasants' Chorus, third act of Cherubini's opera, "Les Deux Journées" (known also in Germany as "Der Wasserträger"), produced 1804.

the drawing-room. Maybe he came yesterday, and I have forgotten about it."

She got up, laid down the guitar, and went into the drawing-room. All the household — tutors, governesses, and guests — were already gathered near the tea-table. The men were standing around the table; but Prince Andreï was not among them, and everything was as usual.

"Ah! there she is," said Count Ilya Andreyitch, as he saw Natasha. "Come here and sit by me!"

But Natasha remained standing near her mother, looking around as if she were in search of some one.

"Mamma!" she murmured. "Give him back to me, mamma, quick, quick!" and again she found it hard to keep from sobbing.

She sat down by the table, and listened to the conversation of her elders, and of Nikolaï, who had also come to the tea-table.

"My God! my God! the same faces, the same small-talk! even papa holds his cup and cools it with his breath just as he always does!" said Natasha, to her horror feeling a dislike rising in her against all the household because they were always the same.

After tea, Nikolaï, Sonya, and Natasha went into the divan-room, to their favorite corner, where they always held their most confidential conversations.

CHAPTER X

"HAS it ever happened to you," asked Natasha of her brother, when they were comfortably settled in the divan-room, "has it ever happened to you that it seemed as if there were nothing, just nothing at all, left in the future for you? that all that was best was past, and that you were not so much bored as disgusted?"

"Have n't I, indeed! Many a time, when everything was going well, and all were gay, it would come into my head that it was all vanity and vexation of spirit, and that all of us would have to die. Once, at the regiment, I did not go out to promenade, though the band was playing, for everything had suddenly become so gloomy...."

"Akh! I know what you mean! I know! I know!" interrupted Natasha. "When I was a tiny bit of a girl, it used to be that way with me. Do you remember I was punished once, on account of those cherries, and you were all dancing, while I had to sit alone in the class-room, and sobbed? I shall never forget how melancholy I felt, and how vexed with you all and with myself! Oh, yes, vexed with you all! all of you! And the worst of it was, I was not to blame," said Natasha; "do you remember?"

"I remember," replied Nikolaï; "and I remember that I went to you and wanted to comfort you; and, do you know, I was ashamed to do it! We were terribly absurd! I had at that time a kind of toy, like a manikin, and I wanted to give it to you! Do you remember?"

"And do you remember," asked Natasha, with a thoughtful smile, "how, once, a long, long time ago, when we were little tots, uncle took us into the library, — that was in the old house and it was dark, — and when we went in, suddenly there stood before us...."

"A negro!" said Nikolaï, taking the word from her mouth, and laughing merrily. "Of course I remember it! And now I can't tell for the life of me that it was a negro, or whether we saw it in a dream, or whether it was something that we were told!"

"He had gray hair, you remember, and white teeth, and he stood and stared at us...."

"Do you remember it, Sonya?" asked Nikolaï.

"Yes, I have a dim recollection of something about it," timidly replied the young girl.

"I have asked both papa and mamma about that negro," said Natasha. "They declare that no negro was ever here. But you see *you* remember about it!"

"Certainly I do! And now I recall his teeth very distinctly."

"How strange! Just as if it were in a dream! I like it!"

"And do you remember how we were rolling eggs in the dining-room, and suddenly two little old women appeared, and began to whirl round on the carpet. That was so, was n't it? Do you remember how fine it was?"

"Yes; and do you remember how papenka, in a blue shuba, used to fire off his musket from the door-steps?"

Thus, smiling with delight, they took turns in calling up, not the reminiscences of a gloomy old age, but the recollections of the poetic days of youth; impressions from the most distant past, dreams fused and confused with reality; and these happy recollections sometimes made them quietly laugh.

Sonya, as usual, sat at a little distance from the other two, though their recollections were not confined to themselves alone. She did not remember much of what the others did, and what came back to her failed to arouse in her that poetic feeling which they experienced. She simply rejoiced in their enjoyment, and tried to take a part in it.

She began to feel a special interest in these reminiscences only when they came to speak of her first coming to their house. Sonya was telling how afraid she was of Nikolaï, because he wore braid on his jacket; and her nurse told her that they were going to sew her up in braid.

"And I remember they told me that you were born under a cabbage," said Natasha. "And I remember, also, that I did not dare to disbelieve it, though I knew that it was a fib, and so I felt uncomfortable."

At this stage of the conversation, a chambermaid thrust her head into the divan-room, at the rear door, and said in a whisper: —

"Baruishnya, they have brought the cock."

"I don't want it, Polya, now; tell them to carry it away again."

While they were still engaged in talking, Dimmler came into the divan-room, and went to the harp which stood in one corner. As he took off the covering, the harp gave forth a discordant sound.

"Eduard Karluitch, please play my favorite nocturne — that one by Monsieur Field," [1] cried the old countess from the drawing-room.

Dimmler struck a chord, and, turning to Natasha, Nikolaï, and Sonya, said, "Young people, how quiet you are sitting!"

"Yes, we are talking philosophy," said Natasha, looking up for an instant, and then pursuing the conversation. It now turned upon dreams.

Dimmler began to play. Natasha noiselessly went on her tiptoes to the table, took the candle, and carried it out; then she came back and sat down quietly in her place.

In the room, especially that part where the divan was on which they were sitting, it was dark, but through the lofty windows the silver light of the full moon fell across the floor.

"Do you know, I think," said Natasha, drawing closer to Nikolaï and Sonya, when Dimmler had now finished his nocturne, and sat lightly thrumming the strings, apparently uncertain whether to cease, or to play something else, — "I think that when you go back, remembering, and remembering, and remembering everything, you remember so far back, that at last you remember what happened even before you were born." ....

"That is metempsychosis," exclaimed Sonya, who always had been distinguished for her scholarship and her good memory. "The Egyptians used to believe that our souls once inhabited the bodies of animals, and will go into animals again."

"Ah, but do you know, I don't believe that we were ever in animals," remarked Natasha, in the same low voice, though the music had ceased. "But I know for certain that we used to be angels in that other world; and, when we come here, we remember about it." ....

[1] John Field, known as "Russian Field," born in Dublin; pupil of Clementi; went from Paris to Germany, from Germany to Russia, where he died in January, 1837.

"May I join you?" asked Dimmler, coming up noiselessly, and taking a seat near them.

"If we were angels, then why have we fallen lower?" suggested Nikolaï. "No, that can't be!"

"Who told you that we are lower than the angels? Because I know what I used to be," objected Natasha, with conviction. "You see the soul is immortal. .... If I am going to live always, it must be that I lived before, lived a whole eternity."

"Yes, but it is hard for us to realize what eternity is," remarked Dimmler, who, when he had joined the group of young people had worn a slightly scornful smile, but now spoke in as low and serious a tone as the rest.

"Why is it hard to realize eternity?" demanded Natasha. "After to-day comes to-morrow, and then the next day, and so on forever; and, in the same way, yesterday was, and then the day before." ....

"Natasha! now it is your turn. Sing me something!" said the countess's voice. "Why are you all sitting there, like conspirators?"

"Mamma! I don't feel like it," said Natasha; but, nevertheless, she got up.

Not one of them, not even Dimmler, who was no longer young, wanted to break off the conversation and leave the corner; but Natasha had arisen, and Nikolaï took his place at the clavichord. Natasha, as usual, going to the center of the music-room, and, choosing the place where her voice sounded best, began to sing her mother's favorite piece.

She had said that she did not feel like singing; but it was long since she had sung as she sang that evening, and long before she sang so well again. Count Ilya Andreyitch listened to it from his library, where he was closeted with Mitenka; and, like a school-boy in haste to go out to play as soon as his lessons are done, he stumbled over his words as he gave his instructions to his overseer, and finally stopped speaking; while Mitenka, also listening, stood silently in front of the count.

Nikolaï did not take his eyes from his sister, and even breathed when she did. Sonya, as she listened, thought what a wide gulf there was between her and her friend, and how impossible it would be to find any one in the world so bewitchingly charming as her cousin. The old countess, with a smile of melancholy pleasure, and with tears in her eyes, sat occasionally shaking her head. She was thinking of Natasha, and of her own youthful days; and of that unnatural and terrible element that seemed to enter into this engagement of her daughter with Prince Andreï.

Dimmler, taking his seat next the countess, and covering his eyes, listened.

"No, countess," said he, finally, "this talent of hers is European; she has nothing to learn; such smoothness, sympathetic quality, power...."

"Akh! How I tremble for her; how worried I am!" said the countess, not realizing to whom she was speaking. Her maternal instinct told her that Natasha had more in her than ordinary girls, and that this would result in unhappiness for her.

Natasha had not quite finished her singing, when fourteen-year-old Petya, all excitement, came running into the room with the news that some maskers had come.

Natasha abruptly stopped.

"Durak! idiot!" she cried to her brother, and, running to a chair, flung herself into it, and sobbed so that it was long before she could recover herself.

"It 's nothing, mamenka; truly it 's nothing; it was only Petya startled me," said she, striving to smile; but her tears still flowed, and her throat was choked by her repressed sobs.

The house servants, who had dressed themselves up as bears, Turks, tavern-keepers, fine ladies, monsters, and ogres, bringing in with them the outside cold and hilarity, at first shyly clustered together in the anteroom; but gradually, hiding one behind the other, they ventured into the ball-room; and at first, timidly, but afterwards with ever-increasing fervor and zeal, began to perform songs, dances, and *khorovods*, and other Christmas games.

The countess, after she had recognized them, and indulged in a hearty laugh at their antics, retired into the drawing-room. Count Ilya Andreyitch, with a radiant smile, took his seat in the ball-room, with approving glances at the masqueraders. Meantime, all the young folks had mysteriously disappeared.

Within half an hour, the other masqueraders in the ball-room were joined by an elderly baruinya, in farthingale, and this was Nikolaï; by a Turkish woman, and this was Petya; by a clown, this was Dimmler; by a hussar, Natasha; and by a Circassian youth, Sonya: both the girls had dark eyebrows and mustaches, contrived with the help of burnt cork.

After well-feigned surprise, and pretended lack of recognition, as well as praise, from those who were not mumming, the young people decided that their costumes were too good to be wasted, and that it was incumbent upon them to go and exhibit them elsewhere.

Nikolaï, who had a strong desire for a troïka ride, the roads being in splendid condition, proposed that they should take with them the ten house serfs who were disguised, and that all should go and visit the "little uncle."

"No, he is an old man, and you will merely disturb him," expostulated the countess. "Why! you could n't all get into his house! If you must go somewhere, then go to the Melyukofs'."

Madame Melyukova was a widow, who, with a host of children of various ages, and with tutors and governesses, lived about four versts from the Rostofs'.

"There! *ma chère*, a good idea!" cried the old count, becoming greatly excited. "Wait till I can get into a costume and I will go with you. I tell you we will wake Pasheta[1] up!"

But the countess was not at all inclined to let the old count go, since, for several days, his leg had been troubling him. It was therefore decided that it was not best for Ilya Andreyitch to go; but that if Luiza Ivanovna, that is to say, Madame Schoss, would act as chaperon, then the young ladies might also go to Melyukova's.

[1] Diminutive of Pelagaya.

Sonya, though generally very timid and shy, now was more urgent than all the others in her entreaties to Luiza Ivanovna not to disappoint them.

Sonya's costume was the best of all. Her mustache and dark brows were extremely becoming to her. All assured her that she was very handsome, and she was keyed up to a state of energy and excitement quite out of her usual manner. Some inner voice told her that now or never her fate was to be decided; and now, in her masculine garb, she seemed like another person. Luiza Ivanovna consented; and in less than half an hour, four troïkas, with jingling bells on shaft-arch[1] and harness, swept, creaking and crunching over the frosty snow, up to the front steps.

Natasha was the first to catch the tone of Christmas festivity, and this jollity was perfectly infectious, growing more and more noisy, and reaching the highest pitch as they all came out into the frosty air, and with shouting and calling, and laughing and screaming, took their places in the sledges.

Two of the three spans were unmatched; the third troïka belonged to the old count, with a racer of the Orlof breed between the thills; the fourth was Nikolaï's own private troïka with a low, shaggy, black shaft-horse. Nikolaï, in his old maid's costume, over which he threw his hussar's riding-cloak, fastened with a belt, took his place in the middle of his sledge, and gathered up the reins. It was so light that he could see the metal of the harness-plates shining in the moonbeams, and the horses' eyes, as they turned them anxiously toward the merry group gathered under the darkness of the porte-cochère.

In Nikolaï's sledge were packed Natasha, Sonya, Madame Schoss, and two of the maid-servants; in the old count's went Dimmler, with his wife and Petya; in the others, the rest of the household serfs were disposed.

"You lead the way, Zakhar!" cried Nikolaï, to his father's coachman; he wished to have a chance to "beat" him on the road.

The old count's troïka, with Dimmler and the other

[1] Called *duga*.

masqueraders, creaked as if its runners were frozen to the snow; and, with a jingling of its deep-toned bell, started forward. The side horses twitched at the shafts, and kicked up the sugar-like gleaming crystals of the snow.

Nikolaï followed Zakhar; behind them, with a creaking and crunching, came the others. At first they went rather gingerly along the narrow driveway. As they passed the park the shadows cast by the bare trees lay across the road and checkered the moonlight; but as soon as they got beyond the park enclosure, the snowy expanse — gleaming like diamonds, with a deep blue phosphorescence, all drenched in moonlight, and motionless — opened out before them in every direction.

All at once, the foremost sledge dipped into a cradle-hole; in exactly the same way the one behind it went down and came up again, and then the next behind; and then, boldly breaking the iron-bound silence, the sledges began to speed along the road one after the other.

"There is a hare track! Ever so many of them!" rang Natasha's voice through the frost-bound air.

"How light is is, Nicolas!" said Sonya's voice.

Nikolaï glanced round, and bent over so as to get a closer look into her face. The pretty face, with an odd and entirely new expression, caused by the black brows and mustache, glanced up at him from under the sables.

"That used to be Sonya," said Nikolaï to himself. He gave her a closer look, and smiled.

"What is the matter, Nicolas?"

"Nothing," said he, and he again gave his attention to his horses.

Having now reached the hard-trodden highroad, stretching away in the moonlight, and polished smooth by numberless runners, and all hacked up by the tracks of horseshoe nails, the horses of their own accord began to pull on the reins, and increase their speed. The off-horse, tossing his head, galloped along, twitching on his traces. The shaft-horse shook out into a trot, laying back his ears as if asking, 'Shall we begin, or is it too early as yet?'

Zakhar's troïka, already a considerable distance ahead, the jingle of its deep-toned bell growing more and more distant, could be seen like a black patch against the whiteness of the snow. Shouts and laughter, and the voices of the party in the distance, could be plainly heard.

"Now then, my darlings!" cried Nikolaï, giving a firm rein with one hand, and raising his hand with the knout. And only by the increase of the wind that blew in their faces, and by the straining of the side horses, which kept springing and galloping faster and more furiously, could it be told at what a pace the troïka was flying. Nikolaï glanced back. With shouts and whistling, with cracking of whips and encouraging words to the horses, followed the other troïka at a flying pace. The back of the shaft-horse rose and fell steadily under the curved duga, but with no thought of breaking, and ready to give more and ever more speed, if it were required of him.

Nikolaï overtook the first troïka. They glided down a little slope, and came out upon a road wide enough for several teams to drive abreast, stretching along the intervale by the river side.

"Where will this take us, I wonder?" queried Nikolaï. "This must be the sloping intervale. But no, it is a place I don't recognize at all! I never saw it before! It is neither the sloping intervale nor the Dyomkin hill; God only knows where we are. It is certainly some new and enchanted place! Well, what difference does it make to us?"

And, shouting at his horses, he began to gain on the first troïka. Zakhar held his team to their work and turned round his face, white with frost even to the eyebrows.

Nikolaï gave his horses rein; Zakhar, reaching out his arms, clucked his tongue, and also gave his free rein.

"Now, steady there, barin!" cried he.

Still swifter flew the two troïkas, side by side; and swiftly the legs of the horses interwove as onward they sped.

Nikolaï began gradually to forge ahead. Zakhar, not changing the position of his outstretched arms, kept the hand that held the reins a little higher.

"You can't come it, barin!" he cried to Nikolaï. Nikolaï urged all three of his horses to gallop, and sped past Zakhar. The horses kicked the fine dry snow into the faces of the party; the bells jingled together as they flew on, side by side; and the swiftly moving legs of the horses mingled together, while the shadows crossed and interlaced on the snow. The runners whizzed along the road, and the shouts and cries of the women were heard in each of the sledges.

Once more reining in his horses, Nikolaï glanced around him. Everywhere was the same magical expanse, flooded deep with the moonbeams, and with millions of stars scattered over it.

"Zakhar is shouting, 'Turn to the left;' but why to the left?" queried Nikolaï. "Are n't we going to the Melyukofs'? Is this the way to Melyukovka's? God knows where we are going, and God knows what is going to become of us, and it is very strange and very pleasant, whatever becomes of us."

He looked down into the sledge.

"Oh, see there! his mustache and eyelashes are all white," said one of the handsome young strangers, with delicate mustaches and eyebrows, who sat in the sledge.

"That, I think, must have been Natasha," said Nikolaï to himself, "and that other is Madame Schoss; and, perhaps I am wrong, but that Circassian with the mustache I never saw before, but I love her all the same!"

"You are n't cold, are you?" he asked. They gave no other answer than a merry laugh. Dimmler was shouting something from the hindmost sledge; it was probably funny, but he could not make out what it was.

"Yes, yes," replied other voices, with a burst of laughter.

"And now here is a sort of enchanted forest, with black shadows interlacing, and the gleams of diamonds, and something like an amphilade of marble steps; and there are the silver roofs of an enchanted castle, and the piercing yells of wild beasts. .... But supposing after all it is Melyukovka's, then it would be still more wonderful that we should have gone, God knows how, and still have come out at Melyukovka's!" said Nikolaï to himself.

In point of fact it was Melyukovka's, and maids and lackeys began to appear on the doorsteps of the entrance, with lights and happy faces.

"Who is it?" asked some one from the front door.

"Masqueraders from the count's, I can tell by the horses," replied various voices.

CHAPTER XI

Pelagaya Danilovna Melyukova, a very stout and energetic woman in spectacles, and wearing a loose-flowing capote, was sitting in the drawing-room, surrounded by her daughters, whom she was doing her best to entertain. They were quietly molding wax, and looking at the shadows cast by passers-by, when the steps and voices of the visitors began to echo through the anteroom.

Hussars, high-born ladies, witches, clowns, bears, coughing and wiping their frost-bound faces, came into the ball-room, where the candelabras were hastily lighted. The clown, that is, Dimmler, with the baruinya, that is, Nikolaï, opened the dance. Surrounded by gleefully shouting children, the masqueraders, hiding their faces and disguising their voices, made low bows before the mistress of the mansion, and then scattered through the room.

"Akh! it's impossible to tell! Ah, that's Natasha! Just see whom she looks like! Truly she reminds me of some one! And there's Eduard Karluitch! How elegant! I should n't have known you. Akh! how elegantly he dances! Akh! Saints preserve us! and who is that Circassian? Indeed, it reminds me of Sonyushka. And who is that? Well, well! this is a kindness! Move out the tables, Nikita, Vanya. And we have been sitting here so solemnly."

"Ha! ha! ha!" .... "What a hussar! What a hussar!" .... "Just like a boy, and what legs!" .... "I can't see!" .... such were the remarks on every side.

Natasha, who was a great favorite with the young Melyukofs, disappeared with them into some distant room, where a burnt cork and dressing-gowns and various articles of masculine attire were immediately in requisition; and these were snatched from the lackey who brought them, through the half-open door, by girlish arms, all bare. Within ten minutes all the young people of the Melyukof family came down, and rejoined the masqueraders.

Pelagaya Danilovna, who had seen that a sufficient place was cleared for her guests, and regalement prepared for the gentlefolk as well as the serfs, went round among the maskers with her spectacles on her nose, and a set smile, looking close into the faces of all, and not recognizing a single one. She neither recognized the Rostofs nor Dimmler, nor could she even distinguish her own daughters, or the masculine dressing-gowns and uniforms which they had put on.

"And who is that one?" she asked of the guvernantka, and looking straight into the face of her daughter, who represented a Kasan Tatar: "I think it must be one of the Rostofs. Well, and you, Mister Hussar, what regiment do you serve in?" she asked of Natasha. "Give that Turk, yes, that Turk, some fruitcake," said she to the butler, who was serving the refreshments; "it is not forbidden by their laws."

Sometimes, looking at the strange but absurd *pas* performed by the dancers, who gave themselves up completely to the idea that they were mumming, that no one would recognize them, and therefore felt no mock modesty, Pelagaya Danilovna would hide her face in her handkerchief, and her whole fat body would shake with the good-natured and uncontrollable laughter of old age.

After they had performed the plyaska, various khorovods and other Russian national dances, Pelagaya Danilovna had all the serfs and the others together form into a great circle; a ring, a rope, and a ruble were brought, and they began to play various games.

By the end of an hour the costumes began to show signs of wear and tear. The charcoal mustaches and eyebrows began to disappear from the sweaty, heated, jolly faces. Pelagaya Danilovna began to recognize the masqueraders, and congratulate them on the skill with which they had made up their costumes, and tell them how very becoming they were to the young ladies, and she thanked them all for having entertained her so well. The guests were invited into the drawing-room, and refreshments were provided in the ball-room for the serfs.

"No, but what a terrible thing to read your fortune in a bath!" exclaimed an old maid, who lived with the Melyukofs.

"Why so?" asked the oldest daughter of the family.

They were now sitting down at supper.

"No, don't think of doing such a thing, it requires so much courage."

"I would just as lief," said Sonya.

"Tell us what happened to that young lady," asked the second Melyukova girl.

"Well, this is the way of it: a certain baruishnya," said the old maid, "took a cock, two plates, knives, and forks, as the way is, and went and sat down. She sat there and sat there, and suddenly she hears some one coming — a sledge drives up, with harness bells jingling; she listens, some one is coming! Some one comes in, absolutely in human form, just like an officer, and sits down with her where the second plate is set."

"Oh! oh!" screamed Natasha, rolling her eyes in horror.

"And how was it — how did he speak to her?"

"Yes, just like a man, everything was just as it should

have been; and he began to talk with her, and all she needed to do was to keep him talking till the cock crowed, but she got frightened; as soon as she got frightened, and hid her face in her hands, then he clasped her in his arms. Luckily, just then, some maids came running in...."

"Now, what is the good of frightening them so!" protested Pelagaya Danilovna.

"Mamasha, you yourself have had your fortune told," exclaimed one of the daughters.

"How is it fortunes are told in a granary?" asked Sonya.

"Well, this is the way of it: you go into the granary and listen. It depends on what you hear: if there is any knocking or tapping, it's a bad sign; but if the wheat drops, then it's for good, and it will come out all right."

"Mamma, tell us what happened to you when you went to the granary."

Pelagaya Danilovna smiled.

"Oh, what's the use! and I have forgotten...." said she. "Besides, you would n't go, would you?"

"Yes, I would go, too; Pelagaya Danilovna, do let me; I certainly will go," said Sonya.

"Very well, then, if you are not afraid."

"Luiza Ivanovna, may I?" asked Sonya of Madame Schoss.

While they were playing the games with the ring, the ruble, and the rope, and now, while they were talking, Nikolaï had not left Sonya's side, and looked at her from wholly new eyes. It seemed to him that this evening, thanks to that charcoal mustache, he, for the first time, knew her as she really was. In reality, Sonya, that evening, was merrier, livelier, and prettier than Nikolaï had ever seen her before.

"Why! what a girl she is, and what an idiot I have been," he said to himself, as he gazed into her gleaming eyes, and saw her radiantly happy and enthusiastic smile dimpling her cheeks under her mustache, and that look which he had never seen before.

"I am not afraid of anything," said Sonya. "May I start now?"

She got up. She was told where the granary was, and how she must stand and listen, and make no noise. The servant brought her shuba. She flung it over her head, and gave a glance at Nikolaï.

"How charming that girl is!" said he to himself. "And what have I been thinking about all this time?"

Sonya stepped out into the corridor on her way to the granary. Nikolaï, making the excuse that he was too warm, hurried to the front steps. It was a fact, the crowd made the air in the rooms close. Out of doors it was as cold and still as ever; the same moon was shining, only it was brighter than before. The brightness was so intense, and there were so many stars in the snow that one had no desire to look at the sky; the real stars were insignificant. In the sky it was almost black and melancholy; on the earth it was gay.

"What an idiot I have been! what an idiot! Why have I waited so long?" mused Nikolaï, and he sprang down the steps and turned the corner of the house by the foot-path that led back to the rear entrance. He knew that Sonya would come that way. Half-way along the path stood a great woodpile covered with snow, and casting a shadow; across it, and beyond it, fell the shadows of the lindens, bare and old, weaving patterns on the snow and the path.

The foot-path led to the granary. The timber walls of the granary and its roofs covered with snow shone in the moonlight like a palace made of precious stone. In the garden a tree cracked, and then everything became absolutely still again. It seemed to Nikolaï that his lungs breathed in, not common air, but the elixir of eternal youth and joy.

Feet were heard stamping on the steps of the servants' entrance. Some one was scraping the snow away from the lower step on which it had drifted, and then the voice of an old maid said: —

"Straight ahead! straight ahead! right along this path, baruishnya. Only you must not look round."

"I am not afraid," replied Sonya's voice; and then toward Nikolaï came Sonya's dainty feet, sliding and squeaking in her thin slippers.

Sonya came along, all muffled up in her shuba, and it was not till she was within two paces of him that she saw him: it seemed to her also that he was different from what she had ever known him before, and that he had nothing of what always made her a bit afraid of him. He was in his feminine costume, with clustering locks, and wearing a blissful smile such as Sonya had never seen before. Sonya swiftly hurried to him.

"She's entirely different; not at all the same," thought Nikolaï, as he looked into her face, all kindled by the moonlight. He put his arms under her shuba, which encircled her head, strained her to his heart, and kissed her lips, which still showed traces of the mustache, and had a faint odor of burnt cork. Sonya returned his kiss full on the lips, and putting up her slender hands laid them on both sides of his face.

"Sonya!"

"Nicolas!"

That was all they said. They ran to the granary, and then they went back into the house by the doors through which they had come.

CHAPTER XII

WHEN they drove home from Pelagaya Danilovna's, Natasha, who had seen and observed everything, made a redistribution of forces; so that Luiza Ivanovna and Dimmler went in the sledge with her, while Sonya and Nikolaï and some of the maids drove together.

Nikolaï, feeling now no anxiety to take the lead, drove deliberately along the homeward road; and as he kept turning to look at Sonya, with the weird moonlight falling on her, he tried to discover in that all-transforming light the Sonya of the past from the Sonya of the moment with her charcoal-penciled brows and mustache, — the Sonya from whom he was determined never to be parted.

As he looked at her, and remembered what she was, and what she had been; as he recalled that odor of the burnt cork — mingling so strangely in his consciousness of her kiss; and as he gazed at the ground swiftly gliding by, and at the glittering sky, — he felt that he was once more in the realm of enchantment.

"Sonya, *art thou* comfortable?" he would occasionally ask.

"Yes," would be Sonya's answer. "And *art thou?*"

When they were half-way home Nikolaï told the coachman to hold the horses, and he ran back for a moment, to Natasha's sledge, and leaned over the side.

"Natasha," he whispered, in French. "Do you know, I have made up my mind in regard to Sonya."

"Have you told her yet?" asked Natasha, becoming all radiant with delight.

"Oh, how strange that mustache and those eyebrows make you look, Natasha! — Are you glad?"

"Oh, I am so glad, so glad! I was beginning to grow angry with you. I have not told you so; but you have n't been treating her fairly. She is such a true-hearted girl, Nicolas. How glad I am! I am often naughty, but I have reproached myself for being selfish in my happiness, and not sharing it with Sonya," pursued Natasha. "But now I am so glad; but you must go back to her."

"No, wait a moment. Fie! how absurd you do look!" exclaimed Nikolaï, still gazing at her, and in his sister also discovering something new and unusual, and bewitchingly lovely, which he had never before noticed in her.

"Natasha! It 's like enchantment, isn 't it?"

"Yes," replied she. "You have done nobly."

"If ever I had seen her like this before," thought Nikolaï, "I should long ago have asked her advice, and what is more should have followed it, and all would have been well. .... So you are glad, and I have done right, have I?"

"Oh, yes, perfectly right. It was only a little while ago that I got vexed with mamasha about this. Mamma said that she was trying to catch you. How could she say such a thing? I almost quarreled with mamma. And I will never allow any one to say anything mean about her, because she is goodness itself."

"All right, then, is it?" exclaimed Nikolaï, giving another searching look at the expression of his sister's face, so as to be sure that she was in earnest; and then, with creaking boots, he jumped down from the runner, and ran to overtake his own sledge. And there still sat the same radiantly happy little Circassian with mustache and gleaming eyes, under her sable hood; and this Circassian was Sonya, and this Sonya was assuredly to be his happy and loving wife in the days to come!

After they had reached home, and had told the countess how they had spent the time at the Melyukofs', the young girls went to their room. Without wiping off their burnt cork mustaches they undressed, and sat together for a long time, talking about their happiness. They had much to say about their future married lives, and what friends their husbands would be, and how happy they should be.

On Natasha's table stood dressing-glasses, placed there early that evening by her maid, Dunyasha.

"But when will all this be? Never, I fear.... it would be too great happiness to come true," said Natasha, as she got up and went over to the mirrors.

"Sit down, Natasha; maybe you will see him," said Sonya. Natasha lighted the candles and sat down.

"I see some one with a mustache," exclaimed Natasha, catching sight of her own face.

"You must not turn it into ridicule, baruishnya!" said Dunyasha.

Natasha, with the help of Sonya and her maid, got into the proper position before the glass; her face assumed a serious expression, and she remained silent. Long she sat there, looking at the row of waning candles in the mirror, wondering, as she remembered the heroines of stories she had heard, whether this mysterious "Twelfth Night" she should see her coffin, or whether she should see *him*, Prince Andreï, in the background of the dark and confused square of glass. But, as she was not ready to mistake the smallest spot or stain on the glass for the form of coffin or of a man, she saw nothing. Her eyes began to grow heavy, and she got up and left the mirror.

"How is it other people see things, and I never see anything?" she asked. "Now you sit down, Sonya. To-day, of course, you must look for yourself; but look for me, too...." said she. "I have such terrible presentiments to-night!"

Sonya sat down in front of the mirrors, arranged herself in the right position, and began to look.

"Now, Sofya Aleksandrovna will surely see something," whispered Dunyasha. "But *you* are always making fun."

Sonya overheard this, and heard Natasha reply:—

"Yes, I know she will see something; she did last year, you remember."

For three minutes all sat in silence. "Of course she will...." whispered Natasha, but she did not finish her sentence. Suddenly Sonya pushed the mirror back, and covered her eyes with her hand.

"Akh! Natasha!" she cried.

"Did you see something? Did you? What did you see?" demanded Natasha, taking the mirror from her.

Sonya had seen nothing; her eyes were simply beginning to grow heavy, and she was just on the point of getting up when she heard Natasha beginning to say, "Of course she will." She had no intention of deceiving either Dunyasha or Natasha, but it was stupid sitting there! She herself did not know how or why it was that the cry had escaped from her when she covered her eyes with her hand.

"Did you see him?" demanded Natasha, seizing her by the arm.

"Yes. Wait.... I.... saw him," said Sonya, led by some unaccountable impulse, but not knowing which Natasha meant by *him*, Nikolaï or Andreï. "But why should I not tell what I saw? Others have seen such things. And who can prove that I did or did n't see something," was the thought that flashed through Sonya's mind.

"Yes, I saw him," said she.

"How was it? was he sitting, or standing? How was it?"

"Now, I saw .... at first I could not see anything, then suddenly I got a glimpse of him, and he was lying down."

"Andreï lying down? Is he ill?" demanded Natasha, gazing at her friend with horror-stricken eyes.

"No, on the contrary, his face was cheerful, and he turned toward me ...."

At that instant it began to seem to her that she had seen what she was telling.

"Well, and then what, Sonya?"....

"Then I did not see anything more! Something blue and red ...."

"Sonya! When will he come back? When shall I see him? My God! How I tremble for him and for myself; and everything fills me with alarm ...." cried Natasha; and, paying no heed to the words of comfort spoken by Sonya, she got into bed; and long after the candles were put out, she lay there motionless, with wide-open eyes, gazing at the frosty moonbeams flooding the icy window-panes.

CHAPTER XIII

SHORTLY after Twelfth Night, Nikolaï announced to his mother his love for Sonya, and his firm determination to make her his wife.

The countess, who had long before that remarked what was going on between the two young people, and who had been expecting this announcement, listened in silence to his words; and then coldly informed him that he might marry any one he pleased, but that neither she nor his father would countenance such a marriage.

For the first time, Nikolaï felt conscious that his mother was offended with him; that, notwithstanding all her love for him, she would not yield to him in this matter. Coldly, not even looking at her son, she sent for her husband; and when he came, she tried, in Nikolaï's presence, to tell him, in a few chilling words, of what her son proposed to do; but she had not the necessary self-control: tears of vexation sprang to her eyes, and she was compelled to leave the room.

The old count tried feebly to reason with Nikolaï, and begged him to give up his intention.

Nikolaï replied that he could not go back on his word; and the father, sighing, and evidently all upset in his mind, hastily put an end to his discourse and went to the countess.

In all his encounters with his son, the count always had the consciousness of his own blameworthiness toward him, in regard to the squandering of his fortune; and, accordingly, he could not show his anger against his son for refusing to wed a rich wife, and for choosing the penniless Sonya; in all this affair, he remembered with the keener sorrow that, if only his estates had not been so ruined, it would be impossible for Nikolaï to find a better wife; and that the only persons responsible for the wasting of this estate were himself and his Mitenka, and their incorrigible habits.

The father and mother had nothing more to say to Nikolaï, in regard to this; but a few days later the countess summoned Sonya, and with a bitterness which no one in the world would have expected of her, reproached her niece with having decoyed her son, and accused her of ingratitude.

Sonya, in silence, and with downcast eyes, listened to the countess's bitter words, and was at a loss to know what was required of her. She was ready for any sacrifice for all of them, in return for their benefits. The thought of self-sacrifice was ever a delight to her; but, in this affair, she could not comprehend what she was required to sacrifice, or for whom. She could not help loving the countess, and all the Rostof family; nor could she help loving Nikolaï, or knowing that his happiness depended on her love for him. She therefore stood silent and sad, and had nothing to reply.

It seemed to Nikolaï that he could no longer endure

this state of things; and he went to his mother to have a final explanation. Nikolaï first besought his mother to be reconciled to him and Sonya, and consent to their marriage; then he threatened her that, if they persecuted Sonya, he would instantly marry her clandestinely.

The countess, with a coldness her son had never experienced before, replied that he was of age, that Prince Andreï was going to marry without his father's sanction, and that he might do the same; but that she would never receive this intrigantka as her daughter.

Angry at her use of the term *intrigantka*, Nikolaï raised his voice, and told his mother that he had never thought that she would oblige him to sacrifice his noblest feelings; and that if this were so, then he would never....

But he did not finish uttering this rash vow, which his mother, judging by the expression of his face, awaited with horror, and which might have forever raised a cruel barrier between them. He did not utter it, because Natasha, with a pale and solemn face, came into the room; she had been listening at the door.

"Nikolinka, you don't know what you are saying; hush! hush! I tell you, hush!" she almost screamed, so as to drown his words. "Mamma, darling, there's no reason in this at all, dushetchka moya — dear heart," said she, turning still paler, and going to her mother, who felt that she was on the very edge of an abyss, and looked with horror at her son; and yet, by reason of her stubbornness, and the impulse of the quarrel, she would not, and could not, give in. "Nikolinka, I beg of you, go away; and you, sweetheart-mamma,[1] listen," she entreated, turning again to her mother.

Her words were incoherent; but they brought about the wished-for result.

The countess, deeply flushed, buried her face in her daughter's bosom; and Nikolaï got up and, clasping his head between his hands, rushed out of the room.

Natasha acted the part of peacemaker so well, that Nikolaï received a promise from his mother that Sonya

[1] *Mama-galubushka.*

should not be annoyed; and he himself swore that he would never do anything without the knowledge of his parents.

With the firm intention of retiring from the service as soon as he could wind up his connection with his regiment, and return and marry Sonya, Nikolaï, melancholy and grave, still under strained relations with his parents, but, as it seemed to him, passionately in love, rejoined his regiment early in January.

After Nikolaï's departure, it became sadder than ever in the house of the Rostofs. The countess, owing to her mental tribulations, was taken seriously ill.

Sonya was depressed, both on account of her separation from Nikolaï, and still more on account of the unfriendly manner in which the countess, in spite of herself, treated her. The count was more than ever occupied by the wretched state of his pecuniary affairs, which demanded of him the most heroic measures. It was absolutely necessary to dispose of their mansion in Moscow, and their pod-Moskovnaya estate: and in order to effectuate this sale, it was essential to go to Moscow. But the state of the countess's health caused him to postpone his departure from day to day.

Natasha, who had easily, and even cheerfully, borne the first weeks of separation from her lover, now every day grew more nervous and impatient. The thought that she was wasting the best time of her life, when she might so much better have been employing it in loving sacrifice for him, constantly tormented her.

His letters generally merely served to annoy her. It revolted her to think that when she was living only in the thought about him, he was living in the great world of action, seeing new places and new people, who were full of interest to him. The more fascinating his letters were, the more they annoyed her.

Her letters to him gave her no consolation; they were nothing but tedious and hypocritical exercises. She was not able to write freely, because she could not realize the possibility of correctly expressing in a letter even the thousandth part of what she was accustomed to express with her voice, her smile, and her glance. She wrote him perfunctory and monotonous letters, the stupidity of which she herself acknowledged; while her mother corrected in the rough draught the mistakes in spelling which she made.

The countess's health was still feeble; but it was now no longer possible to put off the return to Moscow. It was necessary to arrange for the marriage settlement, it was necessary to sell the mansion; and, moreover, Prince Andreï was now expected in Moscow, where his father, Prince Nikolaï Andreyitch, was spending the winter; indeed, Natasha was certain that he had already arrived.

The countess remained in the country; but the count, taking Sonya and Natasha with him, went to Moscow toward the end of January.

PART EIGHTH

CHAPTER I

PIERRE, after the engagement of Prince Andreï and Natasha, suddenly, without any apparent reason, began to find it impossible to pursue his former mode of life. Firmly as he was convinced of the truths revealed by the Benefactor; delightful as had been the first period of enthusiasm for the inward labor of self-improvement, to which he had given himself up with such zeal, — all the charm of this former existence suddenly vanished after the betrothal of his friends, and after the death of Iosiph Alekseyevitch, news of which he received at about the same time. Nothing but the empty skeleton of life remained to him: his mansion, with that brilliant wife of his, who was still enjoying the favors of an influential personage; his acquaintance with all Petersburg; and his duties at court with all their tedious formalities. And this life of his suddenly began to fill Pierre with unexpected loathing; he ceased to write in his diary; he shunned the society of the brethren; he began once more to frequent the club, and to drink heavily; he became intimate with the gay young bachelor set; and his behavior became such that the Countess Elena Vasilyevna found it necessary to give him a stern admonition.

Pierre felt that she was right; and, in order not to compromise her, he decided to go to Moscow.

In Moscow, as soon as he set foot in his enormous house, with the dried-up and withered princesses, and the swarm of menials; as soon as he went out into town and saw the Iverskaya Chapel, with its innumerable tapers burning before the golden shrines, and the Square of the Kreml, with its broad sheet of snow, the izvoshchiks, and the hovels of the Sivtsef Vrazhek; saw the old men of Moscow, who, with never a desire or a quickening of the blood, lived out their days; saw the old ladies, the Moscovite girls, the Moscovite dances, the Moscovite ball-rooms, and the Moscovite English Club, — he felt himself at home in a refuge of quiet. Life in Moscow gave him a sensation of comfort, and warmth, and coziness, such as one has in a dirty old dressing-gown.

Pierre was welcomed by all Moscow society, young and old, as a long-expected guest, whose place was always ready for him and never given to another. In the eyes of Moscow society, Pierre was most kindly, good-natured, intelligent, and benevolent, though eccentric, absent-minded, but cordial; a thoroughgoing Russian barin, of the old stamp. His purse was always empty, because it was opened to all. Benefits, wretched pictures, statuary, benevolent societies, gipsies, schools, subscription dinners, drinking-bouts, the Masons, churches, books, — no one and nothing ever met with a refusal from him; and if it had not been for two friends of his, who had borrowed large sums of him and now took him under their guardianship, he would have had absolutely nothing left. At the club, no dinner or reception was complete without him. As soon as he took his place on the divan, after a couple of bottles of Margeaux, the members would gather round him and vie with one another in all sorts of gossip, discussions, and clever stories. If discussions degenerated into quarrels, he would restore peace by his kindly smile alone, or by a clever jest. The Masonic meetings were tedious and dull if he were absent.

Often after dining with his bachelor friends, he would yield with a genial and weakly smile to their entreaties, and go with them where they went, and help the hilarious young fellows wake the echoes with their wild enthusiastic shouts. At the balls he would never refuse to dance, if partners were scarce. Young matrons and young girls liked him because he was attentive, especially after dinner, to all alike, without making invidious distinctions. It was a common saying of him: "He is charming; he has no sex."

Pierre had become simply a retired court chamberlain, good-naturedly vegetating in Moscow, like so many hundreds of others.

How horror-struck he would have been if, seven years before, when he was just back from abroad, some one had told him that it was idle for him to seek out or find a career; that the ruts in which he would move were long ago made for him, determined before the foundation of the world; and that, in spite of all his struggles, he should be what every one in his position was doomed to be. He would not have been able to believe this.

Had he not, with all his heart, wished at one time that a republic should be established in Russia? then, that he might be a Napoleon? then, a philosopher? then, a general, the conqueror of Napoleon? Had he not seen the possibility, and passionately desired to take part in the mighty task, of regenerating depraved humanity, and of bringing himself to the highest degree of improvement? Had he not established schools and infirmaries, and emancipated his peasantry?

But instead of what he had dreamed, lo! here he was, the rich husband of an unfaithful wife; a court chamberlain retired; a gourmand and wine-bibber, and easily inclined to criticize the government; a member of the Moscow English Club; and a flattered member of Moscow society! It was long before he could reconcile himself to the thought that he himself was a court chamberlain living in Moscow, the very type of what he should have so deeply despised seven years before.

Sometimes he comforted himself with the thought that this mode of life was only temporary; but then he would be terrified by another thought of how many people, just like himself, with all their hair, and their teeth still good, had entered temporarily into this mode of life, and into this club, and were now passing from it, bald and toothless.

In moments of pride, when he thought over his position, it seemed to him that he was of an entirely different nature, distinct from these retired chamberlains, whom he used to despise; that they were insipid and stupid, contented and satisfied with their position: "While I, on the contrary, am utterly dissatisfied; my sole desire is to do something for humanity," he would say to himself, in such moments of pride.

"But perhaps all these colleagues of mine are just like myself, and have been struggling and seeking to *find* some new and original path through life; and, like myself, have, by sheer force of circumstances, by the conditions of society and birth, — that elemental force against which man is powerless, — been brought into the same condition as myself." This he would say to himself in moments of humility; and, after he had lived in Moscow for some time, he ceased to despise his colleagues, the retired courtiers, and began to like them, and to esteem them, and to pity them, as he did himself.

Pierre no longer suffered, as formerly, from moments of despair, hypochondria, and disgust of life; but the same disease, which formerly had been made manifest by occasional attacks, had struck inward, and not for a moment ceased its insidious working.

"For what end? Why? For what purpose were we created in the world?" he would ask himself in perplexity many times every day in spite of himself, beginning to reason out some explanation of life; but as he knew by experience that such questions as these must remain unanswerable, he would strive in all haste to put them out of his mind, — taking up a book, or going over to the club, or calling on Apollon Nikolayevitch, to talk over the gossip of the town.

"Elena Vasilyevna, whom no one ever cared for except for her body's sake, and who is one of the stupidest women in the world," said Pierre to himself, "makes people believe that she is a woman of superior wit and refinement, and they bow down before her. Napoleon Bonaparte was despised by every one until he became great; but since he has become a miserable comedian, the Emperor Franz is trying to make him take his daughter illegally for his wife. The Spaniards, through the Roman Catholic clergy, offered up prayers of thanksgiving to God for granting them a victory over the French on the 26th of June; while the French, through the medium of the same Catholic priesthood, offer up thanksgivings to the same God for having beaten the Spaniards on the 26th of June! My brethren, the Masons, solemnly swear that they will be ready to sacrifice all they possess for their neighbor; but, when the box is passed around, they do not contribute a single ruble for the poor; and the Astræa lodge intrigues against the 'Manna Seekers,' and they toil and moil for the sake of getting a genuine Scotch carpet and a charter, the meaning of which is not known even by the one who copies it off, and which is necessary to no one. All of us profess the Christian law of forgiveness of injuries, and of love for our neighbor, — a law in obedience to which we have erected, here in Moscow, our forty forties of churches; while yesterday a deserter was flogged with the knout, and the priest, the servant of this same law of love and forgiveness, presented the crucifix for the soldier to kiss, before he received his punishment."

Thus mused Pierre; and this whole universal falsehood, acknowledged by every one, amazed him every time he thought of it; just as if he were not used to it, just as if it were some new thing.

"I understand this falsehood and confusion," he thought. "But how can I convince them of what I understand? I have made the experiment, and have always found that they, in the depths of their hearts, understand it just as I do; but they strive not to see it. Of course it must be so. But for me," Pierre asked himself, "what ought I to do?"

He was undergoing the unhappy experience of many people, especially Russians, who have not only the faculty of seeing and realizing the possibility of goodness and right, but of seeing too clearly the falsity and deception of life, to feel able to take any serious part in it.

Every department of activity was, in his eyes, complicated with falsehood and deception. Whatever he had tried to be, whatever he had tried to accomplish, he always found himself jostled by this knavery and falsehood, with his path of activity completely blocked. But, meantime, it was necessary for him to live, necessary for him to find occupation. It was too terrible for him to be under the weight of these unsolvable problems of life; and so he gave himself up to the first temptation, in order to forget them. He frequented the society of all sorts and conditions of men, he drank deeply, he purchased paintings, he built houses, and, chief of all, he read.

He read, and read everything that came into his hands; and he was such an omnivorous reader that even when, on his return home, his valet came in to undress him, he continued his reading, and, after reading till he was tired, he would fall asleep; and the next morning he would go to the club, or call on acquaintances, and talk gossip, and from there go to some wanton rout where wine and women served to occupy his mind; and thus, around the circle again, from spree to reading, and then his idle gossip and his wine.

Strong drink was becoming for him constantly a greater and greater physical, and even moral, necessity. Although the doctors warned him that wine was dangerous to him, on account of his corpulency, he still continued to drink heavily. He felt perfectly happy only when, without knowing or caring how, he had poured down his capacious throat several glasses of wine, and begun to experience the pleasant warmth spreading through his frame, and good-will toward all the human race, and a mental readiness superficially to touch upon any question, without pretending to penetrate deeply into its inner nature. Only after he had drunk a bottle or two of wine, would he vaguely feel that this complicated, terrible coil of life, which had formerly appalled him, was now not so appalling as it had seemed. With a roaring in his ears, as he idly chatted, or listened to stories, or read his books after dinner or supper, he saw this tangle of doubts constantly facing him on every side. But it was only under the influence of wine that he could say to himself: "This is nothing; I will put it away for the present, for I have an explanation all ready. But now is no time; I will think it all out by and by."

This "by and by" never came.

When his stomach was empty, the next morning, all the former questions arose, just as unsolvable and terrible; and Pierre hastened to seize his book, and was delighted when any one came to call on him.

Sometimes Pierre remembered what he had heard of soldiers at war: that when they are lying idle under fire, they eagerly strive to invent some diversion, so as the more easily to forget the threatening danger. And it seemed to Pierre that all men were similar soldiers, distracting themselves from life: some by ambition, some by cards, some by codifying laws, some by women, some by gambling, some by horses, some by politics, some by hunting, some by wine, some by statecraft.

"There is nothing insignificant, there is nothing of great importance; all is the same in the end; only how can I save myself from it?" thought Pierre. "Only by not seeing *it*, this terrible *it*."

CHAPTER II

Early in the winter, Prince Nikolaï Andreyitch Bolkonsky and his daughter took up their residence in Moscow.

The fame of his past life, the keenness of his intellect, and his bold originality immediately caused him to be regarded by the Moscovites with special admiration and respect; and, as the popular enthusiasm for the Emperor Alexander's management of affairs had notoriously cooled down, and as an anti-French and patriotic tendency was now the vogue in Moscow, he had become the center of the opposition to the government.

The prince had aged very considerably during the year past. He now began to manifest some of the acute symptoms of old age: unexpected naps, forgetfulness of recent events and vivid remembrance of those long past, and the childish vanity with which he accepted the *rôle* of chief of the Moscovite opposition. Nevertheless, when the old prince came down to evening tea, in his fur shubka and powdered wig, and at any one's instigation began to tell his pithy anecdotes about the days gone by, or deliver his still pithier and harsher judgments on the present, he inspired in all his guests a single feeling of sincere respect.

In the eyes of visitors, the old-fashioned house, with its huge pier-glasses, its ante-revolutionary furniture, its powdered lackeys, presided over by this severe and intelligent old man of a past generation, with his gentle daughter, and the pretty Frenchwoman, who treated him with such deference, presented an impressive but agreeable spectacle. But these visitors did not realize that, over and above the two or three hours when they saw the household, there were twenty-two more each day, during which the inner life of the house went on unseen.

This inner life had recently, especially during their stay in Moscow, become exceedingly trying for the Princess Mariya. In Moscow she was deprived of her dearest pleasures, — the visits from her pilgrims, and the solitude which gave her such consolation at Luisiya Gorui: she could find no comfort or joy in the crowded city. She did not go into society: everybody knew that her father would not allow her to go without him, and his health was too precarious to permit him to go out; and, consequently, she received no invitations to dinner-parties or balls. She had renounced all hope of ever being married. She had too often witnessed the coldness and irritability with which Prince Nikolaï Andreyitch received and dismissed young men who occasionally came to their house, and who might have been her suitors.

The Princess Mariya had no friends: since her arrival

in Moscow, her eyes had been opened in regard to the two who had been more intimate with her than all the rest. Mlle. Bourienne, in whom, even in times past, she could not feel perfect confidence, had now become positively disagreeable to her; and for several reasons she felt obliged to hold her at a distance.

Julie, with whom she had kept up an uninterrupted correspondence for five years, was in Moscow, but she seemed like an utter stranger to her when they met again face to face. Julie, by the death of her brothers, had become one of the wealthiest girls in Moscow, and was completely absorbed in the pleasures of fashionable society. She was surrounded by young men, who, she said to herself, had suddenly awakened to the appreciation of her merits. She found herself now rapidly growing old, and felt that her last chance of finding a husband was passing, and that now or never her fate must be decided.

The Princess Mariya, with a melancholy smile, remembered, as each Thursday came round, that now she had no one to write to, since Julie, whose presence gave her no delight, was in town and she could see her every week. She, like the old French *émigré* who refused to marry the lady at whose house he had spent all his evenings for a number of years, was sorry that Julie was so near because now she should have no one to write to. She had no one in Moscow to whom she could confide her sorrows, and since coming there these sorrows had increased and multiplied.

The time for Prince Andreï's return and for his marriage was drawing nigh, but his father seemed no more inclined than before to listen to his entreaties and sanction it; on the contrary, he would hear nothing to it; and the mere mention of the young Countess Rostova drove the old prince beside himself, and thus he was in a bad temper the greater part of the time.

The Princess Mariya had a new and additional trial, at this time, in the lessons which she gave her six-year-old nephew. In her treatment of Nikolushka she recognized with dismay that she was liable to fits of irritability similar to her father's. No matter how many times she reproached herself for losing her temper during his lesson hours, it happened almost every time when she sat down with the pointer to teach him his French primer that from her very desire to help him along as rapidly as possible, to make his tasks easy and to give the little fellow all the superfluity of her own knowledge, the slightest inattention on the part of the little boy — who was afraid, to begin with, of an outbreak of his aunt's irascibility — would make her tremble with indignation, lose her patience, grow angry and raise her voice, and sometimes even seize him by the arm and stand him in the corner. After she had stood him in the corner, she would begin to shed tears over her hasty temper, her ugly nature; and Nikolushka, sobbing out of sympathy, would leave his corner without permission, run up to her, and pull her tear-wet hands from her face, and try to comfort her.

But by far the greatest trial of all was caused the princess by her father's irritability, which was always vented upon his daughter, and which of late became even cruelty. If he had compelled her to do penance all night long with prayers and genuflections, if he had struck her, if he had compelled her to draw wood and water, it would never have occurred to her that her position was hard; but this loving tyrant, all the more terrible from the very fact that he loved her, and therefore tormented both himself and her, took especial pains not only to insult and humiliate her, but to make her feel that she was always and forever in the wrong.

And latterly he had discovered a new whim, which tormented the Princess Mariya more than all else put together. This was his constantly increasing intimacy with Mlle. Bourienne. First suggested to his mind by the news of Prince Andreï's engagement, the farcical notion that, if his son were going to marry, then he would marry Bourienne, evidently flattered his fancy, and of late he had stubbornly lavished especial attentions on the Frenchwoman, — for the special purpose, as it seemed to the Princess Mariya, of affronting herself, and of expressing his disapprobation of his daughter by making love to Bourienne.

In Moscow, on one occasion when the Princess Mariya was present, — it seemed to her that her father chose that time on purpose, — the old prince kissed Mlle. Bourienne's hand, and, drawing her to him, embraced and fondled her. The Princess Mariya flushed with anger and left the room.

After a few minutes, Mlle. Bourienne rejoined her, smiling, and began to tell some entertaining story in her agreeable voice. The Princess Mariya hastily wiped away her tears, went with decided steps straight to Bourienne, and, evidently not knowing what she was doing, began to shout at the Frenchwoman in furious haste, and with explosive accents: "It is shameful, contemptible, beastly, to take advantage of a man's weakness...." She did not conclude her sentence. "Leave my room," she fairly screamed, and then burst into tears again.

The following day, the prince said not a word to his daughter; but she observed that at dinner he ordered Mlle. Bourienne to be served in precedence of all others. At the end of the dinner, when the butler, according to his usual custom, handed the coffee round, serving the princess first, the old prince suddenly flew into a passion, flung his cane at Filipp, and instantly gave orders that he should be sent off to the army.

"You did n't obey me!.... Twice I told you!.... You did n't obey me!.... She 's the first person in this house; she is my best friend," screamed the prince. "And if you," he added, in a perfect fury, for the first time addressing his daughter, "if you permit yourself, if you dare, another time, as you did this evening, to forget your duty before her, then I will show you who is master in this house. Away with you! Out of my sight! Here! beg her pardon!"

The Princess Mariya begged Amélie Bourienne's pardon, and then interceded with her father for the butler Filipp.

At such moments there arose in the Princess Mariya's

soul a feeling like the pride of an immolated victim. And then, again, at such moments, this father whom she blamed would either search for his spectacles, not seeing them when they were close at hand, or would forget what had only just happened, or would stagger along on weakening limbs, glancing around lest any one should have seen his feebleness, — or, what was worse than all, after dinner, when there were no guests to keep him awake, would suddenly fall into a doze, dropping his napkin, and nodding his head over his plate. "He is old and feeble, and do I dare to judge him?" she would think at such moments, with revulsion of feeling and disgust at herself.

CHAPTER III

IN 1811 there was living in Moscow a French doctor, Métivier, a handsome man of gigantic frame, amiable after the manner of his nation, and, as was said by every one, a physician of extraordinary skill. He had rapidly become fashionable, and was received in the houses of the highest aristocracy not merely as a doctor, but as an equal.

Prince Nikolaï Andreyitch, who had always scoffed at medical science, had lately, by Mlle. Bourienne's advice, consulted this doctor, and soon became accustomed to him. Métivier used to visit him twice a week.

On the 6th of December (O.S.), — St. Nicholas's Day, — all Moscow called at the prince's door, but he gave orders to admit no one. He commanded, however, that a select few, whose names he handed the Princess Mariya, should be bidden to dinner.

Métivier came that morning with his congratulations, and in his capacity of physician took it upon him to violate the orders, *de forcer la consigne*, as he expressed it to the Princess Mariya, and he went in to see the prince.

It chanced that this morning the old prince was in one of his most detestable moods. The whole morning he wandered up and down the house, finding fault with every one, and pretending not to understand anything that was said to him, and that they would not understand him.

The Princess Mariya knew only too well that this mood of latent and persistent querulousness was certain to flash out into a tempest of fury, and all that morning of the prince's name-day she expected the outbreak, which was as sure to go off as a loaded musket at full cock.

Until the doctor's arrival, the morning passed in comparative serenity. Having admitted the doctor, the Princess Mariya took her book, and sat down in the drawing-room, near a door, where she could hear all that was going on in the prince's cabinet.

At first she heard only Métivier's voice, then her father's, then both voices speaking at once; then the door opened, and the dark-haired Métivier appeared on the threshold, his handsome face expressing alarm, followed by the prince in his nightcap and khalat, his face distorted with passion, and the pupils of his eyes dilated.

"Have you no wits?" screamed the prince. "Well, I have. You French spy! You slave of Bonaparte! Out of my house! Get out, I tell you!" and he slammed the door.

Métivier, shrugging his shoulders, went to Mlle. Bourienne, who, on hearing the loud voices, had rushed in from the adjoining room.

"The prince is not very well.... bilious, and a cerebral congestion. I will come in again to-morrow. Don't be worried," said Métivier; and, laying his fingers on his lips, he hastened out.

The prince was heard walking up and down in his room, in his slippers, and shouting, "Spies!.... Traitors, traitors everywhere! Not a minute's peace even in my own house!"

After Métivier's departure, the old prince summoned his daughter to him, and the whole brunt of his fury fell on her. She was to blame for admitting spies into his presence. Why, he had told her, said he, that she was to write down a list, and not to admit any one who was not on the list. Why, then, had she admitted this scoundrel? It was all her fault. He could not have a moment's rest with her, not even die in peace, said he. "No, matushka, you might as well make up your mind to it: we must part, we must part. I can't stand this sort of thing any more," he exclaimed, and left the room.

And then, as if he feared that she might not understand how thoroughly his mind was made up, he came back to her, and, endeavoring to assume an expression of calmness, he added, "And don't you for a moment imagine that I say this to you in passion; no, I am perfectly calm, and I have made up my mind after full deliberation, and it shall be. We must part. Find a home somewhere else." ....

But he could not restrain himself, and, with a flash of indignation possible only to one who loves, he, though evidently suffering himself, shook his fist in her face and screamed, "And why on earth has n't some idiot taken her for his wife?" He slammed the door after him, had Mlle. Bourienne called to him, and quiet reigned in his cabinet.

At two o'clock the six persons invited to dinner arrived. These guests — the distinguished Count Rostopchin,[1] Prince Lopukhin and his nephew, General Chatrof, an old companion in arms of the prince's, and, for young men, Pierre and Boris Drubetskoï — were waiting for him in the drawing-room.

Having recently come to Moscow on leave of absence, Boris had been anxious to make the acquaintance of Prince Nikolaï Andreyitch, and he had so far succeeded in winning his good graces that the prince made an exception in his case, and received him in spite of his being an eligible young bachelor.

The prince's house was not what one calls "fashion-

[1] Count Feodor Vasilyevitch Rostopchin (1763–1826), the famous governor-general of Moscow. Wrote satires under the pseudonym of Sila Andreyevitch Bogatuiref. His bulletins (*afishi*) were masterpieces of eloquence. While living in Paris he published his denial of having set fire to Moscow (*La Vérité sur l'Incendie de Moscou:* 1823).

able," but it was the center of a small circle, which, though it made little noise in the city, gave a more flattering distinction than any other to those who were admitted to it. This was made evident to Boris a week before, when he overheard Rostopchin tell the governor-general of the city, who invited him to dinner on St. Nicholas's Day, that it was impossible: —

"On that day I always go and worship the relics of Prince Nikolaï Andreyitch."

"Oh, yes, yes," replied the governor-general. "How is he?"

The little company gathered before dinner in the old-fashioned, high-studded drawing-room, with its ancient furniture, was like the gathering of a solemn court of justice. No one had much to say, and if they spoke it was in low tones.

Prince Nikolaï Andreyitch came in, silent and preoccupied. The Princess Mariya seemed even more quiet and timid than usual. The guests took no pains to talk with her, for they saw that she was not attending to what they said. Count Rostopchin was the only one who kept up the thread of conversation, speaking now of the latest news in the city, and now of politics in general. Lopukhin and the old general rarely took any share in it. Prince Nikolaï Andreyitch listened as a superior judge listens to a report presented to him, only showing by his significant silence, or by some curt monosyllable now and then, that he followed the drift of what was said.

The tone of the conversation made it evident that no one took any satisfaction in what was going on in the political world. They spoke of recent events which apparently confirmed the notion that everything was going from bad to worse; but in all their anecdotes and criticisms it was noticeable how each speaker came to a stop, or was brought to a stop, every time at that borderland where there was any possibility of personal reflections on his majesty the emperor.

The conversation at dinner turned on the most recent political news: the seizure by Napoleon of the possessions of the Duke of Oldenburg, and the Russian note — hostile to Napoleon — which had been despatched to all the courts throughout Europe.

"Bonaparte treats Europe as a pirate treats the ships he has captured," said Count Rostopchin, repeating an epigram that he had already got off a number of times before. "You can only marvel at the forbearance or the blindness of the sovereigns. Now it is the pope's turn; and Bonaparte is calmly proceeding to humiliate the head of the Catholic religion; and not a voice is raised in protest! Our sovereign is the only one who protests against the occupation of the duchy of Oldenburg. But then...."

Count Rostopchin came to a pause, conscious of having reached that point where criticism was impossible.

"He was offered other possessions, instead of Oldenburg," said Prince Nikolaï Andreyitch. "Just as I transfer peasants from Luisiya Gorui to Bogucharovo, or to my Riazan estates, he does with dukes."

"The Duke of Oldenburg shows great force of character, and bears his misfortune with admirable resignation," said Boris, modestly joining the conversation. He made this remark because on his way from Petersburg he had been honored with an introduction to the duke. Prince Nikolaï Andreyitch gave the young man a look, as if he had it in mind to make some reply to this, but checked himself, feeling that Boris was too young for him to waste his sarcasm upon.

"I have read our protest in regard to the Oldenburg affair, and was amazed at the bad style in which it was written," said Count Rostopchin, in the easy-going tone of a man who criticizes something which he knows perfectly well.

Pierre looked at Rostopchin in naïve amazement, unable to comprehend why he should be disturbed at the wretched style of the "note."

"What difference does it make how the note was written, count, provided the subject-matter is vigorous?" said he.

"My dear fellow, I think, with our army of five hundred thousand men, it might just as well have been couched in a good style!" said Count Rostopchin.

Pierre understood now why Count Rostopchin was disturbed by the wretched writing of the note.

"It seems to me there's a plentiful crop of penny-a-liners nowadays," said the old prince. "Yonder in Petersburg, everybody is writing not only 'notes,' but new laws, all the time. My Andryusha has been scribbling a whole volume of laws for Russia there. To-day, everybody is scribbling."

And he laughed unnaturally.

The conversation languished for a moment; then the old general called attention to himself, by a preliminary cough.

"Have you heard of what took place recently at a review at Petersburg? — How the new French ambassador acted?"

"What was that? Yes, I heard something about it. He made a very awkward remark in his majesty's presence, I believe."

"His majesty called attention to the division of grenadiers, and their splendid marching," pursued the general; "but it seems the ambassador showed absolute indifference, and permitted himself to say that at home in France they did not waste their time on such trivialities. The sovereign did not deign to give him any answer. But they say that at the subsequent review he did not say a word to him."

All were silent; it was out of the question to make any comment on this occurrence, since it concerned the monarch personally.

"Insolent wretches!" exclaimed the prince. "Do you know Métivier? I drove him out of the house to-day. He came, and was admitted, although I had given special orders to admit no one," said the prince, with an angry look at his daughter. And then he repeated his whole conversation with the French doctor, and gave the reasons that made him think Métivier a spy.

Though these reasons were very unsatisfactory and obscure, no one made any criticism.

After the roast, the champagne was handed around. The guests rose to their feet, offering the old prince their congratulations. The Princess Mariya also went round to him. He gave her a cold, angry look, and put up his wrinkled, clean-shaven cheek for her to kiss. The whole expression of his face told her that their conversation of the morning had not been forgotten, that his mind was just as fully made up, and that only the presence of his guests prevented him from saying the same thing over again.

When they went into the drawing-room for coffee, the older members of the company sat down together.

Prince Nikolaï Andreyitch grew more animated, and expressed his mind freely in regard to the war then just beginning. He declared that our wars with Bonaparte had hitherto been unsuccessful, and would be so long as we tried to make common cause with the Germans, and meddle with European affairs, as we were compelled to do by the peace of Tilsit. There was no sense in our battling either for or against Austria. Our policy lay in the east; and, as far as Bonaparte was concerned, we required only one thing: to protect our frontier, to have some firmness in our policy, and never to let him dare to cross the Russian frontier, as he did in 1807.

"And how is it possible for us to fight against the French, prince?" asked Count Rostopchin. "Can we take up arms against our teachers — our gods? Look at our young men! Look at our young ladies! Our gods are the French! our kingdom of heaven is Paris!"

He had raised his voice, evidently so that all might hear him.

"Our costumes are French, our ideas are French, our sentiments are French. You put out Métivier because he is a Frenchman, a good-for-nothing fellow; but our ladies grovel before him on their very knees. And last evening, at a party, out of five ladies, three were Roman Catholics; and these were working on canvas embroidery, on Sunday, by virtue of a dispensation from the pope! And there they sat, almost naked, for all the world like signboards for a public bath-house, — if I may be allowed the expression. Ekh! when I look at our young dandies, prince, I feel inclined to take the old cudgel of Peter the Great from the museum, and break their ribs for them in good old Russian style; that would put an end to all their whimsies!"

All were silent. The old prince, with a smile on his face, looked at Rostopchin, and nodded his head in assent.

"Well, prashchaïte, — good-by; — your illustriousness, take care of your health," said Rostopchin, rising with the abrupt motions characteristic of him, and offering his hand.

"Good-by, my dear.[1] You 're like a lute, — I always like to hear you," said the old prince, laying his hand on his arm, and offering his cheek for a kiss.

The others also got up with Rostopchin.

CHAPTER IV

The Princess Mariya, as she sat in the drawing-room and listened to the conversation and criticisms of the old men, understood nothing of what she heard; she was thinking only whether these guests had remarked the ill-will that her father showed toward her. She had not even noticed the peculiar attentions and civilities showed her all through the dinner-hour by Drubetskoï, who was now making his third visit to the house.

The princess, with a strangely abstracted and questioning glance, turned to Pierre, who, hat in hand and with a smiling face, was the last of the guests to come and pay her his parting respects after the old prince had retired. Thus it happened the two were left together in the drawing-room.

"May I stay a little longer?" he asked, tumbling his corpulent frame on an easy-chair near the Princess Mariya.

[1] *Prashchaï, galubchik.*

"Oh, yes, certainly!" replied she. Her glance seemed to ask, "Have you remarked anything unusual?"

Pierre was now in a happy after-dinner frame of mind. He gazed musingly straight forward, and smiled gently.

"Have you known that young man long, princess?" he asked.

"What young man?"

"Drubetskoï."

"No, not very long."....

"Well, do you like him?"

"Yes, he is a pleasant young fellow..... Why do you ask?" said the princess, her mind still on her morning's conversation with her father.

"Because I have made a discovery: the young man has come on leave of absence from Petersburg, with the sole and special purpose of marrying a rich wife."

"You have made that discovery?" exclaimed the Princess Mariya.

"Yes," pursued Pierre, with a smile; "and this young man so manages it that where the rich girls are gathered together, there he also is to be found! He is now undecided which to attack: you, or Mlle. Julie Karagina. He's very attentive to her."

"He goes there, then?"

"Yes, very often. And do you know the new way of making love?" inquired Pierre, with a cheery smile, evidently lapsing into that jolly spirit of good-humored ridicule for which he so often had reproached himself in his diary.

"No," replied the princess.

"In these days, in order to please the young ladies of Moscow, one must be melancholy. And he is very melancholy when he is with Mlle. Karagina," said Pierre.

"Really?" exclaimed the princess, gazing into Pierre's good face, and persistently thinking about her trials. "It would be so much easier," she thought, "if I could only make up my mind to confide in some one all my thoughts and feelings. And I should like especially to tell Pierre everything. He is so good and noble. It would certainly be easier for me. He would give me his advice."

"Would you marry him?" asked Pierre.

"Oh, good gracious, count! there are times when I would marry any one," suddenly exclaimed the Princess Mariya, unexpectedly to herself, and with tears in her voice. "Akh! how hard it is to love a near kinsman, and feel that .... no matter, though," she went on to say with trembling voice .... "you cannot do anything for him but only annoy him, and when you know that you cannot help things otherwise .... then, there is one thing, only one thing, to do .... to go away; but where could I go?"....

"What is it? What is the matter with you, princess?"

But the princess, without being able longer to control herself, burst into tears.

"I don't know what is the matter with me to-day. Do not criticize me; forget what I have said to you!"

All Pierre's gayety was gone. He anxiously questioned the princess; begged her to tell him everything, — to confide her trials in him; but her only reply was to beseech him to forget what she had said; that she herself did not remember what she had said, and that she had no trials except the one which he knew about already, that Prince Andreï's marriage threatened to bring about a quarrel between her father and brother.

"Have you heard anything about the Rostofs?" she asked, for the purpose of changing the conversation. "I am told that they will be here soon. André, also, I am expecting any day. I should have liked for them to meet here."

"And how does *he* look upon the matter, now?" asked Pierre, meaning by the pronoun the old prince, her father. The Princess Mariya shook her head.

"But what is to be done? The year will be up now in a few months. And this can never be. I only wish I could spare my brother the first minutes. I wish the Rostofs would come very soon. I hope to make her acquaintance. You have known them for a long time, have you not?" asked the Princess Mariya. "Tell me, with your hand on your heart, exactly the honest truth: what kind of a girl is she, and how do you like her? I want the whole truth, because Andreï, you know, takes such a tremendous risk in doing this against his father's will, that I should like to know just how it is."....

A dull instinct told Pierre that in this repeated demand to hear the whole truth was betrayed the Princess Mariya's ill-will toward her prospective sister-in-law, and that she had an idea that Pierre would not approve of Prince Andreï's choice; but Pierre told her not so much what he thought as felt.

"I don't know how to answer your question," said he, reddening without any reason. "I really don't know what kind of a girl she is. I can never analyze her. She is fascinating. But what makes her so, I can't tell you; that is all that I can say in regard to her."

The Princess Mariya sighed, and the expression of her face said, "Yes, this is what I expected and feared."

"Is she intellectual?" asked the princess. Pierre deliberated.

"I think not," said he, "but perhaps she is. She does not think it necessary to be intellectual .... but no, she is fascinating, nothing more."

The Princess Mariya again shook her head disapprovingly.

"Akh! how I hope that I shall love her! You tell her so if you see her before I do."

"I hear that they will be here in a few days," said Pierre.

The Princess Mariya confided to Pierre her plan for making the acquaintance of her prospective sister-in-law as soon as she came to Moscow, and then trying to reconcile the old prince to her.

CHAPTER V

Boris had not succeeded in making a match with any of the rich Petersburg heiresses, and he had gone to Moscow with the same object in view. There he found himself undecided between two of the wealthiest girls in town, Julie and the Princess Mariya.

Although the Princess Mariya, in spite of her plain features, seemed to him more attractive than Julie Karagina, still there were difficulties in the way of paying his addresses to Bolkonsky's daughter. At his last meeting with her, on the old prince's name-day, she had replied to all his tentative remarks on the subject of the feelings so at haphazard that it was evident she had not heard what he said.

Julie, on the other hand, received his attentions only too gladly, though in a way peculiar to herself alone.

Julie was twenty-seven. After the death of her brothers she had become very rich. She was now far from being a beauty; but she had conceived the idea that not only was she still pretty, but far more captivating than she ever had been before. In this illusion she was sustained by the facts that, in the first place, she had become a very rich maiden, and, in the second place, as she grew older and older, men found her less dangerous, and were able to gather round her with more freedom, since they felt that they were not incurring any obligations in taking advantage of the suppers, receptions, and jollifications which took place at her house. Men who ten years before would have thought a second time about going every day to a house where there was a young girl of seventeen, lest they should compromise her and get entangled themselves, now unhesitatingly appeared there daily, and treated her, not as a marriageable damsel, but as an acquaintance irrespective of sex.

The Karagins' house, that winter, was the gayest and most hospitable in Moscow. Besides the formal receptions and state dinners, they every day entertained a numerous society, especially of men, who ate supper at midnight and broke up at three o'clock in the morning. Nor was Julie willing to miss a ball, an entertainment, or a new play at the theater. Her toilets were always in the height of the fashion. But, nevertheless, Julie pretended to be disenchanted with all life; she told everybody that she had no belief in friendship, or in love, or in any of the pleasures of this world, and hoped for peace only "yonder." She affected the tone of a maiden who has endured great disappointment,— of one, for instance, who had been disappointed in the man she loved, or cruelly deceived in him. Although nothing of the sort had ever happened to her, it began to be thought that such was the case, and she herself came to believe that her sufferings in life had been grievous. This melancholia did not stand in the way of her enjoying herself, or prevent the young men who came to her house from having a delightful time there. Every guest who went there paid his tribute to his hostess's melancholic mood, and then fell to talking about the things of this world, and dancing, and intellectual games, and the capping of verses, — or *bouts rimés*, — which were greatly in vogue at the Karagins'.

Some few of the young men, Boris among them, took a deeper interest in Julie's melancholy moods; and with these young men she had longer and more confidential conversations about the vanity of all things terrestrial, and she showed them her albums, filled with gloomy drawings, apothegms, and couplets.

Julie treated Boris with especial favor; she mourned with him over his lost illusions; she offered him those consolations of friendship which she was so well able to offer, having herself suffered so much in life; she also showed him her album. Boris made a sketch of two trees with the legend: *Arbres rustiques, vos sombres rameaux secouent sur moi les ténèbres et la mélancolie* — "O solitary trees, your dark boughs scatter down upon me gloom and melancholy." On another page, he drew the picture of a tomb, and wrote:—

La mort est sécourable et la mort est tranquille!
Ah, contre les douleurs il n'y a pas d'autre asile.

'Tis death that gives us succor, death that gives us peace!
Alas! 't is then alone that earthly sorrows cease!

Julie declared that couplet to be charming! "There is something so ravishing in the smile of melancholy," said she to Boris, quoting, word for word, a passage from a book she was reading: "'Tis a ray of light falling in darkness, a shadow's difference between sorrow and despair, affording the hope of coming consolation."[1]

Whereupon Boris wrote for her these lines:—

Aliment de poison d'une âme trop sensible,
Toi, sans qui le bonheur me serait impossible,
Tendre mélancolie, ah, viens me consoler,
Viens calmer les tourments de ma tendre retraite,
Et mêle une douceur sécrète
À ces pleurs, que je sens couler.

Oh! poisoned aliment of souls too sensitive,
Thou that alone doth make it sweet for me to live,
Mild melancholy, come! Thy consolation bring!
The torments of my gloomy solitude, oh, calm!
Mingle thy secret soothing balm
With tears that never cease to spring.

Julie played on her harp, for Boris, her most melancholy nocturnes. Boris read aloud to her "Poor Liza,"[2] and more than once had to pause in his reading because of the emotion which overmastered him.

When they met in society, Julie and Boris exchanged glances to signify that they were the only people in the world capable of understanding and appreciating each other.

Anna Mikhaïlovna, who was a frequent visitor at the

[1] *Il y a quelque chose de si ravissant dans le sourire de la mélancolie. C'est un rayon de lumière dans l'ombre, une nuance entre la douleur et le désespoir, qui montre la consolation possible.*

[2] "*Byédnaya Liza*,"—"Poor Liza,"—a famous sentimental romance written by the great historian, Nikolaï Mikhaïlovitch Karamzin (1766–1826) about 1792; the melancholy seduction and suicide of the fascinating heroine being responsible for countless tears shed by the sympathetic maidens of those days.

Karagins', and always managed to be a partner with Julie's mother, took especial pains to procure all possible information in regard to Julie's fortune — which consisted of two estates in the vicinity of Penza, and forest lands near Nizhni-Novgorod. Anna Mikhaïlovna, with humble dependence on the will of Providence, and with deep emotion, looked on the etherealized melancholy which served as a bond between her son and the wealthy Julie.

"Always charming and melancholy, *cette chère Julie*," she would say to the daughter.

"Boris says that here in your house he finds rest for his soul. He has suffered the loss of so many illusions, and he is so sensitive," she would say to the mother.

"Akh! my dear, I cannot tell you how devoted I am to Julie of late," she would say to her son. "And who could help loving her? She is such a celestial creature! Akh! Boris! Boris!" She was silent for a minute. "And how sorry I am for her *maman!*" she went on to say. "To-day she was showing me her accounts and letters from Penza, where they have colossal estates; and it is so trying for her to have no one to help her; they cheat her so!"

Boris's face wore an almost imperceptible smile, as he listened to his mother's words. He was quietly amused at her transparent shrewdness; but he listened to her, and sometimes asked her questions in regard to these Penzensk and Nizhegorodsky properties.

Julie had for some time been looking for a proposal from her melancholy-souled adorer, and she was ready to accept him. But some secret antipathy toward her, a distaste of her evident desire to get married, and of her affectations, and a feeling of horror at thus practically repudiating the bliss of true love, still kept Boris at a distance.

His leave of absence was now drawing to a close. He spent long hours, and every Sunday, at the Karagins'; and every day, when he came to think the matter over, he would decide that his proposal should take place on the morrow. But when he was in Julie's company, and saw her red face and chin, almost always dusted with powder, her moist eyes, and the expression of her face, which seemed ready, at a moment's notice, to fly from melancholy to the equally unnatural enthusiasm and rapture of wedded bliss, Boris could not bring himself to utter the decisive words: although, in his imagination, he had for some time regarded himself as the prospective master of the Karagin estates, and had many times overspent the income arising therefrom.

Julie noticed Boris's infirmity of purpose, and it sometimes occurred to her that he had an antipathy for her; but her feminine vanity quickly restored her confidence, and she would assure herself that it was merely his love that made him so bashful. Her melancholia, however, was beginning to change into vexation; and a short time before the time of Boris's departure, she was thinking of adopting some decisive plan.

Just before Boris's leave of absence drew to a close, Anatol Kuragin made his appearance in Moscow, and, as a matter of course, in the Karagins' drawing-room; and Julie, abruptly arousing from her melancholy, became very cheerful, and manifested great friendliness toward Kuragin.

"*Mon cher*," said Anna Mikhaïlovna to her son, "I know on good authority that Prince Vasili has sent his son to Moscow to make a match with Julie. I am so fond of Julie that I should be very sorry for her. What do you think about it, my dear?" asked Anna Mikhaïlovna.

Boris was thoroughly humiliated at the thought of being left out in the cold, and of having wasted this whole month in arduous, melancholic service of Julie, and of seeing another man — especially such an idiot as Anatol — having control of that income from the Penzensk estates, which he was already, in his imagination, enjoying and profiting by. He went to the Karagins' with a full determination to offer himself. Julie met him with a gay and careless mien, gave him a merry account of what a good time she had enjoyed at the ball the evening before, and asked him when he was going back.

In spite of the fact that Boris had come with the intention of confessing his love, and had, therefore, decided to be tenderly sentimental, he immediately began, in a tone of irritation, to complain of woman's inconstancy, pointing out how easy it was for women to shift from gloom to glee, and that their moods depended wholly on the one who happened to be dancing attendance upon them. Julie took offense at this, and declared that he was right; that women needed variety, and nothing was more annoying to any one than to have a perpetual sameness.

"Then, I should advise you...." began Boris, with the intention of winging a sharp retort; but at that instant came the humiliating thought that he was on the point of leaving Moscow without attaining his wished-for end, and at the cost of wasted labor — a thing to which he was unaccustomed. He paused in the middle of his sentence, dropped his eyes to avoid seeing the look of disagreeable annoyance and indecision on her face, and said: —

"However, it was not at all for the purpose of quarreling with you that I came here. On the contrary...." He looked at her, to see whether she would encourage him to proceed. All expression of annoyance had suddenly vanished, and her restless, imploring eyes were fixed on him with greedy expectation. "I can always manage so as to keep out of her way," thought Boris. "Here I am in for it; might as well finish."

He flushed crimson, raised his eyes to hers, and said: —

"You know my sentiments toward you...."

There was no need of saying more: Julie's face had become radiant with triumph and satisfaction; but she compelled Boris to tell her all that it is customary to say in such circumstances, to tell her that he loved her, and that he had never loved any one else so passionately. She knew that, in exchange for her Penzensk estates and Nizhegorodsky forests, she had a right to exact this; and she obtained what she wished.

The young couple, with no further thoughts of solitary

trees shedding gloom and melancholy, laid their plans for the future establishment of a magnificent home in Petersburg, made calls, and got everything ready for a brilliant wedding.

CHAPTER VI

COUNT ILYA ANDREYEVITCH, together with Natasha and Sonya, arrived in Moscow toward the end of January. The countess was still ailing, and was unable to travel, but it was out of the question to wait for her recovery: Prince Andreï was expected in Moscow every day; and, besides, it was important to purchase Natasha's wedding outfit; it was necessary to sell the pod-Moskovnaya estate; and it was necessary to take advantage of the old prince's presence in Moscow, in order that he might become acquainted with his future daughter-in-law.

The Rostofs' Moscow house had not been warmed. Besides, they were to be in town for only a short time, and the countess was not with them; accordingly, Ilya Andreyitch decided to accept the hospitality of Marya Dmitrievna Akhrosimova, who had long ago urged them to come to her.

Late one evening, the four coaches on runners, conveying the Rostofs, drove into Marya Dmitrievna's courtyard, on the Old Konyushennaya Street.

Marya Dmitrievna lived alone. Her daughter was married. All of her sons were in the government service. She was just as erect as ever; her words were as much to the point; she always expressed her opinion to every one in a loud and decided voice, and her whole personality seemed to be a living reproach against all weaknesses, passions, and impulses, the necessity of which she utterly denied. From early morning, dressed in her jacket, she gave personal attention to the domestic arrangements, and then went out for a drive; if it were a holy day, to mass; and thence to the prisons and jails, where she had business that she never mentioned to any one.

On ordinary days, on finishing her toilet, she received applicants of every rank and condition who chanced to come to her door. Her charities having been dispensed, she dined; and this abundant and well-ordered meal was always shared by three or four guests; after dinner, she made up a table for Boston. Late in the evening, she had newspapers or some new book read aloud to her, while she sat with her knitting. She rarely accepted invitations, and if she ever made any exceptions it was only in favor of the most important personages of the city.

She had not yet retired when the Rostofs arrived; as the door into the hall creaked on its hinges, and admitted the travelers and their retinue of servants, together with a rush of cold air, Marya Dmitrievna, with her spectacles toward the end of her nose, came and stood in the doorway, her head erect, and gazed at the visitors with a stern and solemn face. One might have thought that she was really angry, and was about to turn the intruders out, if she had not been heard at that very instant to give the most urgent orders in regard to the disposition of her guests and their luggage.

"The count's? — bring them this way," said she, indicating certain trunks, and not stopping to greet any of the party. "The young ladies', this way to the left! — Well, and what are you gaping there for?" she cried to the maids. "Have the samovar got ready. — Plumper and prettier than ever!" she cried, taking possession of Natasha, whose face, under her hood, was all rosy with the cold. "Foo! how cold you are! There, get off your wraps as quick as ever you can," she cried to the count, who was bending over to kiss her hand. "You're frozen, most likely! have some rum put in with the tea! Sonyushka, *bon jour!*" said she to Sonya, showing by this French phrase and the pet diminutive her rather condescending, and yet affectionate, relationship to the girl.

When they had taken off their wraps, and put themselves to rights after their journey, they gathered round the tea-table, and Marya Dmitrievna kissed them all in turn.

"I am right glad that you have come, and that you have put up at my house," said she. "It 's high time," she went on, giving Natasha a significant look. "The old man is here, and his son is expected from day to day. You must, you certainly must, make his acquaintance. Well, we 'll talk about all this by and by," she added, giving Sonya a look, as much as to say that she did not care to talk about this in her presence. "Now, listen!" said she, addressing the count. "What are your plans for to-morrow? Whom will you send for? Shinshin?" She doubled over one finger. "Then, that sniveling Anna Mikhaïlovna. — Two. She and her son are here. Son 's to be married. Then, Bezukhoï, I suppose? And he and his wife are here. He ran away from her, but she came trapesing after him. He dined with me on Wednesday. Well, then, and these?" she indicated the young ladies. "I will take them to-morrow to the Iverskaya chapel, and then to Aubert-Chalmé's. Of course, everything will have to be got new for them. Don't judge by me! Such sleeves they wear these days! Recently, the young Princess Irena Vasilyevna came to call on me: she was a marvel to see; she had sleeves like two barrels on her arms. You see, there 's some new fashion every day. And what business have you on hand?" she asked, turning sternly on the count.

"Everything in the quickest possible time," replied the count. "To buy the girls' duds, and to find a purchaser for my pod-Moskovnaya land and house. And so, if you will allow me, I will tear myself away for a little while, and slip off to Marinskoye for a day, and leave my girls with you."

"Very good, very good; they 'll be safe with me. They could n't be safer with the Orphans' Aid Society.[1] I 'll take them wherever they need to go, and scold them, and spoil them with flattery," said Marya Dmitrievna, stroking with her big hand the cheek of her favorite god-daughter, Natasha.

The following morning they went to pray before the

[1] *Opekunsky Sovyet.*

Iverskaya Virgin, and to see Mademoiselle Aubert-Chalmé, who stood in such awe of Marya Dmitrievna that, in order to get rid of her as soon as possible, she would always sell her goods at a positive loss. Marya Dmitrievna ordered there the larger part of the trousseau. On their return, she drove everybody else out of the room, and called Natasha to her arm-chair.

"Now, then, let us have a talk. I congratulate you on your choice. You have secured a fine young man. I am glad for you. I have known him ever since he was so high." She put her hand about thirty inches from the floor. Natasha colored with pleasure. "I am fond of him and of all his family. Now, listen! You know very well that the old Prince Nikolaï is very averse to having his son marry. A whimsical old man! However, Prince Andreï is not a child, and his permission is not necessary; still, it is not pleasant to enter a family against their will. We must act quietly and with tact. You are clever; we will manage to bring him round where he ought to be. You must accomplish it by your sweetness and cleverness. That 's all it requires, and it will come out all right."

Natasha made no reply, — from shyness, Marya Dmitrievna supposed, but in reality because it was annoying to Natasha that any one should meddle with her love-affair with Prince Andreï; for it seemed to her so entirely above and beyond all ordinary human concerns, that no one else, in her opinion, could understand it. She loved and admired Prince Andreï alone; he loved her, and was coming in a few days, and would make her his. That was all-sufficient.

"You see, I have known him for a long time, and Mashenka, also, your future sister-in-law. I am fond of her, in spite of the proverb about husband's sisters.[1] She would not hurt a fly. She asked me to introduce her to you. You and your father must go there to-morrow. Be sure to be very sweet to her, for you are younger than she is. Before your friend comes you

[1] *Zalovki, kalatovki, pobeï galovki:* Husband's sisters are churn-sticks (wranglers) whereby heads are broken.

will have already become acquainted with his sister and his father, and they will have grown fond of you. Am I not right? Is n't that best?"

"Yes," replied Natasha, with little heartiness.

CHAPTER VII

On the following day, by Marya Dmitrievna's advice, Count Ilya Andreyitch and Natasha went to call at Prince Bolkonsky's. The count, in anything but a happy frame of mind, made ready for this call; in fact, he felt terribly about it. He remembered too well his last encounter with the old prince, at the time of the mobilizing of the militia, when, in answer to his invitation to a dinner-party, he had received an angry reprimand for not having furnished his full quota of men.

Natasha, however, having put on her best gown, was in the most radiant spirits. "They cannot help being fond of me," she said to herself. "Every one likes me, and I am so willing to do for them all they could wish! I am so willing to love him because he is his father, and to love her because she is his sister, that they cannot fail to love me."

They drove up to the gloomy old house on Vozdvizhenka Street, and went into the vestibule.

"Well, God have mercy on us!" exclaimed the count, half in jest, half in earnest; but Natasha observed that her father was very much agitated as he hastened into the anteroom and asked, in a timid, faltering voice, if the prince and the princess were at home. After their names had been sent in, the prince's servants seemed to be thrown into great perplexity. The footman, who had hurried off to announce them, was stopped by another footman at the drawing-room door, and the two began to whisper together. A chambermaid came hurrying into the hall, and she also had something to say to them, in reference to the princess. Finally a stern-faced, elderly footman approached the Rostofs and announced that the old prince was unable to receive them, but the princess would be glad to see them.

Mlle. Bourienne first came to receive the visitors. She met them with more than ordinary politeness, and conducted them to the princess. The princess, agitated and nervous, her face covered with crimson patches, hastened forward, stepping heavily, and vainly endeavoring to appear calm and dignified.

At first sight Natasha did not please her. It seemed to her that she was too fashionably dressed, too frivolous, flighty, and conceited. The Princess Mariya did not realize that even before seeing her future sister-in-law she was prejudiced against her through an involuntary envy of her beauty, youth, and happiness, and jealousy of her brother's love for her. Over and above these obscure feelings of antipathy, the Princess Mariya was still more agitated from the fact that when the Rostofs were announced the prince had shouted at the top of his voice that he would not have anything to do with them; that the Princess Mariya might receive them if she so desired, but that they should not come into his presence. The princess determined to receive them, but she was afraid lest at any minute the prince might perform some act of rudeness, since he seemed greatly stirred up by the Rostofs' arrival.

"I have brought my little songstress, my dear princess," said the count, with a bow and a scrape, and looking round anxiously, as if he were afraid of the old prince appearing on the scene. "I am very anxious for you to become acquainted. .... I am sorry, very sorry, that the prince is ill." And, after making a few commonplace remarks, he got up, saying, "If you will excuse me, princess, I will leave my Natasha with you for a brief quarter of an hour, while I slip out and call on Anna Semyonovna, who lives only a couple of steps from here. I will come back for her."

Ilya Andreyitch, as he afterwards told his daughter, conceived this master-stroke of subtile diplomacy for the purpose of giving the future sisters-in-law a chance to get better acquainted; but he had another reason besides, which was that he might escape the possibility of meeting the prince. This reason he did not confess to his daughter, but Natasha perceived this timidity and anxiety of her father's, and felt abused. She blushed for him, and was still more annoyed with herself for having blushed; and she looked straight at the princess with a defiant, challenging expression, which seemed to imply that there was nothing she was afraid of. The princess told the count that he was perfectly excusable, and only hoped that he would make his stay at Anna Semyonovna's as long as possible. Accordingly, Ilya Andreyitch took his departure.

Mlle. Bourienne, in spite of the anxious, beseeching glances given her by the Princess Mariya, who was anxious to have a confidential talk with Natasha, did not see fit to leave the room, and kept up a steady stream of chatter about the delights of Moscow, and the theaters. Natasha was piqued by the confusion that had occurred in the reception-room, by her father's cowardice, and by the unnatural tone affected by the princess, who, it seemed to her, felt that it was an act of condescension to receive her, and, consequently, everything gave her a disagreeable impression. The Princess Mariya displeased her. She thought she was very plain, stubborn, and unsympathetic. Natasha suddenly underwent a moral shrinking, as it were, and, in spite of herself, assumed such a reckless tone that the Princess Mariya was still further alienated from her.

After five minutes of a labored and artificial conversation, slippered feet were heard rapidly approaching. Into the Princess Mariya's face came a sudden look of dismay. The door opened, and the old prince came in, dressed in a white nightcap and khalat.

"Akh! sudaruinya," he exclaimed; "sudaruinya, countess — Countess Rostova, if I am not mistaken — I beg your pardon, I beg your pardon. — I did not know, sudaruinya, 'fore God I did not know that you were honoring us with your presence. I was coming to see my daughter, which explains this costume. I beg you to pardon it. — 'Fore God I did not know," he said for the second time, in such an unnatural tone, laying such a special stress on the word "God," and speaking so disagreeably, that the Princess Mariya got up, and dropped her eyes, not daring to look either at her father or at Natasha. Natasha got up and then sat down again, and likewise knew not what to do. Only Mlle. Bourienne wore a pleasant smile.

"I beg your pardon. I beg your pardon. 'Fore God I did not know," grumbled the old prince, and, after staring at Natasha from head to foot, he left the room. Mlle. Bourienne was the first to recover self-possession after this apparition, and she began to talk about the prince's failing health. Natasha and the princess looked at each other without speaking, and the longer they looked at each other without expressing what they ought to have said, the more they were confirmed in their mutual dislike.

When the count returned, Natasha made an ill-mannered display of relief, and immediately prepared to take her departure. At this moment she almost hated this dried-up old princess, who by her silence had put her in such an awkward position, and who, in half an hour's talk with her, had not once mentioned Prince Andreï. "Of course I can't be the first to speak of him in the presence of that Frenchwoman," said Natasha to herself.

The Princess Mariya, at the same time, was tormented by a similar compunction. She knew that it was her duty to say something to Natasha; but she found it impossible, both because Mlle. Bourienne's presence embarrassed her, and because she herself did not know what made it so difficult to speak on the coming marriage. After the count had already left the room the Princess Mariya went to Natasha with hurried steps, seized her hand, and with a deep sigh said, "Wait a moment, I must...." Natasha gave the Princess Mariya a satirical glance, though she could not have told what made her do so, and listened. "My dear Natalie," said the Princess Mariya, "you must know I am delighted my brother has found happiness." ....

She paused with a consciousness that she was not telling the truth. Natasha noticed this pause, and suspected the cause of it.

"I think, princess, that it is not a propitious time to speak of this," said Natasha, with an appearance of outward dignity and *hauteur*, while the tears almost choked her.

"What have I said? what have I said?" she wondered, as soon as she left the room.

That day they waited for Natasha a long time at dinner. She was sitting in her room, sobbing like a child, blowing her nose, and then beginning to sob again. Sonya stood beside her, and kissed her on the hair.

"Natasha, what is there to cry about?" she asked. "Why should you care about them? It will all pass over, Natasha."

"No; if you only knew how humiliating it was! — I just.... "

"Don't speak of it, Natasha. Of course you were not to blame, then why should you let it trouble you? Kiss me," said Sonya.

Natasha lifted her head and kissed her friend on the lips, laying her tear-wet face next hers.

"I cannot tell you. I do not know. No one is to blame," said Natasha. "If any one is, I am. But all this is terribly painful. Akh! why does he not come?" ....

She went down to dinner with reddened eyes. Marya Dmitrievna, who had learned how the Rostofs had been received at the prince's, pretended to pay no attention to Natasha's disconsolate face, and jested in loud and eager tones with the count and her other guests.

CHAPTER VIII

THAT evening the Rostofs went to the opera, Marya Dmitrievna having secured them tickets. Natasha felt no desire to go, but it was impossible for her to refuse her hostess's kindness, which had been designed expressly for her pleasure. When, after she was already dressed, and had gone into the parlor to wait for her father, she surveyed herself in the great pier-glass, and saw how pretty, how very pretty, she was, she felt even more melancholy than before, but her melancholy was mingled with a feeling of sweet and passionate love.

"Bozhe moï! if he were only here I should not be so stupidly shy before him as I was before. I would throw my arms around him and cling close to him, and make him look at me with those deep, penetrating eyes of his, with which he has so often looked at me; and then I would make him laugh, as he laughed then, and his eyes.... how plainly I can see his eyes even now," said Natasha to herself. "And what do I care for his father and his sister? I love him. I love him, him alone, with his dear face and eyes, with his smile, like that of a man and like that of a child too..... No, it is better not to think about it, to forget him, and to forget that time, too, absolutely. I cannot endure this suspense. I shall be crying again,".... and she turned away from the mirror, exercising all her self-control not to burst into tears. "And how can Sonya be so calm and unconcerned in her love for Nikolenka, and wait so long and patiently?" she wondered, as she saw her cousin coming toward her, also in full dress, and with her fan in her hand. "No, she is entirely different from me. I cannot."

Natasha at that moment felt herself so full of passion and tenderness that it was not enough to love, and to know that she was loved. What she wanted now, at this instant, was to throw her arms around her lover's neck, and speak to him, and hear him speak those words of love of which her heart was full.

As she rode along in the carriage, sitting next to her father, and dreamily looking at the lamplights that flashed through the frost-covered windows, she felt still deeper in love, and still more melancholy than ever, and she quite forgot with whom and where she was going.

Their carriage fell into the long line, and the wheels slowly creaked over the snow as they drew up to the steps of the theater. The two girls gathered up their skirts and quickly jumped out; the count clambered down, supported by the footmen, and, making their way through the throng of ladies and gentlemen and program venders, the three went into the corridor that led to their box. Already the sounds of music were heard through the closed doors.

"Natalie, your hair," whispered Sonya in French. The kapelldiener, hastening past the ladies, politely opened their box door. The music sounded louder; the brightly lighted rows of boxes occupied by ladies with bared shoulders and arms, and the parterre filled with brilliant uniforms, dazzled their eyes. A lady who entered the adjoining box shot a glance of feminine envy at Natasha. The curtain was still down, and the orchestra was playing the overture.

Natasha, shaking out her train, went forward with Sonya and took her seat, glancing at the brightly lighted boxes on the opposite side of the house. The sensation, which she had not experienced for a long time, of having hundreds of eyes staring at her bare arms and neck, suddenly affected her both pleasantly and unpleasantly, and called up a whole swarm of recollections, desires, and emotions associated with that sensation.

Natasha and Sonya, both remarkably pretty girls, and Count Ilya Andreyitch, who had not been seen for a long time in Moscow, naturally attracted general attention. Moreover, every one had a general notion that Natasha was engaged to marry Prince Andreĭ, and everybody knew that ever since the engagement the Rostofs had been residing at their country estate; therefore they looked with much curiosity at the "bride" of one of the most desirable men in Russia.

Natasha's beauty, as everybody told her, had improved during their stay in the country, and that evening, owing to her excited state of mind, she was extraordinarily beautiful. No one could have failed to be struck by her exuberance of life and beauty, and her complete indifference to everything going on around her. Her dark eyes wandered over the throng, not seeking for any one in particular, and her slender arm, bare above the elbow, leaned on the velvet rim of the box, while, with evident unconsciousness of what she was doing, she crumpled her program, folding and unfolding it in time with the orchestra.

"Look, there's Alenina," said Sonya, "with her mother, I think."

"Saints![1] Mikhaïl Kiriluitch has grown fat, though," exclaimed the old count.

"See, there's our Anna Mikhaïlovna. What kind of a head-dress has she on?"

"There are the Karagins, and Boris with them. Evidently enough, an engaged couple. .... Drubetskoï must have proposed."

"What! did n't you know it? 'T was announced to-day," said Shinshin, coming into their box.

Natasha looked in the same direction as her father was looking, and saw Julie, who, with a string of pearls around her fat red neck, — covered with powder, as Natasha knew well, — was sitting next her mother with a radiantly happy face. Behind them could be seen Boris's handsome head, with sleekly brushed hair. He was leaning over so that his ear was close to Julie's mouth, and as he looked askance at the Rostofs he was saying something to his "bride."

"They are talking about us, — about me," thought Natasha, "and she's probably jealous of me, and he is trying to calm her. They need not worry about it. If they only knew how little I cared about them!"

Behind them sat Anna Mikhaïlovna, festive and bliss-

[1] *Batyushki*, — literally, "little fathers."

ful, and wearing her habitual expression of utter resignation to God's will. Their box was redolent of that atmosphere characteristic of a newly engaged couple, which Natasha knew and loved so well. She turned away, and suddenly all the humiliating circumstances of her morning visit recurred to her memory.

"What right has he not to be willing to receive me as a relation? Akh! I 'd best not think about this, at least not till *he* comes back," said she to herself, and she began to scan the faces of strangers or acquaintances in the parterre.

In the front row, in the very middle of the house, leaning his back against the railing, stood Dolokhof in Persian costume, with his curly hair combed back into a strange and enormous ridge. He was standing in full view of the whole theater, knowing that he was attracting the attention of every one in the house, yet looking as unconcerned as if he was in the privacy of his own room. Around him were gathered a throng of the gilded youth of Moscow, and it was evident that he was their leader.

Count Ilya Andreyitch, with a smile, nudged the blushing Sonya, and called her attention to her former suitor.

"Did you recognize him? and where did he turn up from?" asked the count of Shinshin. "He had disappeared entirely, had he not?"

"Yes, completely," replied Shinshin. "While he was in the Caucasus he deserted, and they say he became minister to some reigning prince in Persia. After that he killed the Shah's brother, and now all the young ladies of Moscow have lost their wits over him. *Dolohoff le Persan*, and that 's the end of it. Here with us there 's nothing to be done without Dolokhof. They swear by him. He is made a subject of invitation, as if he were a sterlet," said Shinshin. "Dolokhof and Anatol Kuragin have turned the heads of all our young ladies."

Just then into the next box came a tall, handsome lady with a tremendous plait of hair, and a great display of plump white shoulders and neck, around which she wore a double string of large pearls. She was a long time in settling herself, with a great rustling of her stiff silk dress.

Natasha found herself involuntarily gazing at that neck, those shoulders and pearls, and that head-dress, and she was amazed at their beauty. Just as Natasha was taking a second look at her, the lady glanced round, and, fixing her eyes on Count Ilya Andreyitch, nodded her head and smiled.

It was the Countess Bezukhaya, Pierre's wife.

Ilya Andreyitch, who knew every one in society, leaned over and spoke with her.

"Have you been here long, countess?" he inquired. "I'm coming in, I'm coming in soon to kiss your hand. I'm in town on business, and have got my girls with me. They say Semyonova plays her part superbly," said Ilya Andreyitch. "I hope Count Piotr Kirillovitch has not entirely forgotten us. Is he here?"

"Yes, he was intending to come," said Ellen, and she gave Natasha a scrutinizing look.

Count Ilya Andreyitch again sat back in his place. "Isn't she pretty, though?" asked he of Natasha.

"A perfect marvel," replied the latter. "I could understand falling in love with her."

By this time the last notes of the overture were heard, and the baton of the kapellmeister rapped upon the stand. Those gentlemen who were in late slipped down to their places, and the curtain rose.

As soon as the curtain went up, silence reigned in the parterre and the boxes, and all the gentlemen, young and old, whether in uniforms or in civilian's dress, and all the ladies, with precious stones glittering on their bare bosoms, with eager expectation turned their attention to the stage.

Natasha also tried to look.

CHAPTER IX

SMOOTH boards formed the center of the stage, on the sides stood painted canvases representing trees, in the background a cloth was stretched out on boards, in the foreground girls in red bodices and white petticoats were sitting around. One, who was exceedingly stout, wore a white silk dress. She sat by herself on a low footstool, to the back of which was glued green cardboard. They were all singing something. After they had finished their chorus the girl in white advanced toward the prompter's box, and a man in silk tights on his stout legs, and with a feather and a dagger, joined her, and began to sing and wave his arms.

The man in the tights sang alone, then she sang, then they were both silent. The orchestra played, and the man began to turn down the fingers on the girl's hand, evidently waiting for the beat when they should begin to sing their parts together. They sang a duet, and then all in the audience began to clap and to shout; and the man and woman on the stage, who had been representing lovers, got up, smiling, and, letting go of hands, bowed.

After her country life, and the serious frame of mind into which Natasha had lately fallen, all this seemed to her wild and strange. She was unable to follow the thread of the opera, and it was as much as she could do to listen to the music. She saw only painted canvas and oddly dressed men and women going through strange motions, talking and singing in a blaze of light. She knew what all this was meant to represent; but it all struck her as so affected, unnatural, and absurd, that some of the time she felt ashamed for the actors, and again she felt like laughing at them.

She looked around at the faces of the spectators, to see if she could detect in them any of this feeling of ridicule and perplexity which she felt; but all these faces were absorbed in what was taking place on the stage, or, as it seemed to Natasha, expressed a hypocritical enthusiasm.

"I suppose this must be very lifelike," said Natasha to herself. She kept gazing now at those rows of pomaded heads in the parterre, then at the half-naked women in the boxes, and most of all at her neighbor Ellen, who, as undressed as she could well be, gazed with a faint contented smile at the stage, not dropping her eyes, conscious of the brilliant light that overflowed the auditorium, and the warm atmosphere, heated by the throng.

Natasha gradually began to enter into a state of intoxication which she had not experienced for a long time. She had no idea who she was, or where she was, or of what was going on before her. She gazed, and let her thoughts wander at will, and the strangest, most disconnected ideas flashed unexpectedly through her mind. Now she felt inclined to leap on the edge of the box and sing the aria which the actress had just been singing, then she felt an impulse to tap with her fan a little old man who was sitting not far off, then again to lean over to Ellen and tickle her.

At one time, when there was perfect silence on the stage just before the beginning of an aria, the door that led into the parterre near where the Rostofs were seated creaked on its hinges, and a man who came in late was heard passing down to his seat.

"There goes Kuragin," whispered Shinshin.

The Countess Bezukhaya turned her head and smiled at the newcomer. Natasha followed the direction of the Countess Bezukhaya's eyes, and saw an extraordinarily handsome aide, who, with an air of extreme self-confidence, but at the same time of good breeding, was just passing by their box.

This was Anatol Kuragin, whom she had seen and noticed some time before at a ball in Petersburg. He now wore his aide's uniform, with epaulet and shoulder-knot. He advanced with a supreme air of youthful gallantry, which would have been ludicrous had he not been so handsome, and had his handsome face not worn such an expression of cordial good-humor and merriment.

Although it was during the act, he sauntered along the carpeted corridor, slightly jingling his spurs, and holding his perfumed, graceful head on high with easy grace. Glancing at Natasha, he joined his sister, laid his exquisitely gloved hand on the edge of her box, nodded to her, and bent over to ask some question in reference to Natasha.

"*Mais charmante,*" said he, evidently referring to her. She understood less from hearing his words than from the motion of his lips.

Then he went forward to the front row and took his seat near Dolokhof, giving him a friendly, careless nudge with his elbow, though the others treated him with such worshipful consideration. The other, with a merry lifting of the eyebrows, gave him a smile, and put up his foot against the railing.

"How like brother and sister are!" said the count; "and how handsome they both are!"

Shinshin, in an undertone, began to tell the count some story about Kuragin's intrigues in Moscow, to which Natasha listened simply because he had spoken of her as *charmante.*

The first act was over. All in the parterre got up, mingled together, and began to go and come. Boris came to the Rostofs' box, received their congratulations very simply, and, smiling abstractedly and raising his brows, invited Natasha and Sonya, on behalf of his betrothed, to be present at their wedding, and then left them. Natasha, with a bright, coquettish smile, had talked with him and congratulated him on his engagement, although it was the same Boris with whom she had been in love only a short time before. This, in her intoxicated, excited state, seemed to her perfectly simple and natural.

The bare-bosomed Ellen sat near her, and showered her smiles indiscriminately on all, and in exactly the same way Natasha smiled on Boris.

Ellen's box was crowded by the cleverest and most influential men of the city, who also gathered around the front of it, on the parterre side, vying with one another, apparently, in their desire to let it be known that they were acquainted with her.

Kuragin, throughout that *entr'acte,* stood with Dolokhof, with his back to the stage, in the very front row, and kept his eyes fixed on the Rostofs' box. Natasha felt certain that he was talking about her, and it afforded her gratification. She even turned her head slightly, in a way which, in her opinion, best showed off the beauty of her profile.

Before the beginning of the second act, Pierre, whom the Rostofs had not seen since their arrival, made his appearance. His face was gloomy, and he was still more portly than when Natasha had last seen him. Without recognizing any one, he passed down to the front row. Anatol joined him, and began to make some remark, looking and pointing to the Rostofs' box. A flash of animation passed over Pierre's face as he caught sight of Natasha, and he hastily made his way across through the seats to where she was. Then, leaning his elbows on the edge of her box and smiling, he had a long conversation with her.

While she was talking with Pierre, she heard a man's voice in the Countess Bezukhaya's box, and something told her that it was Anatol Kuragin. She glanced round, and their eyes met. He almost smiled, and looked straight into her eyes with such an admiring, tender gaze that it seemed to her strange to be so near him, to see him, to be so sure that she pleased him, and yet not to be acquainted with him!

In the second act the stage represented a cemetery, and there was a hole in the canvas, which represented the moon, and the footlights were turned down, and the horns and contrabasses began to play in very deep tones, and the stage was invaded from both sides by a throng of men in black mantles. These men began to wave their arms, brandishing what seemed to be daggers. Then some other men rushed forward, and proceeded to drag away by main force that damsel who, in the previous act, had been dressed in white, but was now in a blue dress. But before they dragged her away, they sang with her for a long time, and at the sound of three thumps on something metallic behind the scenes, all fell on their knees and began to sing a prayer. A number of times all these actions were interrupted by the enthusiastic plaudits of the spectators.

Every time during this act that Natasha looked down into the parterre, she saw Anatol Kuragin, with his arm carelessly thrown across the back of his seat, and gazing at her. It was pleasant for her to feel that she had so captivated him, and it never entered her head that in all this there was anything improper.

When the second act was over, the Countess Bezukhaya stood up, leaned over to the Rostofs' box, — thereby exposing her whole bosom, — and with her gloved finger beckoned the old count to come to her; and then, paying no heed to those who came to her box to pay her their homage, she began a smiling, confidential conversation with him.

"You must certainly make me acquainted with your charming girls," said she; "the whole city are talking about them, and I don't know them."

Natasha got up and made a courtesy to this magnificent countess. The flattery of this brilliant beauty was so intoxicating to her that she blushed with pleasure and gratification.

"I mean to be a Muscovite also," said Ellen. "And aren't you ashamed of yourself to hide such pearls in the country?"

The Countess Bezukhaya had, by good rights, the reputation of being a fascinating woman. She could say the opposite of what she thought, and could flatter in the most simple and natural manner.

"Now, my dear count, you must allow me to see something of your daughter. Though I don't expect to be here very long, — you don't either, I believe, — I shall try to make them have a good time. — I heard a good deal about you in Petersburg, and I wanted to make your acquaintance," said she, turning to Natasha with her stereotyped, bewitching smile. "I heard about you from my 'page,' Drubetskoï, — have you heard, by the way, that he is engaged? — and from my husband's friend Bolkonsky, Prince Andreï Bolkonsky," said she, with especial emphasis, signifying thereby that she knew of his relations with Natasha. Then she proposed that, in order to become better acquainted, one of the young ladies should come over into her box for the rest of the performance, and Natasha went.

During the third act the scene represented a palace, wherein many candles were blazing, while on the walls hung paintings representing full-bearded knights. In the center stood, apparently, a tsar and tsaritsa. The tsar was gesticulating with his right hand, and, after singing something with evident timidity, and certainly very wretchedly, he took his seat on a crimson throne.

The damsel who at first had been dressed in white and then in blue was now in nothing but a shift, with disheveled hair, and stood near the throne. She was warbling some doleful ditty addressed to the tsaritsa, but the tsar peremptorily waved his hand, and from the side scenes came a number of bare-legged men and bare-legged women, and began to dance all together.

Then the fiddles played a very dainty and merry tune. One girl, with big bare legs and thin arms, coming out from among the others, went behind the scenes, and, having adjusted her corsage, came into the center of the stage, and began to caper about and knock her feet together.

The whole parterre clapped their hands and shouted, "Bravo!"

Then a man took his stand in one corner. The orchestra played louder than ever, with a clanging of cymbals and blare of horns, and this bare-legged man, alone by himself, began to make very high jumps and kick his feet together. This man was Duport, who earned sixty thousand rubles a year by his art. All in the parterre, in the boxes, and in the "upper paradise" began to thump and shout with all their might, and the man paused and smiled, and bowed to all sides. Then some others danced, — bare-legged men and women; then one of the royal personages shouted something with musical accompaniment, and all began to sing. But suddenly a storm arose. Chromatic scales and diminished sevenths were heard in the orchestra, and all scattered behind the scenes, carrying off with them again one of those who were behind the scenes as spectators, and the curtain fell.

Once more among the audience arose a terrible roar and tumult, and all, with enthusiastic faces, shouted at once, "Duport! Duport! Duport!"

Natasha no longer looked upon this as strange or unusual. With a sense of satisfaction she looked around her, smiling joyously.

"Is n't Duport admirable?" asked Ellen, turning to her.

"Oh, yes!" replied Natasha.

CHAPTER X

DURING the *entr'acte* a draught of cold air made its way into Ellen's box, the door was opened, and Anatol came in, bowing and trying not to disturb any one.

"Allow me to present my brother," said Ellen, uneasily glancing from Natasha to Anatol.

Natasha turned her pretty, graceful head toward the handsome young man, and smiled at him over her shoulder. Anatol, who was as good-looking near at hand as he was at a distance, sat down by her and said that he had been long wishing for the pleasure of her acquaintance, — ever since the Naruishkins' ball, where he had seen her, and never forgotten her.

Kuragin was far cleverer and less affected with women than he was in the society of men. He spoke fluently and simply, and Natasha had a strange and agreeable feeling of ease in the company of this man, about whom so many rumors were current. He was not only not terrible, but his face even wore an innocent, gay, and good-natured smile.

Kuragin asked her how she enjoyed the opera, and told her how Semyonova, at the last performance, had got a fall while on the stage.

"Do you know, countess," said he, suddenly addressing her as if she were an old acquaintance, "we have been arranging a fancy-dress party.[1] You ought to take part in it. It will be very jolly. We shall all rendezvous at the Karagins'. Please come, won't you?" he insisted.

In saying this he did not once take his smiling eyes from her face, her neck, her naked arms. Natasha was not left in doubt of the fact that he admired her. This was agreeable, but somehow she felt constrained and troubled by his presence. When she was not looking at him, she was conscious that he was staring at her shoulders, and she involuntarily tried to catch his eyes, so that he might rather fix them on her face. But while she thus looked him in the eyes, she had a terrified consciousness that that barrier of modesty which, she had always felt before, kept other men at a distance, was down between him and her. Without being in the least able to explain it, she was conscious within five minutes that she was on a dangerously intimate footing with this man. When she looked away from him, she feared he might put his hand on her bare arm, or kiss her on the neck. They talked about the simplest matters, and yet she felt that they were more intimate than she had ever been with any other man. She looked at Ellen and at her father, as if asking them what all this meant; but Ellen was busily engaged in conversation with some general, and paid no heed to her imploring look, and her father's said nothing more to her than what it always said: "Happy? Well, I am glad of it."

During one of those moments of constraint, while Anatol's prominent eyes were calmly and boldly surveying her, Natasha, in order to break the silence, asked him how he liked Moscow. Natasha asked the question, and blushed. It seemed to her all the time

[1] *Karusel f kostumakh.*

that she was doing something unbecoming in talking with him. Anatol smiled, as if to encourage her.

"At first I was not particularly charmed with Moscow, because what a city ought to have, to be agreeable, is pretty women; is n't that so? Well, now I like it very much," said he, giving her a significant look. "Will you come to our party, countess? Please do," said he; and, stretching out his hand toward her bouquet, and lowering his voice, he added in French, "You will be the prettiest. Come, my dear countess, and, as a pledge, give me that flower."

Natasha did not realize what he was saying any more than he did, but she had a consciousness that in his incomprehensible words there was an improper meaning. She knew not what reply to make, and turned away, pretending not to have heard him. But the instant that she turned away the thought came to her that he was there behind her, and so near.

"What is he doing now? Is he ashamed of himself? Is he angry? Is it my business to make amends?" she asked herself. She could not refrain from glancing round.

She looked straight into his eyes, and his nearness and self-possession, and the good-natured warmth of his smile, overcame her.

She gave him an answering smile, and gazed straight into his eyes, and once more she realized, with the feeling of horror, that there was no barrier between them.

The curtain again went up. Anatol left the box, calm and serene. Natasha rejoined her father in her own box, but already she was under the dominion of this world into which she had entered. Everything that passed before her eyes now seemed to her perfectly natural, while all her former thoughts concerning her lover, and the Princess Mariya, and her life in the country, vanished from her mind as if all that had taken place long, long ago.

In the fourth act there was a strange kind of devil, who sang and gesticulated until a trap beneath him was opened, and he disappeared. This was all that Natasha noticed during the fourth act. Something agitated and disturbed her, and the cause of this annoyance was Kuragin, at whom she could not help looking.

When they left the theater Anatol joined them, summoned their carriage, and helped them to get seated. As he was assisting Natasha, he squeezed her arm above the elbow. Startled and blushing, she looked at him. His brilliant eyes returned her gaze, and he gave her a tender smile.

Not until she reached home was Natasha able clearly to realize all that had taken place, and when she suddenly remembered Prince Andreï she was horror-struck; and as they all sat drinking tea she groaned aloud, and, flushing scarlet, ran from the room.

"My God! I am lost," she said to herself. "How could I have let it go so far?" she wondered. Long she sat hiding her flushed face in her hands, striving to give herself a clear account of what had happened to her, and she could not do so, nor could she explain her feelings. Everything seemed to her dark, obscure, and terrible.

Then, in that huge, brilliant auditorium, where Duport, with his bare legs and his spangled jacket, capered about on the dampened boards to the sounds of music, and the girls and the old men and Ellen much *décolletée*, with her calm and haughty smile, were all applauding and enthusiastically shouting bravo, — there, under the protection of this same Ellen, everything was perfectly clear and simple; but now, alone by herself, it became incomprehensible.

"What does it mean? What means this fear that I experience in his presence? What mean these stings of conscience which I experience now?" she asked herself.

If only her mother had been there, Natasha would have made confession of all her thoughts, before going to bed that night. She knew that Sonya, with her strict and wholesome views, would either entirely fail to understand, or would be horrified by, her confession.

Natasha accordingly tried, by her own unaided efforts, to settle the question that tormented her.

"Have I really forfeited Prince Andreï's love, or not?" she asked herself, and then, with a reassuring smile, she replied to her own question: —

"What a fool I am to ask this! What happened to me? Nothing. I have done nothing. I was not to blame for this. No one will know about it, and I shall not see him any more," said she to herself. "Of course it is evident no harm has been done; there 's nothing to repent of, and no reason why Prince Andreï should not love me *just as I am*. But what do I mean by just as I am? O my God! my God! why is he not here?"

Natasha grew calm for an instant, but then some instinct told her that, even though nothing had happened and no harm had been done, still the first purity of her love for Prince Andreï was destroyed.

And once more she let her imagination bring up her whole conversation with Kuragin, and she recalled his face and his motions, and the tender smile that this handsome, impudent man had given her while he was squeezing her arm.

CHAPTER XI

ANATOL KURAGIN was living in Moscow because his father had sent him from Petersburg, where he had been spending more than twenty thousand rubles a year, and had accumulated heavy debts as well, which his creditors were trying to oblige his father to pay.

His father explained to him that he would, for the last time, pay one-half of his debts, but only on condition that he would go to Moscow as aide to the governor-general of the city, an appointment which he obtained for him, and would at last try to win the hand of some rich heiress. He suggested the Princess Mariya or Julie Karagina.

Anatol consented and went to Moscow, where he took up his residence at Pierre's. At first Pierre received him with scant welcome, but at length became accustomed to him, and occasionally accompanied him on his sprees, and, under the pretense of a loan, gave him money.

Anatol, as Shinshin correctly stated the case, had instantly turned the heads of all the young ladies in Moscow, and particularly because he neglected them, and openly neglected them, for gipsy girls and French actresses, with the leading light of whom, Mlle. Georges, it was said, he was on terms of close intimacy. He never failed of a single drinking-bout given by Danilof or the other fast men of Moscow; he could drink steadily from night till morning, out-drinking every one else; moreover, he was always present at all the balls and receptions in the upper circles of society. Rumors were rife of various intrigues of his with married ladies in Moscow, and at the balls he always paid particular court to several.

But from young ladies, particularly those who were rich and in the marriage market, — most of whom were excessively plain, — Anatol kept at a respectful distance, and this arose from the fact, known only to a very few of his most intimate friends, that he had been married two years before. Two years before, while his regiment had been cantoned in Poland, a Polish proprietor of a small estate had forced Anatol to marry his daughter.

Anatol had soon after abandoned his wife, and, by engaging to send money periodically, he persuaded his father-in-law to let him still pass as a bachelor.

Anatol was always satisfied with his situation, with himself, and with other people. He was instinctively, by his whole nature, convinced that it was entirely impossible for him to live otherwise than as he was living, and that he had never in his life done anything wrong. He was in no condition to ponder on the effect that his behavior might have on others, or what might be the result of his behaving in this, that, or the other way. He was persuaded that, just as the duck was so created as always to be in the water, in the same way he was created by God for the purpose of living with an income of thirty thousand rubles a year, and of occupying the highest pinnacle of society. He was so firmly grounded in this opinion, that other people also, when they saw him, shared in his conviction, and never thought of refusing him either the foremost place in society, or the money which he took of any one he met, without ever thinking of repaying it.

He was no gambler; at least, he never showed sordid love for gain. He was not ostentatious. It was absolutely a matter of indifference to him what men thought of him. Still less was he open to the charge of ambition. Many times he had annoyed his father by injuring his own prospects, and he always made sport of dignities. He was not stingy, and he never refused any one who asked a favor of him. All that he cared for was "a good time" and women, and as, according to his opinion, there was nothing ignoble in these tastes, and he could not calculate the consequence for other people of the gratification of these tastes of his, he therefore considered himself irreproachable, sincerely scorned ordinary scoundrels and base men, and held his head high with a tranquil conscience.

Debauchees, those male Magdalens, have a secret feeling of blamelessness, such as is peculiar to the frail sisterhood; and it is based on the same hope of forgiveness. "She shall be forgiven much, for she hath loved much; and he shall be forgiven much, because he hath enjoyed much."

Dolokhof, back again in Moscow, after his exile and his adventures in Persia, and once more leading a dissipated and luxurious life and playing high, naturally became intimate with his old Petersburg companion, Kuragin, and made use of him for his own ends.

Anatol really liked Dolokhof for his wit, intelligence, and audacity. Dolokhof, who found the name, the notability, and the connections of Anatol Kuragin an admirable decoy for attracting rich young fellows into his clutches, made use of him and got enjoyment out of him without letting him suspect it. Besides the financial purpose for which Anatol served him, the act itself of controlling the will of another was an enjoyment, a habit, and a necessity for Dolokhof.

Natasha had made a deep impression on Kuragin. At supper after the opera, with all the enthusiasm of a connoisseur, he praised to Dolokhof her arms, her shoulders, her ankles, and her hair, and he expressed his intention of making love to her. The possible consequences of such love-making Anatol did not stop to consider; nor was it in him to foresee them any more than in any other of his escapades.

"Yes, she's pretty, my dear fellow; but she's not for us," said Dolokhof.

"I am going to tell my sister to invite her to dinner. — How's that?" suggested Anatol.

"You had better wait till she's married."....

"You know," said Anatol, "I adore young girls; you can turn their heads so quickly."

"You have already fallen into the hands of one young girl," said Dolokhof, who knew about Anatol's marriage. "See?"

"Well, can't get caught a second time, — hey?" replied Anatol, good-naturedly laughing.

CHAPTER XII

The next day the Rostofs stayed at home, and no one came to see them. Marya Dmitrievna had a confidential conversation with her father, taking pains to keep it a secret from Natasha. Nevertheless she suspected that they were discussing the old prince, and concocting some scheme. It disquieted and humiliated her. She was every moment expecting Prince Andreï to come, and twice that day she sent the dvornik to the Bolkonskys' to learn if he had arrived. But he had not yet come.

It was now more trying to her than during the first days of his absence. Her impatience and melancholy thoughts about him were intensified by an unpleasant recollection of her interview with the Princess Mariya and the scene with the old prince, as well as by a vague and undefinable fear and uneasiness. She had a notion that either he would not come at all, or that before he came something would happen. She found it impossible, as before, to have calm and collected thoughts about him when alone by herself. As soon as her thoughts turned to him her recollections of him were confused by recollections of the old prince, of the Princess Mariya, of the operatic performance, and of Kuragin. Again the question arose whether she was to blame, whether her troth plighted to Prince Andreï were not already broken; and again she would picture to herself, even to the most trifling details, every word, every gesture, every slightest shadow in the play of expression on the face of that man who had succeeded in arousing in her such a terrible and inexplicable feeling.

In the eyes of the home circle, Natasha seemed livelier than usual, but she was far from being as calm and happy as she had been before.

On Sunday morning Marya Dmitrievna proposed to her guests to attend mass at the parish chapel of Uspenie na Mohiltsakh.

"I don't like these fashionable churches," said she, evidently priding herself on her independence. "God is everywhere One. We have an excellent pope, and deacon as well, and the service is well performed. What kind of worship is it to have concerts given in the choir? I don't like it. It 's mischievous nonsense."

Marya Dmitrievna liked Sundays, and had them kept as high festivals. Her house was thoroughly washed and cleaned on Saturday; neither she nor the people within her gates did any work — they wore their best clothes, and all went to mass. On Sunday she had an extra fine dinner prepared, and her servants were provided with vodka and a roasted goose or a sucking pig.

But nothing in the whole house gave more decided evidence of its being a holiday than Marya Dmitrievna's broad, stern face, which on this occasion wore an unchangeable expression of solemn festivity.

After mass, while they were drinking their coffee in the drawing-room, where the furniture covers had been removed, a servant announced to Marya Dmitrievna that the carriage was at the door. She drew a long face, and, putting on her best shawl, in which she always paid visits, she got up and announced that she was going to see Prince Nikolaï Andreyevitch Bolkonsky, to have an understanding with him in regard to Natasha.

After Marya Dmitrievna had taken her departure, a *modiste* from Madame Chalmé's came, and Natasha, retiring to the next room and shutting the door, occupied herself with trying on her new gowns and was very glad of the diversion.

Just as she had put on a hastily basted and still sleeveless waist, and was standing in front of the mirror, bending her head around to see how the back fitted, she heard in the drawing-room the lively tones of her father's voice, mingled with those of a woman, and it made her blush. It was Ellen's voice.

Natasha had not time to take off the experimental waist before the door opened, and into the room came the Countess Bezukhaya, beaming with a good-natured and flattering smile, and wearing a dark purple velvet dress, with a high collar.

"*Ah, ma délicieuse!*" she exclaimed to the blushing Natasha. "*Charmante!* No, she is quite unlike any one else, my dear count," said she, turning to the count, who followed her in. "The idea of living in Moscow and not going anywhere! No, I shall not let you off. This evening Mlle. Georges is going to recite for me, and we shall have a crowd, and if you don't bring your beauties, who are far better than Mlle. Georges, I shall never forgive you. My husband is away, he is gone to Tver; otherwise I should have sent him to persuade you. Do not fail to come. Don't fail — at ten o'clock."

She nodded to the dressmaker, whom she knew, and received a most respectful courtesy, and then sat down in an arm-chair near the mirror, picturesquely disposing the folds of her velvet dress. She did not cease to chatter with good-natured and merry volubility, constantly saying pleasant, flattering things about Natasha's beauty. She examined her dresses and praised them, and also managed to say a good word for a new dress of her own, *en gaz métallique* — metallic gauze — which she had just received from Paris, and advised Natasha to get one like it.

"Besides, it would be extremely becoming to you, my charmer," said she.

The smile of pleasure did not leave Natasha's face. She felt happy and exhilarated by the praise of this gracious Countess Bezukhaya, who had heretofore seemed to her such an inaccessible, grand lady, and was now so cordial to her. Natasha's spirits rose, and she felt almost in love with this woman, who was so beautiful and so good-natured.

Ellen, on her part, was sincerely enchanted by Natasha, and wanted her to have a good time. Anatol had urged her to help on his acquaintance with her, and it was for this purpose that she called on the Rostofs. The idea of helping her brother in such a flirtation was amusing to her.

Although that winter in Petersburg she had felt a grudge against Natasha for alienating Boris from her, it had now entirely passed from her mind; and, with all her heart, she felt kindly disposed toward Natasha. As she was taking her departure, she called her *protégée* aside: —

"Last evening my brother dined with me — we almost died of laughing — he eats just nothing at all, and can only sigh for you, my charmer! He is in love, madly in love with you, *ma chère.*"

Natasha flushed crimson on hearing those words.

"How she blushes! How she blushes, *ma délicieuse,*" pursued Ellen. "Don't fail to come. Even if you are in love, that is no reason for making a nun of yourself. Even if you are engaged, I am sure that your future husband would prefer to have you go into society, rather than die of tedium in his absence."

"Of course she knows that I am engaged; of course she and her husband, she and Pierre, that good, honest Pierre, have talked and laughed about this," said Natasha to herself. "Of course there is no harm in it."

And again, under Ellen's influence, all that hitherto seemed terrible to her seemed simple and natural.

"And she is such a *grande dame,* and so kind, and she seems to like me so heartily!" said Natasha to herself. "And why should n't I have a good time?" queried Natasha, looking at Ellen with wide eyes full of amazement.

Marya Dmitrievna returned in time for dinner, silent and solemn, having evidently suffered a rebuff at the old prince's. She was still laboring under too much excitement from her encounter to be able to give a calm account of it. To the count's question, she replied that everything would be all right, and she would tell him about it the next day.

When she was informed of the Countess Bezukhaya's visit, and the invitation for the evening, she said: —

"I don't like the idea of your going to Bezukhaya's, and I should advise you not to; however, if you have already promised, go; perhaps you will have some amusement," she added, addressing Natasha.

CHAPTER XIII

Count Ilya Andreyitch took his young ladies to the Countess Bezukhaya's.

The reception was fairly well attended, but the most of the company were strangers to Natasha. Count Ilya Andreyitch saw with dissatisfaction that the larger majority of those present consisted of men and women noted for their free and easy behavior.

Mlle. Georges stood in one corner of the drawing-room surrounded by young men. There were a number of Frenchmen, and among them Métivier, who since Ellen's arrival had become an intimate at her house. Count Ilya Andreyitch decided not to take a hand at the card-table, or to leave the girls, but to take his departure as soon as Mlle. Georges had finished her recitation.

Anatol was at the door, evidently on the lookout for the Rostofs. As soon as he had exchanged greetings with the count, he joined Natasha, and followed her into the room. The moment she saw him, she was assailed, just as she had been at the theater, by a mixed sense of gratified vanity that she pleased him, and of fear, because of the absence of moral barriers between her and him.

Ellen received Natasha effusively, and was loud in praise of her beauty and her toilet.

Soon after their arrival, Mlle. Georges retired from the room to change her costume. In the meantime, chairs were arranged in the drawing-room, and the guests began to take their seats. Anatol procured a chair for Natasha, and was just going to sit next her; but the count, keeping a sharp eye on his daughter, took the seat next her. Anatol sat behind.

Mlle. Georges, with plump and dimpled arms all bare, and with a red shawl flung across one shoulder, came out into the space around which the chairs were ranged, and assumed an unnatural pose. A murmur of admiration was heard.

Mlle. Georges threw a stern and gloomy glance around, and began to recite certain lines in French, in which the guilty love of a mother for her son is delineated. In places she raised her voice; then, again, she spoke in a whisper, triumphantly tossing her head; and in other places she broke short off, or spoke in deep, hoarse tones, rolling her eyes.

"*Adorable!*" .... "*Divin!*" .... "*Délicieux!*" were the encomiums heard on all sides.

Natasha's eyes were fastened on the stout actress, but she heard nothing, saw nothing, understood nothing, of what was going on before her; she felt that she was irrevocably drawn again into that strange, mad world, so far removed from the past world, where it was impossible to know what was right and what was wrong, what was reasonable and what was foolish. Behind her sat Anatol, and she was conscious of his nearness, and with terror awaited what might happen.

After the first monologue, the whole company arose and crowded around Mlle. Georges, expressing their enthusiasm.

" How beautiful she is ! " said Natasha to her father, who had got up with the rest, and was starting to push his way through the throng toward the actress.

"I cannot think so when I look at you," said Anatol, sitting down next Natasha. He spoke so that she only could hear what he said : "You are charming.... Since the first moment that I saw you, I have not ceased...."

"Come, let us go, Natasha," interrupted the count, returning to his daughter. "How pretty she is!"

Natasha, making no reply, followed her father, but gave Anatol a look of wondering amazement.

After several more recitations, Mlle. Georges took her departure, and the Countess Bezukhaya invited her guests into the ball-room.

The count wanted to go home, but Ellen begged him not to spoil her improvised ball. The Rostofs remained. Anatol took Natasha out for a waltz ; and while they were on the floor, and he clasped her waist and hand, he told her that she was *ravissante*, and that he loved her.

During the Écossaise, which she danced with Kuragin also, Anatol said nothing to her while they were by themselves, but merely gazed at her. Natasha was in doubt whether she had not dreamed what he said to her during the waltz.

At the end of the first figure he again pressed her hand. Natasha lifted startled eyes to his ; but his look and his smile had such an expression of self-confidence and flattering tenderness that she found it impossible to look at him and say to him what was on her tongue to say. She dropped her eyes.

"Do not say such things to me ; I am betrothed — I love another," she hurriedly whispered.

She glanced at him. Anatol was not in the least confused or chagrined at what she said.

"Don't speak to me about that. What difference does it make to me?" he asked. "I tell you I am madly, madly in love with you. Am I to blame because you are bewitching?.... It's our turn to lead."

Natasha, excited and anxious, looked around with wide, frightened eyes, and gave the impression of being gayer than usual. She remembered almost nothing of what took place that evening. While they were dancing the Écossaise and the grossvater, her father came and urged her to go home with him, but she begged to stay a little longer.

Wherever she was, whoever engaged her in conversation, she was conscious all the time of *his* eyes upon her. Afterwards she remembered asking her father's permission to go to the dressing-room to adjust her dress, and how Ellen followed her, and told her with a laugh that her brother was in love with her. She remembered how, in the little divan-room, she had again met Anatol, how Ellen had suddenly disappeared, leaving her alone with him, and how Anatol, seizing her hand, had said, in a tender voice:—

"I cannot call on you, but must I never see you? I love you madly, desperately! Can I not see you?".... And then, blocking her way, he had bent down his face close to her face.

His great, gleaming, masculine eyes were so near to her face that she could see nothing else except those eyes of his.

"Natali?" she heard his voice whisper, with a questioning inflection, and her hand was squeezed almost painfully.

"Natali?"

"I do not understand at all; I have nothing to say," said her glance.

His glowing lips approached her lips—but at that instant she felt that her deliverance had come, for the sound of Ellen's footsteps and rustle of her dress were heard in the room.

Natasha glanced at Ellen; then, blushing and trembling, she gave him a terrified, questioning look, and started for the door.

"One word, only one, in God's name!" said Anatol.

She paused. She felt that it was a necessity for her to hear that "single word," which would afford her an explanation of what had happened, and allow her something tangible to answer.

"Natali, one word, only one," he kept repeating, evidently not knowing what to say; and he repeated it until Ellen came close to him.

Ellen and Natasha returned together to the drawing-room. Declining the invitation to stay to supper, the Rostofs went home.

That night Natasha could not sleep at all. She was tormented by the puzzling question, which she loved, Anatol or Prince Andreï? She loved Prince Andreï, — she had a very distinct remembrance of how warmly she loved him.

But she loved Anatol also, there could be no doubt about that. "Otherwise, how could all this have taken place?" she asked herself. "If it was possible for me, on saying good-by to him, to answer his smiles with smiles, — if I could permit myself to go so far, then of course I was in love with him at first sight. He certainly is good and noble and handsome, and it is impossible not to be in love with him. What can I do when I love him and love the other too?" she asked herself, and found no solution to the terrible problem.

CHAPTER XIV

Morning came, with its occupations and bustle. All arose, stirred about, engaged in talk; once more the *modistes* came; again Marya Dmitrievna appeared and summoned them down to tea.

Natasha, with wide-open eyes, as if trying to anticipate and intercept every glance fixed upon her, looked anxiously about, and struggled to seem the same as usual.

After breakfast, which was her favorite time, Marya Dmitrievna sat down in her easy-chair, and called Natasha and the old count to her.

"Well," — with strong emphasis on the word, — "well, my friends, now I have thought the whole matter over, and this is my advice," she began. "Yesterday, as you know, I went to see Prince Nikolaï. Well," again with strong emphasis, "I had an interview with him. He thought to shout me down, but I am not to be shouted down so easily. I had it all out with him."

"Well, what did he do?" asked the count.

"'What did he do?' He is a raving maniac.... won't listen to anything. Well, what 's the use of talking? And, meanwhile, we are tormenting this poor girl so!" said Marya Dmitrievna. "And my advice to you is to transact your business, and go home.... to Otradnoye.... and there wait till...."

"Oh, no!" cried Natasha.

"Yes, you must go," maintained Marya Dmitrievna, "and wait there. If your betrothed should come here now, there would infallibly be a quarrel; but if he is left alone with the old man they will talk the whole thing over calmly, and then he will come for you."

Ilya Andreyitch approved of this plan, which instantly appealed to his good judgment. If the old prince was appeased, then they could rejoin him at Moscow or Luisiya Gorui; if not, as it would be contrary to his wishes, then the wedding could take place at Otradnoye.

"That is true as gospel," said he. "Only I am sorry that I went there and took her," said the old count.

"There 's nothing to be sorry for. As long as you were here you could n't help paying him that mark of respect. Well, if he does not approve, it is his affair," said Marya Dmitrievna, making search for something in her reticule. "Besides, the trousseau is all ready, so what have you to wait for? And what is n't ready I will send to you. Indeed, I am sorry about it, but you would be much better off to return — and God be with you!"

Having succeeded in finding what she was searching

for, she handed it to Natasha. It was a letter from the Princess Mariya.

"She 's written to you. How she torments herself, poor soul! She is afraid you will imagine she does not like you."

"Well, and she does n't like me," said Natasha.

"Nonsense! Don't say such a thing!" cried Marya Dmitrievna.

"I take no one's opinion. I know she does not like me," said Natasha, boldly, snatching the letter, and her face assumed such an expression of hard and angry determination that it caused Marya Dmitrievna to look at her more closely, and frown.

"Don't you contradict me that way, matushka," said she. "What I tell you is the truth. Go and reply to her letter."

Natasha made no rejoinder, and retired to her own room to read the Princess Mariya's letter.

The princess wrote that she was in despair, owing to the misunderstanding that had arisen between them. Whatever were her father's feelings, she wrote, she besought Natasha to be assured that it was impossible for her not to love her, as the choice of her brother, for whose happiness she was ready to sacrifice everything. "Moreover," she wrote, "do not imagine that my father was unkindly disposed toward you. He is old and feeble, and you must excuse him; but he is good and generous, and will not fail to love the one who can make his son happy."

The Princess Mariya further asked Natasha to appoint a time when they could have another meeting.

After reading the letter through, Natasha sat down at the writing-desk to pen a reply.

"*Chère princesse*," she wrote, hastily and mechanically, and paused. What more could she write, after all that had taken place the evening before?

"Yes, yes, all that is past, and now, already, everything is different," she said to herself, as she pondered over the letter thus begun. "Ought I to break our engagement? Is it really my duty? It is frightful!"....

And, to escape from these terrible thoughts, she went to Sonya, and began to help her pick out her embroidery patterns.

After dinner Natasha again retired to her room, and took up the Princess Mariya's letter.

"Can it be that all is really over between us?" she mused. "Can it be that this has happened so quickly, and that all that is past is completely annihilated?"

She recalled, in all its intensity, her love for Prince Andreĭ, and yet, at the same time, she felt that she was in love with Kuragin. She vividly pictured herself as Prince Andreĭ's wife, and recalled those dreams of happiness with him which she had so many times enjoyed in imagination, and at the same time, fired with passionate emotions, she recalled every detail of her last meeting with Anatol.

"Why could it not be possible to love them both at once?" she more than once asked herself, in the depths of perplexity. "Then only could I be perfectly happy; but now I must choose, and I cannot be happy to be deprived of either of them. One thing is certain," she thought, "to tell Prince Andreĭ what has happened, or to hide it from him, is impossible. But as far as *he* is concerned no harm has been done. Can I break off forever, though, with that delicious love for Prince Andreĭ, to whom my life has been devoted so long?"

"Baruishnya," said a maid, in a whisper, and coming into the room with a mysterious face, "a little man told me to give you this."

The maid handed her a note. "Only for Christ's sake...." she exclaimed, as Natasha, without thinking, mechanically broke the seal and began to read. It was a love-letter from Anatol, and, while she did not comprehend a word of it, she comprehended enough to know that it was from him, from the man she loved. Yes, she loved him, else how could happen what had happened? How could she have in her hand a love-letter from him?

With trembling hands Natasha held this passionate love-letter, composed for Anatol by Dolokhof, and in reading it she found it contained what corresponded to everything which it seemed to her she herself felt.

"Last evening decided my fate; you must love me or I die. I have no other alternative." So the letter began. Then he proceeded to say that he knew her parents would not consent to her marriage to him for various secret reasons which he could reveal to her alone, but that if she loved him, it was enough to say the little word *yes*, and no mortal power could suffice to destroy their bliss. Love conquers all. He would spirit her away, and fly with her to the ends of the earth.

"Yes, yes, I love him," mused Natasha, as she read the letter over for the twentieth time, and tried to discover some peculiarly deep meaning in every word.

That evening Marya Dmitrievna was going to the Arkharofs', and she invited the young ladies to accompany her. Natasha, under the pretext of a headache, remained at home.

CHAPTER XV

Sonya, on her return late that evening, went to Natasha's room, and, to her amazement, found her still dressed, and asleep on the divan. On the table near her lay Anatol's letter, wide open. Sonya picked the letter up, and began to read it.

She read it, and gazed at the sleeping Natasha, trying to discover in her face some key to the mystery of what she had read, and finding none. The expression of Natasha's face was calm, sweet, and happy.

Sonya, pale, and trembling with fright and emotion, clutching her breast lest she should choke, sat down in an easy-chair and melted into tears.

"How is it I have seen nothing of this? How can this have gone so far? Is it possible she has ceased to love Prince Andreï? And how can she tolerate this Kuragin? He is a deceiver and a scoundrel — that is evident. What will Nicolas do, dear, noble Nicolas, when he learns of this? So this is what has caused her agitation and unnatural behavior for the last three days," said Sonya to herself. "But it is impossible that she is in love with him. Most likely she opened the letter without knowing from whom it came. In all probability she was offended. She could n't have done such a thing knowingly."

Sonya wiped away her tears, and went close to Natasha, and scrutinized her face.

"Natasha!" she murmured, almost inaudibly.

Natasha awoke and looked at Sonya.

"Ah, are you back already?"

And in the impulse of the sudden awakening she gave her friend a warm and affectionate hug, but, instantly noticing that Sonya's face was troubled, her face also became troubled and suspicious.

"Sonya, have you been reading that letter?" she asked.

"Yes," murmured Sonya.

Natasha smiled triumphantly.

"No, Sonya, it is impossible to hold out any longer," said she. "I cannot hide it from you any more. You know, we love each other. .... Sonya, my darling, he has written me .... Sonya ...."

Sonya, not believing her own ears, stared at Natasha with open eyes.

"But Bolkonsky!" she exclaimed.

"Akh! Sonya — akh! if you could only know how happy I am!" cried Natasha. "You can't imagine what such love is ...."

"But, Natasha, do you mean to say that *the other* is all at an end?"

Natasha gazed at Sonya with wide-open eyes, as if she did not understand her question.

"What, have you broken with Prince Andreï?" demanded Sonya.

"Akh! you can't comprehend it; don't talk nonsense. Listen to me," said Natasha, with a flash of ill-temper.

"No, I cannot believe this," insisted Sonya. "I

cannot understand it. How can you have loved one man a whole year, and then suddenly.... Why, you have only seen him three times! Natasha, I don't believe you. You are joking! In three days to forget everything? and so...."

"Three days!" interrupted Natasha. "It seems to me I have loved him a hundred years. It seems to me I have never loved any one else before him. You cannot comprehend it. Sonya, wait; sit down!" Natasha threw her arms around her, and kissed her. "I have been told, and you have probably heard, that such love as this existed; but now for the first time I experience it. It is not like the one before. The moment I set eyes on him, I felt that he was my master, that I was his slave, and that I could not help loving him. Yes, his slave! Whatever he commands me, I obey him. You can't understand that. What can I do? What can I do, Sonya?" pleaded Natasha, with a happy, frightened face.

"But just think what you are doing," insisted Sonya. "I cannot let this go on. This clandestine correspondence! How could you permit him to go so far?" asked she, with a horror and aversion which she tried in vain to hide.

"I have told you," replied Natasha, "that I have no will about it! Why can't you understand? I love him!"

"Then I will not let it go any farther. I shall tell the whole story," cried Sonya, with a burst of tears.

"For God's sake.... I beg of you.... if you tell, you are my enemy!" exclaimed Natasha. "Do you wish me to be unhappy? Do you wish to separate us...."

Seeing how passionately excited Natasha was, Sonya shed tears of shame and regret for her friend.

"But what has passed between you?" she asked. "What has he said to you? Why does he not come to the house?"

Natasha made no reply to this question.

"For God's sake, Sonya, don't tell any one, don't torment me," entreated Natasha. "Remember, it's never right to interfere in such matters. I have trusted you...."

"But why all this secrecy? Why does n't he come to the house?" insisted Sonya. "Why does he not openly ask for your hand? You know Prince Andreï gave you absolute freedom, if such were the case; but I don't believe in this man. Natasha, have you considered what his *secret reasons* may be?"

Natasha gazed at Sonya with wondering eyes. Evidently this question had not occurred to her before, and she knew not what answer to make.

"What reasons? I don't know. But of course there must be reasons."

Sonya sighed, and shook her head incredulously.

"If there were reasons...." she began; but Natasha, foreseeing her objections, with frightened eagerness interrupted her.

"Sonya, it is impossible to doubt him, impossible, wholly impossible, do you understand?" she cried.

"Does he love you?"

"Love me!" repeated Natasha, with a smile of contemptuous pity for her friend's incredulity. "You have read his letter, you have seen him, have you not?"

"But if he were a dishonorable man?"

"*He!*.... a dishonorable man! If you knew him!" exclaimed Natasha.

"If he were an honorable man, then he ought either to explain his intentions, or else cease to see you; and if you are not willing to do this, then I shall. I shall write him, I shall tell your papa," said Sonya, decidedly.

"But I cannot live without him," cried Natasha.

"Natasha, I don't understand you! What are you saying? Think of your father, think of Nicolas."

"I want no one, I love no one but him! How dare you assert that he is dishonorable? Don't you know that I love him?" cried Natasha. "Sonya, go, I don't wish to quarrel with you! go away, for God's sake, go away! you see how tormented I am," she screamed in a voice of repressed anger and despair. Sonya began to sob, and rushed from the room.

Natasha went to her writing-table, and without pausing a moment wrote the letter to the Princess Mariya which she had not been able to write the morning before. In this letter she laconically informed the princess that all misunderstandings were at an end, that taking advantage of Prince Andreï's generosity in giving her perfect freedom, she begged her to forget all that had happened, and to forgive her if she had been to blame in respect to her; but that she could never be his wife. At that moment all seemed to her so easy, simple, and clear!

The Rostofs were to start for the country on Friday, and on Wednesday the count went with an intending purchaser to his pod-Moskovnaya estate.

On the day of the count's trip, Sonya and Natasha were invited to a great dinner at the Kuragins', and Marya Dmitrievna went as their chaperon.

At this dinner Natasha again met Anatol, and Sonya observed that Natasha had with him some mysterious conversation, which she evidently wished not to be overheard; and during all the dinner-time she seemed to be more agitated than ever. On their return home, Natasha was the first to begin the explanation which her friend was anxious for.

"There, Sonya, you have said all sorts of foolish things about him," Natasha began, in a cajoling tone, such as children use when they want to be flattered. "He and I came to a clear understanding to-day."

"Now, what do you mean? What did he say, Natasha? How glad I am that you are not angry with me! Tell me all, tell me the whole story. What did he say to you?"

Natasha pondered.

"Akh! Sonya, if you only knew him as I do.... he said.... he asked me what sort of an engagement I had with Bolkonsky. He was delighted that it depended on me to break it off."

Sonya sighed mournfully.

"But you have n't broken your engagement with Bolkonsky, have you?"

"Well, perhaps I *have* broken my engagement with Bolkonsky! Perhaps it is all at an end! What makes you have such hard thoughts of me?"

"I have no hard thoughts of you; only I can't understand this...."

"Wait, Sonya, and you will understand the whole thing. You will learn what a man he is! But don't harbor hard thoughts of me, or of him either."

"I harbor no hard thoughts of any one; I love you and I am sorry for you all. But what am I to do?"

Sonya, however, was not blinded by the affectionate manner in which Natasha treated her. The more gentle and insinuating Natasha's face grew, the more stern and serious became Sonya's face.

"Natasha," said she, "you yourself begged me not to say any more about this to you, and I have not; and now you reopen it yourself. Natasha, I have no faith in him. Why all this mystery?"

"There you begin again!" interposed Natasha.

"Natasha, I am afraid for you."

"Afraid of what?"

"I am afraid that you are going to your ruin," said Sonya, in a resolute voice, frightened herself at what she said.

An angry look again came into Natasha's face.

"I will go to my ruin, I certainly will, and the faster the better. It 's no affair of yours. It won't hurt you, even if it does hurt me. Leave me, leave! I hate you!"

"Natasha!" expostulated Sonya, in dismay.

"I hate you! I hate you! We can never be friends any more!"

Natasha rushed out of the room.

Natasha had nothing more to say to Sonya, and avoided her. With that peculiar expression of nervous preoccupation and guilt, she wandered up and down the rooms, trying one occupation after another, and instantly abandoning them.

Hard as this was for Sonya, she did not let her out of her sight for a single moment, but followed her everywhere she went.

On the day before the count's return, Sonya observed that Natasha spent the whole morning at the parlor window, as if in expectation of some one, and that she made some sort of signal to an officer who drove by, and who Sonya thought must have been Anatol.

Sonya began to observe her friend still more closely, and remarked that during all dinner-time and throughout the evening, Natasha was in a strange and unnatural state of excitement, answering at random the questions that were asked her, beginning and not finishing sentences, and laughing at everything.

After tea, Sonya saw a timid chambermaid watching for her at Natasha's door. She let her pass in, and listening at the keyhole discovered that she was the bearer of another letter.

And suddenly it became clear to Sonya that Natasha had some terrible plan on foot for that evening. Sonya knocked loudly at her door. Natasha refused to admit her.

"She is going to elope with him!" said Sonya to herself. "She is quite ready for anything. Her face to-day had a peculiarly pitiful and determined expression. She wept when she said good-by to her father," Sonya remembered. "Yes, it is evident that she is going to elope with him! What can I do about it?" she mused, recalling all of the circumstances that now made her think Natasha had adopted some terrible resolution. "The count is away. What can I do? Write to Kuragin and demand of him an explanation? But who would make him reply to it? Write to Pierre, as Prince Andreï told me to do in case of misfortune?.... But perhaps she has already broken with Bolkonsky! Certainly Natasha sent her letter to the princess last evening..... If her father were only here!"

It seemed terrible to tell Marya Dmitrievna, who had such confidence in Natasha. "But what else can I do?" mused Sonya, as she stood in the dark corridor. "Now or never is the time to show that I am grateful to this dear family, and that I love Nicolas. No! even if I have to stay awake for three nights, I will not leave this corridor, and I will detain her by main force; and I will not allow any scandal to happen to this family," she said to herself.

CHAPTER XVI

ANATOL had recently transferred his lodgings to Dolokhof's house. The plan of abducting the young countess had been suggested and arranged by Dolokhof some days before, and on that day when Sonya, listening at Natasha's door, had determined to protect her, this scheme was all ready to be carried into execution.

Natasha had agreed to meet Kuragin at ten o'clock that evening, at the rear entrance. Kuragin was to place her in a troïka which should be in waiting, and carry her sixty versts to the village of Kamienko, where an unfrocked pope would be in readiness to perform a mock marriage ceremony. At Kamienko a relay would be ready to take them toward Warsaw, and thence by regular stages they would make their escape abroad.

Anatol had his passport and his *padorozhnaya*, or order for post-horses, and ten thousand rubles obtained from his sister, and ten thousand obtained through Dolokhof's mediation.

Two witnesses — Khvostikof, formerly a law clerk, who was now a creature of Dolokhof's, and Makarin, a hussar on the retired list, a weak and good-natured fellow who had an inordinate affection for Kuragin — were sitting in the front room over their tea.

In Dolokhof's large cabinet, the walls of which were hung from floor to ceiling with Persian rugs, bearskins, and weapons, sat Dolokhof himself, in a traveling beshmet and top-boots, before an open desk, on which lay bills and packages of money. Anatol, in his uniform, unbuttoned, came in from the room where the two witnesses were sitting, and was passing through the cabinet into the adjoining room, where his French valet and another servant were packing up the last remaining effects.

Dolokhof was making out the accounts and writing the amounts on a sheet of paper.

"Well!" said he, "you will have to give two thousand to Khvostikof."

"All right, give it to him!" said Anatol.

"Makarka"—this was an affectionate nickname for Makarin—"is so disinterested that he would go through fire and water for you. There now, the accounts are all made out," said Dolokhof, calling his attention to the paper. "Is that right?"

"Yes, of course it is," said Anatol, evidently not heeding what was said, and looking into vacancy with a dreamy expression, and a smile that did not leave his face.

Dolokhof shut the desk with a slam, and turned to Kuragin with an amused smile:—

"But see here, now! you'd better give this up; there's still time," said he.

"Fool! durak!" said Anatol, "stop talking nonsense. If you only knew!.... But only the devil knows what this is to me!"

"Honestly! Throw it up!" said Dolokhof. "I'll tell you the honest truth. Do you imagine that this is a joke that you are going into?"

"There you are stirring me up again. Go to the devil," exclaimed Anatol, scowling; "I have no time to listen to your idiotic twaddle!"

And he started to leave the room.

Dolokhof smiled scornfully and condescendingly as Anatol turned away.

"Wait," he cried after him, "I am not joking, I am telling you the truth; come here, come here, I say!"

Anatol came back into the room again, and trying to concentrate his attention, gazed at Dolokhof, apparently quite under the influence of his will.

"Listen to me, I speak for the last time. Why should I jest with you? Have I done anything to thwart you? Who is it that has made all the arrangements for you who found your priest for you, who procured your passport, who got the money for you? Have n't I done the whole thing?"

"Yes, and I thank you. Do you imagine I am not grateful?"

Anatol sighed and embraced his friend.

"I have been helping you; but it is my place to tell you the truth: it is a dangerous game, and if it misses fire, a stupid one. Suppose you elope with her — well and good. What will be the next step? It will be discovered that you are married. You will be prosecuted as a criminal...."

"Akh! what nonsense! what stupid nonsense!" cried Anatol, frowning again. "Have I not told you again and again? Hey?"

And Anatol, with that peculiar passion for argument characteristic of men of small intellects, when they want to show their wit, reiterated the considerations which he had laid before Dolokhof a hundred times.

"I have told you again and again; my mind is made up: if this marriage is invalid," said he, doubling over his finger, "of course I am not responsible for it; well, then, suppose it is valid; it 's just the same, and, when we are abroad, no one will know the difference; that 's a fact, is it not? So say no more, say no more, say no more!"

"But, really, give it up! You will only get yourself into a scrape...."

"Go to the devil!" screamed Anatol, and, tearing his hair, he rushed into the next room; then he came straight back, and sat down astride of a chair in front of Dolokhof. "The devil only knows what this is to me! Hey? Just see, how it beats!" He took Dolokhof's hand and put it on his heart. "Ah! what an ankle! my dear, what eyes! she 's a goddess! Hey?"

Dolokhof, smiling unsympathetically, looked at him out of his handsome, impudent eyes, evidently feeling inclined to have a little more sport out of him.

"Well, but when your money is gone, what then?"

"What then? Hey?" repeated Anatol, with a touch

of genuine distress at the thought of the future. "What then? I am sure I don't know. But what is the use of talking nonsense?" He looked at his watch. "It's time."

Anatol went into the next room. "Hurry up, there! Are n't you almost ready? What are you dawdling so for?" he cried, addressing the servants.

Dolokhof put up the money, and, shouting to his man to have a luncheon of eatables and drinkables prepared for the travelers for their journey, he went into the room where Khvostikof and Makarin were waiting.

Anatol had flung himself down on the ottoman in the cabinet, and, with his head resting on his hand, was dreamily smiling and whispering tender words.

"Come and have something to eat. Have a drink, then!" cried Dolokhof, from the next room.

"I don't wish anything," replied Anatol, still with the smile on his handsome lips.

"Come, Balaga is here!"

Anatol got up and went into the dining-room. Balaga was a famous troïka driver, who, for half a dozen years, had known Dolokhof and Anatol, and had furnished them with their troïkas. More than once, when Anatol's regiment had been at Tver, he had started at nightfall from Tver, set him down in Moscow before daybreak, and brought him back by the following morning. More than once he had taken Dolokhof out of the reach of pursuers. More than once he had taken them out to drive with gipsies and *damotchki*, — nice little dames, — as Balaga called fast women. More than once at their instigation he had run down pedestrians and izvoshchiks in the Moscow streets, and always his "gentlemen," as he called them, had rescued him from the penalty. More than one horse he had broken down in their service. More than once he had been thrashed by them; many times had they given him champagne and Madeira, which he specially affected, and he knew of escapades of theirs which would have condemned any ordinary man to Siberia.

During their orgies, they had often invited Balaga to

take part, and made him drink and dance with the gipsies, and more than one thousand rubles of theirs had passed through his hands.

In service for them, he had twenty times a year risked life and limb, and in accomplishing their deviltry he had almost killed more horses than their money would ever pay for. But he was fond of them; he was fond of that mad pace of eighteen versts an hour; he was fond of upsetting some harmless izvoshchik from his box, or running down some pedestrian on the street-crossings, and of dashing at full tilt down the Moscow streets. He was fond of hearing behind him that wild cry of drunken voices, "Pashol! pashol!" when it was already a physical impossibility for his horses to carry them a step further; he was fond of winding his whip-lash around a peasant's neck, who shrank back more dead than alive as he passed by. "Real gentlemen," he called them!

Anatol and Dolokhof also were fond of Balaga because of his masterly skill in handling the lines, and because his tastes were similar to theirs. With others he drove hard bargains, charging twenty-five rubles for a two hours' outing, and he himself rarely condescended to drive others, but more frequently sent one of his subordinates. But with his "gentlemen," as he called them, he himself always went, and never charged for his extra labor. Only when he learned through the valets that money was plentiful, he would come, after an interval of many months, and, very soberly and obsequiously, bowing low, would ask to be helped out of his difficulties.

His "gentlemen" always made him take a seat.

"You will excuse me, batyushka Feodor Ivanuitch," or "your illustriousness," he would say, "I am entirely out of horses; I pray you to advance me enough to go to get more at the Yarmanka."[1]

And Anatol and Dolokhof, if they happened to be in funds, would give him a thousand or so of rubles.

Balaga was twenty-seven years old, a stubbed, red-haired, snub-nosed muzhik, with fiery red complexion,

[1] *Yarmanka* for Yarmarka, Jahrmarkt, annual market.

and still more fiery red neck, with glittering little eyes, and a scrubby beard. He wore a fine, blue, silk-lined kaftan, and over that a sheepskin polushubka.

He crossed himself, turning to the shrine corner, as he came in, and advanced toward Dolokhof, holding out a small, black hand.

"Feodor Ivanovitch, your good health," he exclaimed, with a low bow.

"How are you, brother!.... There he is!"

"Good health, your illustriousness," said he, addressing Anatol, who came in at that moment, and offered him also his dirty hand.

"I ask you, Balaga," said Anatol, clapping his hand on his shoulder, "do you love me, or not, hey? Now there's a chance for you to prove it. .... What horses have you come with, hey?"

"Those your man ordered, your own wild ones," said Balaga.

"Now see here, Balaga. No matter if you slaughter all three of your horses, provided you get us there within three hours. Hey?"

"If we slaughter them, how shall we get there?" replied Balaga, with a wink.

"I'll smash your snout for you! A truce to joking," cried Anatol, suddenly, with glaring eyes.

"Who's joking?" exclaimed the driver, with a laugh. "Do I ever grudge anything for my 'gentlemen'? Whatever my horses can show in the way of speed, that we will do."

"Ah!" grunted Anatol. "Sit down, then."

"Yes, why not sit down?" said Dolokhof.

"I will stand, Feodor Ivanovitch."

"Sit down, no nonsense. Have a drink," said Anatol, and poured him out a great glass of Madeira. The driver's eyes flashed at the sight of the wine. Refusing at first, for manners' sake, he drank it down, and wiped his mouth with a red silk handkerchief which he kept in the top of his hat.

"Well, when shall we start, your illustriousness?"

"Let me see," Anatol glanced at his watch; "start

pretty soon now. See here, Balaga, hey! You will get there on time?"

"Well, it depends on the start. If we get off luckily, then we 'll be there in good time. I got you to Tver once, — went there in seven hours. Don't you remember, your illustriousness?"

"Do you know, one Christmas we started from Tver," said Anatol, smiling at the remembrance, and turning to Makarin, who was gazing affectionately at Kuragin with all his eyes. "You would n't believe it, Makarka, we flew so that it quite took away my breath. We came upon a file of carts, and jumped right over two of them. Hey?"

"What horses those were!" interposed Balaga, taking up the thread of the story. "At that time I put in two young side horses with the bay shaft-horse," he said, turning to Dolokhof. "You would hardly believe it, Feodor Ivanuitch, those wild creatures actually flew for sixty versts. It was impossible to hold them. My hands were numb, it was so cold. I threw down the lines. 'Look out for yourself, your illustriousness,' said I, and I rolled over backward into the sledge. It was hopeless to control 'em, or even to stick to my seat. The devils got us there in three hours. Only the left off one was winded."

CHAPTER XVII

ANATOL left the room, and at the end of a few minutes came back in a sable shubka, girdled with a silver-buckled leather belt, and wearing a sable cap, jauntily set on one side, and very becoming to his handsome face. Glancing into the mirror, and then taking the same posture before Dolokhof which the mirror had told him was most effective, he seized a glass of wine.

"Well, Fedya, good-by — prashchaï. Thank you for everything, prashchaï," said Anatol. "Well, comrades, friends," — he pondered a moment, — "friends .... of my

.... youth, prashchaïte," he said, turning to Makarin and the others.

Although they were all going with him, Anatol evidently wanted to do something affecting and solemn on the occasion of this farewell. He spoke in a low, slow, deep voice, and throwing out his chest, he swayed a little as he rested his weight on one leg. "All of you take your glasses! You too, Balaga. Well, comrades.... friends of my youth .... we have had jolly good times together, we have enjoyed life, we have been on many sprees, hey? Now, when shall we meet again? I am going abroad, farewell .... prashchaï, my boys. To your health! Hurrah!" .... he cried, draining his glass and smashing it on the floor.

"To your good health!" exclaimed Balaga, also draining his glass and wiping his mouth with his handkerchief. Makarin, with tears in his eyes, embraced Anatol.

"Ekh! prince, how sad that we should have to part!" he exclaimed.

"Come, let us be off," cried Anatol.

Balaga was on the point of leaving the room.

"Hold on there, wait," said Anatol. "Shut the door. We must sit down first, — there, that 's the way."

They closed the door and sat down, for the sake of the superstition.

"Well, now be off with you, boys," said Anatol, getting up.

Anatol's valet, Joseph, gave him his purse and saber, and all flocked into the anteroom.

"But where is the shuba?" demanded Dolokhof. "Hey, Ignatka, go to Matriona Matveyevna, and ask her for the shuba — the sable cloak. I have heard how girls go off on such occasions," explaïned Dolokhof, with a wink. "She will come running out more dead than alive, dressed for staying in the house, and if you delay a moment too long there will be tears, and 'O papasha!' and 'O mamasha!' and she 'll be cold, and back she 'll go. So be sure you take this shuba with you, and have it all ready in the sledge."

The valet brought a woman's cloak, lined with fox.

"You fool! I told you to get the sable. Hey, Matrioshka, bring the sable," he shouted, his voice ringing down through the rooms.

A handsome gipsy girl, though thin and pale, with brilliant black eyes, and curly, purplish black hair, with a red shawl over her shoulders, came hurrying out with the sable cloak over her arm.

"Why, I don't care; take it," said she, evidently afraid of her master, and yet regretting the cloak.

Dolokhof, without heeding her, took the fox-skin shuba, threw it over Matriosha, and wrapped it round her.

"So," said Dolokhof; "and so," he repeated, as he pulled the collar up above her head, leaving only a small opening for her face.

"That 's the way, do you see?" and he moved Anatol's head towards the opening left by the collar, where Matriosha's brilliant smile could alone be seen.

"Well, good-by, Matriosha, prashchaĭ," said Anatol, kissing her. "Ekh! my follies here are ended. Give my regards to Stioshka. Well, prashchaĭ, Matrioshka. Wish me good luck."

"Well, then, prince, God grant you the best of luck," said Matriosha, in her gipsy accent.

At the doorstep two troĭkas were waiting with two jaunty yamschchiks in attendance. Balaga was on the box of the first sledge, and, with his elbows held high, was deliberately sorting the reins. Anatol and Dolokhof got in behind him; Makarin, Khvostikof, and the valet took their places in the other troĭka.

"All ready?" inquired Balaga. "Let her go!" he cried, twisting the reins round his wrists, and the three horses flew like the wind down the Nikitsky Boulevard.

"Tproo! podi! hey!.... tproo!" rang out Balaga's shout and that of the groom sitting on the box. On the Arbatskaya Square the troĭka ran into a carriage; there was a crash, a shout was heard, and the troĭka flew down over the Arbata. After dashing down the Podno vinsky, Balaga began to draw rein, and, pulling up, halted the horses at the crossing of Staraya Konyushennaya.

The groom leaped down to hold the horses' heads by the curb, while Anatol and Dolokhof strode along the sidewalk. Coming to the gate, Dolokhof gave a low whistle. The whistle was returned, and immediately after a chambermaid came running out.

"Come into the court, else you will be seen; she 'll be down presently," said she.

Dolokhof remained by the gate. Anatol followed the chambermaid into the dvor, turned the corner, and ran up the steps.

Suddenly Gavrilo, Marya Dmitrievna's colossal footman, met Anatol.

"Be good enough to go to my mistress," said the footman, in a deep, bass voice, as he blocked all retreat from the door.

"Who 's your mistress? Who are you?" demanded Anatol, in a breathless whisper.

"If you please, I was ordered to show you...."

"Kuragin! back!" cried Dolokhof. "You are betrayed! back!"

Dolokhof, who had been left at the outside gate, was engaged in a tussle with the dvornik, who was trying to shut it and prevent Anatol from returning through it. Dolokhof, with a final output of force, overturned the dvornik, seized Anatol by the arm, pulled him through the gate, and ran together with him back to their troïka.

CHAPTER XVIII

Marya Dmitrievna, finding the weeping Sonya in the corridor, had obliged her to confess the whole. Having got possession of Natasha's letter, and read it, Marya Dmitrievna took it and confronted Natasha with it.

"Wretched girl! shameless hussy!" said she to her. "I will not listen to a single word!"

Pushing away Natasha, who looked at her with wondering but tearless eyes, she shut her in under lock and key; then she had ordered the dvornik to admit into the courtyard any who might come that evening, but not to let them out again, and she had ordered the footman to show such persons into her presence. Having made these arrangements, she took up her position in the drawing-room and waited for developments.

When Gavrilo came to inform Marya Dmitrievna that the abductors had escaped, she was very indignant; she got up, and for a long time paced up and down the room, with her hands clasped behind her back, deliberating on what she ought to do. At midnight, she got the key out from her pocket, and went to Natasha's room.

Sonya was still sitting in the corridor, sobbing. "Marya Dmitrievna, let me go to her, for God's sake," said she.

Marya Dmitrievna, giving her no reply, opened the door, and went in. "Disgusting! abominable!.... in my house!.... Indecent, shameless wench!.... Only I'm sorry for her father," said Marya Dmitrievna, trying to master her indignation. "Hard as it will be, I will bid them all hold their tongues, and I'll keep it from the count."

Marya Dmitrievna entered the chamber with a firm step. Natasha was lying on the sofa, with her face hidden in her hands; she did not stir, but lay in the same position in which Marya Dmitrievna had left her.

"Pretty conduct; pretty conduct, indeed!" exclaimed Marya Dmitrievna. "To make assignations with your lovers in my house! None of your hypocrisy! Listen when I speak to you!"

Marya Dmitrievna shook her by the arm.

"Listen when I speak to you! You have disgraced yourself, like any common wench! I'd settle this with you, but I have some pity for your father. I shall keep it from him."

Natasha did not change her position, but her whole body began to shake with the noiseless, convulsive sobs that choked her. Marya Dmitrievna glanced at Sonya, and sat down on the sofa near Natasha.

"Lucky for him he escaped me; but I 'll find him," said she, in her harsh voice. "Do you hear what I am saying?" She put her big hand under Natasha's face, and turned it toward her. Both Marya Dmitrievna and Sonya were amazed when they saw her face. Her eyes were dry and glittering, her lips compressed, her cheeks hollow.

"Let .... me .... be! .... What .... do .... I .... care? .... I .... shall die!" she murmured, turning away from Marya Dmitrievna with angry petulance, and hiding her face in her hands again.

"Natalya!" exclaimed Marya Dmitrievna, "I wish you well. Lie there .... lie there if you wish; I won't touch you; but listen to me! .... I am not going to show you how blameworthy you have been. You know. But, don't you see, your father will be back to-morrow; what shall I say to him?"

Again Natasha's form was shaken by sobs.

"He will hear of it; and so will your brother, and so will your betrothed!"

"I have no betrothed; I have broken with him!" cried Natasha.

"That 's immaterial," pursued Marya Dmitrievna. "Well, they will learn of it; do you think they will forgive it? There 's your father, I know him, — if he should challenge him, would it be a good thing? Ha?"

"Akh! leave me! why should you have interfered at all? Why? Why? Who asked you to?" screamed Natasha, sitting up straight on the sofa, and glaring angrily at Marya Dmitrievna.

"But what idea had you?" demanded Marya Dmitrievna, again losing her patience. "Were you kept locked up? Who on earth prevented him from coming to the house? Why must he needs carry you off like a gipsy wench? .... Well, now, suppose he had carried you off, do you suppose we should n't have found him? Either your father, or your brother, or your betrothed? Well, he 's a scoundrel! a knave! that 's what he is!" ....

"He's better than all of you put together," cried Natasha, sitting up very straight. "If you had not meddled!.... Akh! my God, has it come to this, has it come to this? Sonya, what made you?....Go away!"

And she burst into a passion of tears, sobbing with the desperation such as only those feel who know that they are responsible for their own woes.

Marya Dmitrievna began to speak once more, but Natasha cried:—

"Go away, go away! you all hate me! you all despise me!"

And she threw herself on the sofa again.

Marya Dmitrievna continued for some time to give her advice, and assure her that this whole affair ought to be kept a secret from the count; that no one would know anything about it, if only Natasha would try to let it all go, and not betray in any one's presence that anything had happened.

Natasha made no reply. She ceased to sob, but a fit of shivering and trembling came upon her. Marya Dmitrievna put a pillow under her head, covered her up with a couple of comforters, and herself brought her some linden flower; but Natasha had nothing to say to her.

"Now, let her go to sleep," said Marya Dmitrievna, and left the room, thinking that she would soon sleep.

But Natasha did not go to sleep, and with wide, staring eyes gazed into vacancy. She slept none that night, and she did not weep, and she did not speak to Sonya, who several times got up and went to her.

On the following day Count Ilya Andreyitch returned from his pod-Moskovnaya in time for breakfast, as he had promised. He was in a most genial frame of mind. He had come to a satisfactory arrangement with his purchaser, and now there was nothing to detain him in Moscow, and away from his countess, whom he was very anxious to see.

Marya Dmitrievna met him, and informed him that Natasha had been ill the day before, that they had sent for the doctor, and now she was better.

Natasha that morning did not leave her room. With set, cracked lips, with wide, dry eyes, she kept her place by the window, and anxiously gazed at the passers-by in the street, and turned anxiously toward those who entered her room. She was evidently expecting news from him, — expecting that either he would himself come, or send her a letter.

When the count went to her she heard the sound of his heavy steps, and turned round nervously, and then her face assumed its former expression of hauteur, and even anger. She did not get up to meet him.

"What is the matter with thee, my angel? Are you ill?" asked the count.

Natasha hesitated.

"Yes, I am ill," said she.

In reply to the count's anxious questions why she was so cast down, and whether anything had happened to her lover, she assured him that nothing had happened, and begged him not to be disturbed.

Marya Dmitrievna confirmed Natasha's statement that nothing had happened, but the count, judging from the imaginary illness, and by his daughter's absent-mindedness, by the troubled faces of Sonya and Marya Dmitrievna, saw clearly that during his absence something must have happened. It was so terrible, however, for him to think that anything disgraceful had happened to his beloved daughter, he was so happy in his buoyant good spirits, that he avoided asking any pointed questions, and tried hard to assure himself that nothing out of the way could have happened; and his only regret was that, on account of Natasha's indisposition, he was obliged to postpone their return to his country-seat.

CHAPTER XIX

PIERRE, on the day of his wife's arrival at Moscow, had made up his mind to take a journey somewhere, so as to avoid being with her. Then, when the Rostofs came to Moscow, the impression produced upon him by

Natasha made him hasten to carry out his intention. He went to Tver to see Iosiph Alekseyevitch's widow, who had some time since promised to put into his hands her husband's papers.

On Pierre's return to Moscow a letter was handed him from Marya Dmitrievna, who urged him to come and consult with her on some highly important business concerning Andreï Bolkonsky and his betrothed.

Pierre had avoided Natasha. It seemed to him that he felt for her a sentiment stronger than it was justifiable for a married man to harbor for his friend's mistress, and some perverse fate was constantly throwing them together.

"What can have happened? and what can it have to do with me?" he wondered, while dressing to go to Marya Dmitrievna's. "It 's high time for Prince Andreï to be back and marry her," thought Pierre, as he set out for Mrs. Akhrasimova's.

On the Tversky Boulevard some one hailed him.

"Pierre, been back long?" cried a well-known voice.

Pierre raised his head. It was Anatol and his inseparable companion, Makarin, dashing by in a double sledge, drawn by two gray trotters, that sent the snow flinging over the dasher. Anatol sat bolt upright, in the classic pose of dashing warriors, with his neck muffled in a beaver collar, and bending his head a little. His face was fresh and ruddy; his hat, with a white plume, was set jauntily on one side, exposing his curled and pomaded hair, dusted with fine snow.

"Indeed, he 's a real philosopher!" thought Pierre. "He sees nothing beyond the enjoyment of the present moment; nothing annoys him, and consequently he is always jolly, self-satisfied, and calm. What would I not give to be like him!" thought Pierre, with a feeling of envy.

In the anteroom of the Akhrasimova's, a footman, who relieved Pierre of his shuba, told him that Marya Dmitrievna would receive him in her own room.

As he opened the door into the music-room Pierre saw Natasha sitting by the window, with a pale, thin, angry face. She gave him a glance, and frowned, and, with an expression of chilling dignity, left the room.

"What has happened?" asked Pierre, on entering Marya Dmitrievna's room.

"Pretty state of affairs!" replied Marya Dmitrievna. "Fifty-eight years have I lived in this world, and I never saw anything so shameful."

And then, receiving Pierre's word of honor that he would keep secret what he should hear, Marya Dmitrievna confided to him that Natasha had broken her engagement with Prince Andreï without the knowledge of her parents; that the cause of this break was Anatol Kuragin, whom Pierre's wife had introduced to her, and with whom she had promised to elope during her father's absence, in order to enter into a clandestine marriage.

Pierre, with shoulders raised and mouth open, listened to Marya Dmitrievna's story, not believing his own ears. That Prince Andreï's betrothed, that hitherto lovely Natasha Rostova, so passionately beloved, should give up Bolkonsky for that fool of an Anatol, who was a married man, — for Pierre was in the secret of his marriage, — and be so enamoured of him as to consent to elope with him, Pierre could not comprehend and could not imagine.

Natasha's sweetness of character — he had known her since childhood — could not, in his mind, be associated with this new suggestion of baseness, folly, and cruelty in her. He remembered his own wife. "They are all alike," said he to himself, thinking that he was not the only one who had the misfortune to be in the toils of an unworthy woman; and at the same time he could have wept for his friend, Prince Andreï, to whose pride it would be such a grievous blow. And the more he grieved for his friend, the greater scorn, and even aversion, he felt for this Natasha, who had just passed by him, with such an expression of haughty dignity, in the music-room.

He did not know that Natasha's soul was full to overflowing of despair, shame, humiliation; and that she was not to blame for her face expressing, from very despair, that cold dignity and disdain.

"But how could he marry her?" exclaimed Pierre, catching at Marya Dmitrievna's last word. "He could not marry her; he already has a wife."

"Worse and worse!" exclaimed Marya Dmitrievna. "Fine young man!.... What a dastard he is! And she has been waiting here these two days for him to come! At any rate, she must cease expecting him; we must tell her."

When she learned from Pierre all the details of Anatol's marriage, and had poured out the vials of her wrath against him in abusive words, Marya Dmitrievna explained to Pierre why she had asked him to call upon her. She was afraid that the count or Bolkonsky — who was liable to return at any moment — might learn of the affair, in spite of all her efforts to keep it a profound secret, and might challenge Kuragin to a duel; and, therefore, she besought him to add his influence to hers in getting him to leave town and never show himself in her presence again.

Pierre willingly agreed to fulfil her wishes, since now he for the first time realized the danger threatening the old count and Nikolaï and Prince Andreï.

Having preferred her request in short and precise terms, she took him back into the drawing-room.

"Mind you! the count knows nothing of this. You must pretend that you also know nothing about it," said she. "And I am going this instant to tell her that she is to cease expecting him. And stay to dinner if you will," shouted back Marya Dmitrievna to Pierre.

Pierre met the old count. He was disturbed and annoyed. That morning Natasha had told him that she had broken her engagement with Bolkonsky.

"Too bad, too bad, *mon cher*," said he to Pierre. "Too bad for these girls to be away from their mother; how sorry I am that I ever came at all. I am going to be frank with you: she has already broken her engagement, without telling any one of us about it. Now I will admit I have never been over pleased at this engagement; I will agree he's a fine man, and all that; but what would you have? there would not be much happiness if the father was opposed; and Natasha would not lack chances of getting married. Still, the affair has gone on so long, and to have such a step taken without consulting father or mother! And now she's sick, and God knows what's the matter. It's a bad thing, count, a bad thing, for daughters to be without their mother!"

Pierre perceived that the count was very much disconcerted, and he tried to bring the conversation round to other topics; but the count kept returning to his grievance.

Sonya, with anxious face, came into the drawing-room.

"Natasha is not very well to-day; she is in her room, but she would like to see you. Marya Dmitrievna is with her, and would also like you to come."

"Yes, certainly, you and Bolkonsky were good friends; she probably wants to send some message," said the count. "Akh! my God! my God! How good it all was!" And, tearing at the locks of his gray hair, the count left the room.

Marya Dmitrievna had been explaining to Natasha that Anatol was married. Natasha refused to believe her, and insisted on having confirmation of it from Pierre himself. Sonya confided this to Pierre, as they passed along the corridor toward Natasha's room.

Natasha, pale and stern, was sitting next Marya Dmitrievna. The moment Pierre entered the doorway, she met him with feverishly glittering, wildly imploring eyes. She did not smile, she did not even greet him with a nod, she only looked at him eagerly, and her eyes merely demanded if he came as her friend, or, like all the rest, as her enemy, in reference to Anatol. Pierre, in his own personality as Pierre, evidently did not exist for her.

"He knows all about it," said Marya Dmitrievna, indicating Pierre, and addressing Natasha. "Let him tell you if I am not speaking the truth."

Natasha, as a wounded animal at bay glares at the dogs and huntsmen approaching, looked first at the one and then at the other.

"Natalya Ilyinitchna," Pierre began, dropping his eyes, and experiencing a feeling of compunction for her, and of aversion to the operation which he was obliged to perform, "it is true; but whether this is true or not true, as far as you are concerned, it cannot matter, because...."

"Then it is not true that he is married?"

"Nay, it is true."

"Has he been married for some time?" she asked. "On your word of honor!"

Pierre gave her his solemn word of honor.

"Is he still in town?" she asked hurriedly.

"Yes; I have just seen him."

The effort to say more was evidently too much for her, and she made them a sign with her hand to leave her alone.

CHAPTER XX

Pierre did not remain for dinner, but immediately took his leave. He went out for the purpose of finding Anatol Kuragin, the mere thought of whom now made all the blood rush to his heart, and almost choked him. He sought him everywhere: at the ice-hills, among the gipsies, at Comoneno's; but he was nowhere to be found.

Pierre went to the club. There everything was going on in its usual train: the members, who were assembling for dinner, formed little groups, and, greeting Pierre, spoke of various items of city gossip. A servant, who knew his habits and his particular friends, accosted him politely, and informed him that a place was ready for him at the little table, that Prince N. N. was in the library, but that T. T. had not yet come.

One of Pierre's acquaintances, during some talk of the weather, asked him if he had heard of Kuragin's elopement with Rostova, about which the whole city were talking, and if it were true.

Pierre, with a laugh, said that it was all nonsense, because he had just come from the Rostofs'. He inquired of every one if they had seen Anatol; one said that he had not yet come, another that he would be there to dinner. It was strange for Pierre to look at this tranquil, indifferent throng of men, who had not the slightest inkling of what was passing in his mind. He then sauntered through the hall till all had gone in to dinner; and then, giving up expecting Anatol, he did not wait for dinner, but went home.

Anatol, whom he was so anxious to find, dined that day with Dolokhof, and was discussing with him some plan of still carrying out their ill-fated enterprise. It seemed to him absolutely necessary to have an interview with Natasha. In the evening he went to his sister's, in order to arrange with her some means of procuring this interview.

When Pierre, who had vainly ransacked all Moscow, returned home, the footman informed him that Prince Anatol Vasilyitch was with the countess. The countess's drawing-room was crowded with company.

Pierre, not even greeting his wife, whom he had not seen since his return (never had she seemed to him more utterly detestable than at that moment), went into the drawing-room, and, catching sight of Anatol, went straight up to him.

"Ah, Pierre!" cried the countess, approaching her husband. "You don't know in what a position our Anatol...." She paused when she saw, in the forward thrust of her husband's head, in his flashing eyes, and his resolute gait, the same strange, terrible expression of frenzy and might which she had known and experienced after his duel with Dolokhof.

"Sin and lewdness are with you everywhere," said Pierre to his wife. "Anatol, come with me, I want a few words with you," he said, in French.

Anatol glanced at his sister, and boldly rose, ready to follow Pierre.

Pierre took him by the arm and hurried him out of the room.

"If you permit yourself in my salon to ...." exclaimed Ellen, in a whisper; but Pierre made her no reply, and left the room.

Anatol followed him with his usual jaunty gait, but there was a trace of anxiety on his face.

When they reached Pierre's cabinet, he shut the door, and addressed Anatol without looking at him.

"You promised to marry the Countess Rostova, and planned to elope with her?"

"My dear," replied Anatol, in French, in which language indeed the whole conversation was carried on, "I consider myself under no obligation to answer questions asked in such a tone."

Pierre's face, white to begin with, became perfectly distorted with rage. With his huge hand he seized Anatol by the collar of his uniform coat, and proceeded to shake him from side to side until the young man's face expressed a sufficient degree of terror.

"When I tell you that I *must* have an answer from you?"

"Now, look here, this is stupid! Ha?" exclaimed Anatol, looking for the button that had been torn off from his collar.

"You are a scoundrel and a blackguard, and I don't know what restrains me from the satisfaction of smashing your head with this," said Pierre, expressing himself with easy fluency because he spoke in French. He had taken into his hand a heavy paper-weight, and he held it up menacingly, and then slowly laid it back in its place again.

"Did you promise to marry her?"

"I .... I .... I don't think so; besides, I could n't have promised any such thing, be .... because ...."

Pierre interrupted him.

"Have you any of her letters?" he demanded, coming close to him.

Anatol gave him one look, and instantly put his hand into his pocket, and took out a pocket-book.

Pierre seized the letter which he handed to him, and,

violently pushing aside a chair that was in his way, he went to the sofa, and flung himself on it.

"I will not hurt you; have no fear," said he, in reply to Anatol's terrified gesture. "The letters.... one thing," said Pierre, as if he was repeating a lesson for his own edification. "Secondly," he continued, after a moment's silence, getting to his feet again, and beginning to pace up and down the room, "you must leave Moscow to-morrow."

"But how can I...."

"Thirdly," pursued Pierre, not heeding him, "you must never breathe a word about what has taken place between you and the countess. This, I know, I cannot oblige you to do, but if you have a single spark of conscience...."

Pierre walked in silence several times from one end of the room to the other. Anatol had sat down by the table, and was scowling and chewing his lips.

"You must learn sometime that above and beyond your own pleasure the happiness and peace of others are to be considered, that you are ruining a whole life for the sake of having a little amusement. Trifle with women like my wife as much as you please — with such you have fair game; they know what you want of them. They are armed against you by their very experience in lust; but to promise a young girl to marry her.... to deceive her.... to rob her.... why, don't you know that it is as cowardly as to strike an old man or a child?"

Pierre stopped speaking, and looked at Anatol inquiringly; his anger had vanished.

"I don't know, I'm sure; ha?" said Anatol, gaining confidence in proportion as Pierre's anger subsided. "I know nothing about it, and I don't want to know," said he, not looking at Pierre, while at the same time his lower jaw trembled slightly. "But you have spoken to me words so insulting that I as a man of honor cannot think of permitting them."

Pierre looked at him in amazement, perfectly unable to understand what was wanted of him.

"Though we have had no witnesses," continued Anatol, "still I cannot...."

"What! you wish satisfaction?" asked Pierre, scornfully.

"At least, you can retract what you said. Ha? That is, if you expect me to carry out your wishes. Ha?"

"I will! I'll take it back!" exclaimed Pierre. "And I beg you to forgive me." Pierre could not help looking at the torn button. "And money, if you need it for your journey."

Anatol smiled.

This contemptible, villainous smile, which he knew so well in his wife, stirred Pierre's indignation. "Oh! contemptible, heartless race!" he exclaimed, and left the room.

The next day Anatol started for Petersburg.

CHAPTER XXI

Pierre went to Marya Dmitrievna's to inform her how he had accomplished her wishes in regard to Anatol's expulsion from Moscow.

He found the whole house in terror and commotion. Natasha was very ill; and, as Marya Dmitrievna informed him, under seal of secrecy, the night after she had learned that Anatol Kuragin was married, she had poisoned herself with arsenic that she had managed surreptitiously to procure. Having swallowed a considerable quantity, she awakened Sonya and confessed what she had done. The proper antidotes to the poison had been given in time, and she was now out of danger, but she was still so weak that it was out of the question to think of taking her to the country, and the countess had been sent for. Pierre saw the troubled count and the weeping Sonya, but he was not allowed to see Natasha.

Pierre had that day dined at the club, and had heard on all sides gossip about the frustrated elopement; but he strenuously denied these rumors, assuring every one that there was nothing in it, except that his brother-in-law had offered himself to Rostova, and been refused. It seemed plain to Pierre that it was his bounden duty to conceal the whole affair, and save Natasha's reputation.

In the greatest anxiety he waited for Prince Andreï's return, and each day he went to the old prince's to inquire for news of him.

Prince Nikolaï Andreyitch learned through Mlle. Bourienne of all this gossip flying through the city, and he read the letter to the Princess Mariya, in which Natasha broke off her engagement with Prince Andreï. He seemed in better spirits than usual, and with great impatience awaited his son's return.

A few days after Anatol's departure, Pierre received a note from Prince Andreï announcing his arrival, and begging Pierre to come to see him.

When Prince Andreï arrived at Petersburg, his father had immediately handed him Natasha's letter to his sister announcing the discontinuance of her engagement, — this letter Mlle. Bourienne had purloined from the princess and given to the old prince, — and had told him, with additions, the various rumors current concerning the elopement.

Prince Andreï's arrival had been in the evening. Pierre went to see him the next morning. He expected to find him in almost the same state of mind as Natasha was, and, therefore, his amazement was great, when, on being shown into the drawing-room, he heard Prince Andreï, in the adjoining cabinet, telling in a loud, animated manner of some Petersburg intrigue. He was occasionally interrupted by the old prince, and by a third person present.

The Princess Mariya came in to greet Pierre. She sighed as she turned her eyes toward the door of the room where her brother was, evidently anxious to give expression to her sympathy for his affliction, but Pierre detected on her face evidences of her inward gratification at the turn affairs had taken, and at the manner in which her brother had received the news of Natasha's fickleness.

"He told me that he expected this," said she. "I know that his pride would not let him make any show of his feelings, but nevertheless he bears up under it better, far better, than I had any reason to expect. Of course, since it had to be so.... "

"But do you mean to say it is all over between them?"

The Princess Mariya looked at him in amazement. She could not understand how any one should even ask such a question.

Pierre went into the cabinet. Prince Andreĭ, much altered, and apparently restored to perfect health, but with a new and perpendicular wrinkle between his brows, was standing, in civil dress, in front of his father and Prince Meshchersky, and was arguing eagerly, making energetic gestures.

The topic was Speransky, news of whose unexpected banishment and reported treason had only just reached Moscow.

"Now," Prince Andreĭ was saying, "the very men who a month ago were extolling him, and who are wholly incapable of comprehending his aims, are criticizing him and condemning him. To criticize a man in disfavor is very easy, and so it is to make him responsible for the blunders of others; but I tell you, if any one has done any good during this present reign it has been done by him, by him alone."....

He caught sight of Pierre, and paused. His face contracted, and immediately took on an angry expression. "But posterity will do him justice," said he, and with that he turned to greet Pierre.

"Well, how are you? Still stout!" he said in a lively tone, but the newly furrowed frown on his brow grew still deeper. "Yes, I am well," he replied, in answer to Pierre's question, and laughed. Pierre saw clearly that this laugh was affected, and was simply equivalent to saying, "I am well, but who cares whether I am well?"

After exchanging a few words with Pierre in regard to the frightful road from the Polish frontier, and how he met in Switzerland a number of men who had known Pierre, and about Mr. Dessalles, whom he had brought from abroad as his son's tutor, Prince Andreï again, with feverish eagerness, returned to the topic of Speransky, which the two old men were still discussing.

"If there had been any treason, and if there had been any proofs of his secret intercourse with Napoleon, then they would surely have been published broadcast," said he, speaking excitedly and fluently. "Personally I do not like Speransky, and I have not liked him, but I like justice."

Pierre was aware that his friend was now laboring under that necessity, which he himself had only too often experienced, of getting thoroughly stirred up and excited over some alien topic, simply for the purpose of dispelling thoughts too heavy to be endured.

When Prince Meshchersky had taken his departure, Prince Andreï took Pierre's arm, and drew him into the room which had been prepared for him. In this room a bed had been hastily set up; trunks and boxes, opened, were scattered about. Prince Andreï went to one of these and took out a casket, and from the casket a packet wrapped in a paper. All this he did silently and very swiftly. He straightened himself up and cleared his throat. His face was gloomy and his lips compressed.

"Forgive me if I trouble you...."

Pierre perceived that Prince Andreï was going to speak about Natasha, and his broad countenance expressed pity and sympathy. This expression on Pierre's face nettled Prince Andreï. He went on in a loud, decided, and disagreeable voice:—

"I have received my dismissal from the Countess Rostova; and rumors have reached my ears of your brother-in-law having offered himself to her, or something to that effect,—is that true?"

"Whether true or false...." Pierre began, but Prince Andreï interrupted him.

"Here are her letters and her miniature."

He took the packet from the table and handed them to Pierre.

"Give this to the countess .... if you happen to see her."

"She is very ill," said Pierre.

"So she is still here?" inquired Prince Andreï. "And Prince Kuragin?" he asked hastily.

"He went away some time ago. She almost died...."

"I am very sorry for her illness," said Prince Andreï. He smiled coldly, evilly, disagreeably, like his father.

"But Mr. Kuragin did not, then, honor the Countess Rostova with the offer of his hand?" asked Prince Andreï. He snorted several times.

"It is impossible for him to marry, for the reason that he is already married," said Pierre.

Prince Andreï gave a disagreeable laugh, again suggestive of his father.

"And where, pray, is your brother-in-law now to be found — may I ask?" said he.

"He has gone to Peters.... However, I don't really know," said Pierre.

"Well, it's all the same to me," said Prince Andreï. "Assure the Countess Rostova that she has been, and is, perfectly free, and that I wish her all happiness."

Pierre took the package of letters. Prince Andreï, as if trying to make up his mind whether it were not necessary for him to say something, or expecting Pierre to say something, looked at him keenly.

"See here, do you remember a discussion we once had in Petersburg? Do you remember...."

"Yes, I remember," said Prince Andreï, hurriedly. "I said that a fallen woman ought to be forgiven; but I did not say that in my own case I could forgive her. I cannot."

"But wherein is the comparison?".... asked Pierre.

Prince Andreï interrupted him. His voice was loud and sharp: —

"Yes, ask her hand again? Be magnanimous, and all that? .... yes, that would be very noble, but I am not capable of following in this gentleman's footsteps. — If you wish to continue my friend, never mention this to me again .... not a word about it. Now, good-by. You will give that to her?" ....

Pierre left the room, and went to the old prince and the Princess Mariya.

The old prince seemed more animated than usual. The Princess Mariya was her ordinary self, but, back of her sympathy for her brother, Pierre could see that she was delighted at having the engagement broken. As Pierre looked at them, he realized how deep were the scorn and dislike which they all felt for the Rostofs; he realized that it was wholly hopeless even to mention her name, though she might have had any one else in the world in Prince Andreï's place.

At dinner the conversation turned on the war which was unquestionably imminent. Prince Andreï kept up an unceasing stream of talk and discussion with his father, or with Mr. Dessalles, his son's Swiss tutor, and he displayed more excitement than usual; and Pierre knew only too well the moral cause of this excitement.

CHAPTER XXII

THAT same evening Pierre went to call on the Rostofs, to fulfil his commission.

Natasha was in bed, the count had gone to the club, and Pierre, having intrusted the letters into Sonya's hands, went to Marya Dmitrievna, who was greatly interested to know how Prince Andreï had received the news.

Ten minutes later, Sonya appeared.

"Natasha is determined to see Count Piotr Kirillovitch," said she.

"But how can he go to her room? Everything is in disorder there," said Marya Dmitrievna.

"But she is dressed, and has come down into the drawing-room," said Sonya.

Marya Dmitrievna merely shrugged her shoulders.

"If only the countess would come; this is a perfect torture to me. Now be careful, and don't tell her everything, Pierre," she added warningly. "It would break my heart if anything were said to hurt her; she is so to be pitied, so to be pitied!"

Natasha, grown decidedly thin, and with pale, set face — though not at all confused, as Pierre supposed she would be — stood in the middle of the drawing-room. When Pierre made his appearance in the door, she hesitated, evidently undecided whether to go to him or to wait for him.

Pierre hastened forward. He supposed that she would, as usual, give him her hand. But she stood motionless, sighing deeply, and with her arms hanging lifelessly, in exactly the same pose that she always took when she went into the middle of the music-room to sing, only with an entirely different expression.

"Piotr Kiriluitch," she began, speaking very rapidly, "Prince Bolkonsky was your friend, and is still your friend," she added, by an afterthought; for it seemed to her that everything was past, and all things had changed. "He told me once to turn to you if...."

Pierre quietly blew his nose as he looked at her. Till that moment he had, in his heart, blamed her, and tried to despise her; but now she seemed to him so eminently deserving of pity, that there was no room in his heart for reproach.

"He is here now; please ask him to for.... forgive...."

She paused, and breathed still faster, but she did not weep.

"Yes.... I will tell him," said Pierre, "but...."

He knew not what to say.

Natasha was evidently terrified by what Pierre might have thought she meant.

"Yes, I know that all is over between us," said she, hurriedly. "No, it can never be. All that tortures me is the wrong that I have done him. Only ask him to forgive, forgive, forgive me for all...."

Her whole frame trembled, and she sat down in a chair.

Never before had Pierre experienced such a feeling of compassion as now came over him.

"I will tell him, I will certainly tell him all,".... said Pierre. "But.... I should like to know one thing."....

"What?" asked Natasha.

"I should like to ask if you loved...." Pierre did not know what term to use in speaking of Anatol, and reddened at the thought of him. "Did you *love* that vile man?"

"Don't call him vile," exclaimed Natasha. "But I .... I don't know; I don't know at all."....

Then the tears came again.

And a still more intense feeling of pity, affectionate compassion, and love came over Pierre. He heard the tears welling out from under his spectacles and dropping, and he hoped that they would not be noticed.

"Let us say no more about it, my dear," said Pierre.

Strange indeed suddenly seemed to Natasha the sound of his voice, so sweet, so tender, so sincere.

"Let us say no more about it, my dear, I will tell him all; but one thing I want to ask you: consider me your friend, and if you need any help or advice, or simply if you need some one in whom you can confide—not now, but by and by, when everything is clear to your own mind, remember me." He took her hand and kissed it. "I shall be happy, if I am in the position to...."

Pierre grew confused.

"Do not speak to me so, I cannot bear it!" cried Natasha, and she started to leave the room; but Pierre detained her by the hand. He knew that there was something more he must tell her. But when he had spoken it, he was amazed at his own words.

"Wait, wait! all the future is yours," said he.

"Mine! Only ruin is for me!" she exclaimed, in shame and self-reproach.

"Ruin!" he repeated; "if I were not myself, but the handsomest, wisest, and best man in the world, and were free, I would this very instant, on my knees, sue for your hand and your love."

Natasha, for the first time in many days, wept tears

of gratitude and emotion; and, giving Pierre one look, she fled from the room.

Pierre immediately afterwards almost ran out into the anteroom, and, restraining the tears of tenderness and happiness that choked him, he threw his shuba over his shoulders, but without putting his arms through the sleeves, and got into his sledge.

"Where now?" asked the driver.

"Where?" repeated Pierre to himself. "Where can I go now? To the club, or to make some calls?"

All men, at this moment, seemed to him so contemptible, so mean, in comparison with that feeling of emotion and love which overmastered him — in comparison with that softened glance of gratitude which she had given him just now through her tears.

"Home," said Pierre, throwing back his bearskin shuba, over his broad, joyfully throbbing chest, though the mercury marked ten degrees of frost.

It was cold and clear. Above the dirty, half-lighted streets, above the black roofs of the houses, stretched the dark, starry heavens. Only as Pierre gazed at the heavens above, he ceased to feel the humiliating pettiness of everything earthly in comparison with the height to which his soul aspired. As he drove out on the Arbatskaya Square, the mighty expanse of the dark, starry sky spread out before Pierre's eyes. Almost in the zenith of this sky, — above the Pretchistensky Boulevard, — convoyed and surrounded on every side by stars, but distinguished from all the rest by its nearness to the earth, and by its white light, and by its long, curling tail, stood the tremendous brilliant comet of 1812, — the very comet which men thought presaged all manner of woes and the end of the world.

But in Pierre, this brilliant luminary, with its long train of light, awoke no terror. On the contrary, rapturously, his eyes wet with tears, he contemplated this glorious star which seemed to him to have come flying with inconceivable swiftness through measureless space, straight toward the earth, there to strike like an enormous arrow, and remain in that one fate-designated spot upon the dark sky; and, pausing, raise aloft with monstrous force its curling tail, flashing and playing with white light, amid the countless other twinkling stars. It seemed to Pierre that this star was the complete reply to all that was in his soul as it blossomed into new life, filled with tenderness and love.

END OF VOL. III.